Praise for J. Courtney Sullivan's

COMMENCEMENT

"Entertaining. . . . A smart, discerning book about school years. . . . Gloria Steinem likes *Commencement*. She ought to; the women of *Commencement* are big fans of hers."
—*The New York Times*

"This story about four Smith College students and the paths they follow post-graduation celebrates friendship and explores modern-day feminism. At the same time, it's just a really devourable read—think a 2009 version of Mary McCarthy's *The Group*." —*Cookie* magazine

"*Commencement* is much more than a novel about academia or young women. It's a thoughtful, engrossing study in lives transformed and relationships realigned, full of details and dilemmas that speak to a broad audience."
—*The Onion*'s A.V. Club

"Sullivan is a keen observer, with a wry sense of humor."
—*Chicago Tribune*

"Garnering rave reviews . . . [*Commencement*] delves into the complex choices young women face today."
—*The Boston Globe*

"Sullivan tells an involving story of four students from different backgrounds who share quarters at Smith College. . . . Chick lit with depth and engagement."

—*New York Daily News*

"Totally entertaining." —*New Haven Register*

"[*Commencement* is] layered with love and honesty and promises that friendship perseveres when nothing else might or seems to." —Glamour.com

"Sullivan's debut novel, *Commencement,* works like a backstage pass to a world I barely knew existed—the elite contemporary women's college, the world of Smithies—with their rampant anagrams (including my favorite, S.L.U.G., Smith Lesbian Until Graduation), fluid and complex sexuality, eccentric traditions, arch politics, and, most of all, incredibly deep and enduring friendships."

—Bridget Asher, author of *My Husband's Sweethearts*

"Many writers have tried to duplicate *The Group* . . . J. Courtney Sullivan comes admirably close. McCarthy was very much of her era, and so is Sullivan."

—*Entertainment Weekly*

"Sullivan has homed in on so much of the utter anguish of adolescence and young adulthood. Her characters are brilliantly flawed, intensely realistic, thoroughly compassionate, and often incredibly funny." —*BookPage*

J. Courtney Sullivan

COMMENCEMENT

J. Courtney Sullivan's work has appeared in *The New York Times*, *New York*, *Elle*, *Cosmopolitan*, *Allure*, *Men's Vogue*, the *New York Observer*, *Tango*, and in the essay anthology *The Secret Currency of Love*. She is a graduate of Smith College, lives in Brooklyn, and works in the editorial department of *The New York Times*. *Commencement* is her first novel.

www.jcourtneysullivan.com

COMMENCEMENT

COMMENCEMENT

J. Courtney Sullivan

Vintage Contemporaries
Vintage Books
A Division of Random House, Inc.
New York

FIRST VINTAGE CONTEMPORARIES EDITION, MAY 2010

The Library of Congress has cataloged the Knopf edition as follows:
Sullivan, J. Courtney.
Commencement : a novel / by J. Courtney Sullivan. —1st ed.
p. cm.
1. Women college students—Fiction. 2. Female friendship—Fiction.
3. Young women—United States—Social conditions—Fiction. I. Title.
PS3619.U43C66 2009
813.6—dc22
2008054386

Vintage ISBN: 978-0-307-45496-6

www.vintagebooks.com

Printed in the United States of America
10 9 8 7 6 5 4 3 2 1

For my parents,
Eugene F. Sullivan Jr. and Joyce Gallagher Sullivan

PART ONE

Spring 2006 Class Notes

CLASS OF '02

Robin Hughes graduates from Northwestern this May with a master's in public health. She lives in Chicago with fellow Hopkins House alum Gretchen (Gretch) Anderson . . . Natalie Goldberg (Emerson House) and her partner, Gina Black (class of '99), have finally realized their dream of moving to Finland and opening a karaoke bar! So far, they say, Emersonians Emma Bramley-Hawke and Joy Watkins have already stopped in for several verses of "Total Eclipse of the Heart". . . After four years of working in a health clinic in her native Malaysia, Jia-Yi Moa has been accepted to NYU Medical School! . . . And now, news from my own darling group of girls: Sally Werner, who works as a researcher in a medical lab at Harvard, is getting married (on the Smith campus!) this May to longtime boyfriend Jake Brown. Fellow King House alums Bree Miller (Stanford Law '05), April Adams (intrepid research assistant for Women in Peril, Inc.), and yours truly will be serving as bridesmaids. Look out for the embarrassing drunken photos in the next issue. Until then, happy spring to all and keep sending me those updates.

Your class secretary,
Celia Donnelly
(celiad@alumnae.smith.edu)

CELIA

Celia woke with a gasp.

Her head was throbbing, her throat was dry, and it was already nine o'clock. She was late for Sally's wedding or, at least, for the bus that would take her there. She silently cursed herself for going out the night before. What the hell kind of a bridesmaid showed up late to the wedding of a dear friend, and hungover at that?

Sun streamed through the windows of her little alcove studio. From her spot in bed, Celia could see two beer bottles and an open bag of tortilla chips on the coffee table by the couch, and, oh Jesus, there was a condom wrapper on the floor. Well then, that answered that.

The guy lying next to her was named either Brian or Ryan; that much she remembered. Everything else was a bit of a blur. She vaguely recollected kissing him on the front stoop of her building, fumbling for the keys, his hand already moving up her leg and under her skirt. She did not recall having sex or, for that matter, eating tortilla chips.

She was lucky not to have been chopped up into little bits. Her sober self needed to somehow get the message to her drunk self that it was entirely unadvisable to bring strange men home. You saw it in the papers all the time—*They met at a party, he asked her to go for a stroll, two days later the police found her torso in a dumpster in Queens.* She wished that casual sex wasn't so intimately connected to the possibility of being murdered, but there you had it.

Celia leaned toward him now and kissed his cheek, trying to affect an air of calm.

"I've got to leave soon," she said softly. "Do you want to hop in the shower?"

He shook his head. "I don't have to go into the office today," he said. "Got a golf date with some clients this afternoon. Mind if I sleep in?"

"Umm, no," she said. "That's fine."

Celia looked him over. Blond hair, perfect skin, chiseled arms, dimples. He was cute, suspiciously cute. Too attractive for his own good, as her mother would say.

Before she left, she kissed him again. "The door will lock automatically behind you. And there's coffee on the counter if you want it."

"Thanks," he said. "So I'll call you?"

"Good. Well, see you later, then."

From his tone, she figured the odds of his actually calling were about fifty-fifty, not bad for a drunken hookup.

Celia headed toward the subway. Was it weird that he had

asked to stay in her apartment? Should she have demanded that he leave with her? He looked clean-cut, and he said he worked in finance. He didn't seem like the type who would go home with a girl just to rob her, but what did she really know about him anyway? Celia was twenty-six years old. Now into what she considered her late twenties, she had begun compiling a mental inventory of men she should not sleep with. As she stepped onto the A train, she added *Guys who might be suspected of stealing my belongings* to the list.

Twenty minutes later, she was sprinting through Port Authority, praying for the bus to be five minutes late. Just five extra minutes, that was all she needed.

"Hail Mary, full of grace, the Lord is with thee, blessed art thou amongst women," she muttered. "Come on, come on."

It was a habit of hers, a remnant of a time when she actually believed in God and would say a Hail Mary whenever she was in trouble. Celia realized now that what she had once thought of as prayers were in fact just wishes. She didn't expect the Virgin to actually *do* anything—even if she did exist, she probably wouldn't be in the business of controlling buses running express from Manhattan to Northampton, Mass. All the same, the familiar words calmed Celia down. She tried to use them sparingly so as not to offend the Mother of God, a woman she didn't believe in, but even so.

Her mother revered the Virgin Mary, saying the rosary in her car on the way to work each morning, keeping a statue of the Madonna in the front garden for years, until a Presbyterian family moved in across the street (not wanting to offend them, she dug up the statue and put it out back). She believed that Mary had all the power, that Jesus was secondary to her, because he had come from her womb. Celia often marveled at how her mother was perhaps the only person on earth to perceive Catholicism as matriarchal.

She reached the gate just as the bus driver was collecting the last of the tickets and closing the door.

"Wait!" she shouted. "Wait! Please!"

The driver looked up in sleepy-eyed surprise. She hoped he wasn't as hungover as she was.

"Please! I have to get on that bus!" she said.

"Hurry up, then," he said. "There's one seat left."

It wasn't like Celia to draw attention to herself in public, but the thought of Sally's disappointment if she had to call and say she was running late was just too much to bear. Besides, Celia had been looking forward to this weekend for months. She did not want to miss a moment with the girls.

She pushed through the aisle, past mothers bouncing crying babies on their laps, teenagers with their headphones blaring, and twenty-somethings having loud cell phone conversations about insanely private matters. *Bringing new meaning to hell on wheels,* that ought to be Greyhound's slogan. She was desperate for more coffee and as much Advil as she could take without killing herself.

Despite the four-and-a-half-hour bus ride that lay ahead, Celia smiled. Soon she would be with them again—Sally, impeccable and impulsive, a twenty-five-year-old millionaire in a thrift-store wedding gown; April, brave and opinionated, with that sometimes reckless air that worried them all; and Bree, beautiful and bright eyed and mired in a doomed love affair—she was still Celia's favorite, despite all the changes and distance between them.

Celia sat down beside a pimply teenager reading a comic book. She closed her eyes and breathed in deep.

Eight years earlier, on Orientation Day, Celia wept in the backseat of her father's Lincoln Town Car all the way out to Smith. The family had to pull over in a Taco Bell parking lot so she could get herself together before meeting her house-mates. By the time she arrived at the front door of Franklin King House, she was fixed with a big fake smile and half a tube of her sister's Maybelline concealer. (Celia had always prided herself on being a girl who didn't wear makeup, but she realized at that moment that she did in fact apply pow-der and mascara and eye shadow most mornings, she just never bought any of it herself.) She held back tears for hours as they carried boxes upstairs and mingled with other new students and their families on the lawn of the science quad. Then, at last, it was time for the family to go, and there was an embarrassing, agonizing moment in which the four of them—Celia, Violet, and their parents—stood in a circle and embraced, everyone crying except for Violet, who was fif-teen and eager to get back home in time to see her boy-friend's ska band play at the Knights of Columbus Hall. (The band was called For Christ's Sake, and Celia's mother thought they were a Christian rock group. She didn't know that the last word was pronounced with an emphasis on the *e*, like the Japanese wine.)

After they left, Celia cried until she felt as hollow as a jack-o'-lantern. College had snuck up on her, and unlike so many of her friends, who had been dying to leave home,

Celia liked her life just fine as it was. She couldn't imagine going to sleep at night without first creeping into her parents' room, curling up with the dogs at the foot of their bed as her father watched Letterman and her mother read some trashy novel. She couldn't picture herself sharing a bathroom with anyone but Violet—you couldn't yell at a dorm mate for using up all the hot water the way you could your sister. You couldn't squeeze your blackheads in front of the mirror, wrapped in a towel and dripping wet from a shower while she sat on the edge of the tub and clipped her toenails.

At Smith, Celia worried that she would never again feel truly comfortable.

Along with a month's worth of groceries for a family of five, her mother had given her a prayer card with a picture of the Virgin printed on the front and her great-grandmother's golden wall cross.

"You know this isn't a convent, right?" her father teased his wife.

After a lifetime of Catholic school, Celia considered herself an atheist, but she was still terrified to throw these things in the trash—it seemed like a surefire way to get struck by lightning. Instead, she shoved them in the back of her top drawer and covered them over with underwear and socks.

Celia pulled two bottles of vodka from her suitcase, where they lay wrapped in a Snoopy bath towel that she'd had since she was eight. As she placed them in her mini-fridge, she realized with some delight that she didn't have to hide them from anyone.

She unpacked the rest of her clothes and filled the closet. The room was small, with plain white wallpaper, a single bed, an oak dresser, a nightstand, and a dingy little mirror with a faded CLINTON/GORE '96 sticker stuck to the bottom. Having seen friends' rooms at Holy Cross and BC, Celia knew that this one was cozy and clean by comparison. Smith had free cable TV in every room, and private phones for each student, and huge windows with thick sills you could sit on, reading for hours. Her parents were going into crazy debt so she could be here. ("We'll be paying the loans off until *your* kids are in college," her father had said the previous spring, in one final attempt to make her go to a state school.) She knew she ought to feel grateful. Still, Celia got a little hysterical, imagining living the next four years between these walls.

She tried to go as long as she could without calling her mother. She lasted three hours.

"I started to drive on the way back here so your father could rest his eyes," her mother said. "I didn't even make it to exit eighteen before I was crying so hard that I had to pull over and switch seats with Daddy."

Celia laughed. "I miss you guys so much already."

Just then, a girl appeared outside the open door to her room. She looked like a middle-aged man, with a huge beer gut hanging over her khakis and a small brown stain on her white T-shirt. Her hair was slicked back, and she held a clipboard in her hand.

Celia hoped she hadn't heard her blubbering away to her mother like a five-year-old.

"I gotta go," she said into the phone.

"Celia Donnelly?" the girl said, looking down at her list. Her voice was deep and gravelly. "Pleased to meet you. I'm your HP—that's house president—Jenna the Monster Truck Collins. First-year meeting in the living room in five."

Downstairs in the living room a few minutes later, they sat in a circle on the floor, and Celia took stock of the other new girls. There were fifteen of them in all, and they mostly looked like the girls she'd known in high school. They wore jeans or cotton sundresses; they had touches of lip gloss and mascara on their faces, and smooth, long hair. Then there were the girls leading the meeting: Jenna the Monster Truck; two other seniors about her size, both named Lisa, both with cropped boy haircuts; and a junior named Becky, who looked like she might be positively gorgeous if only she gave a damn about her appearance. Her shoulder-length hair lay flat, clumped with grease, and her face was so shiny that, for the first time ever, Celia envisioned herself taking a little witch hazel to a stranger's skin. With the exception of Jenna, they all wore flannel pajamas.

Is this what she and the others would become? Celia wondered. Did attending a women's college make you relinquish all grooming products and embrace carbohydrates like you only had a week left to live? (Later she would learn that if you weren't careful, the answers to these questions were yes and yes. After one semester, about a quarter of the girls would be going crazy, filling out transfer applications to Wesleyan or Swarthmore or any coed school that would take them midway through the year.)

Jenna the Monster Truck started the meeting off by making introductions. She was HP, the Lisas were HONS (heads of new students), and Becky was an SAA (student academic adviser). Everything had an acronym, even in cases where it probably would have been easier to just use the words. Jenna ran down the list of new names, pointing out after she did so, "You're the *first years* by the way. Never let me hear you calling yourself freshmen—there are clearly no men here."

A thin girl with a sleek brown ponytail and a Lilly Pulitzer dress raised her hand. Celia recognized her from earlier in the day. Her room was just three doors down from Celia's, and she had arrived alone, lugging an oversize trunk, which Celia's father had quickly swooped in to help her carry.

"You didn't call my name," the girl said. "It's Sally Werner."

Jenna the Monster Truck checked her sheet. "It says here you withdrew."

"I did, but then I unwithdrew," Sally said, with a sad smile. "It's a long story."

Celia wanted to know it immediately. Her mother always said she had a novelist's fascination with other people's tragic tales. A year earlier, she had had to stop accompanying her family to the soup kitchen where they volunteered because with each person who walked by, she would imagine a more terrible and heartbreaking scenario: A man in a tattered Ralph Lauren jacket was a former banker who had lost his family and his fortune in a house fire (in fact, her mother said, he was just a mean old drunk). A young woman with a sorrowful smile had a sick child somewhere out there, whom she supported by selling her body (no, her mother said, that was *Les Misérables*).

"The thing is," Sally said, "my mom died, so my plans sort of changed at the last minute."

"When did it happen?" Celia blurted out.

Everyone turned to look at her for a moment, and then all eyes were on Sally.

"Almost four months ago. May seventeenth. That's why I withdrew. She was sick, and we thought she had about nine more months, so I decided I'd just start college a year late. But then she died, and there really wasn't anything for me to do at home, so . . ." she trailed off.

"I'm so sorry," Jenna the Monster Truck said, and several girls in the circle echoed her.

"Thanks," Sally said meekly, and Celia wondered what on earth one was supposed to say at a time like this that didn't sound completely stupid.

Celia wished she were brave enough to stand up and give this stranger a hug. She should go to Sally later, sit beside her on her narrow bed, and become her friend, a shoulder to cry on.

The meeting went on, with a discussion of dining hall hours and information on where to get the morning-after pill and birth control and dental dams. (What the hell were dental dams? Celia wondered. She made a mental note to look them up online when she got back to her room.) Jenna distributed what seemed like hundreds of brightly colored pamphlets for campus clubs and teams and stores and publications, all of which Celia knew she would throw away as soon as she went back upstairs.

Her legs began to fall asleep beneath her. She stretched them out and glanced around the room. It was full of ritzy-looking couches and a huge Oriental rug, with a real working fireplace and an enormous chandelier. It looked like one of the mansions in Newport that her mother loved to tour, oohing and aahing over ottomans and armoires, before returning to their modest suburban house, where the beat-up Crate and Barrel couches were covered in paw prints and the oily traces of decade-old peanut-butter stains.

"Oh, I forgot to mention shower hours," Jenna said, just as it seemed things were drawing to an end. "Basically, don't shower with your significant other during prime traffic flow—usually about eight to ten a.m. It's really disrespectful, and, honestly, who wants to hear two dykes going at it first thing in the morning?"

Some of the first years began to squirm a little, and Celia wondered if this was just a seniority tactic—they'd all heard the lore about Smith lesbians, but was girl-on-girl shower sex really such an issue that it necessitated a house rule?

A beautiful, movie-star blonde across the circle seemed startled, her body jolting upright. Celia looked her over and noticed a small, sparkly diamond ring wrapped around one of her delicate fingers. Jesus, what was she, some sort of child bride? An eighteen-year-old girl, engaged. That was going to work out great.

The girl caught Celia's eye, and Celia shot her a huge smile and even, regrettably, gave her a little wave. She always overcompensated when she got nervous or had just been caught snooping.

As they climbed the stairs back up to their rooms after the meeting, Celia watched the three girls with whom she'd be sharing a hallway: Bree, the beautiful engaged blonde; Sally, whose mother had just died; and a third girl named April, with an eyebrow ring and a T-shirt that said RIOT: DON'T DIET across the front.

The four of them were assigned to the worst rooms in King House—third-floor maids' quarters. Everyone in King had a single, and most of the rooms were huge, big enough for a king-size bed, with two or three windows each. But a few unlucky first years had to sleep in the dim corridors of four rooms off the main floors, where students had once housed their live-in servants.

That first night, each of them went to her room and closed the door, a mystery.

Later, around eleven o'clock, Celia could hear Bree sobbing through the wall that separated their rooms. She put on an Indigo Girls CD to block out the noise and told herself not to be nosy, but halfway through the first song, she could no longer take the sound of a stranger in pain, and also, she was dying to know if Bree and her fiancé had broken up. She scribbled a note on the back of one of the house meeting flyers (*Join the Radical Cheerleaders and Pummel the Patriarchy with Pep!*) and slid it under Bree's door: *I feel your pain. Want to come next door for vodka and Oreos? —Celia D. Room 323*

The crying stopped. Ten minutes later, there was a knock at Celia's door.

Bree poked her blonde head in and waved Celia's note in the air. "Thanks for this," she said in a sweet Southern drawl. "Is the offer still good?"

Celia smiled. "Of course."

She wondered whether Bree felt the same way she did about the house meeting. Celia had stayed dressed in her dark jeans and emerald green wrap dress on principle: Just because there were no guys around did not mean she was going to become a total slob. Bree wore pink flannel pajama pants and a plain white tank top, but Celia could tell that she had just applied a fresh coat of eye shadow and lip gloss, and something about that struck her as both funny and touching.

"I'm sorry I was crying so loud," Bree said. "My brothers call me the Drama Queen of Rosewood Court. That's the street we live on back home."

"No worries," Celia said. "I think I've cried more since I got here this morning than I have in the last year. So are you homesick or boy sick?"

"A bit of both," Bree said, walking to the desk and taking a seat.

"Can I get you some vodka or Oreos?" Celia said.

"A bit of both," Bree said again, and Celia laughed for the first time all day.

They drank their vodka out of paper cups Celia's mother had tucked into a grocery bag, along with plastic cutlery and paper napkins and Tupperware containers, as if Celia were going off on a picnic instead of to college.

Bree downed the contents of her cup, and then refilled it to the brim.

Was this girl a big drinker, or just nervous? Celia figured the latter—big drinkers didn't tend to swig straight vodka by the gulpful. They knew it was all about pacing yourself. She thought back to the parties she had attended senior year—red plastic cups and vodka that felt warm in her throat, consumed in countless musty basements while someone's unwitting parents watched 20/20 upstairs; tequila shots taken in Reggie Yablonski's mother's hot tub when she was visiting her sister in Kittery; and a bottle of champagne with the girls from the neighborhood on prom night.

"What about you?" Bree asked. "Did you leave someone back home?"

"I broke up with a guy right after graduation," Celia said. "We'd been seeing each other for like four months. He was going off to be a camp counselor for the summer, and I just knew that that whole long-distance thing was a disaster waiting to happen."

She instantly regretted saying it.

"For me," she stumbled. "A disaster for me. I'm just not cut out for all that."

"Why a disaster?" Bree said with wide eyes, like Celia was an oracle who could predict the fate of her engagement.

At Celia's high school, girls called September 1 "D-day," as in the day your boyfriend went off to college and dumped you. She had always sympathized when this happened to friends, secretly reminding herself to never let it happen to her.

And so she had ended it with Matt Dougherty at the graduation night lock-in at St. Catherine's. In the gym, everyone was dancing and drinking punch and sneaking beers, giddy with excitement. Celia and Matt sat just outside the fray on an old treadmill in the weight room. They had lost their virginity to each other right there in that sweaty, windowless space between lunch and fourth period, just one month earlier. He was captain of the wrestling team, and as such, he had a key. They had snuck in during the lock-in to fool around, but Celia thought she saw something in his eyes: She knew this would not last. And wasn't it better to end something while it was still in your control than to have it yanked out from under you when you weren't expecting it?

"Can't we even give it a chance?" he had asked.

"What's the point?" Celia said. He was going all the way to Berkeley, and who knew when they'd see each other again.

They spent the rest of the lock-in apart, talking to their respective friends, with Celia crying into Molly Sweeney's jean jacket in the bleachers at one point, knowing all the while that it wasn't really about Matt, at least not entirely. It was the fear of the new and the unfamiliar, the surprising sorrow of knowing that she would probably never stand in this gym again, even though she had always hated gym class and skipped it at least twice a month, either hiding out with Sharon Oliver in the handicap stall or telling the teacher—a balding guy in a polyester tracksuit—that she had cramps. (This always seemed to gross him out sufficiently, and she would get to spend the hour napping on a cot in the nurse's office, sipping Tropicana from a tiny carton and reading pamphlets on abstinence and the proper way to use an inhaler.)

"Do you miss him?" Bree asked now.

"Not really," Celia said. "Maybe just the thought of him. I have this problem where when I'm single, I am really happy, but I feel like something's missing. Then when I'm coupled up, nothing's missing, but I'm just sort of sad and insane. It's fucked up, right?"

For a split second, Bree looked taken aback, and Celia wished that she hadn't said "fuck."

Then Bree said, "Yes, I've never heard it put that way, but I know exactly what you mean."

"I've always been a little boy crazy," Celia confessed. "But then once I get the boy I'm never quite sure what to do with him."

Bree laughed. "If you're so boy crazy, can I ask what in God's name brought you to Smith?"

Celia took a little sip of her vodka. "I'm from just outside of Boston, and I knew that I wanted to go to school close to home. Basically, Smith was the best place I got into. I guess the all-women's thing kind of freaked me out at first, but as long as there are parties with men in attendance, I'll be fine here. Truth be told, I've never really understood women who want to be friends with men. I only have a sister, and I grew up with a bunch of girls on my street, and I don't know—female friendships have always been my thing."

Bree nodded her head. "Mine, too."

She ran her finger over her engagement ring.

"Anyway, what about you?" Celia asked. "Why Smith?"

"My mom and my grandmother both went here," Bree said. "When I was little, every summer my mother and I would fly to Boston for a long weekend, and then we'd rent a car and drive out here to Northampton. My mom was always telling me about ball gowns and fancy dress dances with the Amherst boys and candlelit dinners in the dining hall. I've been in love with the idea of Smith ever since."

"Huh," Celia said. "I have to admit, I was almost scared off by all the tea parties and formals and stuff."

Bree laughed. "They were a big selling point for me."

"Isn't it a bit odd that the same school that has a weekly tea party in every house also has rules about lesbian shower hours?" Celia said.

"Yeah, I don't think that was part of Mom's and Nana's experience," Bree said.

"What do they do now?" Celia asked.

"Do?" Bree said.

"For work."

"Oh. Well, they were both homemakers. But they've always done a lot of volunteer work in the community," Bree said. "Does your mother work?"

"Yes," Celia said. "She's a VP at an ad agency in Boston."

Bree's eyes grew wide. "Oh wow," she said. "That's great. I don't know—I couldn't wait to come here, but the past couple months my boyfriend, uhh, my fiancé, has been pressuring me to transfer."

"Already?" Celia asked. She tried to envision Matt Dougherty begging her to transfer to Berkeley, but that was beyond imagining. Where she came from, no one got engaged out of high school. If she had even tried something like that, her parents would no doubt have staged an intervention.

Bree nodded.

"How long have you been together?" Celia asked.

"Almost three and a half years," Bree said.

"Wow." Celia's longest relationship had lasted six months, and that had seemed like an eternity. When it ended, all she could manage to do for weeks was go to school and write her little column for the student newspaper. The rest of the time she lay in bed, with her father bringing her bowls of ice cream and trying to make her laugh, her sister reporting on all the choicest gossip from the freshman class, as if Celia cared. Suddenly, she saw why Bree would want to hold on to her boy back home.

"It's like it's 1952 and I'm just here to get a degree in home ec," Bree said. "I sometimes think love has a hard time catching on to social change, because part of me really wants to go be with him."

"Well, what part of you wants to stay?" Celia asked.

"The part that gave birth to me," Bree said. "My mother loves Doug, but she just about threw a walleyed fit when I told her I might transfer. She really wants me to give this place a chance. And I want to, too. At least I think I do."

"Ahh, mothers," Celia said. "Mine tied a string bracelet onto my wrist this morning, and an hour later my little sister goes, 'It's a WHAT WOULD JESUS DO? BRACELET!' My mom had put the letters facedown, so I wouldn't know. Subliminal Jesus power or something, I guess."

Bree laughed. "Some of the girls running registration were wearing WHAT WOULD JANE AUSTEN DO shirts."

"That's awesome," Celia said. "I'll have to send one to my mom."

After a long pause, Bree thanked Celia for the cookies. Her voice wavered, and Celia could tell she was getting tipsy.

"I should be thanking you," Celia said. "You're actually helping me to not set a record for the fastest freshman fifteen ever gained."

"You mean *first-year* fifteen," Bree said with a smile.

"Oh, right. And from the look of those upperclass-women, maybe I should amend that to first-year fifty."

Celia wrinkled her brow in thought. "Too mean?" she asked.

"No, I was thinking the exact same thing," Bree said.

Her voice turned to a whisper, as if maybe someone were listening. "Have you met April yet?" she said. "The girl who lives on the other side of me."

"No," Celia said. "Not yet."

"I met her in the bathroom before dinner," Bree said. "She kinda freaked me out. She's a real hippie type, you know? They just don't make 'em like that where I come from."

Celia laughed. "She did look—interesting."

Bree started to giggle. "I'd secretly love to tie her down and give her a makeover. The right shadow and blush, and that girl would be downright lovely," she said. "Speaking of, I like your coloring. I was thinking that at the meeting earlier."

"My coloring?" Celia said.

Truly beautiful women were always complimenting average-looking women on the strangest qualities: *Oh, I'd kill for your small feet. Your coloring is divine.*

"Yeah, I always wanted that exotic Black Irish look. That's what you call it, right?" Bree asked. "That's not offensive, is it?"

Celia laughed. "No, it's not offensive. But where I come from it's hardly exotic. Every girl I grew up with looks exactly the same: Black hair. Pasty white skin. Freckles. We had one fake ID that started off with my friend Liz's older sister and got passed around among five of us neighborhood girls."

"You're not pasty!" Bree said. "You're fair skinned. Anyway. Growing up in Irish Boston must have been so cool."

Irish Boston. Celia had to stifle a laugh. She wondered if Bree was picturing her family wearing scally caps and talking in thick Southie accents, when really they lived on a sleepy suburban street like everyone else. They did have the cast-of-thousands Irish clan, with cousins all over Massachusetts, who gathered nearly every weekend in someone's backyard to celebrate something—a birthday, a communion, a wedding anniversary. And in a brief burst of pride after a trip to Galway (as well as a fruitless attempt to fix Celia's incurable clumsiness), her mother had forced her and Violet to take step-dancing classes, which Celia now credited with her perfect posture and complete inability to dance like a normal person. But other than that, she was no more Irish than anyone else.

Of course, she was doing the same thing to Bree: She could easily imagine this girl at high school cotillions and debutante balls. All they knew of each other, really, were the sharp edges. The middle parts and blurry lines were yet to be filled in.

Celia missed her friends back home. Liz Hastings, with her wicked sense of humor and childlike fear of the dark. Lauren O'Neil, who had been raised with six brothers and always had the wildest slumber parties as a kid—the brothers scaring and delighting them, popping into the room in clown masks, or telling them ghost stories until they cried. Those girls knew Celia, all the way through. How long would it be before she could sit down with someone and just have a conversation without small talk or backstory, without having to worry about what words she used?

An hour later, before she went back to her room, Bree hugged her and said, "I'm so glad you're right next door. Have you ever been to Savannah, Celia? It's beautiful there. These gorgeous droopy trees, and purple Spanish moss hanging all over the place. Oh, I'll bring you there one of these days. I know you'll just eat it up with a spoon."

Then she gave a dainty little drunken hiccup. "I don't really drink very much."

Celia laughed. "I'm glad you're next door, too."

The following morning, on the first full day at Smith, Celia woke before eight o'clock. There was still a day to go before classes began, but she could not get back to sleep. She opened her bedroom door and looked out into the empty hallway. She wished she knew Bree well enough to go wake her up for an early breakfast or a long walk around campus. Instead, she left the door open and sat alone on the bed, writing in her journal.

A while later, there was a movement in the hall, and Celia caught a glimpse of red hair. "Hey!" she called out. "April, is it?"

April's head popped in. "Yes, it is," she said.

She entered the room in cutoffs and a faded tank top, and Celia saw that her calves were covered in thick, brown hair. It wasn't stubble, she realized. The girl had never shaved. Her dyed red hair was up in a messy ponytail, and she wore no makeup. She was about five foot eight and very skinny, with long legs that were surprisingly sexy in spite of the hair.

Typical, Celia thought. It was always the girls who didn't give a damn about how they looked who got to be tall and thin without even trying. April's face was pretty enough, but her features were sharp—she had a slightly pointy nose and prominent cheekbones that gave her a sort of harsh look when she wasn't smiling.

"Have you already been out and about this morning?" Celia asked.

April nodded. "I went to help set up for a lecture from the director of Equality Now later today," she said. "It's gonna be amazing. Here, take this."

She handed Celia a pamphlet. Celia's eyes scanned it:

STOP HONOR KILLINGS NOW! DID YOU KNOW:
In Pakistan, under the Hudood Ordinances, a woman needs either the confession of her rapist

or the eyewitness testimony of at least four Muslim adult males to prove she has been raped? Otherwise, she can be prosecuted for fornication or adultery, or murdered by her husband, brothers, and father for having dishonored the family's name. An average of one thousand women die in honor killings in Pakistan each year. HELP US STOP THE CRUELTY AND THE SUFFERING!

Celia blinked. She felt overwhelmed just being in this dorm and meeting all these strange new women. How on earth had April already taken it upon herself to join in the fight against honor killings?

April came and sat beside her on the bed. She had the body odor of a Boston street person—pungent and spicy and raw. Celia suddenly remembered how one summer in high school, her mother had read a magazine article about chemicals in household products that cause cancer and insisted that the family go organic. She made them start using all-natural toothpaste and shampoo and even deodorant. Celia wondered now if this was the way she had smelled up until she started dating Joey Murray the fall of her junior year. That was when she began to sneak Soft & Dri, hair spray, and Noxzema into the house the way other kids might smuggle in bags of pot or shrink-wrapped copies of *Hustler*.

April eyed the glass Absolut bottle from the night before in Celia's garbage can, and Celia immediately felt guilty for not asking her to join them.

"You know Smith recycles, right?" April said.

Celia diligently took the bottle from the trash and placed

it in the blue bin behind the door, reminding herself to tell Bree about the interaction later. Who the hell was this girl? she wondered.

"Do you feel like grabbing breakfast?" April asked after an awkward pause.

"Sure," Celia said.

"On the walk home from town I couldn't stop thinking about potato hash and a huge fucking plate of Fakin' Bacon," April said.

"What's Fakin' Bacon?" Celia said.

April laughed. "It's a soy-based product that tastes like the real thing. Well, kind of. I'm a vegan," she said. "But I really like to eat."

Celia smiled. At least they had that in common.

They walked downstairs to the dining room. Celia was relieved to have someone, anyone, to go with. Though her sister was three years younger, and they had different groups of friends, she had always had Violet by her side when she started something new—summer camp, or softball, or even just a stupid snorkeling class at Club Med. Her whole life she had wanted privacy, imagined a Saturday when she wouldn't have to go along to some boring family party. Now, alone for the first time, Celia had no clue what to do with herself.

The dining hall was dotted here and there with girls in flannel pajama pants and tank tops, or baggy T-shirts and boxers. Most of the upperclasswomen still hadn't arrived on campus, and the majority of the tables were empty.

Celia wore jeans and a red cardigan, with socks and Keds.

"Do you think it's a little odd how everyone here dresses

like they're in a mental hospital?" Celia whispered to April, wanting a laugh.

April just shrugged. She gestured toward her cutoffs. "Not exactly a fashion expert, now, am I?"

Celia hoped she hadn't offended her. "I'm trying to fight the power and not wear my pajamas in public for as long as I can," she said.

April raised an eyebrow.

They took plates from the table at the end of the buffet line and surveyed the food. There were platters heaped with doughnuts and bagels and pastries; a huge tureen of steaming oatmeal; and pans full of bacon, sausage, eggs, French toast, waffles, and hash browns. Beside each meat product was a vegan alternative.

Celia had never heard of such a thing. Had there been any vegans in her high school? No, she decided. Definitely not. The two or three vegetarians she knew just ate the cafeteria pizza every day, so they never really stood out.

April loaded her plate with a green-hued egg substitute and Fakin' Bacon that reminded Celia of the rubber food she had had in her Fisher-Price kitchen as a kid.

"You should try this, it's good, and no animals had to die gruesome deaths for it to be made," April said.

Celia was holding a sausage between tongs in midair. Oh, brother. She put the sausage on her plate and took two Danishes from the pastry tray—one raspberry, one cheese. If there was ever a perfect time for comfort food, this was it.

They sat down and began to talk about the house meeting the night before.

"What did you think of the shower hour rules?" Celia asked.

April shrugged.

Jeez, this girl was going to make her work for it.

"Do you have a boyfriend back home?" Celia asked.

April sputtered a little and said no, as if Celia had asked her whether she had a My Little Pony collection in her purse.

"A girlfriend?" Celia asked. Oh, what the hell.

"No," April said. "Not to sound like an asshole, but I thought the whole meeting was kind of juvenile. I am pretty sure the fact that I was assigned to live in King must have been some big prank on the part of the Housing Office."

"What do you mean?" Celia asked.

"I'm just not really Quad material," April said. "I'm not into all the sorority bullshit and the keg parties with white-hats. That's not why I came here. I could have gone to any state school in Illinois if I'd wanted that."

"Oh, you're from Illinois?" Celia said, in a tone that was far too eager for someone who had never actually been there.

"Chicago," April said.

Celia nodded. "So why did you come here anyway?" she asked. "If not for parties and all that normal college stuff."

"I came here because it was the alma mater of Gloria Steinem and Molly Ivins. I thought it was the most effective place to fight the patriarchy in this godforsaken country," April said. Then she took a bite of her Fakin' Bacon and said, "Also, I like the dining hall food."

Celia wondered for a moment whether she was the only normal person at Smith College. At home, she had always been thought of as slightly odd, because unlike her girl-friends she preferred Victorian novels and Dorothy Parker poems to women's magazines, and Technicolor musicals to any modern movie. But now, she felt like Joe Normal—no teenage wedding, no rage at the establishment—which at Smith apparently meant she was a freak.

As they bused their dishes, April mentioned that she would be spending the afternoon volunteering with an anti-sweatshop group on campus before attending her Equality Now lecture. It sounded admirable, of course, but Celia just wanted to crawl back into bed and talk to friends from home on the phone for the rest of the day.

"I think it's really important to reach out and help people, to realize that it's not all about our own petty bullshit," April said. "Most women our age will cry over a guy not calling them back, but they don't give a flying fuck about real human suffering."

Celia told herself that April was just speaking generally, that she hadn't meant anything about her necessarily. Even so, she felt her cheeks burning red and cursed her stupid pale skin for always betraying her emotions.

"Sorry," April said. "I'm working on trying to control my soapbox."

Celia smiled. "That's okay."

She wondered what April's friends back home were like.

"So what kind of music are you into?" April said.

"Oh, all kinds. I like old stuff—Billie Holiday and all that. But I'm starting to get really into folk, like Bob Dylan and Joni Mitchell."

"Now you're talking," April said with a grin. "I love both of them. How about Elliott Smith, or Kris Delmhorst?"

"I don't know much of their stuff," Celia said, though the truth was she didn't know any.

"Ahh, well then, I'll burn you a CD that will blow your fucking mind," April said.

Later that day, April plastered the outside of her door with bumper stickers that said things like FEMINISM IS THE RADICAL NOTION THAT WOMEN ARE PEOPLE and IN GODDESS WE TRUST. She wrote a quote from *Mary Poppins* right on the hall-way wallpaper in permanent red ink: THOUGH WE ADORE MEN INDIVIDUALLY, WE AGREE THAT AS A GROUP THEY'RE RATHER STUPID.

Celia slipped another note under Bree's door: *Check out what Crazypants did in the hall.*

A while later, Bree slid a note back: *I told you. She's bonkers!*

The next day, Celia was getting ready to walk to her first class, when April came into her room.

"Do you have a nine o'clock?" she said.

Celia nodded.

"Me too. Want to walk together?"

"Sure," Celia said. She picked up her backpack, and they made their way into the hall. As they did this, four moving men carrying enormous boxes burst through the maids' quarters doors.

"Sally Werner?" one of them said.

Celia pointed to Sally's room at the end of the hall.

"It looks like she's moving into a four-bedroom house," April said.

Celia smiled. She had chosen her outfit for the first day of classes sometime in mid-August—a black A-line dress with a long-sleeved purple shirt underneath, black tights, and purple ballet flats. April was wearing scrubs and a T-shirt that said IT'S A BLACK THING, YOU WOULDN'T UNDERSTAND. She had let her red hair air-dry, and it fell in unruly waves around her shoulders. Celia couldn't help it: She wondered what people would think when they saw the two of them crossing campus together.

As soon as they were out of the Quad, a student with a green mohawk descended the stairs of Chapin House and called out, "April, baby!"

"Lookin' good, Miss April," said another, whom they passed in front of Bass Hall. She planted a big kiss on April's cheek.

"Did you guys know each other before you got here?" Celia asked.

"No, I just met them last night at the Feminists of Smith Unite welcome party," April said. "You should come with me to the next meeting."

Celia smiled weakly. At her high school, those sorts of girls would have held dominion over the smoke-filled ladies' room and the drama club, and little else. Her outfit, which had seemed sophisticated and pretty a month earlier, suddenly felt like something you would wear on the first day of second grade. She felt like she ought to be skipping rope and sucking on a giant lollipop.

After class, Celia made her way back to King House alone. April had invited her to come hear Rebecca Walker speak about the intersection of sexism and racism during the lunch hour, but Celia just wanted to get back to her room—to her familiar bedspread that still smelled like home, to her e-mails from old friends, and to her own private telephone from which she planned to call Liz, who had grown up next door and just started her freshman year at Trinity. The dorm, which had seemed foreign and strange only a day earlier, suddenly felt like a refuge from the campus beyond, full of unknown girls and scarily long reading assignments.

When she reached their little hallway, there were cardboard boxes outside Sally's room, overflowing with clothes and books and CDs. A lot of the girls who were from distant states and countries were only receiving their belongings now.

Celia could hear a Supremes CD playing in Sally's room, and the door was open, so she went to it. She had wanted to introduce herself ever since the house meeting, but Sally seemed always to be on the phone, talking in hushed tones.

She stood on a chair, in perfect jeans and a plain gray T-shirt. Behind her, long floral curtains billowed in the breeze. She was hammering a huge picture frame to the wall—it contained ten or so photos, cut into the shapes of ovals or stars, with bright-eyed, preppy types holding up their diplomas at high school graduation or lying in a row in two-piece bathing suits. There were more of these frames lined up on the bed, waiting to be hung, next to neat piles of button-down shirts and sundresses and pressed pants, which made it look as though Sally might be operating a J.Crew franchise out of her room.

"Hi," Celia said to get her attention.

"Oh God, I'm sorry for the mess," Sally said. "My stuff just arrived today."

"Don't worry about it," Celia said. "Where are you from?"

It was perhaps the fifty-ninth time she had asked that question in three days. Who really gave a crap where anyone was from anyway? Albuquerque or Tokyo, New Jersey or the moon? What difference did it make?

"I'm from outside of Boston," Sally said.

"Oh, me too," Celia said. "What town?"

"Wellesley. You?"

"Milton." Celia thought for a moment, and then said, "You didn't drive out here?"

Sally shook her head. "Took the train. My father is on a business trip, and my brother is so undependable, I'd sooner rely on a unicorn arriving at my front door, pulling a U-Haul behind it."

There was a long beat of silence as Celia took this in and thought about the one thing Sally wasn't saying. Whose family lived just a two-hour drive from school and didn't want to bring her there themselves?

"I'm really sorry about your mother," Celia said. "If you ever want to talk, my door is always open. And my mom has stocked my closet with more food than I could eat before graduation."

She suddenly felt guilty for even mentioning the word "mom," but Sally smiled and said thank you.

"Do you need some help unpacking?" Celia asked.

"Oh, no thanks," Sally said. "I'm kind of anal. I like my things just so. But if you wanted to keep me company, that would be great."

"Sure," Celia said.

There wasn't any room on the bed, and the desk and chair were stacked high with boxes, so Celia took a seat on the floor. She noticed that each of Sally's boxes had been carefully labeled—BOOKS, HAIRCARE, FILES AND PAPERS, SNEAKERS, HEELS. Had Sally done all this herself? Or was it the last project her mother took on before she died?

Sally started removing shirts from a box on the desk. Each one was individually wrapped in tissue paper.

"Nice weather out there today?" she asked.

Celia nodded. "Still a little hot."

"I haven't been out yet," Sally said.

"Have you met the other two on our hall?" Celia asked. "Bree and April."

Sally nodded. "April, yeah. We spent the whole first night talking."

Even though Celia hadn't invited them to come join her and Bree, she felt a little sting at knowing she had been excluded from their conversation.

Sally laughed. "I don't think I've ever had less in common with a person in my life, but I really like her. It's a cliché, but I just felt like I could say anything to her."

You can say anything to me, Celia thought, and then she realized she was competing for closeness in a place where no one had known each other for more than a minute and a half.

"So do you know what you want to major in?" Sally asked.

She was much more formal than the other girls Celia had met so far, asking the types of questions one might usually expect from a friend's great-aunt.

"English lit," Celia said. "What about you?"

"Oh, I'm premed. Or will be anyway," Sally said. "I'll be majoring in bio. I took a couple of classes over the summer, just to get a head start. It's pretty fascinating stuff."

She lifted an enormous Chock full o'Nuts can from a pink shopping bag. "My mom's ashes," she said, nodding down at the can.

Jesus, Mary, and Joseph.

Celia nodded. "Oh. Well, it's nice that you can have her close."

"Yup, that's exactly what I was thinking," Sally said.

She put the coffee can on the floor of her closet and shut the door gently. As she did this, Celia had a horrible vision of herself going in there months later, after all the awkwardness had ended and they'd become friends. She imagined herself looking for a dress, say, and absentmindedly kicking Sally's mother over, the ashes spreading everywhere—into the cracks in the hard wood and onto Sally's pristine footwear collection.

"Do you know Jacob Wolf?" Sally asked. "He went to Milton High."

Celia shook her head. "I went to Catholic school my whole life, so—"

The phone rang. If it had been Celia's, she would have let it go, but Sally picked up.

She put her hand over the mouthpiece. "I have to take this," she said to Celia. "It's my best friend Monica. Can I catch up with you later?"

"Oh, of course," Celia said, awkwardly climbing to her feet.

"Would you mind shutting the door?" Sally said.

Celia didn't see Sally again that day, or that night. When she got up to use the bathroom around 3:00 a.m., she passed Sally's room and heard her talking.

Celia knew she shouldn't, but she pressed her ear to the door.

"I can't do this, Mon," Sally was saying, her voice thick and desperate. "I think coming here so soon after everything was just a huge mistake. Will you stay on the phone with me? Please don't hang up, sugar. Please."

.   .   .

The next day was convocation. The first years had received flyers under their doors reminding them that everyone was to meet in the lobby at four o'clock to process to John M. Greene Hall (JMG, as they of course called it) as a house.

By then, all the upperclasswomen had moved in, and the halls of King House were jammed with suitcases and bulging garbage bags full of winter clothes hauled up from the storage space in the basement.

From her bedroom, Celia could hear them. The seniors, many just back from junior year abroad in Geneva or Florence or Sydney, screeched and hollered and kissed each other all over the face, sounding like the year apart had almost killed them. The sophomores were giddy, too. They hugged each other for longer than seemed natural. They left their doors open and played music while they unpacked— the soft sounds of Jeff Buckley and the Beatles and sweet, girlie music that Celia had never heard before.

She paused as she walked by them in the bathroom, lining up jars of Jolen bleach and boxes of tampons in their cubbies. The older girls hung hand-printed signs above the toilets for visitors: WELCOME TO OUR HOUSE, BUT REMEMBER THAT REAL MEN PUT THE SEAT DOWN. Even after an entire lifetime of living with a mother and a sister, Celia had never been anyplace so entirely and unabashedly feminine.

The weather had turned steamy, a mid-August day at the start of September.

As Bree had put it over breakfast: "It's hot as Georgia asphalt."

Some of the older girls walked around in just bras on top and panties or boxer shorts on the bottom. A few of them had gorgeous bodies—toned abs and long, lean legs. But most of them did not. They let their guts hang out as they ripped open packing boxes or hung curtains.

Celia told herself that a year from now, she'd probably be like them: comfortable here, at home. Though she wasn't sure about the intensity of the bonding, or the extent of the nakedness. Other than at the beach, she had never seen her own mother in less than a floor-length terry-cloth robe and slippers.

At four o'clock on the dot, a chanting voice boomed up the central staircase and down the fluorescent-lit halls.

"Everybody do the King House Rumble, Everybody do the King House Rumble. Everybody! Rumble! Everybody! Rumble!"

The sound got louder and louder, until Jenna the Monster Truck and a gaggle of other girls came to the first-year rooms one by one and pulled them out into the hall.

Celia saw Sally, Bree, and April getting pulled toward the stairs as she was and laughed as she made eye contact with each of them.

"What in the Lord's name is this?" Bree said, as they were shepherded downstairs.

"It's convocation," Sally said. "There'll be speeches and singing and appearances by famous alums. It's the first time we'll get to be with the entire school, all at once."

Sally seemed like the sort of girl who would have joined a sorority, if she'd gone to a college that didn't forbid them completely.

All seventy-five King House residents were packed into the foyer, and Jenna the Monster Truck was handing out

Burger King crowns. Another girl was pulling sparkly purple bedsheets from a giant cardboard box.

"Okay, girls," Jenna said. "This is it! Our first chance to show Smith what the new King House is all about."

"What's with the costumes?" said one of the first years in the crowd.

"It's tradition that each house gets dressed up for convocation," Jenna said. "We wear crowns and robes, because we're the queens of King."

"Holla!" screamed an upperclasswoman named JoAnn. Celia had met her getting coffee that morning, and on her own she had seemed rather mousy and slight. But standing among her friends, she looked altogether different.

"I want everyone to grab a cape, grab a crown, and meet us back down here in five," Jenna the Monster Truck said.

"We're supposed to go all the way back upstairs just to put on a cape?" April asked.

Some of the older girls started to laugh.

"You left out the best part, Monster Truck!" someone yelled.

"Oh yeah," Jenna said. "We do it in our underwear."

A few of the first years squealed with delight. A few others uttered concerned murmurs.

April said, "You're fucking kidding me."

"Nope, baby, it's true," Jenna said, walking over to April and draping an arm over her shoulder. "Of course, you don't have to, but most of us think it's more fun that way."

Everyone started rushing back up the stairs. Celia felt like her blood was coursing faster than usual. She was supposed to get into her underwear around hundreds of women she didn't even know? She grabbed Bree's hand, hoping maybe she had Southern modesty on her side—if someone other than April refused, Celia would, too. She really didn't care on what grounds.

"Are you gonna do it?" she asked Bree.

"Not in my skivvies." Bree smiled. "I think I'll just wear a bikini."

Well sure, why not, when you look like a freaking movie star?

"Sally?" Celia said, as the four of them followed the crowd upstairs.

"I guess so," Sally said. "Yeah, why not. When in Rome, right?"

Celia faked a smile. "Right."

When she got to her room and opened up the top drawer of her dresser, Celia thought she might pass out. She owned a couple pairs of sexy, tiny underwear, suitable only for the eyes of teenage boys who were so happy to see a girl undressed that they simply did not notice her fat thighs or stretch marks. Other than that, she wore cotton granny panties, covered in little-girl prints. She sighed, and then dropped her clothes. She was wearing a red cotton bra and the Friday pair of panties from her days-of-the-week underwear collection, even though it was Wednesday. She looked stupid, but no worse than she would in anything else she owned.

Celia glanced down in horror to see a tiny little tuft of black hair poking out against her white leg. Did she have time to shave? Why the fuck hadn't the older girls warned them?

A moment later, Sally stood in the doorway with a bottle

of tequila in one hand and a digital camera in the other. She wore a perfect black satin bra and matching panties. Behind her was Bree in a pale pink bikini, and April dressed exactly as she had been, in khaki shorts and a black T-shirt, with the purple cape draped over the top.

Celia quickly grabbed her cape and wrapped it around herself.

"I think we should each take a swig," Sally said.

"I second that," Bree said.

They passed the bottle among the four of them, quickly gulping down the burning liquid.

"Let me get a picture!" Sally said.

"No, no," Celia said with a laugh.

"I'll take it," April said.

"No, you won't," Sally said. "I want all four of us in it."

So they stood in a huddle, and Sally held the camera out far in front of them with her outstretched arm.

"Say 'naked'!" she said, and they all screamed, "Naked!"

Downstairs, girls fat and thin stood shuffling around in their underwear, not even bothering to cover themselves up. Jenna the Monster Truck taught all the first years the words to the King House Rumble, and they practiced out in the driveway four or five times.

Finally, it was time to go to JMG, and they marched along the sidewalks two by two: Celia arm in arm with Bree, and Sally and April close behind. Men driving along Elm Street beeped their horns, and from every corner of campus, other girls from other houses could be heard chanting their own house cheers, the collective sound getting louder and louder, until they filled the auditorium.

Banners for each house on campus hung from the rafters,

and all you could see and hear were girls—their screaming voices, their flesh everywhere. Some wore just pasties and thongs (Celia thanked God himself for not placing her in whatever house that was). Others wore gold bras and underpants, with angel wings stuck to their backs. The soccer team wore Smith thongs, sports bras, and sliced soccer balls on their heads. Compared with most women in the room, the King House girls were overdressed.

"Don't stop the Rumble!" Jenna shouted.

They kept going, as the girls to the left cheered for Jordan House, and the girls to the right cheered for Morrow. Even April was getting into it.

The room shook and echoed, the energy like nothing Celia had ever felt before. She let it smother her for a moment. Twenty-four hundred young things, all of them energized, all of them proud, joined together by this place.

Bree grabbed her arm and pointed at Sally, who was trying to tell them something. Celia struggled to make out her words.

"What?" she shouted, leaning in to listen along with Bree and April.

"I said I think we're officially Smithies now," Sally called over the din.

Their first few weeks at Smith were full of parties, teas, lectures, plays, and concerts, just for the first years. Celia wondered if the school did this by design to make them forget their collective loneliness.

She was pleased to have been placed in maids' quarters, because there was something much more manageable about having to learn the ways of only three hall mates. Also, they had their very own bathroom, instead of having to share the big bathroom down the hall with everyone else. Celia was endlessly relieved by this. In high school, she couldn't even use the ladies' room at Saint Catherine's if there was someone else in there. Celia would sit silent in the stall, willing the other person to leave, then peeing quickly and yanking up her tights before anyone came in. She had always been outgoing and friendly, but there were some things that just seemed wrong any place but home.

The maids' quarters bathroom had two stalls, two showers, and two sinks, all crowded with beauty products of Bree's. (None of the others complained about this, because they enjoyed using her expensive avocado scrubs and lavender conditioning treatments and hot-oil hair masks.)

One night in early December, Bree and April had both come down with colds, and Celia could hear them hacking away in their rooms. She grabbed her first-aid kit and knocked on their doors.

"Into the bathroom with you," she commanded, feeling like her mother, and both girls followed, looking pathetic and splotchy. Sally came, too, though she wasn't sick and made a great show of popping a vitamin C pill to indicate that she intended to stay healthy.

"What are we doing?" April said.

"Sit down," Celia said. The girls sat on the windowsill and watched as she turned the shower taps to the highest setting and poured eucalyptus oil into the streams of hot water. She turned the sinks on, too.

"Close the window," she told Sally.

"What are we doing?" April said again.

Celia blinked. "I'm steaming your colds away. Didn't your mom ever do that when you were a kid?"

April laughed. "Umm, no. My mother's not exactly that type."

They sat in the bathroom for one full hour. Celia made the girls take a tablespoon each of the cough syrup her mother bought on trips to Ireland—it tasted foul, but it had codeine in it. She read to them from a paper she was writing about Edna St. Vincent Millay, her all-time favorite poet, whose poems she had copied furiously into her journal in high school, alongside song lyrics from the Indigo Girls and Sarah McLachlan, hoping that inspiration might strike if she filled her brain with enough beautiful words written by other people.

"Listen to this," she said now. "It's from an essay written about Millay in 1937 by this guy named John Crowe Ransom, and here's why he says she's not truly talented: 'A woman lives for love . . . Man distinguishes himself by intellect . . . If I must express it in a word, I feel still obliged to say it is her lack of intellectual interest . . . which the male reader misses in her poetry . . . I used a conventional symbol, which I hope was not objectionable, when I phrased this lack of hers: deficiency in masculinity.' "

"So not much has changed since 1937, I guess," April said.

"What do you mean?" Bree said.

"Well, when a woman writes a book that has anything to do with feelings or relationships, it's either called chick lit or women's fiction, right? But look at Updike, or Irving. Imagine if they'd been women. Just imagine. Someone would have slapped a pink cover onto *Rabbit at Rest,* and poof, there goes the fucking Pulitzer."

Sally laughed. "Okay, but I think you're forgetting Jane Smiley and Marilynne Robinson and a whole host of women writers who have gotten every bit as much attention as men."

April threw up her hands. "You must be joking!"

Celia smiled. These girls were smart, she thought, much smarter than she was. They weren't even planning to be English majors, yet here they stood, on the linoleum in socked feet, discussing the state of American literature.

"What were your high schools like?" Celia asked, when what she really meant was *How do you know all this? Should I know the nuances of your worlds—of science and politics? Because I don't.*

"I'm a public school girl," April said.

"Me too!" Bree piped up. "But it was a really nice public school, right on the main street in Savannah, and just the nicest teachers, and almost everyone in my group took only AP classes."

Even when she had a fever of 102, Bree's skin was lovely, her eyes stayed bright. Celia would sell her soul to the devil to look like Bree on even her ugliest day. No man passed by her without staring, and though there was something predictable and gross in this (April always screamed out, "Take a fucking picture, it'll last longer!"), Celia understood why they couldn't look away. Bree was funny and kind and happy, so much happier than most intelligent people Celia knew. She loved her parents and her brothers and—for a time, anyway—her fiancé. She loved Savannah and dancing and blasting country music in her room. (She often quoted old

Dolly Parton songs in casual conversation, though hardly anyone ever realized she was doing it.) Her room always smelled like strawberry lip balm and lilacs, and each time Celia entered it and saw the pale pink carpet, the rows of glass perfume bottles on the dresser, the framed antique black-and-white photos, she was struck with a grade-school-like urge to be just like Bree in every way.

"My high school was one of those dingy Chicago schools with gum stuck to every surface and two-hundred-year-old textbooks," April said. "The teachers were either spiteful old lifers or, worse, perky little Teach For America volunteers who thought they could lift us out of our miserable existences in nine months or less."

Sally sputtered. "You're exaggerating."

"I'm not," April said.

"Did you grow up in a bad neighborhood?" Bree said, in a tone that made it sound as though she herself had never even set foot in one, the term "bad neighborhood" merely something she had heard about on the evening news.

"No," April said. "But my mother thought it was important for me to experience real life and not be so fucking pampered. I was probably the only kid in Chicago who was bused out of a good neighborhood and into a bad one."

Celia was always riveted when April spoke of her single mother, who took her to protests in her baby stroller, smoked joints all day long, and believed that the government had been listening in on her phone calls ever since she was arrested at a demonstration in 1973.

While the other girls in King House were still breaking apart from their high school boyfriends, or trying desperately to avoid gaining weight from all the carbs in the dining hall, April was working two campus jobs, because she was putting herself through Smith and needed the money. Celia believed, perhaps naïvely, that class was indistinguishable at Smith—it wasn't like in high school when you could tell whose parents had money based on the size of their house, or the cars they drove. Here, most people didn't drive, and everyone dressed in tattered jeans and Nikes. But when she told April this, April just laughed and said, "Everyone here goes to Smith. Therefore, their parents have money. Other than the five of us who are paying our own way."

"What about you, Sal?" Bree asked now.

"Oh, I went to a school called Patterson," Sally said.

"Private?" Bree said.

"Yeah."

Celia knew a few girls who had gone there. They came from the wealthiest families in Milton. They wore uniforms made by some fancy-pants designer and were forced to play a sport each semester—lacrosse or tennis or soccer or golf. Celia made a mental note to tell her parents this bit of information. It only confirmed what she had suspected from the beginning: Sally's dad was loaded.

In some ways, it seemed like Sally had been raised to coexist. If she ran into town for shampoo, she asked the other girls if they needed anything, and she'd gladly lug back huge bottles of detergent and Poland Springs for them all to share. ("Good exercise!" she would say with a smile.) Every Sunday, she knocked on their doors to check and see whether their carpets needed cleaning, since she had the vacuum out and was going to do hers anyway. She spoke in what April called Sallyisms, always adding a ridiculous "sweetpea" or "lemon drop" or "sugarplum" at the end of every sentence, addressing them as if she were their friendly cookie-baking grandma. (For every time Sally said "sweetpea," April said "fuck." It was her favorite word, used to emphasize anger, enthusiasm, and any other emotion possible.)

Of all of them, Sally was the most serious about her work. She logged in countless morning hours in the biology lab and studied alone in her room at night with the door closed, while the others engaged in a combination of reading and gossip out in the hall. She was going to be a doctor someday, she said, and she needed to focus.

But Sally was peculiar. She did not go home for Thanksgiving, choosing instead to pay the two-hundred-dollar boarding fee to stay alone in her dorm room, drinking red wine and watching *Golden Girls* reruns on Lifetime. She called her father Fred to his face, though one got the impression it hadn't always been that way.

"So two public school kids, a private school snoot, and our little Celia went to Catholic school," April said. "I do believe it turned her into the gin-swilling saint she is today."

Celia batted her eyelashes and did a dramatic sign of the cross.

"Peace be with you all," she said, and they laughed.

That's what Catholic school was good for—self-deprecation and nun jokes and not much else.

"I can't believe you'd call me a snoot!" Sally said, with fake indignation.

After a while, Sally crept out and brewed tea in her hot pot, and brought them each a cup.

April had a strange, almost sad look on her face.

"Are you okay?" Celia asked.

"Yeah," April said. "It's just I've never had the kind of friends who would actually steam up a bathroom for me before."

Celia could not wait to tell her mother. Despite April's frequent complaints that she didn't belong in the Quad, Celia noticed, she never applied for a room change.

Celia gave her a hug, holding on tight even though April stiffened.

"I'm glad we all found our way to each other," she said.

(Later, April would blame her uncharacteristic mushiness on the codeine.)

April was a die-hard MacKinnonite, an association Celia had never even heard of before her Smith days. Even most Smith feminists thought she was too strident, which was really saying something. She believed that porn and strip clubs were bad for women and men alike—degrading to those who took part in them, and for those who watched. She thought the women's movement was run by a bunch of rich, white ladies who cried about being tethered to domestic lives of dinner parties and tennis lessons while most of the world's women were struggling to make minimum wage and feed their children.

During that first year, along with some of her more radical friends from outside the dorm, April led the transpositive campus movement. In her opinion, there was discrimination against women who came to Smith and then underwent gender reassignment surgery. These transgendered men, she said, should be acknowledged as such. She started a petition to change the wording of the student constitution from "she" to "the student" and got so many signatures that the school senate agreed to vote on it.

After much debate, Sally said she agreed with April's point, but Bree and Celia just couldn't. It was a person's right to change his or her gender, they said (though Celia wasn't totally sure what she really thought about this), but Smith was a *women's* college, and if you were born a woman and chose to become a man, you should pick another school. Once they said it, April acted aloof around them for two full weeks, until her bill got passed without their support.

Soon after, April joined in with the vegan club on campus and went around the dining hall during Parents' Weekend affixing PETA stickers onto the mink coats of four mothers, including Bree's, while everyone was eating grasshopper pie. (Bree didn't want to forgive April, but then April appeared at her door with a bouquet of daisies stolen from the president's garden and a roll of Toll House cookie dough. The two of them devoured the dough, and April told Bree dirty jokes until she nearly choked from laughing, and forgot why she had been angry in the first place.)

Sally never got mad at April. She seemed thrilled by April's enthusiasm for causes that she herself had never even thought about. April took her to rallies and lectures; she put piles of books outside Sally's bedroom door, with private notes attached—*The Beauty Myth* and *Backlash, Only Words,* and *Sisterhood Is Powerful.* Sally studied each one of them, growing ever more incensed by the sexism all around, which she said she had hardly ever noticed before. April saw sexism everywhere—in the movies, on the radio, in TV ads for dish soap and fast food, in political elections and toys and corporations and elementary schools, in packages of red meat wrapped in cellophane at the grocery store.

By the end of their first year, April had been arrested for

disorderly conduct twice—once during a protest in Boston, and once for starting a fight with the right-wing crazies outside a clinic in Amherst. Each time, Sally drove to wherever April was and paid the fifty-dollar fee to get her out. Hours later, they would return to the dorm holding hands, like they'd been off at some ice-cream social.

"The odd couple's at it again," Bree would whisper to Celia.

There was something magnetic between April and Sally. Maybe they were so perfect for each other because both of them were strange, and neither ever seemed to notice the other's strangeness, or at least never seemed bothered by it. Or maybe, as Bree said, it was because they mothered each other. Sally often got terrified by nightmares, or even pleasant dreams, about her mother. She said it was unbearable to dream of her mother doing something mundane—taking a run, say, or picking her up at school—only to wake up and realize that what she had dreamed of was impossible now. Bree told Celia that all Sally's talk about death made her insanely uncomfortable, but April spent whole nights lying next to Sally in bed, softly singing Bob Dylan songs, holding Sally's hand while she slept so that if she woke up scared, it wouldn't last for long. She said she had seen her mother through "Many a bad trip," and compared with that, Sally was nothing.

"What kind of a bad trip?" Bree had hissed at Celia after April said it.

Celia just shrugged.

There was something unsettling about having to take a Greyhound bus to a close friend's wedding. It was a concrete reminder of how much Sally had changed in these past four years, and how much Celia had stayed the same. The train would have been far more dignified, but Celia couldn't bring herself to pay a hundred dollars each way just to prove she was a grown-up.

The bus stopped at a Roy Rogers somewhere outside Hartford. She had no idea that Roy Rogers even existed anymore. Celia bought a Diet Coke and reluctantly climbed back onto the bus, newly awash in the smell of fried food. The woman in front of her had bought a fish sandwich. A goddamn fish sandwich! Was there anything more offensive to eat on a bus full of people at eleven-thirty in the morning?

As they turned back onto the road, the kid beside her took a notebook from his backpack, with the words "Freshman English" printed on the front in droopy letters.

Celia remembered how Bree used to refer to their first year out of college as their freshman year of life. Celia might call her crying from a bathroom stall at work, complaining about her boss, or she might send a pained text message from yet another ill-fated first date, and Bree would soothe her gently, saying, "You're only a freshman. It's going to get better. I swear."

Celia's freshman year of life had amounted to nothing much besides going on a string of comically bad dates, forging a stormy yet intense bond with New York that she knew would last for decades, and taking a job as an assistant at a mass-market book publisher that was far from the novel-writing career she really wanted. Circus Books published mostly self-help guides and pink anthologies about shoes and breakups. It was the sort of place where, when you told someone at a cocktail party that you worked there, you had to roll your eyes. (At the recommendation of the Smith Career Development Office, Celia had asked in her first interview whether her predecessors had been promoted—the girl before her, they said, was backpacking through Nepal, and the one before that had joined the Peace Corps. Celia now thought she should have taken it as a sign that the place would suck the soul out of anyone who dared to work there, driving the dreamers out to the farthest corners of the earth for some sort of fulfillment.)

They would remember Bree's freshman year of life as the time when she left for Stanford Law and threw herself into her studies. That was the same year that she became more or less estranged from her Southern family. "She's lost her sparkle," April said to Celia on the phone one night, and Celia agreed.

For Sally, freshman year of life had meant meeting Jake, falling in love, and planning her world around their relationship, so that she even forestalled applying to med school, the one thing she had always planned to do. Bree and April thought Sally was trying too hard to replace her lost mother, convincing herself that what was comfortable must be right. They feared she would be disappointed if she hoped to get a real commitment out of such a young guy. Even three years later, Jake's proposal shocked them all—all but Sally, who had never doubted it for an instant. Sally was the head fund-raiser for their class and a volunteer at the Boston chapter of the National Organization for Women. Twice a week after work, she organized mailings and set up lectures and served as the youngest board member in New England. She helped write the group's monthly newsletter, updating members on women's issues around the globe.

(April gave her most of the ideas, and Sally toned them down so the sixty-year-old women of Brookline, Massachusetts, wouldn't have a collective heart attack while reading about fistulas in developing nations.)

Celia thought of how NOW and other groups like it were the perfect logical next step for Smithies so accustomed to acronyms. And she was proud of Sally for actually getting out there and doing something positive in her free time. But April rolled her eyes at this. "Could she *be* any more of an establishment feminist?" she had once said to Celia, who wasn't quite sure what that even meant.

April's freshman year of life was about joining forces with the legendary Ronnie Munro to form Women in Peril, Inc. Ronnie was one of Smith's most talked about alums, right alongside Julia Child and Gloria Steinem, but unlike them, she was something of a villain in the eyes of most Smithies. Ronnie was a militant feminist and a filmmaker who had dedicated her life to social activism and women's rights. She was also slightly insane.

Once, she had been a pioneer—she was a major player in the early fight against domestic violence and a big proponent of equal pay for equal work. But at some point in the late seventies, she was at the center of a scandal. She had convinced some horrible wife beater in Indiana to let her make a film about his life, including footage from a hidden camera of him punching, hitting, and whipping his wife. From the interviews she did with him, it seemed like Ronnie was in love with the guy. She egged him on on camera, asking him to describe the thrill he got from keeping his woman in her place. Then one day, Ronnie told him a secret: His wife was planning to leave. That night, he murdered her.

He stabbed her through the heart right on the kitchen floor. Ronnie wasn't there, but she got the whole thing on tape and used it as the opening scene of her movie.

Her supporters said she was drawing attention to the issue, and that she did—with articles in every major paper and secret screenings of the film on college campuses after it had been banned and even a few lawmakers trying to initiate legislation to protect women in the transition out of abusive homes. But most people inside the movement thought Ronnie's methods were dangerous and sucked credibility out of the whole debate. If she had seen this man beating his wife, if she even had it all on tape, why hadn't she gone to the police sooner? Why had she told him of his wife's plan to leave him when she knew it might cost the woman her life?

After that, most mainstream feminists broke ties with Ronnie; some even called her a murderer. Ever since, her tactics had grown stranger and riskier. She had fewer allies and an increasing number of critics. During their first year at Smith, she had come to campus to give a talk on female genital mutilation, and three hundred girls turned out to protest. Still, April spoke about her as if she were a goddess.

It was obvious why Ronnie had hired April to be her assistant. She took advantage of April, asking her to do all sorts of dangerous and stupid things in the name of women's liberation. The two of them made films about misogyny and sexual violence all over the world—important films that explored the lives of women who were victims of previously untold horrors. Ronnie made April live with her and seemed to be April's only friend in Chicago.

The rest of the girls were proud of April. They knew that this was her life's work, and that it was endlessly important, but they worried about her, too. Especially Celia, who knew the most about April's exploits and the lengths she was willing to go to to make Ronnie happy.

The latest scare had come just two days earlier, when April called from some army base in Illinois to say that a military guard had beaten the shit out of her when he caught her stealing classified files. She thought her arm might be broken, she said, and there was blood in her eyes, blurring her sight.

Celia had felt paralyzed, listening to April cry on the phone like that. Before she picked up, she had been sitting at her desk drinking an iced tea and reading *Us Weekly* online, trying to block out the guilt she felt over the stack of unread manuscripts on the floor by her side.

"Where was Ronnie while all this was going on?" she asked in a rush.

"She ran," April said.

"She left you?"

"She didn't leave me," April said. "She just needed to protect herself. But anyway, she's driven off now and I don't know how the fuck I'm gonna get home."

"What can I do?" Celia said.

"I don't know. Just stay on the phone with me for a minute, okay? You should see me, I'm all bloody and gross and I need to get to the hospital so someone can check out my arm."

Celia was silent, shocked. She did not know what to say.

"Please don't tell Sally about any of this," April said at last. "She'll flip."

Celia thought of the wedding, of April walking down the aisle with bruises all over her face. Sally was bound to find out what had happened. Still, Celia promised that she would keep April's secret, just as she always kept April's secrets.

Bree never referred to them as sophomores or juniors in life, but even so, Celia had thought of their second and third years away from Smith in exactly that way. And now it was May of their fourth year, and Sally was getting married. Married, Celia could hardly believe the word applied to one of them. It was only fitting that Sally had decided to have the wedding right on campus, because if this was the end of their senior year of life, then the weekend would be a sort of commencement, a beginning and an end.

As the bus turned onto Route 9, Celia pulled a fat slice of sour cream coffee cake from her purse. She was almost there. She took a big bite and closed her eyes. She had a blurry memory of buying the cake at the little corner store by her apartment just before heading upstairs with What's-His-Name. She never ate that sort of crap anymore, but she had figured that you'd really have to hate yourself to ride the bus hungover for four hours without some kind of indulgence. Or, for that matter, to be even remotely food deprived for the wedding of a friend whose birthday was six months after yours when you didn't even have a date.

There had been pretty slim pickings on the New York dating scene lately. There was the guy she met at the movies, who referred to her vagina as her "cave of pleasure" (not okay). And the candidate for a doctorate in English at Columbia, who could not help but reference the names of modern novelists in every casual conversation. (Example: "Whatcha doin', Ian McEwan?" Blech.) In a cabinet in his apartment, hidden behind his Fassbinder video collection, Celia had found dozens of pornos with literary names—*A*

Midsummer Night's Cream, A Tale of Two Titties. The porn itself didn't bother her, but the titles were simply too much. She decided to break up with him then and there.

Celia looked at the trees that lined the road leading into town. She took another bite of cake and reminded herself to ask Bree how she'd thought of it, the freshman-year-of-life idea. Especially since at Smith they were never allowed to use the term "freshman."

It was the kind of subtle distinction that made outsiders groan.

When the topic of Smith came up at a family Christmas party her sophomore year, Celia's uncle Monty said, "You can always tell a Smith student because she's the one who refers to it as a *women's college* instead of a girls' school."

"Whenever I picture Celia there, I think of the proper ladies from my old parish who went to Smith in the forties," her grandmother said. "Cee, is it still that way? Tea parties and pearls and pinkies up and all that?"

Her least-favorite cousin, Al, piped up, likening attending a women's college in the twenty-first century to reenacting Civil War battles on Sunday afternoons: "It's outdated," he said. "But it's sort of kooky and quaint, so let them have it."

"We're so glad you approve," Celia said. She turned and walked into the dining room in a rage.

In high school, Celia excelled in English without really trying and filled countless notebooks with short stories and poems. But she maintained a solid C average in most of her math and science classes, in some cases only after begging and flirting and crying her way up from a D.

Celia lacks focus, her senior-year biology teacher had written in a note to her parents. *If only Celia could put the energy she puts into boys into her studies, she'd no doubt be an A student,* wrote that little hobbit of a geometry teacher, who probably lived in his mother's basement and would most likely die a virgin.

Still, somehow, miraculously, she had gotten into Smith. Her mother told everyone that it was because Celia had written an admissions essay that had made the review board cry, and it was true that they had said this in her acceptance letter. But Celia always suspected that the real reason she got into Smith was that it had snowed on the day of her interview with the head of admissions. The woman had to bring her two little daughters to work with her, and when Celia arrived, they were sitting in the waiting area, looking bored. Instinctually, she got down on her knees beside them, right on the floor, dug some pens out of her purse, and started drawing with them, much to their delight. She honestly hadn't meant it as a kiss-ass move, but when their mother came out of her office, she beamed and said, "Tell me, Celia, do you babysit?"

Celia realized then that years of taking care of her sister and little cousins had served her better than an SAT prep course ever could.

The all-women aspect of Smith had freaked her out in the beginning, but she reasoned that there were Amherst men to be found nearby. This had proven to be wildly untrue, but she came to love the place anyway, and defending it to the members of her extended family—who had all attended Trinity and Holy Cross and were no doubt wondering if she was a lesbian—sometimes got exhausting.

In the four years since she left Northampton, she had met all sorts of women who raised their eyebrows when they heard she'd gone to Smith; and she had been on dates with dozens of men who seemed to think she was joking when she told them that she had attended one of the Seven Sisters.

They'd say things like, "Oh my God, it's *still* all girls?" or "How sweet. I didn't even know Smith existed anymore!" Or worse. Just last month, out for drinks with some friend of a friend, a balding guy who wrote for *Sports Illustrated,* she had talked wistfully about her college days. Halfway through the story of how she and the girls had gotten caught in a thunderstorm during Celebration of Sisterhood, she felt his hand touch her thigh under the table as he said, "Aww, don't tell me this! You're way too hot to be a feminazi."

After that, she ignored his calls. Men like that were not to be tolerated, according to April. Celia agreed, but sometimes she thought to herself that between Smith and Women in Peril, Inc., April had had so little contact with real, red-blooded American men that perhaps she wasn't exactly an authority on the topic of what one could expect from them.

Outside the bus window, Celia began to recognize buildings—Fitzwilly's restaurant with its bright green awning, the Calvin Theatre, where she had once made out with a Hampshire film student in the balcony during a Lucinda Williams concert.

The bus rolled into the depot. As passengers began to disembark, Celia sat back for a minute, looking at the crowd gathered outside—there were a few Smithies, chubby cheeked and dressed in sweatshirts and jeans. Probably headed to the mall in Holyoke, she thought. Beside them were the Springfield-bound hippies who came to play sidewalk music in town or worked at the organic cafés on Main

Street. She inhaled, steadying herself as she stood up, and pulled her duffel bag from the overhead rack.

Celia got off the bus and made her way up the hill toward campus. The air smelled different here. It was cleaner, more alive than in Manhattan. She had remembered everything about the look of the place—the lush New England mountains that circled the valley; the smooth, glassy perfection of Paradise Pond. But the once familiar smell was a startling surprise, like a forgotten love letter peeking out from under a mattress.

When she reached campus, she walked around the Grecourt Gates. It was superstition that if you went through them before graduation you would never get married. She had graduated now, and she wasn't even sure she wanted to get married, but, still, better to be safe than sorry. She walked by the old art museum and the new student center and John M. Greene Hall, past Haven House with its wide yellow front porch, and Park Annex, with its neat red bricks and white trim. Each house on campus was from a different time period in American history, and a girl could usually be described by whichever one she lived in—the houses on Green Street were home to the vegan/lesbian/armpit-hair crowd. Chapin, Capen, and Sessions housed a lot of left-wing party girls who smoked weed and dated each other, though they'd only ever slept with men before college. The big dykes on campus (BDOCs) usually lived in Haven-Wesley. These were the women whom even the straightest of Smithies fantasized about and blushed over when they saw them walk by.

Celia and Bree were typical Quad bunnies—the type who

loved boys, kissed girls only when they'd had a lot of tequila, and might go to a frat party if such a thing existed at Smith, and if the men were not utter pigs.

Celia crossed Paradise Road, walked past Scales House, and, finally, there she stood, in front of King, staring at the door she had gone in and out of so many times that she could feel its exact weight just by looking at it. The back of King House opened out to the Quad—wide green lawns and ivy-covered brick buildings. But she stood now at the front of the house, facing Elm Street, where two lanes of traffic separated the campus from the world and seemed to provide a sort of force field to adulthood. On the other side of Elm Street, there were people pushing baby strollers; lawn mowers and dog toys left in yards; houses with two-car garages—all the trappings of real life that had seemed so trivial and distant in college, and that seemed distant still.

In the midst of it all, directly across from King and wedged oddly between two houses, was the Autumn Inn, where they'd be staying for the wedding. A few months earlier, Sally had announced that she would be putting them all up at the Hotel Northampton. Even though Sal could clearly afford it, the other girls had said no. It wasn't right for her to pay for them to come to her wedding. So Sally settled on the Autumn Inn, reasoning that a three-night stay at the Hotel Northampton was too expensive for Celia and April even if they shared a room, and that every other place in town was a dump.

When Sally suggested the inn, April and Bree had both immediately pointed out to Celia, who was already thinking the same, how inappropriate it was: In college, the Autumn Inn was where Sally would go with Bill Lambert when the

Neilson Library offices were too crowded, and the two of them just had to see each other. And now she was staying there with poor Jake on their wedding night. Leave it to Sally.

Celia had never been inside the inn, but she had had a view of it both first year and senior year, when she lived in street-facing rooms. Some nights she would look across Elm Street and imagine the people who were staying there— married couples in town to enjoy the foliage, Smith parents visiting their daughters, lovers like Sally and Bill hiding away. Tonight, Celia thought, she would do just the opposite: check into the Autumn Inn, and gaze over at King House, imagining the students who filled those rooms, no longer hers now.

For the next three days, the girls would envelop her.

Of the four of them, only Celia had made several close girlfriends since leaving Smith. Sometimes she thought New York resembled a women's college in the way that it brought women together, in part because of a lack of decent men. In the last four years, she had spent more happy nights drinking wine at the Temple Bar with Lila Bonner and Laura Friedman, or out dancing in Chelsea with Kayla from the office, than she had with all the men she had dated combined.

But although she had made plenty of friends in the city, it still felt like each of them was alone, their lives running parallel, but never quite touching. With the Smithies, it was different. There was sometimes no telling where one of them began and the others left off.

BREE

The bridesmaid dress hung on the back of a kitchen chair, pale pink cotton with a halter neck, and a skirt that fell limp to the floor like one of Bree's mother's old nightgowns. She ran her palm over the light fabric as she waited for the water to boil. It wasn't really appropriate for a wedding, even an outdoor wedding in May.

"My money's on pouffy peach taffeta with shoulder bows," Bree had joked when Celia called her to say that Sally had gotten engaged, and that she was asking them as well as April to be her bridesmaids, and that Bree needed to sound utterly surprised upon pain of death when Sally called, because Sally had sworn Celia to secrecy.

"I have a plan," Bree went on. "I'm going to get married after everyone else I know, and then make each of my bridesmaids wear the exact dress they made me wear in their wedding. That way if they were fair, they'll get to look good. If they made me wear pouffy peach, well then, now they get to wear pouffy peach."

Bree was trying to sound breezy and happy, but she wondered why Sally hadn't called her yet.

She didn't call for two more days. Bree thought it was strange and sad, but she knew things had changed between them since college. And maybe it was foolish to think she was still Sally's priority the way she had been at Smith, when there was so little to distract them. Back then, they had expanses of time in which to memorize one another's routines and favorite songs and worst heartaches and greatest days. It felt something like being in love, but without the weight of having to choose just one heart to hold on to, and without the fear of ever losing it. They had spent so many evenings together on the front porch of King House with the world all before them. Maybe it was just impossible to recreate that sort of closeness in real life.

Or maybe Sally had been afraid to tell Bree about the wedding because she knew how much it would hurt. Whatever the reason, when she called with the news, she said it in a rush, like a confession or an apology, instead of an announcement.

Everyone knew that once upon a time Bree thought she'd be first. But now it looked like she'd never get married, at least not in the way she had planned—no white dress and long aisle strewn with a flower girl's rose petals. Her father wouldn't give her away in a big Savannah chapel, her mother wouldn't stand by in a pale suit, like she had always imagined. Bree knew that the surprise of it shouldn't be so surprising—who ever imagined herself into a life?

She lifted the kettle from the stove and poured water into twin red mugs in two even streams.

Lately, whenever she felt confused or depressed, she would compare her life with Sally's—*Here I am, lying on the couch stressing out about my relationship. I bet Sally's looking at wedding gowns. Here I am making yet another pro-and-con list on a Sunday morning. Sally is probably serving Jake French toast in bed, to be followed by hours of mind-numbing sex.* No matter what the imagined comparison, Sally always came out ahead.

Bree plopped a peppermint tea bag and honey into one cup, and the regular old Lipton with milk and sugar in the other for herself. Their bedroom was just off the kitchen, and from the tone of the snoring—gentle, morning gurgles, instead of those late-night blasts that required her to sleep with earplugs—Bree knew she had a while to go before she'd be disturbed. She looked at the clock on the microwave. Their flight wasn't for a few more hours.

Her BlackBerry buzzed on the table. Bree tried to resist the urge, but opened the frantic e-mail from her boss, asking about a brief she'd filed the day before. She dashed off a quick reply. It was the first time she'd taken any vacation since she started at the firm a year earlier, and the way they were freaking out about it, you would have thought she was taking a month off instead of two lousy days.

Bree pulled out a chair and sat down, gathering her long blonde hair into a knot.

Sally was getting married. Sally, who had always somehow been both the most sensible and the craziest of them all, the girl who set a record for streaking across the Quad; who carried on an affair with a professor who was more than twice her age; who drank so much at winter formal junior year that she had to be rushed to Cooley Dickinson in an ambulance to have her stomach pumped. It had only been four years since all of that. How could so much have changed so quickly?

Bree realized it was nasty to think anything but wonderful thoughts about the marriage of one of her best friends. She never wanted to be the sort of woman who measured everyone else's happiness against her own. And of course, in some ways, she could picture Sally married—she was, after all, the only woman in America under sixty who had voluntarily enrolled in a flower-arranging class. In college, she had taken the role of neat freak to levels Bree never knew existed. She laundered her sheets and comforter every Sunday morning, flipping her mattress while they dried. She regularly cleaned the tub with bleach, even though the housekeeper did the same. She occasionally washed her keys in boiling, soapy water. She decorated her room for every holiday: red paper hearts on the windows in February, a tiny Christmas tree with working lights and a shining gold star. And it was more than just that. Sally had lost her mother, and she'd been aching for a family ever since. Unlike the rest of them, Sally wanted to start having kids by the time she was thirty. Overplanner that she was, she had decided long ago that she wanted a few years alone with Jake before her babies came along.

Bree genuinely liked Jake; they all did, although she and April agreed he wasn't exactly the sharpest knife in the drawer. They had been e-mailing back and forth with Celia, all three of them trying to decide what to get Sally for a wedding present, when April sent a message saying, *Not to be an asshole, but remember when Sal and Jake were first dating and she went to his place, and she told us he only owned two books—*

the Bible and something by John Grisham? Should we be worried about that?

Bree had responded immediately: Well that depends on whether you think there's cause for concern when our best friend is about to marry someone whose favorite author is Dr. Seuss.

April shot back: Maybe we should get them his complete works as a wedding gift? Or a first edition of Green Eggs and Ham.

Bree laughed as she read this, but just as she hit REPLY she got an e-mail from Celia, ever the den mother.

Stop it, you two, she wrote. How dumb can he be? He went to Georgetown for Christ's sake! Jake is a great guy. He's just . . . uncomplicated. And Sally loves him, so he's off-limits for mocking now.

April replied: Uncomplicated? And that's a good thing?

Celia wrote back: For Sally, yes.

The correspondence turned to other topics then—Celia's date the night before, the fact that April had been arrested again and Ronnie had had to bail her out. Then they began to discuss boring wedding details—how they'd wear their hair, whether Sally had a preference about shoes. Without thinking, Bree forwarded the entire exchange on to Sally, and wrote: See below . . . your thoughts on shoes?

As soon as she hit SEND she clapped a hand over her mouth.

"Shit," she said. She hoped Sally wouldn't read farther than the first message. Bree assumed she hadn't, because two days later, Sally just wrote back: Sweetpea, sorry for the delayed response. Work has been CRAZY. You guys should wear whatever you want, unless you want to wear Doc Martens. XO

Celia, who had minored in psych in college and seemed to think that made her an authority on human behavior, said she thought Bree had done it on purpose.

"Why would I do that?" Bree asked.

"Maybe because you want her to know how you feel, but you're afraid to tell her."

"Why would I want her to know that I think Jake is stupid?"

"That's not what I meant," Celia said.

It was true that for some reason Bree couldn't make it through a conversation with Sally about Jake without snapping at her. Sally just acted so smug about it all, so over the top when she described how happy they were together. The extent of Bree's disappointment shocked her. It felt almost physical, like a broken rib poking through the skin, so that every time her thoughts twisted this way or that, a horrible pain spread through her whole body.

When she was fifteen years old, Bree bought a two-foot stack of bridal magazines at the A&P and hid them under her bed like porn, so her brothers wouldn't make fun. At night, she folded down the edges of each page that featured a dress like the one she wanted—ivory, with a full-on Bo Peep skirt and a row of silk-covered buttons from the base of her spine to the top of her neck.

She and Doug Anderson got engaged right after high school graduation. All through the ceremony, across the rows of bleachers, she could see that he was sweating. Anyone else might have thought it was from wearing a black cap and gown in the Savannah heat, but Bree knew better—something had him terrified. A few hours later, at the picnic their fathers threw at Forsyth Park, Doug took her over to a row of oak trees and propped her up against one as though she might lose control of her bones. He still looked afraid, even after drinking two beers.

"You okay?" she asked him, and just as the words came out of her mouth, he fell to one knee. He didn't have the ring in a velvet box, the way she had pictured. Instead, he uncurled his fingers and the diamond band sat right in the palm of his hand. He reminded Bree of a little boy bringing his mama a treasure from the garden, a ladybug or a double-headed acorn.

She said yes before he could even ask. Doug jumped to his feet and squeezed her tight. He kissed her until she felt like the sun was shining out from inside of her and she might actually burst into a thousand glittering shards of light. And then their families gathered around them, and everyone toasted with good champagne, and Bree realized that they had all known. This was meant to be her engagement party. She could still remember the proud look on her daddy's face, her grandmother's giddy chatter about whether Bree ought to carry red roses or calla lilies when she walked down the aisle. Only her mother stood back from the crowd, her lips pressed tightly together, a gesture that she had once told Bree was the true secret to a happy marriage. Later though, when plans were being ironed out, she spoke up. While Doug thought Bree ought to transfer to the University of Georgia so that they could be married within the year, her mother insisted that she give Smith a fair shot, and that they make the engagement a long one.

When Bree was in grade school, she and her mother would go to Northampton for a few days every summer. They'd walk around campus, eat fancy dinners downtown, get manicures and blowouts, buy tiny soaps in the shape of fish or hearts or elephants at the Cedar Chest on Main Street. Her brothers would have to stay behind.

Bree had been romanticizing the Smith Sisterhood ever since. She loved the idea of living in a land of women, rich in tradition. Tea parties and candlelight dinners and friends you'd keep for a lifetime. When it came time to think about college, she applied only to Smith, early decision, and was accepted within a week.

Doug and Bree both wanted to be lawyers, someday going into practice together. Her secret wish was to go to Stanford Law, and not wanting to jinx herself, she had told no one but Doug.

He teased her, saying over and over, "No trusting Southerner is gonna want a lawyer who ran off to some Yankee college and then got a law degree in hippie-dippy California."

Bree knew he was scared. He didn't want her to go so far away. She tried to reassure him, even though all summer long she felt like a pioneer: She was the only person they knew who was leaving the South for college.

But when it came time to say good-bye, Bree suddenly grew terrified. She held his hands so tight that her fingernails left ten perfect moons on his palms when she let go.

Her parents had the car all loaded up and were sitting in the front seat trying to give them their privacy. Eventually, her father beeped the horn, and she and Doug embraced long and hard. He kissed the diamond on her hand as a sort of seal on the promise they'd made. They had already planned their reunion over Bree's fall break, imagining out loud how they would run to each other in the airport, just like characters in an old movie (her vision), and have sex in his dad's Oldsmobile before even leaving the parking garage (his).

Bree had seen him almost every day of her life since kindergarten. They had been a couple for more than three years.

"I can't believe I have to wait until October to be with you again," she said.

"Well, if you stay here with me, you won't have to," he said.

Two flights and several hours later, Bree arrived in Northampton, just in time to register and run to the first house meeting. It was time enough to determine that this was not her mother's Smith College and that she wanted out. Back in the seventies, good Southern parents sent their girls off to the Seven Sisters to stay out of trouble and away from men. Bree would bet anything that her mother had never heard about shower hours, and if she did now, she'd yank Bree right out of this place.

On her way into registration, Bree had seen someone's dad point at a group of shaved-headed lesbians sitting in the grass. He said to his daughter, "I don't think you'll have trouble meeting boys around here. They're everywhere."

"Those are women!" the girl hissed.

The father looked like he'd been shot.

Bree skipped dinner that night and called her parents, and then Doug, from her room.

"Jacobson and Jones are having a kegger in their suite tonight," Doug said excitedly. "All the guys from home will be there, and Kathleen said to tell you we'll give you a good drunk dialing later."

"Oh," Bree said. "Sounds fun."

She had watched these boys drink beers on countless nights, in parking lots, and at the drive-in, and out at the old stone quarry. Would their next four years be any different from their last? She felt jealous of and sorry for them all at once.

"I miss you," she said.

"Hey," he said. "Me too, babydoll. I hate hearing you so sad."

Doug tried to sound soothing, but in the background people were laughing and yelling and shouting his name, and he had to keep asking her to repeat herself.

Eventually Bree said, "I'm fine, baby. Go have fun."

He didn't argue.

Bree went to the bathroom with a towel slung over her shoulder, and her little pink shower caddy in her hand. She stood alone before a row of sinks, bathed in fluorescent light, and scrubbed off her eye makeup, her blush. She flossed her teeth and thought—she couldn't help it— about how fat all the older girls at the house meeting had been.

Down the hall, someone let out a squeal of recognition, the sound you make when you see a familiar face that you haven't seen in ages. Bree's loneliness was so strong that she half expected it to take the form of another person and materialize there beside her, perched on the ugly Formica countertop in a fuzzy bathrobe and hot rollers.

She walked back to her room and shut the door. Before leaving home she had ripped dozens of pages out of her bridal magazines and placed them in an envelope marked *Wedding Inspiration*. She pulled them out now, lovingly smoothing the pages as if they were photographs of old friends. She tacked them to her bulletin board, one by one.

She tried calling Doug again, but the phone just rang and rang. Back in Georgia, she knew, he was off to the party, probably surrounded by gorgeous Southern college girls with their fine summer dresses and smooth, glossy hair.

It was only ten-thirty when Bree crawled into bed, intent on crying herself to sleep. As she always did when she was scared or sad, she tried to mentally recall each and every date she and Doug had ever been on. (She usually fell asleep or calmed down by about the fifth or sixth.) First date: They went to the movies with Melissa Fairbanks and Chris Carlson. Doug paid for her ticket; Chris did not pay for Melissa's. Second date: The Sadie Hawkins dance. She had asked him, as was the custom, and instead of some dopey corsage he had sent roses to the house, something he would continue to do on the first Saturday of every month, right up until the previous day, the last day at home before Bree came to Smith. The third date: Their first kiss, and Doug had said right then and there, "Bree Miller, you're the girl I'm gonna marry."

Thinking on this, Bree began to weep. She stared up at the ceiling, where someone had left behind a constellation of tiny glow-in-the-dark stars. She ran her ring over her lips. Why hadn't she listened to Doug when he told her to come with him? What was so great about this place that she had left him and all their friends behind? Doug had been talking about wanting to get married and have babies since freshman year of high school. If two people loved each other enough, couldn't they overcome anything—even distance, even their own goddamn youth?

After a short while, Celia slid a note under the door.

They liked each other immediately. In the weeks that followed, Bree taught Celia how to create a smoky eye using just one gray shadow, and Celia taught Bree how to make an Irish car bomb, a drink so potent that it sent Bree into hysterics, and made her drunk dial Doug at 4:00 a.m. to tell him she had a feeling all their babies would be born with freckles.

She often thought of her auntie Sue and auntie Kitty—not really aunts at all, but her mother's Smith roommates and lifelong best friends. She knew almost from the start that Celia would be that person for her. The godmother to her children, the maid of honor when she married Doug, although the one thing Celia didn't seem to understand about her was the engagement.

"You'll never have sex with anyone but him as long as you live," Celia said in wonderment one night in late September. "Doesn't that scare you?"

Bree said no, but admitted that she was afraid she might be changing, while Doug was staying just the same. As soon as the words were out of her mouth, she felt guilty and changed the subject.

Being together from a distance wasn't as easy as she had imagined it would be. It got harder and harder just to find time to talk on the phone at night. By the time Doug got home from class, she was off to some lecture or a movie with the girls. As she lay down to sleep, he was just heading out to a party.

On the first Saturday in October, Bree dashed to the front

door of King House every time the doorbell rang, but it was never for her.

"You didn't send me roses," she said to Doug on the phone that night.

"Is it October already?" he said. "Sorry, baby, I didn't even realize."

He was disappointed when she didn't come home for fall break, but she'd had two midterms that following Tuesday, and she couldn't afford not to spend the whole weekend studying. She had asked him to fly out to Northampton the next weekend instead. They could go apple picking, she said, take a hayride.

Doug scoffed a little. "A hayride?" he said. "I can't, babe. We've got tickets for the game on Saturday, and we're prepartying in my suite."

She knew he didn't mean to be hurtful, but his quick dismissal made Bree burst into tears.

When she hung up, she went straight to Celia's room. The door was open, so she walked right in and flopped down on the bed. Celia was sitting at her desk reading *The Canterbury Tales* for her Chaucer class, her bare feet propped up on the edge of an open drawer.

"What's the matter?" she said.

Bree sniffled. "I just feel like I'm losing him."

Celia didn't look all that surprised, and she didn't say a word about Doug. Instead, she said, "Put on your jacket, little lady. I'm taking you to lunch."

Celia never wanted anyone to be left out. Sometimes, Bree selfishly wished that she didn't always feel the need to invite

Sally and April everywhere. But then Bree would remember how Celia had saved her from her loneliness that first night, and grow guilty for not thinking of the others—especially poor Sally, whose mother had died.

Celia was the one who had reached out to each of them initially, the glue that held them all together. Did that have something to do with the fact that she was Catholic? Bree wondered, though she knew Celia would laugh at the suggestion. Celia rarely talked about religion, except to make a joke about Catholic school every now and then, or to break out her old uniform for a costume party in the Quad. She seemed determined to prove to everyone, maybe even herself, that she was an atheist. Still, Bree believed that Celia's religion must be in her somewhere, deep down, which accounted for the fact that Celia was so good, so worried about everyone else, so eager to make them all happy. Bree's own parents were lapsed Baptists. The last time she had been in a church was at her great-aunt's funeral three years earlier.

They were discussing this one lazy Sunday afternoon. Sally, Celia, and Bree were lying in Bree's bed, eating a tin of Savannah lemon cookies that her mother had sent, and Celia was talking about how she didn't believe in God.

"How can you not believe in God?" Sally asked, looking mesmerized.

"I might ask you how you *can* believe," Celia said.

"I guess because if I didn't, I'd go crazy," Sally replied.

Bree imagined that Sally must be thinking about her mother, and so, although she wasn't sure what she believed, she said, "I agree with Sally. There's definitely more than this out there somewhere."

Sally gave her a little smile.

Bree watched as she nibbled on her bite-size cookie, eating it at one-millionth the rate of a normal person. This was how Sally stayed so skinny, of course. Bree placed the cookie she was holding back in the tin. After just a couple of months at Smith, her pants were fitting tighter, and she couldn't even get into the dress she'd worn to her high school graduation. Celia was puffing up too, her cheeks growing full, a soft little roll forming at her belly. Bree had been voted Most Beautiful and Best Dressed in her senior yearbook, and now look at her, plump and decked out in flannel pajama pants and a Smith sweatshirt, with the hood pulled up over her head because she hadn't washed her hair in two days. She was afraid of what her mother would say when she saw her for the first time at Thanksgiving. Not to mention Doug.

The phone rang then, and Bree leaned over to pick it up. When she heard Doug's voice, she laughed.

"I was just thinking about you," she said.

"Bree, we need to talk," he said, and she felt like someone had dropped a brick into her stomach.

She asked the girls to leave, and shut the door. She took a long deep breath before picking up the phone again.

"What's wrong?" she said, her heart racing.

His confession came fast. The night before, he said, he had gotten drunk at a party and made out with someone, a girl Bree had never heard of named Laney Price. ("She sounds like a hooker," Celia said later.) It was a stupid mistake, he said, and it would never happen again.

Bree sobbed into the phone while Doug apologized over and over.

"Tell me everything," she said. "Every detail."

"Bree—," he said in his sweet little baby voice, making her heart ache. "It was nothing, I swear. Just kissing, pretty much."

"Pretty much?" She was growing hysterical now. "What is *pretty much*? Were you in a bed?" She braced herself against his reply: *Say no, say no, say no.* If they had been standing up at a dark party somewhere, maybe it wasn't such a big deal.

He sighed. "Yes, we were in my bed."

"Did you have your shoes on?" she asked.

Doug laughed. "Baby! Come on. It was just a stupid mistake."

"Tell me," she said. "Were there shoes? Were you naked?"

"Jesus, no," he said. "She had her top off. That was it."

Bree felt like she had been kicked hard in the gut. This was supposed to put her at ease? When he suggested that they talk about something else, she screamed "No!" so loud that April, Sally, and Celia all came running in.

"He cheated on me," she said to them, her hand pressed over the receiver.

The girls left the room, Celia squeezing her hand and whispering, "I'll be right next door if you need me."

They talked for hours. Doug kept saying maybe they should cool off for a while, but Bree didn't want to hang up the phone. She wanted him to hear what he had done to her, to suffer for his stupid, meaningless mistake the way she would suffer for it. Eventually, she let him go, said she'd call again after dinner. He told her he loved her, and even after what had happened, Bree believed him. She said she loved him, too.

That night, alone in her room, she stared at her engage-ment ring for a long time. He had said he wanted her for-giveness, that he still wanted to marry her. Maybe they could find a way to put this behind them. Doug had warned her not to move so far away, but she hadn't listened. Maybe this was just her punishment for leaving.

Bree went to the bulletin board and ran her hand over the glossy photos of happy brides in flowing gowns. This life—Doug, marriage—was what she had always wanted, wasn't it? But if she wanted it that badly, would she really have left?

The door was cracked open, and she could hear footsteps on the other side.

April poked her head in, wearing her apron from her shift in the dining hall. She was the only one of them on work-study, and though Bree knew it wasn't really all that tragic, she still felt sorry for April sometimes.

"You okay?" April asked from the doorway. "Need me to kill anyone?"

She entered the room and saw what Bree had been staring at.

"Wedding dresses, huh?" she said.

Bree nodded.

"You know what could be therapeutic?" April said, her eyes widening. "If we set them on fire."

Bree shook her head, laughing. But then, something shifted in her. The sadness seemed to drop out of her, and in its place was a rage so strong it nearly knocked her down. She had asked him for all the details thinking that knowing would somehow make it better. But now she had this visual—her fiancé making out with some topless girl in his bed, a bed Bree had never even seen. While he was doing that, she had been lying in her own bed with Celia, talking about her wedding. She had always dreamed of going to Smith College. If Doug felt the need to spread his stupid seed all over the University of Georgia just because they'd been apart for two months, there was nothing for her to do.

Bree reached up toward the board. Her hand gripped the top of a page—her favorite, the Priscilla gown with the six-foot train. Gently, delicately, Bree tore it in two, and then began to rip the pieces into tiny squares, the size of sugar cubes.

A moment later, she and April were tearing the pages off the board, running to the bathroom, dumping them by the handful into the sink.

"You should do the honors," April said, and she handed Bree a book of matches from inside her coat pocket.

Bree struck a match and dropped it onto the papers, watching all the white gowns burn.

April's face glowed with approval. She had never had a boyfriend. She had met her own father only once. Bree suspected that this void was responsible for making April who she was, though April rarely spoke about trouble in her life. Unlike the rest of them, she kept her secrets to herself.

To April this small fire was probably a statement about the patriarchy, a stab at capitalism, something like that. But to Bree, it was simply surrender—a giving over of herself to this new life. In the days that followed, she tried to listen to Doug, tried to see things from his perspective, tried to imagine her life without him, and wept over the prospect. But she could never quite manage to get the disappointment and doubt out of her head.

By the time November arrived, her engagement was off.

. . .

By sophomore year, Bree, Celia, April, and Sally had moved out of maids' quarters and into the main hall, but they still lived next door to one another. They left their doors open during the day, yelling from one room to the next. They lingered on the couches in the living room after dinner, gossiping and reading aloud to one another from *The New Yorker* and *Vogue*. Once a week they ordered dumplings and fried rice and lo mein from the takeout place on Main Street and had a feast while they studied, taking sips from a bottle of Boone's Farm that Celia had gotten with her fake ID. They ate the rest of their meals at the corner table in the dining hall.

It had felt liberating to leave Doug, but even a year later, it wasn't easy for Bree to be without him. At Smith, it seemed to her, hearts broke quickly and stayed that way too long. There was no distraction, no rebound guy to speed your recovery. She thought about him all the time—not so much about Doug the individual, but rather about the nature of love, and the shock of learning how quickly it could disappear. About the fact that some girl she had never met, never even seen, had perhaps changed the whole course of her life. She cried about him more than was healthy, despite the fact that the Smith girls kept saying she had dodged a bullet, and despite the support of her family. (Her parents now sent her flowers on the first Saturday of every month, and her brother Roger had offered to have Doug beaten to a pulp by some frat guys he knew. Bree turned him down, but she was grateful for the sentiment.)

She had always been a happy person, but that year she began to worry that something inside her had changed. Was it her, she wondered, or was it the girls? All of them worried a lot, and all of them cried. Over ex-boyfriends and Sally's mother and sexism in America and a fear of eventually leaving one another. Sometimes Bree wondered if they all loved crying just a little too much.

At first, she thought of it as a pure outpouring of emotion. There was something wonderful about living among women and only women, about having your own little family of friends where honesty and true feeling reigned. It was exactly what she had imagined as a little girl. But somewhere along the way she began to feel stifled. Though they were sociable with other girls in the house, the four of them rarely spent time with anyone except one another. Her role in the group was neatly defined as the pretty Southern belle to whom nothing bad had ever happened. The one who was just so darn naïve and adorable that she'd actually arrived at Smith with a diamond ring on her finger.

The one-year anniversary of Sally's mother's death came and went, and as her shrink had predicted, things only got harder. Sally never spoke about her friends from home anymore. During their first year, her friend Monica had come for the weekend once or twice, and called fairly often, but now she seemed to have vanished, and so it was up to the Smithies to care for Sally. They spent so many nights just comforting her. Celia was a natural at this. April, with her matter-of-factness about the terrible ways of the world, was also well equipped to help.

But Bree found it unbearable. As soon as she offered a

single word of counsel, she imagined what life would be like without her own mother, and just wanted to crumble. How on earth could she help Sally?

Bree had once whispered to Sally late at night that she admired her so much, because losing a parent was her greatest fear in life.

Sally had snapped at her: "Why would you say that, Bree? My reality is your greatest fear. What am I supposed to do with that information?"

Bree had also said aloud more than once that she and Sally had lived almost the same life, except for the fact that Sally lost her mother. By this, Bree meant that they had both lived in privilege with mothers who ran their worlds, and so she understood how Sally must feel. Afterward, when she saw the stung expression on Sally's face, she knew it was a stupid thing to say. But she could not help saying it—the constant reminder that one cosmic toss of the dice had left Sally in misery and Bree the same as ever was just too much.

She told her mother all of this over the phone one night, whispering in case any of the girls were outside the door.

"Maybe you just need a breather," her mother said. "Join a club the girls would never want to be a part of or something."

Sometimes talking to her mother made Bree realize how easy she had it. Her breathy tone seemed to imply that she would kill for silly problems like Bree's. Then again, her mother did not know the girls. There was no club she could join that Sally or April wasn't already a member of. Sally had all of the social committees and student government positions wrapped up, and April would join any group with the word "radical" or "unite" in the title.

Then, in the post office one morning, Bree spotted a flyer listing job openings on campus. She applied to be a clerk in the college bookstore, which was where, on her first day, she met her Lara.

Celia thought she was crazy for taking a job that ate up her free afternoons, especially when she didn't really need the money. But Bree loved the steady pace of the work, the sense of accomplishment she got from alphabetizing the stacks or hanging T-shirts in the correct order—smallest to largest starting from the front. Her hours in the bookstore felt controllable because each task had an end point, unlike her classes, where reading a book only led to writing a long paper which led to class discussions which led to exams. And unlike the dorm, where their problems, trivial or enormous, seemed all but unsolvable.

Lara was what Celia called a conveyor belt lesbian, by which she meant one of the dozens of girls on campus whose sexuality was evidenced through their short, spiky hair, bodies either spindly or massive (never anything in between), and a uniform of white tank tops over cargo shorts, as if they had all been mass-produced in a factory somewhere in New Jersey.

This was a part of Smith that Bree knew very little about. In the Quad, all the girls kissed one another all the time. (Well, not all the girls. Sally, for one, thought it was just plain gross.) Bree had kissed Celia plenty of times after a few rounds of vodka tonics, and once Deborah Cohen, who lived next door in Scales, had kissed Bree on the mouth after a barbecue, and moved her lips down Bree's neck and onto her breasts, sloppily licking one nipple and then the other. Two mornings later at breakfast, Bree ran into Deborah, who happened to be with her boyfriend, and quickly got a craving for pancakes from the diner on Pearl Street. It was as if they were all playing at being gay, though they knew it was only a pose. Or perhaps some of them were trying it on for real. Others, Bree imagined, treated Smith like prison— they needed some bodily contact during these years, but once they were set free, they'd return to the opposite sex.

April, who said it was a strange joke that she'd been assigned to live in the Quad, was a member of every human rights group on campus and knew a lot of the famous Smith lesbians—the Bull, a giant girl with a ring through her nose; Little Lefty, a bony thing who sang a cappella with the Smiff-enpoofs and had once thrown a cream pie in Ann Coulter's face; Elania, head of the BDOCs who needed no last name, she was just that cool. But those girls were like celebrities to the Quad bunnies. They presented themselves as untouch-able, or at least Bree perceived them that way.

("If we went to any other school, can you imagine April and the Bull being the most popular girls?" Celia had once asked her, and Bree just laughed.)

Lara was different. On the afternoon Bree started at the bookstore, she could not stop watching her—the way Lara sang under her breath at the register, how she read a paper-back hidden behind the inventory list. She was Asian, with hair like a black cat's and dark brown eyes. Her arms and legs were tan and lean but sinewy, in a way that the gym never provided. She looked as if she used her body for work—a fisherwoman, Bree thought, though she recognized Lara as one of the cute lesbians from the soccer team, who were forever crashing formal events by running through in their panties, banging pots and pans and singing *Olé*. (Sally, who was cochair of the Recreation Council, despised them for it.)

They both had a three o'clock break.

"You want to grab a coffee?" Lara asked, and Bree was shocked to hear a Southern accent.

They walked down Green Street talking about home. Lara was from Virginia, a state that had once seemed as far from Savannah as the moon, but now felt like right next door.

They joked about how different it was up north.

"My father always says 'Up at Smith, they think okra is a black talk-show host,' " Lara said, and Bree laughed so hard that she spat coffee onto the sidewalk.

"I guess the biggest difference for me is how everyone here is all emotions all the time," Bree said, and she couldn't help but feel a little guilty. "I get exhausted talking about other people's feelings. I grew up with two younger brothers in Georgia—there wasn't a whole lot of soul-searching going on. At least not out loud."

Lara nodded. "Tell me about it. My mother is from Singapore, and my father is the son of a white, Christian tobacco farmer. They don't talk about feelings. Although I think it's less about the North and more about what happens when you isolate twenty-four hundred self-obsessed women for four years. I mean, isn't it a little bit creepy how enmeshed in our friends' lives we all are? I get my period the exact same day as everyone else in my house. That's just weird."

"Exactly," Bree said. "Sometimes I need a break from the girls I live with, as much as I love them."

"I think it's just sophomore slump," Lara said. "But

maybe we can break through it by hanging out together. I promise not to ask you about your feelings or to sync my menstrual cycle up with yours."

Bree laughed. "Deal," she said, lifting her eyes to meet Lara's. She could feel her face go red.

They worked the noon-to-six shift together every Tuesday, Thursday, and Saturday. Soon they were meeting for three o'clock coffee every day, even when they were off. They both loved Southern writers—Flannery O'Connor, Eudora Welty. Lara introduced Bree to novels by newer authors like Ellen Gilchrist, and Bree stayed up long into the night trying to finish each one as fast as she could so that they could discuss it.

The King House girls, especially Celia, seemed a little bit jealous.

"Haven't you had enough coffee?" they'd call as she bounded down the staircase each afternoon.

The way Bree felt about Lara was similar to the way she felt about the girls, but there was something else there, too. She wanted to be with her every second. In the beginning she wondered if it was just that she and Lara had more in common—they were both from down south, they didn't take it all so damn seriously. But at some point, Bree found herself thinking about Lara the way she once had about Doug or George Clooney. She'd get distracted by the thought of Lara's long legs for a minute in class, or sit on the windowsill in her room and recall every word of their last conversation, cringing retroactively at something dumb she had said. Once she even lay in bed, moving her hand up under her cotton nightgown, imagining Lara's long fingers on her thigh. A minute later April was banging on the door, looking for a notebook she'd left behind earlier. Bree felt herself blushing as she called out, "Come in!"

She almost told April then. Out of all of them, she would probably be the most understanding. But Bree could not say the words.

Not long after, as they waited for a traffic light to change on a walk into town, Lara took Bree's hand, leaned over, and kissed her gently on the lips.

Kissing Lara felt nothing like kissing the Quad girls. That had always seemed like a dumb joke. This was simply magic.

"I've been wanting to do that since the first time we worked together," Lara said with a huge smile. "But I wasn't sure."

The WALK signal flashed, and Bree stumbled backward a bit, something in her insisting that she stop this. Lara began to cross the street.

"I don't know. I'm just not—," Bree sputtered. "I have to go."

She turned and ran up the hill, back toward campus, with Lara behind her, calling out to her to slow down.

"Leave me alone," Bree shouted over her shoulder. "Just get away from me!"

They didn't speak again for four days. Bree called in sick to work and skipped the classes where she had a chance of running into her. The entire time they were apart, Bree thought of Lara, missed her, dreamed about her.

Finally, she called her and asked her to meet up.

When they did, Bree said, "I'm terrified."

Lara squeezed her hand tight. "I shouldn't have done that. We're friends and that's all, okay?"

Bree felt strangely disappointed by this. She had hoped for something else.

For the next few weeks, Bree longed for contact. She shivered when their hands accidentally brushed at the cash register at work. She let her head fall against Lara's shoulder at the movies, reasoning that she would do the same thing if Celia were there.

Then, one Friday night, they were in Lara's dorm room talking, sitting on the bed with Alison Krauss singing in the background. Lara leaned over and kissed Bree's neck gently, moving her lips over Bree's jawbone and onto her face, up to her lips.

"Is this okay?" Lara whispered.

Bree couldn't say anything but yes.

As they kissed, Lara moved her hands under Bree's dress and over her skin, making her tremble. "Take it off please," Lara said.

Nervous and exhilarated, Bree slid the dress over her head and let Lara unhook her bra. She didn't know what she was doing. It seemed that this should be easier, more intuitive than fooling around with a guy. After all, Lara's body was so much like her own. But everyone around her— friends, cousins, hell, even Judy Blume—had prepared her early for what boys wanted. This time, there was no map.

Lara ran her fingers over Bree's nipples, making them hard, and then down, down into her panties. Bree didn't breathe. She sat still as a post, feeling herself get wet. Lara kept her hand there, moving slowly, kissing Bree's neck until she moaned.

"Lie down," Lara instructed. Bree did as she said.

Lara moved her lips toward her hand, and pulled down Bree's underwear with her teeth, letting it fall to the floor, laughing.

"Slick move, huh?"

She ran her tongue over Bree's wet flesh, in slow, intoxicating circles. No one had ever done this to Bree before, and she felt like she might pass out from the joy of it.

"Don't stop," she gasped. "Lara, don't stop."

After Bree came, Lara pulled off her T-shirt. She wore no bra. Her small, pert breasts looked like two white peaches. She took Bree's hand and guided it over her body. Bree had never touched another woman's breasts. Lara's skin was smooth and soft, like nothing she had ever felt.

"I want your lips on me," Lara whispered, and Bree took Lara's breasts into her mouth, one by one, licking the nipples, sucking them hard. Shaking, she reached into Lara's jeans. She couldn't help but let out a surprised "Oh!" at the soft hair between Lara's legs. Her own had always been well manicured, clipped close or shaved off completely, as per her brother's *Playboy* magazines, her go-to source for what other women looked like down there.

Bree had lost her virginity to Doug Anderson in his family rec room their junior year. Sex with Doug had always been exciting, dangerous. But there was little real pleasure in it. Neither of them knew what they were doing, and poor Doug came after a minute or two every time, yelling out "Sorry!" with his final thrust. This thing with Lara was another world completely. They continued for hours, with lips and fingers everywhere, and when they were done, they lay naked, exhausted, wound together in Lara's bed until morning.

At first, Bree could not bring herself to tell the girls. Not because she thought they would judge her, but because she knew that they would want to talk about it constantly, to analyze it like they did all their other relationships. They would want the story of Bree and Lara to belong to the group, while Bree believed it should be hers alone.

Lara didn't buy it. She had always known she preferred women, and she'd come out to everyone in her life back in high school. "You're afraid that if their perception of you changes, you'll have to change your perception of you," she said, not harshly, but with understanding. And of course it was true. During the first couple of months they were together, Bree would only allow Lara to sleep over if she snuck through the back door after everyone was asleep. Once, a fire alarm sounded in the middle of the night. Bree begged Lara to stay in the house, picturing the looks on her friends' faces if they were to run outside together. It was only a drill, but she instantly regretted what she had done.

The next day over lunch, Bree decided to come out to her friends. But it wasn't a coming-out, not really, she told them. She broke the news quickly—she and Lara were now a couple—and then, before taking a big bite of her turkey club, she said, "So. What's doing with everyone else?"

"What's doing?" Celia said. "Umm hello, you're a lesbian. That's what's doing."

"I am not a lesbian," Bree said with a smile.

"Did you have sex with a woman last night?" April said.

"Yes. And this morning."

"Show-off," April said.

"Then you're a lesbian," Celia said.

Bree laughed. "But how can I be a lesbian if I still really really want to marry Brad Pitt?"

"Good question. I'll have to get back to you," Celia said.

And that was more or less that.

What followed was a blur of parties and concerts and dinners in the dining hall spent holding hands, unafraid. Bree knew they were one of those couples that were so touchy-feely that other people had to look away. She didn't care. This feeling was what she had always dreamed of.

They were together for the rest of their time at Smith and achieved all the milestones of a couple, while posing as friends to the world outside the college. They met each other's families, they said *I love you,* they read aloud in bed, and made love for hours on end. They fought sometimes, but mostly they laughed. No one had ever made Bree laugh the way Lara did. They shared a Southern sensibility, inherited from their fathers, that was devoid of the political correctness that saturated most conversations at Smith. They laughed over how their grandparents would react to typical Smith terms like "heteronormative" and phrases like "Gender is fluid." They agreed that women who started off any comment in class with the words "I feel" deserved to be dragged out and shot. "It's not a therapy session, it's History 203," Lara would say.

Bree had always told the girls that commencement would mark the end of her relationship with Lara. She had told Lara this, too, but Lara never seemed to believe her, or if she did, she didn't want to think about it. Some women came to Smith and realized that they had been lesbians all along. Bree was not one of them. There was a name for girls like her: SLUG. It stood for Smith Lesbian Until Graduation. She wasn't the only straight woman on campus in a full-fledged relationship with a gay woman. Most straight Smithies had kissed women, but that didn't count. SLUGs went on dates and held hands and had sex with women—*they took it a step beyond,* as Sally put it. But they did not take it beyond the college gates.

Celia seemed comforted by the thought that Bree would soon return to the world of men. Bree knew it was hard for Celia to understand that she was not a lesbian, but that she had fallen in love with a woman. It was hard for her, too. The thought of ever trying to make her parents understand this seemed impossible. She had taken Lara to the family beach house off the coast of Charleston two summers in a row for the Fourth of July, and they had shared her bed. Bree knew her family liked Lara fine, but when she pictured them realizing what this had meant, she feared they would never forgive her.

She broke up with Lara as planned, late one night in May. They sat on the edge of Paradise Pond in the dark and wept into each other's hair, and Lara kept begging Bree to change her mind.

"I know you're afraid, but we can do this," she said. "We've done it here, and these have been the best years of our lives."

"I know," Bree said. "But that was here, Northampton. Not the real world."

"You think I'll ever find someone as great as you, B.?" Lara shook her head, and in an imitation of her father's Southern drawl, she said, "I'm sorry, baby, but that dog just won't hunt."

Bree laughed weakly.

"I love you," Lara said. "I can't lose you because you're afraid of what other people will think."

"It's not just any old people," she said. "It's my parents, my grandparents. The people who love me the most."

"Will we still be friends?" Lara asked.

"We will always be best friends," Bree said, though in truth she did not know.

"Can I still kiss you?" Lara said.

Bree shook her head. She thought of seeing Lara and not being able to kiss her or touch her soft skin. Bree sobbed into her hands, the hot tears puddling in her palms. Eventually, she got up, brushed the dirt from her pants, and said she had to go.

"I think you did the right thing," Celia said when Bree returned to the dorm.

Bree gulped. "I can fall in love again, but I'll never find another family."

As soon as she said it, she realized that she didn't believe herself. She would never fall in love like this again. And so, she went to Lara's dorm, dialed up from downstairs, and screamed "I'm an idiot! I was wrong!" into the intercom, as a trio of baffled first years looked on, smoking their cigarettes with wide eyes.

They were briefly elated, but then graduation came. The most stinging memory of all was the look on her mother's face when, just after the ceremony, Bree pulled her aside and told her the truth.

"I don't understand," her mother said. She looked like she might faint. "Not you, Bree."

Not you. It was, Bree thought, as if she had admitted to being a serial killer.

"It's my own fault," her mother whispered. "Why did I

insist on you coming here? You could be home safe and married to Doug Anderson by now."

Bree had hardly thought of him since she met Lara. It shocked her to hear his name. And how many times had her mother told her that she had made the best decision of her life letting him go?

"Please, Mama," Bree said. "Try to understand."

The rest of the family joined them then, the boys whooping and hollering over Bree's diploma. Her mother smiled in the pictures her father insisted on taking, but afterward she sent Bree's brothers away and said, "Tell your father what you've done."

Bree could feel herself turning red. She recited the words she had practiced with Lara the night before. "Daddy, I'm in a committed relationship with Lara and we're in love," she said.

Her father looked baffled. "What do you mean?" he said.

"They're a couple!" her mother shouted, hysterical. "She's telling us she's a lesbian! She's telling us that her little Chinese friend is her *girlfriend!*"

All around them, people stared. *Her little Chinese friend,* Bree thought, and she didn't know whether to laugh or cry. Did it bother her mother more that she was in love with a woman or that she was in love with an Asian?

Bree graduated magna cum laude from Smith College that day and received her diploma and her Phi Beta Kappa key. But in her parents' eyes, it would always be the day she had broken their hearts in a sea of folding chairs, right in the middle of the Quad.

Things had been strained between them ever since.

Lara followed her to Stanford, taking a job as a coordinator at the local Boys & Girls Club while Bree finished law school. Lara's patience always amazed Bree. When she stressed over an exam or a paper, Lara would say, "You need carbs," then busy herself in the kitchen making banana bread or pasta in a thick, creamy Parmesan sauce. She quizzed Bree every morning, reading questions off of note cards and sitting on Bree's feet as she did her sit-ups. If Bree expressed a moment's doubt over whether she could handle the workload, Lara would smooth her hair and say, "Come on now, cowgirl, you can do this. You were born to be a lawyer. Look how you argue me into submission all the time."

After Bree passed the bar, they moved down to San Francisco where they could both find better jobs. Bree knew it was thanks to the Old Girls Network that she landed her fantasy gig as an associate at Morris & White (White being Katherine White, Smith Class of '68, who loved hiring smart women's college grads).

At first, it was wonderful, being with Lara in the wide world, making a life together. But as years passed, her parents' disapproval took a greater and greater toll on Bree. Each time she was asked to declare their relationship for what it was, she hesitated. It made Lara livid that Bree's coworkers didn't know she had a girlfriend and that, a year after college graduation, she had faked food poisoning to get out of going to her high school reunion, picturing the looks on the faces of her former classmates when she strolled through the doors of the high school gymnasium with Lara on her arm.

Lately they were lucky if they could go twenty-four hours without a fight, despite the fact that Lara still made Bree laugh more than anyone; despite the fact that the sex was amazing as ever; despite the fact that they fell asleep each night pressed together, with Lara's hand on her belly, whispering nonstop about politics and books and celebrities and their days until they were too tired to say one more word.

In theory, Bree thought, it was bold and brave and right to choose love and fight for it. But how could love survive when it necessitated giving up so much? Since telling them about Lara, Bree spoke to her parents once every month or so, instead of four or five times a week like she used to. Her brothers e-mailed her and sent drunken text messages, but that was about it. She did not go home for holidays. She knew this hurt her parents, but she also knew that they wouldn't want Lara in their house. So they spent holidays with Lara's parents in Virginia, eating fried shrimp wontons and playing mah-jongg around a card table, with Lara's mother and aunts lapsing into Mandarin every so often, and Lara whispering, "They're talking about you."

Lara's mother went to Catholic Mass every morning, and on Christmas she insisted that they all go with her, even her husband, who had fought in Vietnam and was a staunch atheist, and Lara's brother, who was in some sort of cult, though they really never talked about it. Bree would get lost in the sound of organ music and the sight of sunlight passing through a stained-glass window behind the altar and the strange, funny feeling that you just never knew what the hell life was going to bring. She tried to ignore how much she missed being home with her own family.

Lara's mom would squeeze her hand as they walked out of church, and say, "Next year, you'll bring your parents with you, okay?"

It embarrassed Bree that her family wanted nothing to do

with these people, that her own mother had no interest in meeting Lara's parents. When Lara had come out in high school, she said, her mother had been devastated, saying Hail Marys and lighting candles, trying to undo what had been done. For a year, they hardly spoke. But then, Lara said, one day her mother returned home from church and said, "When I was twenty-five, I met your father. And I brought him to my parents, and they said if you marry this man, we will disown you. He was white, a non-Catholic. I married him anyway. My father died without ever speaking to me again, my mother missed my wedding, and your birth. We don't always do the things our parents want us to do, but it is their mistake if they can't find a way to love us anyway."

Bree only wished her own parents would realize this.

"They'll come around," Lara said. "You just have to let them in a little."

Bree was ashamed to tell her that she suspected they didn't want to be let in.

April had been supportive of their relationship. She sent cards addressed to both Bree and Lara; she always asked after Lara when she called or e-mailed. But Bree could tell that Celia—and Sally, too, to some extent—felt mystified. They had never really taken to Lara, never quite understood why Bree was willing to risk everything to be with her.

Sometimes just knowing this felt as real and painful as a dog bite. She was in love, but hers was a relationship that would always require explanation, that few people—even her dearest friends, even she herself—could really understand. After all this time, she still wished for a normal life, for the kind of love that would please her parents, for a moment like she'd had with Doug Anderson in Forsyth Park all those years ago, but with the person she actually loved. Part of her wanted to break away and find what Sally had found—normal, understandable love. She knew she could never have that, as long as she and Lara were together.

The alarm went off in the bedroom—a jarring, moaning sound. There was a grunt of protest, and then the noise stopped. A moment later, Lara emerged in her cotton bra and panties, her short, spiky hair sticking up in the back like Dennis the Menace's. Her soccer player's body—all muscle and curve—looked golden in the morning light.

She rubbed her eyes, walked over to the back of Bree's chair, and wrapped her arms around her from behind.

"You okay, baby?" she asked, and Bree shrugged.

"You were tossing and turning all night, and then you got up before the alarm even went off," Lara said, crouching down and kissing Bree's neck. "This can only mean one thing: We're about to see Sally get married."

"Yup," Bree said. "Buckle up."

"Oh, I'm ready for it," Lara said. In a sudden burst of energy, she started moving around the kitchen, hopping from one foot to the other, arms outstretched as if she were on the soccer field, trying to block a goal.

"Hit me with your best shot," Lara said, still moving. "I'm ready for the Bree Miller supersize emotional roller coaster, to be endured and dealt with by yours truly, and made up for by you with hours of mind-blowing sex when we get home."

Bree couldn't help it. She burst out laughing.

"Do you know that I love you?" she said.

"Why yes," Lara answered. "As a matter of fact, I do."

APRIL

I n her entire life, April had been to only one wedding, on her mother's friend's emu farm in Colorado. They had called it a Cherish Ceremony, and—not wanting to adhere to any patriarchal customs—they'd done away with rings, a white dress, attendants, and all of that. Really it was just a bunch of hippies out in a damp field, smoking joints and dancing circles around a couple who were blissfully in love and six months pregnant. April was only seven at the time, but she still remembered parts of it—her mother's long, tangled red hair, a strapping guy with a beard who scooped her up and put her on his shoulders, a cake covered in honey and sunflower seeds.

When she'd e-mailed Sally about it in an effort to explain why she had no business being a bridesmaid, Sally had written back just one short line, a classic Sallyism: *Sweetums, I need you there.*

April had to hand it to her—she would have envisioned Sally as a Princess Diana sort of bride, all done up in a meringuelike dress and veil, a church full of people, bagpipers on the front steps. But Sally had told her that the wedding was to be a simple, small outdoor ceremony and reception with absolutely no meringue.

April was glad for that, at least, though she still could not believe that after all their Smith training in independence and self-reliance Sally had decided to get married at twenty-five.

She arrived at the hotel slightly on edge. In the cab from the airport she had popped a Xanax Ronnie had given her, washing it down with the last of the bottled water she'd gotten on her flight. It wasn't helping. Despite all the crazy things she had done without fear in the past four years—hiding out in African villages, watching little girls endure the agony of genital mutilation in Indonesia, going to a maximum-security prison in Mississippi to interview a serial rapist—being her best friend's bridesmaid was still threatening to give her a full-blown panic attack.

She had felt this way for weeks, but now, having been punched in the stomach by a military guard two days earlier and forced to sit in a hospital waiting room for five hours just to learn that her arm was not, in fact, broken, April wanted nothing more than to spend the weekend lying in bed. She knew it was the jackass's job to protect government files, but he seemed to recognize her and Ronnie, and took genuine pleasure in beating her up, when he could have just escorted them off the premises. It was exciting, in a way, because it meant that the army was scared of what they knew was about to be exposed.

She was lucky that none of her bruises showed. Most were hidden by her T-shirt. Her dreadlocks, which she had once feared might anger Sally, actually covered a welt on her neck quite nicely.

It annoyed her that Sally and Jake were getting married in Northampton, because it hinted at the fact that Sally knew she was losing herself, and so she was grasping for their Smith days; for the last time in her entire life she would get to be an individual. And then there was the wastefulness of making all those people trek out to the middle of nowhere, increasing their collective carbon footprint and decreasing April's personal bank account.

All through college, April had marveled at the way her fellow students threw their—or, more accurately, their parents'—money around. She did ten shifts a week in the dining hall, washing dishes, peeling seemingly endless bags of potatoes, listening to the full-time staff talk about car payments or their kids' ear infections. She worked mornings in the admissions office, sorting through applications. She was the only one of the girls who paid for school entirely through work-study and loans in her own name. (Sally and Bree's fathers had paid their tuition in full. Celia had loans, but April knew for a fact that her parents made all the payments.)

Not much had changed since. The other girls still received financial help of some sort or another from their parents, though as open as they were about everything else, this was one area in which specifics never came up. She knew that Bree and Celia paid their own rent. And she was proud of Sally, because even though she could live comfortably off her mother's malpractice money for the rest of her life, she went to work every day just the same.

April knew it wasn't the money that was bothering her. In fact, the girls had been incredibly generous and thoughtful when it came to this weekend. Celia and Bree knew that Ronnie wasn't paying her much, so they had insisted on covering her third of the costs for Sally's presents—which, by the way, were a goddamn Cuisinart and a KitchenAid mixer, *hello 1952*.

The simple fact was, weddings were just not her thing, and this one was going to be particularly strange. She liked Jake, but she didn't think he was smart enough for her Sally, and she couldn't stand his frat-boy friends.

Plus, Ronnie had made her swear not to tell the girls the full extent of their next project, which would be hard, if not impossible.

"People like that don't understand," Ronnie said. "They'll try to talk you out of it, and I need you to be in it with me, one hundred percent."

"I'm in it," April said, annoyed because as long as she had worked for Ronnie, as many sacrifices as she had made, Ronnie never quite seemed to think she was dedicated enough.

For months after she graduated from Smith, April was working in the Chicago headquarters of Senator Dick Durbin, answering phones, fetching sandwiches, sorting mail. She told herself that these little tasks were an essential part of getting the greater work done, but she was dying to do something more radical, more real. Then came the phone call that changed her life. Ronnie Munro—whose picture April had had taped to her bedroom wall since middle school—called her up and asked her to meet for a drink.

April's mother had always talked about Ronnie Munro's

true devotion to the cause. They kept her book, *Woman Scorned,* in an exalted position in the center of the mantel.

Months before she even graduated, April had sent Ronnie her résumé and a heartfelt letter, in the hopes that she might at least keep it on file until the next time she needed an assistant. But job searching had led her to the conclusion that no one actually kept anything on file—they just threw résumés in the trash, until the day they happened to be hiring. She had long ago given up on the idea of hearing from Ronnie, so when she suddenly did, April felt elated.

She went to meet Ronnie at a dark wine bar two days after getting the call. Ronnie ordered them a bottle of Cabernet and laid out her plan, step by step. She was starting a Chicago-based company called Women in Peril, Inc. They would make films about misogyny all over the world—covering honor killings in Pakistan; genital mutilation in Africa; sex tourism in Asia and Eastern Europe; and the epidemics of rape and eating disorders right here in the United States—culminating in something huge, explosive, a few years down the road, once they had established a reputation.

"You don't have as much experience as I usually like in an assistant," Ronnie said. "But your letter really stayed with me."

Then Ronnie Munro actually quoted April to herself: *There's nothing I wouldn't do to help girls and women who are suffering in this world.*"

She looked April in the eye and said, "I couldn't have put it better myself. Tell me, April, do you really mean it?"

"Of course," April said, feeling giddy with excitement. She had never been this close to one of her role models, and for the first time in her semi-adult life, she couldn't think of a thing to say.

"You're bright as hell, that's clear," Ronnie said. "And I like that you're a Smithie, even though there are Smithies and there are *Smithies.*"

April laughed. "Right," she said.

"But I can tell which kind you are already," Ronnie said. "This isn't going to be a job like any job you've ever had. You're going to be right in the thick of it, all wrapped up in it. It might be scary sometimes. Hell, even I get scared, and I've been doing this for years."

"I'm not scared," April said. "It sounds really exciting."

"And I'll admit I can be a pain in the ass," Ronnie said with a smile. "I'm not what you would call an agreeable lady, as you might have heard." She took a sip of wine. "But I can promise you that working with me on this project will change your life and accelerate your role as a revolutionary."

April grinned, not sure whether or not Ronnie was being serious.

But Ronnie went on. "I mean that quite literally, April. When we are done, everyone who matters will know your name."

April was thrilled, calling Sally as soon as she got home, telling her the entire story.

"Do you get benefits?" Sally had asked.

April sputtered, "*That's* your first question?"

"Well. Do you?" Sally asked.

"I have no fucking clue," April said.

"What is she paying you?" Sally said.

"Sal, why aren't you happy for me?" April said, though of course she knew why.

All young feminists studied and revered the work of Gloria Steinem and Susan Faludi and women like that. They were beyond reproach. But most of the feminists who had made a real impact—Dworkin, MacKinnon, Brownmiller, Munro—were divisive figures.

"I'm a member of NOW, even though its milksop politics deeply offend me," Dworkin had written in an essay about attending a conference in the eighties and trying to get support for antipornography laws. "Guts were sorely lacking even back then." April had had this quote written on a scrap of paper and tucked into her wallet since her junior year at Smith.

All anyone ever thought about when they heard Ronnie Munro's name was the damn movie she'd made in which a woman ended up being killed by her husband. But that was thirty years ago, and in the meantime she had done so much good. People April's age, having heard the story secondhand, acted like Ronnie herself had killed that Indiana housewife, for fuck's sake. Anytime some Smith girl said bad things about Ronnie, April thought of how, when they were just babies, Ronnie was in China, raising awareness of female infanticide and trying to keep little girls alive, even though no one in the press gave a shit or did a thing.

April suspected that the real reason Ronnie had been cut out of most popular feminist circles was that her views and her methods were considered too extreme. It sickened her that to feminists like Sally, "extreme" meant that you didn't want women to be forced to have sex, forced to have their genitals carved up, forced to starve themselves in the name of beauty. If it was radical to think that all women should be

free and safe in the world, then why have a women's movement in the first place?

Despite Sally's trepidation, April accepted the job the
very next day. She sometimes joked to the Smithies that in
her entire time working for Ronnie, that first night in the
bar constituted the wooing phase. Ever since, it had been
all-consuming, heart-wrenching, and often dangerous
work. Ronnie wanted their minds to be in sync, for the two
of them to share not only a job but a life. So much of their
work was a secret, she said, that having an office away from
home made no sense at all. They should have their projects
with them always. April moved into Ronnie's apartment at
her request shortly after they started working together. She
knew the girls thought this was crazy.

"What do you two do after work?" Sally said. "Do you play
Scrabble and watch *Entertainment Tonight* at the end of the
day, or what?"

She was joking, of course, but it wasn't so far from the
truth. Ronnie was rich, and they each had an enormous
bedroom at opposite ends of an enormous apartment. But
they did tend to spend their free time together, drinking
wine on the couch, watching PBS, and shouting at the television set. While they were working, Ronnie was all business,
and she was nuts about her work—sometimes she would
shake April awake at four in the morning because she had a
brilliant idea and wanted them to get started on it right
away. But most of their free time was spent pleasantly
enough, eating alone together or else with Ronnie's incredible friends, who were all scholars and activists April had
long admired. She often thought that if she were working for
some Hollywood starlet and getting to mingle with famous

actors, the girls wouldn't bat an eye at her boss's odd behavior. Ronnie and her friends were April's icons, and having the chance to live among them was an honor.

As Ronnie had envisioned, Women in Peril, Inc., was their whole life now. It wasn't the big company it sounded like. Instead, it was just April and Ronnie, and the occasional contracted film crew or editor. Ronnie didn't trust anyone but April and herself to do the real work of interviewing women who'd been beaten or who had starved themselves nearly to death; of photographing the frightening aftermath of botched vaginal mutilation; of wooing brutal rapists into telling their stories; of stealing—Ronnie said "liberating"— files from government offices to get to the bottom of exactly how many female soldiers in Iraq had been raped by their own and then made to shut up about it.

Their work had been mentioned in *Ms.* magazine and praised by a handful of prominent radical feminists. Now it was finally time for the big, explosive project Ronnie had hinted at that night, more than three years earlier. She told April that this was her moment to shine, the point at which her name would be mentioned right alongside Ronnie's, a cocreator instead of an assistant, which she had never really been in the first place.

April knew the girls would disapprove, find the whole idea of it dangerous and risky. But what the hell was the point of life without a little danger and risk?

She was different from the others. They had all known it from the start. The summer before first year, they had had to fill out a form stating their preferences on dozens of questions—*Do you smoke? What kind of music do you like? What are your politics? Do you have a significant other?*

April had described herself as a vegan, an anarchist, a lover of sixties folk music. She wrote that she identified as an F-to-M transgendered person. That last part wasn't true, but she had added it for good measure, thinking that it would assure her a single on Green Street with a window seat and radicals all around.

April knew after taking just one look at Sally, Celia, and Bree on the first day of college that all three of them had been popular in high school. Maybe not the most popular girls in the class, certainly not the bitchy ones who made fun of the nerds. But she could tell they had been invited to dances and sleepovers. That they had the sort of mothers who always picked out the perfect birthday presents for their friends and braided their hair before school.

Sally hung Monet and Renoir posters on every wall of her dorm room: pretty, benign images of crowded cafés and blooming water lilies. All of the girls had framed photos of classmates and friends in their rooms—shots of boys grilling burgers on the beach; prom pictures, posed and stiff, their hair shellacked into what looked to April like cotton candy on a stick. When they asked April why she never put pictures up, she just shrugged and said she had been a loner in high school. It seemed a very James Dean—like alternative to saying that she had no friends, that she had longed for someone to talk to but no one ever invited her out, that other parents found her mother inappropriate, and so most of her Friday nights were spent reading tattered copies of *Backlash* and *The Feminine Mystique* at home on the couch. (*Cry me a river, Mrs. Astor!* her mother had written in the margins of the latter. April had no idea what it meant at the time, but she adopted the phrase as her own, and still used it to this day.)

April had convinced herself as a kid that she didn't need anyone, and she was standoffish with the girls at first, assuming that the three of them would form a little clique, leaving her to be the outcast on the hall. She was drawn instead to the radicals on campus, who accepted her as one of their own from the start. But to her surprise, the King House girls treated her like a true friend. Even more surprising to April was the way she took to this—loving it when they confided in her or knocked on her door each night at six for dinner. She had imagined, rightly so, that she would be able to bond with the good lefties on campus over social issues. But now, for the first time in her life, she had three friends who liked her, just because.

April had to work hard to catch up to the girls socially. She studied them—the way they interacted with ease, their ability to feel out one another's needs. She carved places for herself where she could: She was the one who listened to Sally cry, the one who made mistakes but always tried to repair things with cookie dough. And sometimes, she could even get them excited about her causes and convictions, especially Sally, who it seemed had never thought much about feminism or racism, or any ism besides maybe Impressionism, before coming to Smith.

Though she complained about having to live in the Quad, April knew she'd gotten the best of both worlds on the Smith campus—at meetings and in class she had met rebellious feminists who wanted to help her take down the patriarchy, and back home at the dorm she had three friends who offered safety and laughter and concern, the sort of family she had never known.

But ever since graduation, the girls' indifference to the world beyond their own love lives rankled her. She had imagined that four years out of college they'd be saving the world, not planning a fucking wedding. All over the planet women were being tormented, yet if you took sexism seriously, you were a bore, an idiot, or a pain in the ass. How the hell could anyone keep quiet? Why did so many women do nothing?

A feminist anthropologist friend of Ronnie's had come to their place for dinner one night while she was in Chicago for a conference. She told them about her research on rape in the animal kingdom. Nearly every species had some form of rape, she said, except for the bonobos, a group of primates similar to chimpanzees. Somewhere along the line, the female bonobos decided that they would no longer tolerate sexual violence. So when a male attacked one of them, she emitted a sound to draw attention to herself. The other female bonobos would drop what they were doing, rush toward the sound, and together they would tear the offending male limb from limb. She knew Sally would roll her eyes if she ever said so out loud, but that sounded perfect to April. Why couldn't women be more like that?

At the front desk of the Autumn Inn, she picked up the spare key to the room she'd be sharing with Celia and made her way to the elevator. The bellhop looked past her, out at the circular driveway, as if her steamer trunks might be stacked up on the curb.

"It's just this," she said, patting her backpack. She had managed to cram in video equipment, two pairs of jeans, and her bridesmaid dress and shoes, though the dress was now in a ball at the bottom of the bag. Did cotton wrinkle? That was one of those things that people like Sally and Bree knew off the top of their heads, and that she herself would never make room for in her memory bank.

She had e-mailed Sally earlier that week, asking who was coming. Sally said it would just be Jake's parents, grandparents, aunts, uncles, and sister; a few of his friends and cousins and fraternity brothers from Georgetown; Sally's father (Fred, as Sally called him) and brother; and a young married couple Jake and Sally had befriended in Boston. The young married couple was actually named Jack and Jill. April snorted when she read this, and she could almost feel Sally's eyes on her, begging her to shut up.

She inhaled deeply now. *Behave,* she told herself. She knew it wouldn't be easy.

Sally was what always kept her from hollering inappropriate things at strangers—just the mere thought of Sally's face were she there to witness it. Every morning in the coffee shop at the end of the block, April overheard the old men at the counter talking politics. They weren't enraged or even unhappy with the state of the country. Instead, they worried about a Democrat being elected in 2008; they talked loudly about how some antitorture pansy-ass wasn't going to protect the country from another terrorist attack. April wanted to scream, *Don't you know our evil president is eavesdropping on your phone calls and monitoring every library book you take out and killing thousands of your sons and daughters in a war that serves no earthly fucking purpose?* But because of Sally, she settled for just slamming the door as hard as she could when she left.

The elevator opened, and April made her way toward room 493. She could hear the girls laughing from five doors away. When she stepped into the room, all three of them were there, lying in bed, watching *Golden Girls* on TV.

"I see you three are as wild as ever," April said with a smile. "Some things never change."

Sally ran to her first, and then the others. April's ribs throbbed as they hugged her, and she had to pull away.

Celia wore a pale blue tank top and jeans. She had probably lost twenty pounds since college. She looked thinner every time April saw her. Her cheeks and collarbone were dramatically sharp, so different from the soft, cloud face she had had at Smith. The two of them exchanged a look, and April knew that Celia had not said anything about the fight she had been in. April gave her a grateful smile.

Bree still had the look of someone's trophy wife—long blonde hair and a tiny waist, full lips, and bright blue eyes. April found it satisfying, in a way, that no man would ever have her.

"Where's Lara?" April asked.

"We had a fight," Bree said. "But I know she'll be thrilled to see you."

"And Jake's golfing with his dad," Sal said. "Why do men always feel the need to golf before they get married?"

April shrugged. "Don't ask me."

The four of them crawled back under the covers for a bit, and the girls asked her about her flight, about Ronnie.

"We've been waiting for you to get here so we can all go

down to the bar in the lobby and drink champagne," Celia said. "Are you ready yet?"

"I'm always ready for champagne with my ladies," April said.

"Good. I'll get Lara," Bree said, as they climbed out of bed. "She could use a drink."

A few minutes later, April sat between Sally and Celia at the hotel bar. It was two o'clock, and they were the only people in the room besides the balding bartender. He looked about forty-five years old. Celia befriended him immediately, and they started talking about life in New York City. He asked her who the last famous person she'd seen was, and Celia shrugged. "I saw Joan Rivers at the movies this past weekend. Does she count?"

He said that yes, indeed, Joan Rivers qualified as famous. Celia laughed, throwing her head back as if they were having the funniest exchange in the history of funny exchanges. The girl could flirt with an oak tree, April thought, though she was grateful to have a few moments alone with Sally.

"How's work?" Sally asked.

"Forget work. How are you feeling about everything?" April said.

Sally beamed. "Honestly? The fact that I get to marry Jake and see you guys—it's like I'm on *The Price Is Right* and I just won the Showcase Showdown."

April remembered long hours back in college spent listening to Sally talk about how much she loved Bill. That had always been a bittersweet union, a love that caused Sal more pain than joy. This one was different, but still, April was not sure that Jake could really make Sally happy in the long run.

Would she wake up one morning fifteen years from now and be mad that April hadn't stopped her?

"I can't believe you are getting married in two days," she said, kissing Sally on the forehead.

"Me neither," Sally said. "I'm so glad you guys are here."

A moment later, Sally's face turned sad, and April leaned in, preparing to hear the confession she'd been waiting for all year—Sally wanted out. But instead, she said, "I really miss my mom."

"Of course you do," April said.

"The thought of stupid Rosemary being my kids' only grandmother is so upsetting," Sally said. "My mother would have been the absolute best."

April nodded sympathetically.

"It just feels totally wrong that my mother never knew Jake, or any of you. The woman kept every macaroni collage I made in preschool, but she never got to meet my best friends or have a conversation with my husband."

April squeezed her hand. "It feels totally wrong because it is totally wrong," she said.

A while later, Bree joined them, alone. Her eyes looked puffy.

"She's pissed," she said, before ordering an extra-strong gin and tonic.

They moved to a tiny table, with last night's bowl of nuts still sitting on it.

For the past six months, April and Ronnie had been busy tying up loose ends on their latest documentary. She realized now that it had been forever since she last spoke to Bree. April had no idea things had gotten so bad.

"Lara wants Bree to marry her," Sally whispered, loudly.

April laughed. Sally, ever the lightweight, was already way beyond tipsy.

"Sal, that was more of a stage whisper than an actual whisper, just FYI," Bree said.

"Well, I'm sorry," Sally said. "But it's just—is that a great idea for you guys right now? You seem to be fighting all the time."

Bree sighed. "I don't know."

April wondered if Sally still secretly found the idea of Bree and Lara hard to comprehend: She was constantly telling Bree that maybe it was time to move on. April thought it strange that Sally had no problem saying so, though she saw her own relationship as beyond reproach. It was as if having a ring on her finger had elevated her above the level of critique, even though Bree and Lara had been together far longer than Sally and Jake.

"What more does Lara want?" Sally said. "You live together, you're out to your family and friends."

"It's more complicated than that," Bree said. "It's like she thinks I resent her for putting me in this position in the first place. And maybe I kind of do. I love her, but I wish it could just be easy."

"Love's never easy," Sally said.

"*Easier* then," Bree said. "Why do relationships have to be so damn complicated?"

Back in college, they had talked about marriage so many times that April could almost recite the conversation she knew they were about to have. Of course, as with most things in life, everything always came back to their parents. Sally's had had a sad, strained marriage. Her mother was ten years younger than her father, and he had always been a cold, removed sort of man. He'd had affairs, too, and never really bothered to keep them quiet.

In her mother's last days, Sally had asked her why she ever married him in the first place. She didn't really expect her to respond, but her mother had answered quickly, without having to think.

"I loved the idea of him," she said. "The wisdom he had, the life he could give me. By the time I realized what he was made of inside, it was too late."

April had always wondered why she didn't just leave him, but even she knew that wasn't the sort of question you could ask someone about her dead mother.

Bree and Celia both had happily married parents. Celia's had met in the stands at a Boston College football game their junior year, and Bree's had known each other since grade school. It seemed to make the two of them believe in some sort of guaranteed, endless human connection, though since moving to New York, Celia claimed not to anymore. If April knew anything for sure, it was that bonds like that didn't exist. Your husband could walk out of work one day after twenty years of marriage and an air conditioner could fall on his head from the fifty-second story, and you'd be alone again. Or, more likely, he could walk out of work, bump into a twenty-two-year-old dental hygienist, and the next thing you knew you'd be standing at your front door exposed in your mom jeans and your homemade Christmas sweater, as you were served with divorce papers.

Even as a little girl, April had had no illusions about a big white wedding. Other girls' mothers had told them about Prince Charming, so as adults they still searched for salvation in the form of some man. April's mother had told her about self-sufficient princesses who wore painter's pants and had adventures on the high seas. The story never included men, though she knew that her mother craved male approval, male companionship, even as she railed on about misogyny. In the years since college, she had grown further and further from her mother, so that now, even though they both lived in Chicago, they no longer spoke. The girls did not know this, and April thought it was for the best: It would scare them to have to think of her as parentless, though April had long since thought of herself that way.

All that April had ever heard about her father was that he was an artist who had shown at the Saatchi Gallery and the Guggenheim. Her mother had loved him terribly, "like a sickness," she said. He left her anyway when she was eight months pregnant with April, for some art student.

Like all little girls whose mothers refused to talk much about their fathers, April imagined that hers wasn't quite so bad. Perhaps he'd had that silly, selfish artist phase for a while, but then he'd had a change of heart. She imagined him living in a warm cottage somewhere in France, jammed full of old teapots and copper pans and dried flowers hanging from the rafters. He had married a fat French painter, and they did watercolors together for hours and baked bread and played with their seven children. April imagined that he thought of her every day, that he longed for her, searched for her. And that one day, he would find her.

"Don't take my April away," her mother would scream, but he would say softly, "I must, Lydia. I've missed her too much all these years to let her go now."

And April would go with him, to sleep in a big bed the size

of their whole apartment in Chicago, alongside her brothers and sisters and ten or twenty dogs.

When she was in fifth grade, her mother called school one day to say that April was home sick, and then dragged her to a no-grapes rally in Madison. She spent the entire car ride smoking a joint with her friends while April read in the backseat.

When they got there, April was hungry and needed to pee.

Her mother told her to go ahead and go, but April was scared she might get lost in the crowd.

"Please, Momma," she whined over and over, shifting from one leg to the other.

"In a minute," her mother kept saying. "Hold your horses."

Finally, she took April to the port-o-potties by the road.

There was a couple in front of them in line, holding hands. The woman had long black hair and wore a tiny dress. April's mother kept staring at them with squinty eyes. At first, April thought it was just because she was stoned, but then her mother began to cry.

April felt embarrassed. Her mother was known for silly, weed-induced moodiness among her hippie friends. It was a joke to them, but to April it was increasingly mortifying. No one else had a mother like hers. When she was very small, this had seemed like a wonderful gift—her mother pulled her out of school to drive to the lake and watch lightning storms. She served frozen waffles with Reddi-wip for dinner. She sometimes stayed out until dawn painting with friends and decorated their apartment with her homemade artwork. But April had begun to long for a normal mother, the type who checked your math homework and made you eat your vegetables.

Now, in the port-o-potty line, she thought of how her classmates were probably just heading out to recess, and here she was, watching her mother cry before a protest.

"Mom, are you okay?" April asked.

But her mother was still staring at the couple. "Richard?" she said loudly.

The man and woman turned around, as did several others. April's heart sped up.

"Lydia," the man said. He had long sideburns and thick black hair. He looked like he might say more, but April's mother leaned toward him first and whispered something in his ear. He stared at April, his face a knot of confusion.

"April," he said softly.

The next thing she knew, her mother was yanking her away from the line and back toward her friends.

"You're hurting me!" April said.

The man called after them, but April couldn't make out his words. Then the crowd closed up around them like an ocean, and he was gone.

"I have to pee!" she shouted. "Mom, what are you doing?"

Her mother kept crying. "I don't like that man," she said. "Now let's please not talk about it anymore, not until we're back home."

April knew better than to argue with her when she got like this. The rest of the day and the drive back to Chicago felt endless. April stayed quiet, buried in her book, while her mother shouted along with the crowds, while she and her friends stopped at a diner for grilled cheese sandwiches and talked about George Bush, that oil-guzzling, money-grubbing motherfucker.

When the two of them finally reached their apartment, April asked, "What did you whisper to that man in the bathroom line? He knew my name."

Her mother frowned. "I said, *Take a good long look at your daughter.*"

April was confused for a moment. "You mean, that was my father?" she asked.

"I wouldn't call him a father, would you?" her mother said.

April held her breath, trying not to cry. If she had known, then she could have said something to him; she could have memorized his face, his hands. Something. She said nothing to her mother, though she wanted to know why there had been no introduction, no exchange of phone numbers. Now how would he ever find her again, if in fact he had been looking?

"I think I'll go to bed," April said.

She waited until she was under the covers to let the tears flow. They didn't believe in God, not really, though her mother sometimes claimed to be a Buddhist. But on that night and what seemed like a million nights that followed, April prayed for her father to come back to her.

She never saw him again.

April had slept with only two men in her life. Her junior year of college, there was Steven, the sweet Hampshire student who had been raised by a pair of Reaganites and rebelled by becoming a Trotskyist. They met at a rally at Smith (she couldn't remember what the rally was for now). He was tender, the softest kisser in the world, and his mere existence put a spring in Sally's step. ("You're going to marry him," she kept saying. "You're the kind of girl who sees what she wants and sticks with it.") Their affair was charming, but it lasted only four months. April still e-mailed with him every now and then. He had given up on becoming a playwright and gone to work in his father's architectural firm. He was engaged to someone named Bitsy or Betsy or Bunny whom his parents had introduced him to at a country club Easter brunch.

April's first, when she was just thirteen, was Gabriel. In all the years since, she hadn't told a soul about him. She didn't know how the girls would react. But one night, after too much wine, she told Ronnie the story.

He was a poet friend of her mother's who hung around a lot that summer. He had a long brown ponytail and broad shoulders, and April thought he was the most attractive man she had ever met in real life. One night, he offered to pick up the Chinese food and casually asked April if she wanted to come along for the ride. To her mother, only half listening, it sounded entirely harmless. Kids loved to go along for the ride, after all; they liked the attention.

Gabriel parked his van in the Cathay Pacific lot, and they climbed into the back. She suddenly longed for the safety of her bed, for the pale blue Care Bear with a picture of a rain cloud on its belly that she kept hidden under her pillow. April was terrified, even though she had been dreaming of this, imagining what he would do.

He had been hinting at it for weeks.

"April, you look good enough to eat," he said once, running his hand along the small of her back.

When he saw her in her bathing suit on her way to the community pool, he said, "Don't tell anyone, but I just got hard from looking at you. Face it, April, you're gorgeous."

In the back of his van outside of the Chinese place, he told her to lie down. Silently, he pulled down her khaki shorts, her pink cotton underpants. He gently spread her legs apart, kissing the insides of her thighs. He proceeded to go down on her until she felt like she might burst. Then he flipped her over onto her hands and knees, and entered her from behind. It hurt, but she pursed her lips together, forcing herself to stay silent, lest he decide to stop.

When they returned home with dinner, her mother had the table set. She sat there, with her bare feet perched on the windowsill, a glass of wine in one hand and a cigarette in the other. She smiled at them, and April knew she was pretending they were a family, father and daughter home from a brief road trip, mom ready to welcome them back.

At the time, April believed that Gabriel was her boyfriend, or at least that he loved her. She understood that nobody must know about them. He was forty years old, her mother's age. And anyway, the secret was delicious. A part of her that her mother could not own.

They had sex in her bedroom while her mother painted in the kitchen. She gave him a blow job in the mailroom of their apartment building. He stared at her naked body for hours, touching every curve, every bump and hair. He told her she was beautiful.

She hoped they would go on like that forever, but then something happened. April got pregnant. Her mother handled it disturbingly well, taking her to get the abortion, making her Ramen noodles and Jell-O afterward. She did not know that Gabriel was the father, of course, or if she suspected she didn't mention it. April never saw him again. Her mother said later that he had gone to Denver in search of his ex-wife and teenage son. It shocked April to hear that he had a child, especially a child who was older than her.

As an adult, April had tried to get her mother to talk about Gabriel, but her mother always changed the subject or just said, "Please, April, I can't discuss this now."

The girls said she was too cynical about love, but how could you not be? On the surface, relations between men and women were all soft kisses and white gowns and hand-holding. But underneath they were a scary, complicated, ugly mess, just waiting to rise to the surface.

Of course, she wouldn't say that now. This was Sally's wedding, and April loved Sally. She sat back, took a long sip of champagne, and vowed to shut the fuck up.

Back in college, April's favorite month was November. A chill set in and left the Northampton air smelling clear and crisp. The leaves all fell to the ground so that on cloudy days the campus looked like a black-and-white photograph, with dark buildings and trees set against a pale gray sky. Women on campus started bundling up in gloves and hats, and at the first dusting of snow, trucks from Residence Life poured gallons of soy sauce on the walkways. (The salty liquid melted the ice without polluting the ground, and the entire Quad smelled like a Thai restaurant until February.)

November was also the time for Celebration of Sisterhood, the festival of sexual diversity that was April's favorite Smith tradition. It had started back in the early 1990s after a group of lesbians were attacked on campus.

Some of the popular Smith customs left her feeling over-privileged and ridiculous. Each fall the president called Mountain Day, which meant that classes were canceled and everyone could go out and enjoy nature (or, more likely, take the shuttle to the Holyoke Mall). Mountain Day was always a surprise, announced in the Quad by someone blaring Madonna's "Holiday" out an open window first thing in the morning. Students signaled that they wanted Mountain Day to come by holding Quad Riot—a massive food fight in the middle of the Quad, where women hurled long-stored moldy leftovers and shaving cream and soda and God only knew what else at one another for hours. The next morning, the grounds crew would have to come and clean it all up. April thought the classism in this was simply nauseating, and every year she'd be out there with them, filling her recycling bin with dirty noodles and old toothbrushes and all the remains of the fight, just to prove that not all Smith women were thoughtless ninnies.

Then there was Immorality, the notorious clothing-optional party held in Tyler House every Halloween. Women attended in nothing but lingerie, or body paint, or Saran Wrap. In theory, maybe it wasn't such a bad idea. But in reality, it was just an excuse for hundreds of fully clothed college boys to swarm the campus and gawk (they were bused in from as far away as Florida). The women on campus didn't seem to mind being stared at and prodded by fat fratty fingers all night, even though every year at least one woman got assaulted.

When April posted flyers attempting to ban the party, she only got one reply, a voice mail from the freak who led the Smith Christian Fellowship. (Who even knew that group existed?) "Hey April," the girl said in a voice that sounded like audible sunshine. "I was so glad to see your flyers this morning. All semester, the fellowship has been lifting up the prayer that Immorality will be stopped. Perhaps you're just the gift from God we needed." April shuddered at the thought. She erased the message immediately. (This was before she learned about the unholy matrimony between antiporn feminists on the far left and conservative Christians on the far right.)

But Celebration of Sisterhood was purely wonderful. Senior year, April was cochairing the event with her friend Toby Jones, a junior transman who had been taking testosterone for two years and had made a full top transition the previous summer, having his breasts removed entirely. A few weeks before the event, Toby suggested to April and the committee that they change its name to just Celebration, in an attempt to be more inclusive of Smith's transgender population. Everyone in the meeting thought it was a fantastic idea.

April's first inkling that others might not agree came while she was working a brunch shift in the King House dining room one Sunday morning. As she scrubbed the tables, she watched a sophomore named Christine Lansky eyeing the plates of the other women in the buffet line, scooping half the scrambled eggs on her plate back into the serving dish.

Celia and Sally were in the corner, and April walked over to their table, wiping her hands on her apron. She bit into a slice of pineapple from Celia's plate.

"Look at that," she said, nodding toward Christine. "It's like if she eats fewer eggs than anyone else, she wins."

Celia wasn't paying attention. Instead, she stared in the direction of the doorway. "Oh my Lord," she said under her breath.

Bree and Lara had come in holding hands, still wearing pajamas with messy make-out hair and big smiles on their faces.

"I cannot deal!" Celia said in a whisper. "It's too early in the morning for lesbianism."

"What?" April asked. She was pretending to be washing their tabletop, though if there had been a single crumb on it, Sally would have cleaned it up immediately.

"Oh, come on!" Celia said. "You have to admit it's weird."

Even though Bree and Lara had been dating for two years, their relationship still shocked Celia. April thought it was fantastic. It's hard enough to find a soul mate, she had said to Celia on the night Bree first told them about the relationship. Why limit yourself to only a little sliver of the population?

Of course, Celia disagreed. She could sometimes be unbelievably possessive of Bree, though she said that wasn't it; she just could not figure out how Bree was straight yet actually dating Lara.

"They have sex?" Celia asked.

"I would assume so," April said.

"Jesus, I just can't imagine," Celia said with a shudder.

"Well, what's the big deal? You've kissed girls."

"That was different! Anything above the belt is child's play compared to, well, you know," Celia said.

"Anything below the belt?" April said.

"Yes!" Celia said, her cheeks growing red.

Celia had never liked the idea of Lara to begin with—she wanted to be the most important woman in Bree's life, and it was clear that Lara had won that title. April always marveled at how competitive some Smith women could be, over friendships, and boyfriends, and grades, and weight, and pretty much everything else. What the hell was the point?

The two of them sat down, and Lara put her feet in Bree's lap. April always thought they looked happy together, really happy. She had never felt that way about anyone, male or female.

"Maybe you're a lesbian, gumdrop," Sally had said, on one of the countless nights when they were discussing her relationship with Bill, and Sally just had to turn the conversation to April's lack of a love life.

"What's a lesbian gumdrop?" April said.

"You know what I mean," Sally said.

April sighed. "I wish I were a lesbian. That would make life a hell of a lot easier. But distrusting men doesn't necessarily make you attracted to women, you know?"

Sally nodded. "I'd like to be a lesbian, too," she said. "Except for the sex part."

Never having been in love didn't bother April. When she saw the way her friends let it overtake them—the crying, the obsessing, the analyzing, the endless phone calls—she was glad that no person had ever brought that out in her. Friends were enough, she thought. With friends there was no game playing or power struggle or need to fit into some precise model of womanhood—doting cheerleader, or longing lover, or scolding mommy. You could just be yourself.

"What's shaking, girls?" Lara said.

"*Nada mucho,*" Celia said.

"Bree, baby, you want me to get you some food?" Lara said.

"Nah," Bree said. She turned to the others. "We ate leftover dining hall cake in bed this morning. And I for one am full as a tick."

"That's a great image," Celia said. "I'm so glad you could put that in my head while I'm eating."

"That's real Georgia talk for you," Lara said.

April smiled, thinking of how funny it was that two Southern girls had come to the East Coast and found each other.

She looked outside. It was beginning to rain.

"I have a Celebration meeting in an hour in Duckett. Think it will stop raining by then?" she asked.

"This morning the Weather Channel said it's going to rain until early evening," Sally said.

"Who watches the Weather Channel?" Bree said with a laugh.

"I do!" Sally said, taking a blueberry from her fruit salad and throwing it at Bree.

"I really hope it doesn't rain for Celebration," April said. "We have so many amazing things planned this year!" She smiled, thinking about Toby's idea. To leave a mark on Smith College, this place that she loved so much, was one of the best things she could imagine.

"Okay, why do you keep calling it Celebration?" Celia said. "We know you're one of the cool kids, but must you abbreviate *everything*? Oh sorry, I mean must you abbreviate *ev*?"

"We're changing the name to be more inclusive," April said proudly.

"More inclusive of whom?" Lara asked.

"More inclusive of our trans population," April said.

"Not this again," Celia said. "It wasn't enough to change the student constitution to accommodate the trannies? Now you're taking Celebration of Sisterhood away, too?".

"She's not taking anything away," Sally said, jumping to April's defense. "She's making it better! Inclusiveness is what the whole thing is supposed to be about."

April gave her a smile. When she had first talked to Sally about transgender issues, Sally had been resistant, freaked out. But ultimately, she said, "You're right, April. Why shouldn't these people have the right to be all that they can be?" (April had had to stop herself then from humming the old Army Reserves theme song that started off just that way.)

"But this is a *women's* college," Celia said now. "One of the very last ones. Smithies have fought to keep it that way for ages. And now, in the name of political correctness, you're taking the femaleness out of it so that a few confused people can feel included?"

"It's more than a few," April said. "We have thirty-four transmen on this campus, and they love Smith as much as we do. Think about Toby! Don't you think he's worth fighting for?"

"I like Toby," Celia said. "And I remember first year, when he was Theresa. But if he wants to be a man, why does he want to do it here, at a women's college?"

"Because we're welcoming," April sputtered. "You know, most women on this campus aren't as closed minded as some of the women sitting around this table."

"Don't you mean the *people* sitting around this table?" Celia said. "You never know, Sally might decide to become a man. Nothing will have to change, of course. We can just keep calling her Sal."

April knew that Celia was making a joke, attempting to end the debate so they could get on with their brunch. But she could not laugh it off.

"Have a good day, everyone," she said, turning to leave.

A chorus of "Come back here!" arose from the girls, but April was already making her way back into the stockroom. She could feel the hot tears in her eyes.

"We have to do inventory before noon," she called, not looking back at them.

She walked into the stockroom and shut the door behind her. The shelves were lined with huge tins of pineapple and baked beans, boxes of cereal and bagels wrapped up in plastic bags, salt and flour and sugar in plain economy-size sacks.

April remembered the night that Toby told her how he had known since preschool, maybe earlier, that he was meant to be a boy. His parents tried to force him to grow out his long ringlets and wear little jumpers and dresses. He would cry, always finding a pair of scissors and chopping his hair off. His parents locked him in his room until he promised to stop acting like such a tomboy. In high school, they sent him away to a school for emotionally disturbed kids. They had meant it as a form of punishment, he said, a way to straighten him out. Instead, he met doctors who recognized his condition, the first people he had met who took him seriously.

"I'm out of place in my own skin," Toby had told her with tears in his eyes. "Can you imagine that? I literally know that this body I'm in is not my body."

April had felt out of place more times than she cared to recall—back in high school, and even now, at the ridiculous tea parties they held in the King House parlor every Friday at four, on Saturday nights when Amherst frat boys filled the halls. But she could not imagine what it would be like to feel out of place in her body. She thought Toby was a hero. Life would never be easy for him, because he had chosen to be honest about who he was. If Smith could provide a respite from judgment, a four-year break from hardship, why did someone as kind as Celia care about the language in some stupid student constitution?

Sometimes April worried that she'd been built without some fundamental piece that everyone else had that just let them deal. Even her mother, who got involved in every lefty cause she could, seemed to be able to shake it all off at the end of the day and enjoy life. But the evil in the world, every-where you looked, was always on April's mind. She had been that way ever since she was a child. She had to force herself to watch the news. Every night it was the same thing—bomb-ings, genocide, children abducted or murdered on the way home from school, freak car accidents that killed entire families on vacation. The reporters would tell these stories in somber, important tones, as if they mattered, but the next day they became worthless.

She thought about the women she lived with at Smith. They were probably some of the most privileged people in this world, yet the sadness they had known was immense; the injury they had experienced at the hands of themselves and others could break your heart.

She remembered the night junior year when Celia had accompanied some of the other King House girls to a formal at Dartmouth. Dates had been arranged by someone or other, and Celia had Googled her guy a hundred times. His name was Rob Johann. He was a senior majoring in business who played for the soccer team and had already made half a million dollars in the stock market somehow. Celia spent hours the day of the formal primping in her room, singing along to the Dixie Chicks. She borrowed an old girdle from Bree's homecoming-queen days. ("It's *called* a waist cincher!" Bree said, when April said she hadn't realized anyone had worn a girdle in the last hundred years.) When Celia emerged, she looked like a princess—her hair was up in an elegant twist, her makeup was perfectly applied, and her black sleeveless cocktail dress magically disguised every last lump and bump.

Sally, April, and Bree took pictures, fawning over her like parents before the prom.

"You're going to marry Rob Johann," Sally squealed. "I just know it."

April rolled her eyes, but she had to admit that Celia looked stunning.

"Knock him dead," she said.

The following morning, April, Bree, and Lara were studying in the hallway and eating animal crackers out of an enormous bear-shaped tub that Bree's mother had sent. Sally was off somewhere with Bill.

"Celia's not up yet?" April asked, looking at her watch.

"I don't think she ever came home last night," Bree said.

"I'm so glad that I can have sexual adventures vicariously through the rest of you," April said.

Bree laughed. "Happy to oblige," she said, wrapping an arm around Lara, and planting a kiss on her cheek.

Celia arrived home around eleven, her black eyeliner smudged. She smiled weakly at the three of them.

"Long night," she said. "I need a little disco nap."

April noticed a row of light blue bruises on each of her upper arms and another large bruise on her knee. But before she could say anything, Celia walked right past them and into her room.

Bree and April followed her, knocking on the door. "Can we come in, sweetie?" Bree said. She didn't wait for an answer. When they opened the door, Celia was already under the covers, still in her dress, with the light off and the shades pulled down.

"Please leave me alone, you guys," she said. "Really. Please go."

April felt a gnawing in her stomach as they closed the door and returned to their spots in the hall. This wasn't like Celia. Happy or sad, she was not the type who ever wanted to be alone. If she took a nap during the day, she always left her door wide open because she said she wanted to hear what was going on with everyone else, even if she was unconscious.

"I'm worried," Bree whispered. "Remember when she fell down the stairs at Wilder?"

April nodded. There had been a few times, in fact, but it seemed cruel to mention it. A couple of drinks only made Celia want more and more, until she was drowning in it. She had once joked about how it was illegal to buy liquor in Massachusetts on Sundays or on holidays, so her Irish relatives would always stock up beforehand. (Right before Independence Day each year, Celia said, her grandfather would announce, "If you want to have a great Fourth, buy a fifth on the third!")

When Sally came home around dinnertime that night, Celia still hadn't emerged. They told Sally what had happened, and she shook her head. "Have you asked around the house to see what went on last night?"

They had, but none of the other girls had seen Celia since about midnight the night before, when they got on the road to head home, and she insisted on staying behind. She told them she was bunking in with a girlfriend from high school.

Celia slept right through dinner and into the next morning, but when she finally came out of her room, headed to the shower and wrapped in her Snoopy towel, she looked happy enough.

"Sweetie, are you okay?" Sally asked. "Where did you get those bruises?"

"I'm fine." Celia smiled, but April thought it didn't look quite real.

"So," Sally said, "any word from Mr. Johann?"

"Yup, he e-mailed me," Celia said. " He said he had a great time, and wished we didn't live so far apart. He kept calling me Snow White all night, and the e-mail started off *Dear Snow.*"

Sally squealed. "Oh, I knew he couldn't resist you in that dress! No man could. Mrs. Celia Johann, I can just see it now."

"Oh, I'll never take his name," Celia said with a wink. "Well, maybe we will hyphenate."

After that, she didn't mention him.

Weeks passed before Celia told them the real story. It was a Thursday night. The four of them sat on the braided rug in Sally's room, drinking wine and talking. Sally mentioned that her brother had a cute hippie friend at Dartmouth who April might like. April responded that she didn't like guys from Ivy League schools, and Celia suddenly started to cry.

"When I hear the word 'Dartmouth,' it makes me want to throw up," she said. "Like truly, even if I just see it printed on someone's sweatshirt, I have to fight to keep myself from vomiting."

She told them that the night of the formal, she and Rob Johann had gotten along from the start, making jokes and talking about their families and never having so much as a single awkward silence. He was gorgeous. Way out of her league, she thought. But he seemed to think she was pretty. They drank champagne, they danced, and at some point they snuck off to a coatroom to kiss.

"He said he thought kissing a girl he really liked on the dance floor was tacky, but that he had been dying to kiss me since I walked in the door," Celia said.

Around midnight, the other Smithies wanted to leave, she said, so she told Rob good-bye. But he begged her to stay and take a walk around campus with him. He had a car, he said, and he would gladly drive her home in a couple of hours. Celia was elated.

"I had pretty much already picked out the bridesmaid dresses," she said sarcastically, but April knew there was a grain of truth to it. Progressive as they were, in some ways her friends still lived in a Jane Austen novel.

Celia went on. After the Smithies left, Rob swiped a bottle of Veuve Clicquot from the bar at the party, and they walked around campus, holding hands and swigging champagne. They emptied the bottle and kept walking, giggling with drunken delight at each other's stories, talking about how many kids they wanted to have, and how they both hoped to settle in New York City.

"I won't ever be able to sleep if my daughters look like you," he said at some point. "You're too gorgeous."

She couldn't remember what time it was when he asked her to come back to his apartment, but she knew that it was late and that he was in no shape to drive.

"You can take the bed and I'll take the floor," he had said with a smile. "I'll be a perfect gentleman, I swear. I'll drive you home first thing in the morning."

Celia kissed him. "Deal," she said. "As long as we can get pancakes at Sylvester's. You'll love it. It's the best breakfast spot in Northampton."

As they made their way to his place, she thought of how she had always longed to be part of one of those couples that goes out to brunch together, reading the newspaper over French toast and coffee. Perhaps she had finally met him— the one she was meant to be with.

When they got to the apartment, Rob's three roommates were sitting on the couch, drinking beer and watching a repeat of *Saturday Night Live.* The lights were off, and she could hardly make out their faces in the blue glow of the TV screen. Celia started to introduce herself to them, but suddenly she felt Rob pushing her from behind. "They're a bore," he said. "Let's go to bed."

Celia said that's when she began to panic. They got into his bed and started kissing, gently at first, and then harder. He took off his pants. He put his hands under her dress and squeezed her breasts.

"No bra," he said mischievously. "You're naughty, aren't you?"

Celia felt her head spinning. "I'd like to go to sleep now. I'm exhausted," she said, still flirting, not wanting to upset him. Even as her fear rose, she thought about that damn girdle, and willed him not to see it.

"Oh come on," he said. He reached for a drawer in his bedside table and pulled out a blue condom in a clear wrapper, the kind they give away at safe sex lectures and AIDS Action rallies. He climbed on top of her.

"No," Celia said sweetly. "Not tonight. Next time, okay?"

"Come on," he said in a whisper. He was still on top of her, but she could feel his hand putting the condom on.

"No, Rob," she said. "I'm so sleepy."

He held her arms against the mattress. Celia tried to pull out from under him, but he pinned her knee down hard with his leg. A moment later, he yanked her girdle and panties over with one hand, stinging the inside of her leg. He entered her, the pain of it like nothing she had ever felt, not even her first time. She told the girls that at that point she thought to herself, This isn't happening, and for the rest of it she just lay there with her eyes closed, not fighting him, not making a sound. When it was over, he kissed her cheek lightly, rolled into the space beside her, put his arm around her, and fell asleep.

She lay awake until morning. His alarm clock sounded at nine, and he reached up to turn it off without even opening his eyes.

"Rob, I want to go now," she said.

He squinted at her. "Okay," he said. "Get home safe."

"I thought you were going to drive me," she said.

"I forgot I have soccer practice today. There's a bus schedule in the drawer under the microwave."

She got up silently and put her shoes on, straightened her dress.

"Good-bye," she said, starting to cry.

"Hey," he said. "I had a great time last night."

After she finished telling them the story, Celia looked up from her glass of wine. Bree, Sally, and April were all crying.

"Oh, you guys," she said, wiping away her own tears. "I was so fucking stupid. There were three other people there, and I didn't even scream. I didn't fight him. I just sort of left my body and floated up to the ceiling. And I stayed all night in his goddamn bed! Why didn't I run? And then he sent me that e-mail the next day and I felt happy! Can you believe it? Happy. I thought to myself, Maybe it was just a misunderstanding. We were both drunk. Maybe we'll laugh at this later, after we've been dating for years. I am so fucked up."

"You are not fucked up," Bree said plainly. "Celia, you were raped. I think we need to get in Sally's car right now and go chop this guy's balls off."

Celia smiled faintly. "But don't you see? I was partly to blame. I went home with him, I didn't scream for help."

April took Celia's hands, which were clammy and cold. "You did not do anything wrong," she said. She couldn't help but think of the statistic they'd heard in her Women and Sexuality class—one out of every four American women has been raped. Here it was, painted clearly in her own group of dear friends.

"Do you want to press charges?" April asked gently. "You know we'd stand behind you."

"No, no," Celia said. "I couldn't put my parents through that. I never want my father to know that this happened to me."

They were all silent for a moment. Finally, Sally piped up. "The sickest part of it is that this dirtbag looks like a catch on paper—good education, self-made fortune. In two years he will probably be married to a supermodel, and she'll never know her husband is a rapist."

Celia nodded. "I doubt he even thinks of himself that way. I just wish that I had never gone to Dartmouth, or that you guys had been with me. You wouldn't have let me just take off like that. Not that I should need someone else to watch me, but you know."

It was true. They all took care of one another around men and alcohol, which said something when you thought about it. It was sad that they needed to do it in the first place. April thought about what Sally had said. How many other men like Rob Johann were out there? Most rapists probably seemed like upstanding guys, they had jobs and families and friends. They couldn't all be psychos in ski masks lingering in dark alleys.

Ultimately, April and Toby changed the name of the event to just Celebration. There was a minor protest on campus, people chanting things like "Keep the women in a women's college." But everyone came out for it anyway, just like always.

April wore a long-sleeved red wrap dress that had belonged to her mother in the sixties. Toby was dressed in a full tuxedo, his boy-short hair frizzing around her face. It was spitting rain when they took the stage that had been erected at the front of the Quad.

"Welcome to Celebration!" April said into the microphone. Two thousand Smithies stood before her, cheering.

She felt a lump in her throat. This would be her last Celebration as a Smith student. For the first time, she had no idea what she'd be doing at this time next year.

That night was still one of April's happiest memories. Watching the house skits that she and Toby had chosen, seeing the faces of her fellow students laughing in the crowd. Celebration was meant to observe all different types of sexual freedom, but most of the skits (all performed by straight Quad girls) took a similar form: A few girls would dress up in khakis and popped collars, pretending to be Amherst frat boys. A few others would play the Smithies who meet them, date them, and then decide to dump them and date one another instead. The crowd would whoop with glee when the dejected frat boys walked offstage and the newly minted lesbians embraced.

After the skits, everyone walked through campus, holding candles, sipping cider, and admiring the twinkling lights that lit the pathways. Each house made a contribution to the event—some had set up trays of baked goods outside; some had gotten one of the campus a cappella groups to gather on the front porch and sing; others had made art or keepsakes or staged elaborate performances.

April walked arm in arm with Toby, savoring every second. The King House girls had gone ahead, hearing that Chapin was offering a Smith-themed mix CD but probably hadn't made enough for everyone.

"I'm proud of us," Toby said.

"Me too," April said. "I'm going to miss all this so much."
Toby squeezed her arm. "You have no idea. I'm really
scared to think about what comes next."

Outside of Duckett House, they had set up a head-shaving
booth, meant to look like an old-fashioned barbershop,
with a red-and-white pole and everything.

Toby looked at April. "What do you say? Something to
remember this night by?"

April's heart sped up. Maybe she'd regret it tomorrow, but
right at that moment it seemed like the perfect thing. She
thought of Toby as a child, cutting off his golden locks in
secret. Now, in a way, maybe he could reclaim that memory
and turn it into something good.

They sat in dining hall chairs out on the sidewalk, holding
hands as two first years took out electric razors and set to
work. A crowd gathered around and everyone cheered. April
closed her eyes, feeling the buzz of the razor against her
scalp, as her long red hair fell to the ground in chunks.
When she got back to King House, the girls would surely
make a fuss, screaming at her that she had lost her mind, but
totally enjoying the shock of it all. April felt at peace.

Something to remember this night by, Toby had said. As if
she could ever forget.

SALLY

Sally listened from inside the closet, covering her face in Jake's suit so his mother wouldn't hear her breathing. She had gotten slightly tipsy during afternoon drinks with the girls, and they had all decided to part ways for a nap. But Sally couldn't sleep. She had been in the closet, drunkenly steaming Jake's clothes for the wedding, when she heard a key in the hotel room door. She knew it couldn't be Jake—he was out golfing in Amherst with his father all day. For a moment, Sally wondered if it might be Bill, but that was ridiculous. He had no idea she was even in town. She had been thinking too much about Bill in the month or so leading up to the wedding. Those long hours spent making love in his office in Neilson Library, his silver hair and itchy sweaters. His favorite poem repeated over and over in her head, Auden's "Brussels in Winter." *Ridges of rich apartments loom tonight / Where isolated windows glow like farms, / A phrase goes packed with meaning like a van, / A look contains the history of man.*

When Rosemary came into the room and yelled out, "Anyone home?" Sally slid the closet door shut, closing herself inside without thinking. A moment later, it felt ridiculous and childish, but she couldn't very well emerge from the closet now.

Who did Rosemary think she was, anyway, just walking right in without even knocking? That was Jake's family—they had no concept of doors or walls or personal space. Sally hoped she'd find whatever it was she wanted and get out. She wasn't in the mood for Rosemary right now. But instead, Rosemary sat down on the bed, started poking through Jake's suitcase, and called her sister Anna on the telephone.

"The maid's in our room, and I don't want to be in there while she's cleaning," Rosemary said into the phone. "I don't know. I just don't feel comfortable going for a walk downtown without Joe. Wait until you get here, Anna. There are lesbians everywhere you look—I am telling you, everywhere!"

There was a pause, and then Rosemary said, "No, I am *not* afraid they're going to try and convert me."

Sally had to bite down on the sleeve of Jake's suit to keep from laughing.

"I told Jake he should put his foot down about this idiotic outdoor wedding idea six months ago. And now look—it's going to rain on Sunday!" Rosemary was screaming into the telephone as if the receiver itself had defied her. She took a deep breath, composing herself.

"You know I love Sally, but she's not very bridely, is all. First, she didn't want a proper wedding gown. Then she ruled out the church ceremony. And then she announced that she was having the wedding here. What kind of girl wants to get married at her college, anyway? What's wrong with her hometown—or ours, for that matter? Two perfectly nice Boston suburbs to choose from, and she makes us all schlep out here to the boonies. Lord knows she could afford a big wedding with all that money of hers. And so could Jake. You marry a boy who's made a little fortune in banking, and then you don't let him show it off? I mean, it's not five million, but it's something."

Sally's hands formed two tight fists. The last thing Jake cared about was showing off by having a big wedding. They were spending their money on more practical things—the new house in Cambridge, their car payments, their kids' college funds. Rosemary knew all that. *It's not five million,* she had said. Five million, Sally's cut of the blood money. The number that had followed her around like a ghost ever since her father settled with the oncologist at Mass General. Five million dollars that made people think she was the luckiest twenty-five-year-old on earth, when of course she would give it all back and then some if she had the choice of seeing her mother for one more day, one more hour.

After all the legal fees had been paid, there was ten million left. Her father said that she and her brother should split it down the middle. She had told him that she didn't want it, but he refused to take no for an answer, talking at her about investment options for far longer than he'd ever bothered to talk to her about her mother's death. ("Men are emotional fuckwits," April had said. "He doesn't know how to help you, but he wants you to know that he wishes he could.") The money felt like a bribe. Sally tried her hardest always to act as though she didn't even have it—until a month ago, she had lived in a shabby apartment in Central Square with three roommates. And here was Rosemary, rubbing it in her face.

She had tried many times to consider things from Rosemary's point of view, really tried. A woman has a son and loves him and raises him up and thinks he's a prince, and then one day another woman comes along to steal him away. That must feel awful. But shouldn't Rosemary want Jake to find happiness? Shouldn't she have pushed him out of the nest a bit more to begin with? He was thirty years old, and when he and Sally met four years earlier, his mother was still filling his fridge with seven homemade meals every Sunday night when she came over to drop off his laundry, folded neatly with double fabric softener on the sheets. If that part wasn't Freudian, Sally thought, she didn't know what was.

The first time she and Jake had a fight, it was because Rosemary had gone into his room while he was at work and actually made his bed for him, then mentioned that it was a bit unseemly for one of Sally's bras to be hanging on the headboard where everyone could see it. When Jake related this story to Sally the next time they were alone in his room, he didn't roll his eyes or look embarrassed by his mother's intrusion. Instead, he meant it as an actual word of warning: *Don't hang your unseemly bra on my pristine, handpicked-by-Mommy headboard.*

"What is your mother even doing in here?" Sally had snapped. "Does she have a key to your apartment?"

"What's wrong with that?" Jake's face always crumpled when he felt hurt, like a child in the sandbox in that instant right after the shovel has been snatched from his hand, and right before he begins to wail. His expression made Sally want to drop the whole issue, but she couldn't.

"I'm surprised she doesn't just jump right into the goddamn bed after she makes it," she shouted. "I'm surprised *her* bra's not hanging on the headboard."

She knew that she had taken it too far. Any other guy might have stormed right out of there, but Jake just laughed and pulled her onto the bed with his big bear arms, and rolled her body into the sheets. "Admit it," he said. "You like these sheets as much as I do. You're just using me for my double fabric softener."

Sometimes Sally wondered if she found Rosemary so unbearable because she herself would never again experience that smothering, safe brand of love that only comes from the woman who has known you since the beginning of you, since even before the beginning.

She missed everything about her mother. The brown waves she pushed back with a plain tortoiseshell headband; the rows of pressed cardigans and cable knits that hung in her closet; her perfume, something discontinued called Creation that she had to buy in a little specialty shop in Harvard Square. She ran eight miles every morning before breakfast and had what Sally considered the perfect figure for a mother—trim and strong with a tiny soft belly where her babies had grown. When Sally and her brother were kids, she used to drive them out to the beach in Cohasset for a picnic on sunny Saturdays. Their father was usually at work, or flying to some conference or other. "Wave hello to Daddy!" their mother would shout when a plane flew overhead, and they would wave, all three of them pumping their arms as if he really could see them. To Sally, even now, her mother's body seemed like a place where cancer would not dare to dwell.

The fall of Sally's junior year of high school, her mother had been losing weight.

"You look good," Sally said before dinner one night, as they were chopping vegetables for a salad and watching the evening news.

"Really?" her mother said.

"Yeah, you look thin," Sally said.

Her mother said she hadn't noticed, but she seemed pleased, and Sally assumed that she was back on one of her crazy lemon juice or cabbage soup diets.

In November, she found a lump, a hard, round, pea-size nuisance, between her armpit and her breast. The doctor said it was nothing, a benign cyst. He told her that the blood work showed she was anemic, and so she and Sally started taking iron pills, which they agreed tasted like sucking on a penny.

For a while, her mother felt better. But the lump remained, and finally, months later, she had another round of tests with another doctor. It was breast cancer, this second doctor said, and it had spread to the lymph nodes and bone. He was sorry, so very sorry, that the first doctor had missed it, because her chances of survival now were small. Had they caught it sooner, well—why wonder?

During her year of chemo, she insisted on wearing lipstick and taking a long walk every morning. She wore a designer wig that cost a fortune and looked almost like her real hair. Afterward, though the treatments weren't successful, the doctors said they were impressed by her stamina. Perhaps she had longer than they had first predicted—possibly nine months, instead of three. But then things seemed to backslide. She was in and out of the hospital. Still, she stayed cheerful and brave. On good mornings, she made casseroles, which she froze "for later," she said.

"You mean when you're dead," Sally's brother had said once, starting to cry, and even though Sally knew he was hurting and that he was probably right, she hated him for saying it. (No one ever ate those casseroles. As far as Sally knew, they were still in her father's freezer, an icy monument that none of them could bear to throw away.) Her mother took out old shoe boxes full of photographs and pasted the best ones into albums. She wrote long letters to family and friends. Her spark did not die until the moment the rest of her gave out, two days before Sally's high school graduation.

Had her mother lived, Sally thought, she would probably have been one of those Smith girls who wears pearls and keeps her own horse at the campus stables and goes home every other Sunday for family dinner. She recognized much of what she had done since her mother's death as an attempt to shock her back to life—the affair with Bill, not applying to medical school, even this bare-bones wedding in the Smith College Quad, were all actions that her mother would have protested and eventually nixed. And then there were the things Sally knew her mother would have loved. Those, too, made it easy to imagine how she might come back to life, since nothing good seemed quite real without her there to approve of it.

She would have loved Jake.

"He's not good enough for you" had been her rally cry all

through Sally's high school years whenever she brought home another cocky football player or debate team captain. Jake was good enough for her. He was the kindest man Sally had ever known. He wanted kids, lots of them, and he wanted to be there for every day. Not like Sally's father, who always boasted that he was in China signing his first million-dollar deal the moment Sally took her first steps, on the front lawn back home. Jake laughed at her when anyone else might get frustrated and walk away, which was good, because Sally knew that she could be exasperating some-times.

Jake always remembered when it was her mother's birth-day and how old she would have been. He understood Sally's rituals, which anyone else but April would probably find creepy—some of her mother's ashes were in a coffee can under her bed, and Sally still had one voice-mail message from her left on her cell phone, which she saved each month and listened to all the time.

"Hey," her mother said. "Hope you guys are having fun. Can you bring home a quart of milk? Oh, and wear your seat belt. Love you." In the background, you could hear the open-ing strains of the nightly news theme song. This message was Sally's most treasured possession, and she planned to carry her outdated cell phone as long as she possibly could, so that she would never lose it.

No matter how many times Sally woke up sobbing over missing her, Jake just smoothed her hair and drew her close. He would never ask, *When are you going to move on?* In the years to come, he would help Sally keep her mother's mem-ory alive, even when it seemed like her father and brother were intent on erasing it. They refused to speak about her mother now, as if she had simply never existed. Ever since her death, Sally felt like she had no family at all.

Rosemary's heated voice interrupted Sally's thoughts.

"Yes, Anna, I understand that, but what I'm saying is you just don't serve prime rib at a ninetieth birthday party—half the people couldn't even chew. It was an embarrassment. And Dottie paid eighty-five dollars a plate. Oh? She told you seventy? She told me eighty-five."

At least they had moved on from the wedding, Sally thought. She looked at her watch in the dim light of the closet. Rosemary had been out there for twelve minutes.

"Okay, I'm gonna scoot," she said after a while. "We'll see you tomorrow for the rehearsal dinner, if not before. What? Oh wear whatever you want—Lord knows the bride will probably be sporting a tie-dye T-shirt."

Sally watched through the slits in the door as Rosemary went to the dresser and looked long and hard at herself in the mirror. She spotted Jake's roll of Life Savers, untwirled the silver wrapping, and popped one into her mouth. Then she slipped out into the hall, the door closing with a thud behind her.

Sally opened the closet and fell onto the bed. A tie-dye T-shirt? She was tempted to run right out and buy one to wear tomorrow. She sighed. She was less and less like her old self every day—years ago, she would have been horrified by the mere idea of insulting her mother-in-law. Now it gave her a little thrill.

Oh well. She was marrying Jake, not his family. That's what Celia reminded her whenever Sally called her to complain after a long dinner with Rosemary and Joe. She knew it wasn't strictly true, but still, the thought was comforting.

Sally switched on the TV and started flipping through the channels. By this time on Sunday, she would be married. Just forty-eight hours and everything would be different. A shiver went through her—equal parts panic and excitement.

Suddenly the door opened again, and Rosemary stepped back into the room. Sally held her breath. She watched Rosemary's expression change when she saw her there, lying on the bed. It had only been thirty seconds or so since Rosemary left, and she looked horrified.

"Hi, Sal," she said, glancing around the room as if trying to find a clue about where Sally had come from. "I left my reading glasses on your nightstand earlier. I just wanted to come get them."

"Oh," Sally said calmly, reaching for the red-framed glasses and handing them to her. "Here you go."

"Thanks." Rosemary walked toward the door, and then paused for a long moment, perhaps debating whether or not to say something. She smiled over her shoulder instead. "See you later, honey."

Sally waved. She could barely manage to hold in her laughter until Rosemary was back in the hall. She thought of calling one of the girls in their rooms to tell the story, but decided to wait until dinner. It would be better to see the looks on their faces. She got to do that so rarely now. It had been two years since they were all together in one place. She remembered telling Celia once how Jake and his friends from Georgetown had shared an apartment after graduation.

"Why didn't we ever think to do that?" Sally asked.

It had broken their hearts to be apart, she thought, and she still hadn't found a single friend besides Jake who could compare with any one of them. So why had they been so intent on going their own ways?

"We could have all moved into a big house and taken turns cooking dinner," Sally said. "Why couldn't we be those kind of people?"

"Because people like that never grow," Celia said quickly, which made Sally think she had probably asked herself the same question in the past.

"Sometimes I think growth is overrated," Sally said then.

"Me too," Celia said.

Sally knew that splitting up had been hardest for her. The first year out of school, the four of them had talked on the phone to one another almost every night. They had a mini-reunion in Vegas the summer after graduation, and another the following year at her father's new six-bedroom estate on the Cape. (He called it a cottage, which just made the place all the more ridiculous.) She saw Celia every time she came home to Massachusetts to visit her family, and she went out to Chicago once to spend time with April. But lately, they had begun to fall away from one another. Sally had listened to Celia's outgoing voice-mail message so many times that she sometimes heard the whole thing, note for note, in her head as she was dialing. She knew that Celia spent too many hours at work, and that that was just the nature of the book publishing business. She knew that Celia's social life was different from her own. While she and Jake spent most nights going to the gym, cooking dinner, and watching ESPN, Celia lived the life of a Manhattan chick-lit heroine— cocktail parties, long dinners in trendy restaurants she couldn't really afford, and date after date after date with the wrong guys.

But still, Sally often remarked to Jake, doesn't *everyone* have a few minutes a night to just pick up the phone? Sally suspected that the girls had distanced themselves from her because she was in love and about to get married. April disapproved of marriage in general. The others, Sally assumed, were jealous. Bree had Lara, of course, but ever since graduation she seemed to cause Bree more misery than anything else. And Celia was alone. Neither of them wanted to hear about how good things were with Jake.

Once, as she recounted to Bree the story of a trip they'd taken to Maine for their six-month anniversary, Bree had snapped: "I get it, Sal. You're perfect."

After Jake proposed, she had dialed the first few digits of Bree's number twelve times before finally making the call.

The real sting in it came from the fact that the same women who had counseled her through her grief for four years at college wanted nothing to do with her joy. Perhaps it took more to feel truly happy for a friend than it did to feel sympathy for her. She remembered how many times in college Bree had pointed out that, until her mother died, they had been the same, as though in the lottery of life, Bree had won out, and needed to mention it.

All of the girls had gotten a bit of a thrill out of her relationship with Bill. They had hours and hours to talk about *that*, to advise her against it and tell her what a terrible cliché it was, but then also to devour the stories like candy. She knew that if she told them how much she'd been thinking about him lately, they would suddenly have plenty to say.

Then again, they probably already knew.

.   .   .

Three weeks into the second semester of her sophomore year, Sally had a C average in Modern British Poetry. She had never gotten a grade lower than an A-minus in any class she'd ever taken in her life.

She had already aced Molecular Physics and Chemistry 206 and Advanced Biology with Lauder, a course/professor combo that other premed Smithies considered a death wish. So when Celia suggested that they take a class together for fun, Sally enrolled in the only poetry course Celia still needed to complete her major. Five minutes into the first class session, she knew it was a mistake. Celia had failed to mention that she and every other English department nerd had memorized all of Yeats in second grade. Of course, Sally should have known better: After all, Celia often spent hours copying poems into her journal, and she actually read poetry for fun on many a rainy Sunday.

The class was a lark for Celia and the others, one of those "put your feet up and discuss what you already know" deals. For Sally, who had always loved novels but found poetry sort of goofy, looking at words clumped together in that way was as incomprehensible as calculus would have been to Celia. For a few days, she considered dropping the class. But all the science courses she wanted were already full, and the only other English class she could take was a seminar on Milton. She would have to stick with it, but she could at least take the course pass-fail if Professor Lambert would sign the form.

It was a Tuesday morning when she first knocked on his office door—*Neilson B106,* she had written on her hand so she wouldn't forget. Later, she'd wonder how she had ever not known where he sat and studied and, sometimes, lived.

He called out, "Come in!" and when Sally entered the

room, he sat there looking like a professor in a school play, a perfect portrait of the intellectual would-be poet. He held a thick leather book and wore a heavy cardigan over a button-down shirt. His shaggy, silver hair looked wet and disheveled, and he probably hadn't shaved in a week—not to make a statement, Sally thought, but just because it hadn't crossed his mind. She glanced at his ring finger and noticed that he was married. How on earth could his wife let him out of the house looking so messy? Unless she was an academic, too, one of those women who stuck a pencil into her hair to keep it out of her eyes while she was reading and then, hours later as she lay down to sleep, found the pencil again with great bewilderment. Celia told Sally that Professor Lambert had been published three times by small university presses back in the seventies, and that he was something of a legend in the literary community. Sally had her doubts. Those who can do, and all that, she had said to Celia the night before. Celia had pointed out that some of the world's greatest poets probably lived on less money than the average fourteen-year-old with a paper route. From the look of Bill Lambert, this seemed about right.

Celia had also told Sally to watch out when she went to see him. "I hear he makes passes at anything with a pulse," she said. "Did you ever meet Rose Driscoll? She graduated last year, and word is they slept together, then she tried to end it, and he basically stalked her until she got a restraining order."

Sally sighed. The gossip about Smith girls and their professors always seemed improbable to her, like something out of a bad Harlequin novel. There were stories about lots of the male professors, and they always conveniently included some girl who was no longer around to tell the tale.

His office was dim and windowless, lit only by a small green desk lamp. The desk and tables and couch were cluttered with papers and books halfway to the ceiling, and a million yellow Post-it notes stuck out here and there.

When he looked at Sally, he did not seem to recognize her right away. "How can I help you?" he said.

"Professor Lambert, my name is Sally Werner. I'm in your British poetry course. And I'm here because—"

He raised a hand to interrupt her. "Sally, I know who you are. Please. Sit. And call me Bill. Professor Lambert was my father."

Sally didn't really go in for these professors who went by their first names. They were always men, intent on staying young forever, despite the fact that they had achieved a tremendously adult career goal.

She sat down across from him, taking care to remove some papers from the chair and place them in a small pile on the floor. She smiled without showing her teeth.

"I'm here because I desperately need to change my status in British poetry to pass-fail," she said.

"And why is that?" he asked.

"I'm a science person. I'm in way over my head."

He nodded. "Poetry is something of a science, you know," he said. "The elements have to be perfect, exact, in order for the experiment to succeed."

Sally fought the urge to roll her eyes. He was officially getting on her nerves. Next he'd be telling her that each stanza was like a beaker, full of powerful chemicals called words.

"In any case," she said. "I guess poetry is just a language I don't speak. I read the poems you assign each night, four or five times at least. But it's just a jumble of words to me. The next day, I'm sitting there listening to what the other girls say in class, and wondering if we even read the same stuff. They understand so much of it, and I just . . ." She trailed off, unable to get the words out. In all her life, Sally Werner had never had to admit that she didn't get something.

He nodded, looking past her at the door. "Do you enjoy the poems?" he asked.

"Oh yes," she said quickly, then, "Well, to tell you the truth, no. It all seems a bit ridiculous to me."

"How so?" he asked.

"It's all so over the top. If you're going to say something, why not just say it?" she said, before adding, "No offense."

"None taken," he said.

He furrowed his brow and cleared his throat. *"Side by side, their faces blurred, / The earl and countess lie in stone,"* he began, in a lofty voice that let her know he was reciting something. *"Their proper habits vaguely shown / As jointed armour, stiffened pleat / And that faint hint of the absurd—The little dogs under their feet."*

Sally stared blankly. "Is that one of yours?" she asked.

He sputtered, laughing. "I wish," he said. "That's Philip Larkin. 'An Arundel Tomb.' This couple has been buried, and their tomb is built to look like them, yet it bears no real resemblance to what they were like in life."

He continued his recitation. Sally glanced up at the clock over his head. She needed to be in bio, on the other side of the library and across the Science Quad, in eight minutes. If he would just sign the damn form, she could still get a seat in the front row. She'd have to interrupt him.

"Professor Lam—uhh, Bill," she started, but he raised his hand and kept on.

"*Time has transfigured them into / Untruth,*" he said.

Sally thought of her mother. It was the perfect way to describe what had happened to her.

Bill went on. "*The stone fidelity / They hardly meant has come to be / Their final blazon, and to prove / Our almost-instinct almost true: / What will survive of us is love.*"

Sally pictured her mother's plain headstone. It conveyed nothing of the woman she had been, of the life that was gone forever. She remembered driving out to the cemetery after work on summer evenings before the school year began, sitting in the grass in a skirt and heels, searching, searching for a hint of her.

"It reminds you of someone," he said.

Sally nodded.

"Me too," he said. "That's what poems can do. I'm not saying you'll get every single one of them. Hell, I have an MFA in poetry from Columbia, and I'm lucky if I understand one-tenth of what a poem means. Poems are like people, like lovers. If you try to understand them all at once, your head's gonna spin. But if you let them take you in, piece by piece, they can move you. Transform you. Thanks for tidying up, by the way," he said with a grin, and Sally noticed in horror that she'd been absentmindedly forming piles out of the papers heaped on top of his desk. This was a habit of hers around messy people, inherited from her mother, who had once insulted a neighbor by mopping her kitchen floor unasked at a dinner party.

"Oh God, sorry!" she said. "I'm a neat freak."

"You never need to apologize for cleaning off my desk," he said. "In fact, if you like, we could make a deal."

Sally looked at him, and in place of his face she saw her

unblemished academic transcript floating in space. What-ever he wanted, he could have.

"The department lets me hire a work-study assistant each year," he said. "Someone to help me with research and filing and all that jazz. As you can see, I've never actually taken them up on the offer. I don't need much in the way of research, but I could sure use some help with the organiza-tion stuff."

"Okay," she said, not sure where he was going with this.

"I don't really give a damn about papers or grades. I just want every student to connect to a poem—if that happens, my job is done. So. If you could help me out a couple times a week, I might promise to give you a good grade, provided we talk poetry when you're here."

"You might?" she said.

He smiled. "I will."

Sally inhaled deeply. "It's a deal," she said. "Thank you."

They shook hands across the desk. He held hers much longer than she thought seemed normal, and she couldn't help but think of the story Celia told about the girl he had stalked.

"Who did the poem remind you of?" he asked before let-ting go.

"My mother," she said. "You?"

"My wife."

A widower. It made all the sense in the world. It explained why he was so disheveled, so scattered. He was suffering from a broken heart of the highest order, just like Sally. Bill Lambert needed looking after, and who better to under-stand him than her? She decided then and there that Celia had been wrong about him.

She came to him for an hour on Monday mornings, after he finished swimming laps in the faculty pool and before her biology class. She came on Wednesday afternoons at three, and sometimes stayed long into the evening, past closing time in the dining hall. On those nights, Bill opened the little mini-fridge beside his desk and brought out food from campus events he'd been to during the week—cold chicken and cucumber sandwiches from a lunch at the president's house, chocolate soufflé from an English department tea, and, occasionally, tiny bottles of red wine that he pocketed at an alumnae fund-raiser. He sometimes spoke of his house on Paradise Road, a long stretch of Victorians all owned by professors. But from what Sally could see, he seemed to live in his office. She imagined him terrified to go back to the bed he had once shared with his wife. He rarely mentioned her to Sally, but he often referenced her in class: *My wife, Janice, used to stay up nights rereading* Bleak House *and eating poppy-seed crackers. When my wife, Jan, and I bought the house on Paradise, we used the pages of old Norton anthologies to plug the leaks in the roof.*

Sally wanted to squeeze his hand at those moments. A few times, she caught Celia giving her a look and realized she must be making her pitying face.

She was supposed to be getting Bill organized, but mostly they just sat in the dim office and talked. He said he'd never talked to anyone that way, especially a student. He recited poems to her, looking straight into her face for her reaction as he spoke. Sally knew she ought to feel moved by the words, but her mind always wandered to other things. She would get distracted by the rhythm of his voice or the smell of his skin, a mix of chlorine and Ivory soap that caught in the air whenever he gestured with his hands.

Bill kept his favorite lines of poetry scribbled on Post-its all around the office, so that inspiration might catch him by surprise. Sometimes when he wasn't looking, Sally would snatch a Post-it from a book or file folder on his desk and slip it into her pocket. She left them in a little stack on the nightstand in her dorm room, piled neatly and hidden under the alarm clock. Before she went to sleep at night she'd take them out and line them up on the bedspread, reading them over, again and again, committing the words to memory:

> *I sometimes hold it half a sin to put in words the grief I feel; For words, like Nature, half reveal and half conceal the Soul within.*

> *Too common! Never morning wore to evening, but some heart did break.*

> *I have hoisted sail to all the winds which should transport me farthest from your sight.*

The Post-its were the only way Sally enjoyed poetry—distilled down to the most beautiful lines, absent of any context besides the one she created. She wondered what they meant to Bill, and sometimes imagined that they were something like a love letter, a confession of the feelings that he could not speak out loud.

He never read her any of his own poems, but one day

when he left her alone in his office for a moment, Sally slid one of his books down off the shelf. *Five Seasons,* by William Lambert. Inside there was an old black-and-white shot of Bill, looking handsome and young. The back cover was sprinkled with quotes: "*Five Seasons* is poetry the way poetry should be written. It took my breath away," wrote someone she had never heard of from *The New York Times.* "An exquisite rendering of the ongoing battles between men and women, lust and reason," said Ted Hughes. Ted Hughes! Even Sally knew who he was.

The most famous Smith suicide was Sylvia Plath. Morbid Goth girls who lived on Elm Street always claimed that they had the dorm room that had once belonged to her. April said *The Bell Jar* was her all-time favorite novel, and that Plath had probably always been a little bit off—a poet, a visionary, too smart for her own good. But of course, there was also a man. Ted Hughes. As fucking usual, April would say. According to April, Plath's was a typical female death. She didn't rage in the streets, or kill her unfaithful husband and cut out his heart for a trophy. She simply shut her children up safe in their bedrooms, got down on her knees in front of her oven, and slowly, silently gassed herself to death. She was thirty-one years old.

Sally thought about how, back then, Bill really had been something of a celebrity, a *real* poet, whatever that meant. She wondered why he had stopped writing when he came to Smith. Did it have to do with his wife getting ill? A moment later, she could hear his heavy footsteps coming back toward her, and she slipped the book back onto the shelf.

On the way to the Quad from his office that night, Sally

realized that she might be falling in love with him. It wasn't the poems that made her heart swell—it was the way his fingers wrinkled after a swim, the ink stains on his forearm, even the little bald patch on the back of his head, which he seemed not to notice, or in any case not to care about. Bill was an adult, a real man. He made her feel safe somehow. Sally knew April would probably call it a daddy complex, but that wasn't it. She knew he felt it, too. There was that energy between them.

But weeks passed, then a month, then two, and he never so much as touched her hand. They talked for hours about movies and novels, poetry and science and family, about Northampton and its strange blend of beautiful nature, true art, and goofy, hippie liberalism. She left his office with a lightness in her stomach and head every time.

On Friday nights she'd go along to Quad parties with Celia. The previous year, all the King House first years had gone in a big group to every gathering on frat row at UMass, every Amherst College tap, and every Smith Quad party, in the hopes of meeting men. They'd preparty in the dorm, drinking gin and tonics and singing their hearts out to some CD by Tom Petty or the Beatles. They'd dance, and laugh, and take their pick of outfits from all sixteen of the first-year closets—the next day no one could remember whose black pants they'd borrowed, whose droopy earrings they'd accidentally left on the bus. At the parties, they spent hours talking to Amherst boys and townies who were probably still in high school, drinking warm keg beer from plastic cups. They rarely met anyone worth calling, let alone sleeping with. At two or three, they would head home, scrub off their makeup, and huddle together in the living room, drinking tea, watching Brat Pack movies or *Breakfast at Tiffany's,* thrilled to be back in the land of Girls Only.

By sophomore year, the enthusiasm had faded. Bree had started dating Lara, and they hardly ever went out to parties. April had stopped attending on principle, complaining that the strong, independent Smithies she knew during the week seemed to be replaced by tube-top-wearing fembots whenever men and beer entered into the equation. Plus, the kind of guys she always went for—skinny, brooding types in Clark Kent glasses and holey sweaters—never attended these sorts of gatherings. For most of the girls in the house, the jig was simply up. They'd met enough unremarkable men at frat parties to know that off-campus husband searching was just a plain old waste of time. Like most sophomores, Sally and Celia never left campus on the weekends anymore. Celia now refused to attend a Smith house party unless they had an invitation to a private party upstairs. Down below, the dining hall furniture had been stacked against the walls, and guys were trying to score, making awkward conversation, dancing with the first years, pumping the keg. Upstairs, upperclasswomen were taking tequila shots, shooting Polaroids of one another topless to determine who had the best breasts, climbing naked onto the roof to smoke a joint and sing to the moon, starting all-female make-out sessions that they would never speak of again after graduation day.

Sally took it in, and played the role of caretaker—holding back other girls' hair while they puked, fetching them glasses of water, and tucking them into bed with their heads elevated so they wouldn't choke on their own vomit during the night. All the while, she thought of Bill alone in his office. She would have so preferred to be with him, listening to him weigh the virtues of Keats versus Byron, or discussing their childhood summers, both spent on Cape Cod. Occasionally, after those private parties, Celia brought boys home, lanky Amherst students who came to brunch in the dining hall the next morning with their collared shirts untucked and sheepish grins on their faces. Once or twice she even brought home a girl, some straight Quad bunny or other. Later she would report that they had made out for hours, breaking every so often to discuss how neither one of them had gotten over her high school crush yet. (It wasn't meant to be romantic, Sally thought. It was more like an experience, the sort of thing girls like Celia did just to say that they had done it.)

Sally never so much as kissed someone on those nights. She preferred her thoughts and her Post-its, as pathetic as she knew that was. When she saw Bill again on Monday, he'd ask her about her weekend. Sally wouldn't mention the parties. They seemed to exist in another universe from him, his poetry, his office, which she thought of, in a way, as theirs.

Finally there came a Monday morning when he asked her how she'd spent her weekend, and she could no longer hold it in. Some guy had grabbed her ass at a party and acted like she ought to be grateful, as if he'd given her a diamond ring. She went home and cried herself to sleep.

"I went to some stupid party, the same sort of stupid party we've been going to for two years," she told Bill.

He raised his eyebrows. "What's stupid about it?"

She sighed. "Oh, I don't know. Everything. My best friend April always complains that we Smith girls tend to transform ourselves into these trampy tarts whenever men are around."

"*Tarts,*" he said with a smile. "Good word. Go on."

"We wear these skimpy little skirts and halter tops," she said, feeling her heart in her chest.

"*We?*" he said, eyeing her cable-knit sweater.

Sally ignored the implication. She'd never worn a skimpy skirt or a halter top in her life, but she needed to get this point across, and now she had his attention.

"And for what? The guys at these things are just so unevolved. They're embryos, really."

"So you need someone more mature," he said in a detached, almost uninterested voice. Then he met her eyes, and Sally felt something pass between them. Was he going to say the words that would change everything?

But he looked down again and only said, "It is the plight of many an intelligent young woman."

She told herself that this was for the best; that what she had been imagining was altogether ridiculous anyway. But then, at last—

"You could try wearing that tiny skirt here some time if you're looking for something a little more grown-up," he said, and she felt a rush of energy shoot from her belly to her groin.

She took a deep breath. He had made the attempt, laughing so that she might pass it off as a joke if she wanted to. Sally hadn't lusted after anyone since high school. She hoped middle-aged men could be seduced with the same tricks as teenage boys. She soon found that indeed they could.

"What will this grown-up something entail?" she said with a coy smile, cocking her head.

She felt like she was in a movie, the sort of movie no director would ever cast her in because she was too wholesome looking.

Bill rose from his chair, walked around the desk, and then perched on her side of it, so that his warm body was all before her. He reached down and cupped her chin in his hands, lifted it gently, and then kissed her so hard that later that day she could swear her lips were swollen, puffed up, though no one seemed to notice.

He was the first man to undress her. Before, it had always been the quick and awkward routine of yanking one's own clothes off while the guy did the same. But Bill ran his hands over her, peeling off first her pink sweater and then her tank top, as though they were layers of delicate tissue paper, rather than cotton blends from Banana Republic. He unbuttoned her jeans so slowly that she moaned, wanting his hands on her, inside of her. He pulled her pants down and dropped to the floor with them, kissing her ankles, and then the insides of her knees, and up and up until she gasped for breath and dug her hands into the arms of his old wing chair. They made love against the door to his office, and Sally thought with panic about that little square of glass in the door, wondering if some unsuspecting English major had spotted the tops of their heads and figured it all out. A moment later, lost in the feeling of his skin against hers, she had forgotten her fear. She wanted to scream out that she loved him, but she knew it was way too soon. Instead she said it silently, in her head, over and over.

That week, she went to his office every afternoon. By Wednesday, he had covered the window in the door with duct tape. She assigned this act too much meaning, knowing she was doing so, but not caring in the least. The fact that he had covered the window said that he wasn't in this for the stupid thrill of sleeping with a student, but because what they shared was irresistible, Sally reasoned. For once in her life, she had been the aggressor. They had sex in the wing chair, and behind the desk, and on the sheepskin rug that he once told her he and Jan had bought on their honeymoon in Scotland. When she was with him, she was in heaven, and when she wasn't, she only thought about seeing him again.

By dinner the following Thursday, the girls were beginning to get suspicious. The four of them plus Lara sat at their corner table, which was piled high with a platter of turkey and bowls of thick gravy, stuffing, mashed potatoes, and steamed squash. April loved to horrify Sally with tales of what went into their meals—huge bricks of butter in the shepherd's pie, a whole can of Crisco in the chicken and wild rice casserole.

Usually Sally would steer clear of this sort of glop. She was terrified of turning into one of those Smithies who sat in the living room watching TV with her pants unbuttoned, seeming not to notice the rolls of fat growing around her middle. Celia and Bree had both put on weight in the previous two years, and they talked about it as if it were inevitable: "Look at my gobble chin," Celia would say, pulling at the skin under her neck with one hand as she took a bite of cherry cobbler with the other.

Sally spent two hours a day minimum in the gym in the basement and ate a Lean Cuisine with a salad from the veggie bar for dinner almost every night. But tonight she felt famished, and she filled her plate and began eating before anyone else had even been served.

"Whoa there," Bree said. "Sally, you're eating like Lara—like you only have a day left to live."

"Thanks, sweetie," Lara said, patting Bree on the knee.

Sally caught Celia rolling her eyes. This was shortly before Bree and Lara announced that they were a couple, and apparently Celia thought that only she was allowed to call Bree sweetie. Or maybe it annoyed her that Bree felt comfortable enough around this new friend to tease her as the King House girls might tease one another.

"I'm hungry," Sally said with a shrug. "You guys are always telling me to eat more, so I'm eating more."

They changed the subject. There would be banana-cream pie for dessert, and despite the fact that she usually ate a vegan diet, April leaned over to the table beside theirs to tell a junior named Lily Martin that she thought tonight might be her night for beating Lily's record—five pieces of pie in a sitting.

Jenny Reynolds, a first year who had already gained BDOC status, dinged her water glass with her fork, a Smithie signal that meant she had an announcement to make. The room grew quiet.

"The Smiffenpoofs will be having an a cappella concert tonight in the archway by Public Safety to celebrate Coming Out Day," she said. "Come one, come all, come out!"

The whole room laughed and cheered.

"That girl could announce National Teeth Cleaning Day and people would applaud," Celia said. "But is it Coming Out Day today? I didn't see any chalkings."

Usually on Coming Out Day there were colorful chalkings on the pathways all over campus—SO AND SO IS OUT AND PROUD OR SILENT NO MORE! OR COME OUT, COME OUT, WHOEVER YOU ARE! The previous year, Sally had walked over so many of them that she dragged what looked like four pounds of chalk into the house and onto her brand-new throw rug.

"It's actually Coming Out Day Eve," Lara said. "We're chalking after dinner tonight. Speaking as the token lesbian at the table, I thought I'd let you know. Oh, and we're decorating the whole campus with paper lanterns later."

"During that last part, were you speaking as the token Asian at the table?" Bree said.

Sally gasped a little—wasn't it sort of racist to say something like that? But Lara laughed, and said, "Oh, yes, I take all my minority roles very seriously."

Sally reached for the gravy. She accidentally spilled a huge dollop onto the white tablecloth, but she ignored the mess and poured gravy over her potatoes. Lara kept talking, but the other three were instantly silent.

Bree squealed, "Sally, what is going on?"

"What happened?" Lara asked, looking confused.

"The Sally Werner we know is physically incapable of spilling anything onto linen without at the very least running for seltzer," Bree said.

All eyes were on Sally, who was shoveling a forkful of stuffing into her mouth. "What?" she said with a smile.

The truth was, she was dying to tell them. She swallowed and started to laugh. "Lean in," she said, wishing that Lara weren't around. She hardly knew the girl, but what the hell?

"You must all promise to never ever tell a soul what I'm about to tell you," she said, knowing that she could roughly estimate that each of them would tell at least three people. "Promise!"

"We promise!" they said in unison.

"Tell us, I'm dying here," Bree added.

"I am sleeping with someone," she said, taking in a deep breath. "And don't laugh, but I think I'm in love."

"This just happened today?" April asked.

"No," Sally said. "It's been going on for a while, but it's only been—well, you know, physical—since Monday. He is just so—"

"*He?*" Bree and April blurted out, because it was more plausible that their straightest friend might have fallen for a woman than that she could have found a man to love on the Smith campus in the middle of the week.

"Yes, *he.*" Sally laughed. "Jesus, what do you think I am?"

She noticed Lara's face tighten a bit and felt a little guilty. She hadn't meant anything against lesbians. She thought that perhaps she ought to say so, but couldn't bear to let it take away from the exquisite fun of the conversation. She would just have to send her a note in the campus mail the next day. Did Hallmark make Coming Out Day cards?

"Well, who the hell is he?" Bree asked.

"Please don't say Bill Lambert," Celia said quietly.

"Who's Bill Lambert?" Lara asked.

"Some old poetry prof," April said.

Celia's eyes were trained on Sally. "He's a creep," she said.

Sally felt herself harden. "Yes, it's Bill," she said. "But you don't know anything about what he's really like, sweetheart."

Bree slapped the table. "What? Oh my *goodness,* Sal, way to spice up a Thursday dinner! Details!"

"This is some seriously old-school women's college shit,"

April said. "Do you realize that once you become a faculty wife, your old professors won't even acknowledge that they ever taught you? My mom's friend married her adviser from Radcliffe, and that's how it went down."

Sally giggled. She was grateful for their excitement or amusement or whatever it was, but she could feel Celia's disdain from across the table. "Well, we're not exactly getting married yet."

Finally, Celia spoke. "This is just too clichéd for words," she snapped. "This doesn't happen at Smith. It's the kind of thing people fantasize about, not the kind of thing they actually do. I mean, seriously. The whole thing is like a parody of itself. Was he reciting Tennyson when he came on to you?"

Sally fumed. "It's nothing like that. We just—connect."

April took her hand in a rare show of romantic enthusiasm. It had been a long, dry semester for them all.

"You're like old souls maybe," April said. "Age be damned. Seniority be damned. Fuck it. All that stuff is bullshit anyway."

"Exactly." Sally smiled. "Thank you, my love."

"Previous history of stalking be damned, too," Celia said.

"That's just a nasty rumor, and you know it," Sally said.

"April, I'm surprised at you," Celia said. "You don't think this is wrong?"

April shrugged. "No, not really. It sounds like old Sally here is more than into it. It's not like he coerced her."

"And what about the fact that he's married?" Celia said.

"His wife is dead, for God's sake!" Sally said.

"Jan Lambert isn't dead," Celia said. "She's a Victorian lit professor at Mount Holyoke. She was signing books at Beyond Words on Sunday afternoon."

Everything began to blur in front of Sally's eyes—the food and her friends and the room around them.

She heard Bree whisper, "Are you sure it's the same person?"

The next thing she knew she was running in her T-shirt, pajama pants, and flip-flops, out of the dining hall, and then out of the house, past the president's home and Paradise Pond and the greenhouse and Chapin, until finally she got to the steps of the library. The campus had grown dark and all but deserted at only six-fifteen. Nearly everyone was inside, listening for the squeaky wheels of carts, pushed by friendly old ladies and laden with thick slices of banana-cream pie.

Sally did not stop to catch her breath. She pushed through the doors and went straight to his office.

There he sat, with his door open, the sight of that duct tape making her feel slightly ill now. His feet were up on the desk, and he was reading *The New York Times* in the dim lamplight.

She knocked at the open door.

He turned his eyes upward without moving his head, and when he saw her there, he grinned. "Well, aren't you a vision," he said.

Sally suddenly realized what she was wearing, and she felt embarrassed in spite of herself. "I was in a rush," she mumbled.

"I'm serious," he said, putting down the paper and beckoning her to him. "You look radiant. Have you been running?"

"Are you married?" she interrupted.

"What?" he said with a chuckle.

Rage was coming over her now. He had made her the kind of woman she despised without so much as letting her know. She thought of her own father's affairs, how she had overheard her mother weeping into the phone one night in high school, something about business trips and the credit card statements and how had she possibly not realized before?

"Are. You. Married." Sally said it more sternly than she'd ever said anything in her life.

"You know I'm married," Bill said. "Darling, come in. What is this about?"

She wanted to be immune to the power of that *darling,* yet already she felt herself slipping. She did not want to hate him, or for this to end. She just wanted it all to be a big misunderstanding.

She tried again. "The poem about the tomb. I thought you said it reminded you of your wife."

"It does," he said, not seeming to understand her point.

"Oh," Sally said. "I guess I just assumed that . . ."

"What?" he said, looking genuinely confused. Then a grin spread over his face, and he began to laugh, a deep belly laugh as if she had said the most hilarious thing in the world. "You thought Janice was dead."

"Well, yes," Sally said, her heart beating quickly as she took this information in fully. His wife was alive. She was someone's mistress.

"It's a poem about dead lovers, isn't it?" she said finally.

He looked to the ceiling, his way of telling her he was giving this some thought. Then he said, "To me, it's a poem about pure feeling, pure love that is lost, and a sad shell that remains."

"Your wife is alive," Sally said. She immediately wished she hadn't. Obviously she was alive; he had just said so.

"Sally," he said, pulling her to him and running his palm over her scalp as if she were a cocker spaniel. She had an incredible urge to punch him in the jaw. "Janice and I are separated. Have been for a year now."

"Separated," she said. She felt slightly relieved, though she knew separated could mean a great many things. "Separated, as in—"

"Separated as in we're about to get divorced. Separated as in a poem about a tomb reminds me of her. Separated as in I'm in love with you."

It was the first time he had ever said it.

"I love you, too," she said, and then borrowing a favorite phrase of her mother's, she whispered, "I love you to the moon and back."

That night they slept together, curled into each other on the carpeted office floor. When she woke alone the next morning, Bill had left a Post-it stuck to her purse: *Went swimming. Love you.*

Seeing the words written out that way startled her. She threw on her coat and headed to the Quad, her breath forming tiny clouds in the frigid February air. It was still early, the middle of the night by college sophomore standards.

When she got to her room, another note was waiting, this one from April: *Where did you go, Lady Chatterley? Come see me when you get home. I'm worried about you.*

She crept into April's room. The shades were drawn, and the heavy smell of sleeping breath hung in the air. Sally slipped off her flip-flops and crawled under the covers. A moment later, she felt April roll over and nestle in beside her.

"What time is it?" she whispered.

"Seven-thirty," Sally said.

"And are you still in love, even at this early hour?" April asked.

"Mmm-hmm," she said.

"Have you been out having a big lovers' quarrel and amazing makeup sex?"

"Yes."

"Fabulous," April said, pressing her face into Sally's hair. "Can we discuss it after ten-thirty?"

"We don't need to discuss it at all," Sally said.

"Like hell we're not gonna discuss it," April said. "I suspect we'll discuss nothing but for some time."

She reached over and wrapped her arm around Sally.

"Do you think Celia hates me now?" Sally asked.

"She'll get over it," April said. Soon after, her breathing grew steady, and Sally knew she had fallen back to sleep.

Sally closed her eyes, but she couldn't help saying one more thing. "They're separated," she whispered. "It's not what Celia thinks."

The morning before her wedding day, Sally awoke from a dream covered in sweat. Jake's arms were wrapped around her, his chest pressed to her back, and something in this sweet, unknowing gesture made her want to cry. How on earth could she let herself dream about Bill with Jake lying right there beside her? She closed her eyes and tried to think about tomorrow—she was marrying Jake, at last. The wedding itself seemed less exciting than what would come after, and Sally took this as a good sign. One more day and they'd be in the car on their way to Maine, holding hands and singing songs like they did on any road trip, but this time would be different. This time they would check into the bed-and-breakfast as Mr. and Mrs. Jake Brown.

Sally had always known she would take her husband's last name. She couldn't stand it when women made their children walk around using clunky hyphenates just out of some misguided nod to feminism. She considered herself a feminist, but why did it matter to anyone—how did it further the cause?—for her to distance herself from the person to whom she felt the closest? A few of the older women she volunteered with at NOW had even told her that trying to keep your maiden name was more trouble than it was worth—people were always going to call you Mrs. So-and-So anyway, so why not just make it official? Everyone had to have some man's last name, and Sally reasoned that she would far prefer to have Jake's over her father's.

She knew April would be mortified by the thought of her taking Jake's name. But then, April had never really agreed with Sally's brand of feminism. "That's great, but you need to think bigger!" she said, when Sally told her that she was volunteering at NOW and, more recently, in a domestic violence shelter. "Those sorts of solutions are just Band-Aids. We have to attack this thing from the roots up."

Sally said she realized this, but in the meantime women needed a safe place to call home. They needed warm meals and clean blankets and someone to talk to late at night. The women's movement couldn't be all about radical action and immediate change. That just wasn't how the world worked.

Her ultimate hero was Gloria Steinem. She had improved countless lives, with actions as simple as setting up networks of women who would have otherwise never found one another and starting a magazine devoted to feminism. She always stood up for what was right and never compromised her principles, but she also didn't offend the average person's sensibilities and wasn't afraid to highlight her hair. She liked men! She dated. She got married, though it ended tragically. She was a real woman who believed in equality. Wasn't that a hundred times more powerful than the contributions of someone divisive and scary like Ronnie Munro?

Sally sat on the edge of the bed now, her clammy palms facing upward in her lap. She wasn't going to be able to fall back to sleep. She walked quietly to the bathroom and turned on the shower, stepping into the stream of water before it even had a chance to warm up.

The problem with her memory was that it was always too sharp, too clear. It seemed proper to recall an old lover's scent, maybe, or the sound of his laugh. But Sally could not stop thinking about the precision of Bill's teeth, two perfectly even rows tinged gray from tobacco. She remembered his penis, the exact width of it, and the long blue vein that rose above the pink flesh when she stroked it with her tongue. It wasn't that she missed him exactly, only that she could not forget.

She had known for a long while what the other girls were just beginning to find out—that ideologies were nice, but they didn't serve you very well when it came to having a real life. Perhaps when a person found lasting love, she was supposed to forget all about the men who had come before. But being engaged had only made Sally think more about Bill, and now, being here at the Autumn Inn, she remembered the nights they had spent together under this roof, making love in secret while her housemates were watching *The Real World* across the street.

After her shower, Sally blew her hair out straight and applied a coat of red lipstick and some mascara. She slid into the red sundress and sandals she had gotten for the rehearsal dinner later that night, knowing that it was far too early to be primping for dinner, and that she was really doing all this in case she ran into him.

As she picked up her purse from the nightstand, Jake stirred.

"Where you going?" he said, his eyes still closed.

"To take a walk around campus," she said, suddenly feeling guilty.

"I'll come if you want company," Jake said. He rolled over so he was facedown in the pillow.

"No, no, you sleep," she said.

Finally, Jake turned his head and opened his eyes. He whistled, taking her in. "You're a knockout. I can't believe I get to marry you tomorrow."

Sally went to him and kissed his cheek. He tried to pull her down into the bed, but she resisted. "I'll be back in a bit," she said with a laugh.

"I love you," she said as she opened the door to the hall.

"To the moon and back?" Jake mumbled, his smile audible.

"You know it, babe," she said.

Outside, the air was just turning warm, and clouds were giving way to clear blue sky. Sally crossed the street toward King House and thought of all the students still asleep in their twin beds.

In college, half of what they had talked about was what came next—what would they do for work, where would they live, whom would they fall in love with? They recognized that they were the first generation of women whose struggle with choice had nothing to do with getting it and everything to do with having too much of it—there were so many options that it felt impossible and exhausting to pick the right ones. She almost wanted to rouse those new King House girls from sleep and let them know that, most of the time, the choices just made themselves. She had gone back to Boston because of the offer of work in a cancer research lab at Harvard. And so she had met Jake, standing in line for a tuna sandwich at Au Bon Pain.

She always brought her lunch from home, but that morning on the bus she had been reading a sign above the heads of other passengers: SICK OF THE BAY STATE DATING SCENE? WANT TO MEET FABULOUS MEN WHO ARE LOOKING FOR A COMMITMENT? THEN LOOK NO FURTHER THAN DATEBOSTON.COM. Sally was considering this, thinking of how Celia had met a couple of guys on Match.com, and maybe it wouldn't hurt to try something new and get her mind off Bill. She fished for a pen in her purse and wrote the name of the site on her palm. Then she looked up and saw two high school kids snickering at her. She felt her cheeks grow red. She was officially pathetic and would most definitely die alone. When the bus pulled over, she quickly got off, even though they were still three stops away from her office. Later, after e-mailing the girls about the whole mortifying ordeal, she realized that she must have left her salad on the seat beside her. She decided to treat herself to a big fattening sandwich and a lemonade, and because of that, she had found Jake.

. . .

The Smith campus had not changed a bit since Sally had last been there. The grass was neatly trimmed, the pond sparkled, the ivy-covered brick buildings stood proud and tall. Making her way toward the library, she wondered whether she would see him.

The affair had lasted three years. Since they couldn't be together every night, Sally filled her free time with parties and concerts, growing wilder than she ever had been, or might have otherwise become. She streaked across the Quad in the snow with a group of King House first years, she danced until dawn at every campus party, flirting with the townies and the Hampshire boys without consequence—now that she had someone, it was all just for fun and didn't seem half as bleak as it had when she was looking for love.

"It's called the Absentee Boyfriend Theory," April said. "Having a guy in your life at a distance allows you to be free to explore who you are without the fear or the stigma of being alone."

"But Bill's not at a distance," Sally said.

"Well, you know—a *distance*," April said, as if that cleared things up.

In the beginning, their hours together were exhilarating. They'd make love in his office, at the Autumn Inn, and once, recklessly, in her dorm room. They would go for beers at a dark, smoke-filled bar out by the car dealerships in Florence and play darts, his hand up under her dress as she aimed for the bull's-eye.

But Bill was also prone to long, dark periods of sadness, during which he would ignore Sally altogether or tell her that she was just a foolish, twitty little girl who couldn't understand his pain. Sometimes he said that he wanted his wife back more than anything, that Jan was brilliant and beautiful, and that someone like Sally could never compare with her. He attempted three or four times during their relationship to reconcile with his wife, and each time Jan refused him, leading him to call Sally sobbing in the middle of the night, begging her to meet him at the Autumn Inn. (When she did, he would apologize over and over, holding her close to his chest until she promised to forgive him.)

When she set their time together against the years she had spent with Jake, it seemed absurd. Three years of sneaking around like criminals. She never met Bill's friends, and when they ran into his oldest son walking home from high school one day, Bill introduced her as "Sally, one of my students." She searched the kid's face for some sign that he had heard her name before, but of course he had not, and he only said, "Hey."

Their relationship ended just before graduation. Bill handed her a fat envelope as she left his office one day during finals. Inside was a letter, written in that self-important tone he took whenever she asked anything of him. He wrote about how he would remember her forever—the young beauty who had captured his heart. It hurt him to have to release her into the world, which was sometimes cruel and cold.

"Release you into the world!" April had snapped when Sally showed the letter to the girls. "What are you, a fucking ladybug in a mayonnaise jar?"

"This is typical Bill," Bree said. "No discussion, just a note. That man makes me sick."

Sally knew that Bree was partially just feeling stressed over how she herself had ended things with Lara, only to change her mind at the last second. Sally imagined that by August, Bree would come to her senses. This thing with Lara was just Bree trying to hold on to Smith, when she couldn't, not really. They were all leaving their little bubble of a world, and what lay beyond was anyone's guess.

Also, the girls had come to dislike Bill a great deal—they found him controlling, manipulative, and slightly ridiculous, with his unpredictable bouts of moodiness and brooding. Celia said he still acted like a teenage boy who writes poems about death and wears a lot of black and hates his parents.

Sally never told them what she had once overheard during a student senate meeting at Seelye Hall.

"Did you know Bill Lambert attacked her and that's why she transferred to Wellesley?" one girl said to another.

"Well, I heard that they had slept together, but that was it," the other girl said.

Sally left the auditorium and went straight to the second-floor ladies' room, where she proceeded to breathe hard into her cupped hands until a janitor came in wanting to scrub the floor.

"Just a minute," she said, trying to sound calm and cheerful. She told herself that it was just more vicious gossip, and that she must put it from her head. She had heard all kinds of things about professors and students that were simply untrue. Like the rumor April was spreading the previous semester, that a sixty-year-old guy had been fired from his post in the art library after receiving a blow job from a first year in the stacks while a halogen lamp slowly burned the entire D-through-F section to dust. (Sally had gone herself to check it out, and no such fire had ever taken place.)

Bill insisted that there had been no one else, besides Sally and Jan. For a time, she reasoned that if he was honest about Jan, he was honest, period. But as months passed, her doubts only grew. When Sally tried to end things with Bill after junior year, he stuffed her campus mailbox with love letters and poems, and his much-underlined first edition of W. H. Auden. The girls thought she ought to bring all of it right to the Public Safety office. But Sally still loved him. It amazed her how chemical a feeling love could be, how it could take hold of you even when you had come to despise its object. She kept the letters and the book in a Stride Rite shoe box full of keepsakes that she had had since fourth grade. She went to his office and sat in the old wing chair, and he sat on the floor with his head in her lap, actually crying as she smoothed his hair. Other than Bill, Sally had never seen a grown man cry, not even her father at her mother's funeral.

In their last year together (and this was something that no one—not even the girls—knew about), Sally had lent him a quarter of a million dollars for various things: home repairs and back taxes and legal fees and God knows what else. He swore up and down that he would pay her back by the end of the semester, though she knew he never would. She was fine with this, too: Bill had fallen in love with her long before she got the money. She knew the girls would say he was using her, but Sally disagreed. Money wasn't meant to be shut up in some cold box. If you needed it, you hoped someone would give it to you. If you had it, you ought to give it away.

After his letter, she demanded that they talk about the

breakup he had simply announced. Bill said there was nothing to talk about. She was leaving Smith and needed to move on with her life. Sally had assumed that they would stay together—she was only moving two hours away, and now that she was no longer a Smith student, they could bring their relationship out into the open. She imagined long dinners in little Italian restaurants in Harvard Square, weekends spent on the Cape. But Bill said he wouldn't talk about it any longer. He had made up his mind. He was getting old now, he said, and needed to start acting like it. He would convince Jan to give it another try, and they would have their family again.

"And what about me, sweetheart?" Sally said with tears in her eyes.

"I'm not worried about you," he told her. "Girls like you land on their feet."

She hated him for putting it like that. *Girls like you*, he had said, as though the specifics of what they shared were irrelevant.

At graduation, she cried as he processed in with all the other professors in his academic regalia. When she shook the president's hand after accepting her diploma, she gazed over at him to see if he was watching, but he just stared out at the crowd, straight ahead.

Six months later, right after she met Jake, Bill made a bizarre attempt to win her back, flooding her office phone with messages, and even driving out to Cambridge to meet her. When she refused to come see him, he screamed, "Sally, I will throw myself into the Charles if you deny me." She hung up the phone gently and shut off the ringer for the remainder of the afternoon.

She had thought of it as a romantic gesture, until she told Jake about it. He sputtered with laughter. He nicknamed Bill "Old Man River."

She realized then that she had found someone a million times better.

Sally loved Jake. He was the kind of guy who, when asked to sum up his thoughts on poetry, would probably call it gay (a word she had tried to get him to stop using roughly one thousand times, without success). He showed his love by patching the window screens in her apartment, installing the air conditioner on his lunch break, or taking her out for a homemade picnic. His moods were predictable. He seemed to wake up happy every day—happy to be with her, happy to be alive. To her surprise, this was everything she needed.

As Sally approached the library in her red dress, she paused for a moment, remembering all that had passed inside that building. She had thought at the time that Bill elevated her, gave her an adultness that would have otherwise taken years to develop. But now she wondered if perhaps he had robbed her of something, and she was grateful for what she shared with Jake, a union in which there was nothing secretive or ugly about being in love.

She was glad that she had decided to break from tradition and spend the night before the wedding with Jake, because sleeping close beside him always calmed her nerves. She took off her heels and walked barefoot back to the inn.

Sally had decided to have her wedding at Smith and the rehearsal dinner in the wine cellar at Pizza Paradiso long before she and Jake got engaged. On their fifth date, to be precise. She had been in the wine cellar only once before, at the farewell Rec Council dinner right before graduation. She recalled thinking then that she wished she had some special occasion to commemorate there. After Jake proposed, she had first wanted to do the traditional Smithie thing and get married at Helen Hills Hills. (That was the name of the campus chapel. The story was that Helen Hills had married her cousin, but Sally couldn't remember now if it was a fact or just a dumb joke.)

But then one night she had the idea of getting married in the Quad, on the very grass she had looked out at from her college dorm room, everything coming back around to this place where her adult life began. She and Jake agreed that a wedding should be simple and small. Without her mother there, she didn't feel the need to throw some fifty-thousand-dollar parade.

Sally was eager for Jake to spend more time with the girls. They had all met him before, but she wanted them to really *know* Jake, to see in him all the wonderful things she saw. She knew they didn't quite get him yet—well, maybe Celia, but not the others. He wasn't any of the things that the girls usually went for—tortured, dramatic, doomed to disappoint. Nor was he particularly complex, something that Sally appreciated, though the others seemed to find this quality suspect. She was self-conscious about talking too much about Jake to any of them, or acting like she had to have him around. In this respect only, she preferred the company of her work friend Jill, who had been married to her husband, Jack, for two years and hardly ever used the word "I." Instead it was always "We'd love to" or "Sorry, we're busy."

"We-speak," Celia called it with disdain.

But Sally found it comforting to be around a woman who was in a committed relationship and always thought of herself as one half of a pair. She imagined that even if they did get married, her Smith friends would never be that way.

Before dinner, they practiced the ceremony out in the Quad—the girls walked with her brother and two of Jake's college buddies, and Jake stood at the end of the path, right in front of Wilson House, the same path they had walked when they graduated. As Sally moved toward him on her father's arm, tears filled her eyes. It finally felt real.

She had thought about walking down the aisle alone, of asking her father to do something else, like hand out programs. He hadn't been involved at all during the planning process. Plus, eight years of being friends with April had made its mark on Sally, and the thought of having one man hand her over to another was vaguely nauseating, especially when one of them was her father, who could never have laid claim to her in the first place. It would have been different if her mother were there, Sally thought, but then again, so would everything else. Ultimately, Jake said he thought she ought to just bite the bullet and let her father walk her down the aisle, and Sally agreed.

After they rehearsed, Sally and the girls stayed behind in the Quad to take pictures for the *Alumnae Quarterly*. Celia said she wanted shots of them both in and out of their formalwear, so she could show the progression of the weekend. Sally loved the idea, but after a while of posing, she started to get antsy. She never liked arriving late to anything, let alone her own rehearsal dinner, and she couldn't help but feel a little pulled between past and future—the girls still wanted her to belong to them, but any part of her that could belong to someone was Jake's now.

Finally she said, "Okay, my loves, let's go. I'm nervous about leaving my father alone with the in-laws for too long."

They walked into Pizza Paradiso twenty minutes behind everyone else and saw the familiar wood-burning oven, its flames shooting up around bubbling pies. A family sat in the booth by the door, two mothers and their toddler son.

"It's good to be back in Northampton," April said, casting an eye their way.

Sally laughed, but she hoped Jake's grandparents hadn't noticed.

When they got downstairs, she started to direct the girls to the chairs right beside Jake's, but Celia took April's hand and said, "Come sit by me!" and they squeezed in beside Anthony, an investment banker who had grown up with Jake, and whom Celia had decided to make out with when they met at the hotel bar the night before.

"April, you didn't get to meet Morgan Stanley last night," Celia said, presenting her to Anthony. "Morgan, this is my dear friend April, the hardest-working girl in America. Would you believe her boss had her editing movie footage in her hotel room last night while the rest of us were getting hammered?"

Sally sat down beside Jake, with her eyes still on Celia. Lara came over and kissed Sally's cheek. She had slicked back her hair, and she was wearing a black pantsuit.

Sally eyed her mother-in-law and wished for the first time ever that her friends could be a little less like themselves, just for one night.

Lara apologized for not being around all day and said she had a headache. Sally smiled. "Not to worry, tulip," she said, though she was already imagining the conversation she would have with Jake later: What was Bree doing in this ridiculous relationship, where she was always miserable, and someone always had to pretend to have a headache or a big work project, or *something,* because they couldn't stand to be together in the same room most of the time? They'd had fun together in college, but ever since they had been totally unable to make it work. In Sally's opinion, Bree was wasting her most beautiful years on a relationship that had been doomed from the start. Whenever she tried to talk to April about it, April immediately accused her of being homophobic, but Sally knew that wasn't it—Bree wasn't even gay, for Christ's sake! Sally had once asked her whether she would date men or women if she ever broke up with Lara, and Bree had said, "Oh men, definitely," without even having to think.

Sally gave Lara credit, though, for coming all the way from California, for sending flowers when she got engaged, which was more than any of the others had done.

She had to stifle a laugh when she saw Jake's mother staring at Lara's getup.

"This crowd loves you, huh?" Sally whispered.

"Oh yeah," Lara said. "Since I got to the restaurant, I've already been asked if I was in a fraternity in college by one guy, and whether I like k.d. lang by another. And Jake's grandmother asked if I just moved here from Japan. When I said I'm from Virginia, she said, 'There's a Virginia in Japan?' "

Sally cringed. "Oh God, I'm so sorry."

"Not a problem," Lara said. "I just can't wait to see you get hitched. Anyway, now that April's here she'll probably take some of the heat off."

"Yeah, those dreads are my mother-in-law's worst nightmare," Sally said.

She watched Celia fill a wineglass and hand it to April before filling up her own and downing half of it in one gulp. Just as she started to get annoyed, Jake leaned over and took her hand.

"I'm glad you're here," he said.

"Why? Has my father been misbehaving?" she asked.

"Nah," Jake said. "I just missed you."

The waiters arrived, carrying trays piled high with Caesar salad, antipasti, and chicken parmigiana over spaghetti. Sally had special-ordered a plate of roasted eggplant over whole wheat ziti for April.

"You have the vegan entrée, right?" a waiter asked her, and April turned to Sally and smiled.

"You're amazing," April said.

Out of the corner of her eye, Sally saw Jake's parents kiss. As annoying as they could often be, Rosemary and Joe clearly still loved each other. Sally knew that, statistically speaking, this probably increased Jake's odds of being a good husband, but it made her sad when she set them against her own parents and thought of how her mother had never really known love like that. This was something Sally hadn't realized about weddings until she started planning one—no matter how simple, they were never just about the bride and groom. Those in attendance who were in love felt all the happier; their love strengthened by being in the presence of a new, hopeful marriage. For those who hadn't been lucky in love, a wedding was like a bad paper cut—annoying and painful and impossible to ignore.

The dinner raced by, with speeches from Jake's dad and grandfather, and a few awkward words from Sally's brother ("Jake's a really good guy, and we hope he's going to make Sally real happy, and, umm, yeah"). He did not mention their mother once. Celia talked drunkenly and a little too freely about their college days—about dear Sally and how she had always been the sweetest and wildest girl around. How everyone in King House went to convocation in their underwear each fall, and how Sally had hand-painted Burger King crowns for them all with the words BEST F.KING HOUSE ON CAMPUS splayed across them in glitter. How she once did a series of keg stands at a luau with some Amherst frat guy and gave up on breaking the school record with just one keg stand to go, because said frat guy got a barbecue sauce stain on his Hawaiian shirt and Sally insisted on cleaning it up immediately, before it had time to set.

Sally saw Jake's mother's eyebrows rise as she listened in on this, looking a little too delighted by her own shock. She pictured Rosemary storing this information away as future ammunition, and willed Celia to stop talking.

"Now Sally's making the craziest move of all—she's getting married!" Celia said. "We couldn't be happier for her. It takes a lot for us to approve of a man, but Jake, as Sally would say, we love you to the moon and back."

Sally smiled. That made her happy, at least, because she knew Celia wouldn't say it unless she actually meant it.

Finally, Jake stood up. "Thanks, Cee," he said. "Wow. I'm not so great at speeches. But here in front of everyone we love, I have to say something about Sally, this girl—sorry Smithies, this *woman*—who has totally changed my life. I've always been a pretty happy-go-lucky guy, but I never knew how happy I could be until I met Sally. She is my best friend, the love of my life, the smartest person I know, and apparently a keg stand champion. Ever since we met, I wake up with butterflies in my stomach every morning, excited just to see her again. And I know I'm still going to wake up with butterflies when we're ninety-three years old and both of us have lost our teeth, and Sally's brown hair has turned white. I'm so glad you are all here with us as we start our journey together, and I know Sally's mom is here, too, guiding us along. Thank you all for coming and for not throwing up—one other thing I know is how nauseating cute couples can be and, well, we're pretty damn cute."

He leaned down and kissed Sally. Her eyes filled with tears.

Their courtship ran through her head like a cheesy montage in a Meg Ryan movie—meeting in the sandwich line at Au Bon Pain, Jake stumbling over his words and saying, "I'm not a crazy person, I swear, and I never talk to strangers, but you're beautiful. Can I buy you lunch?" Then there was their first date, and their second, and all the hundreds of dinners and movies that came after; the car rides spent singing Elvis songs to each other; the long talks about family and friends; the trips to the Cape with Jack and Jill, sipping Coronas on the beach, grilling hamburgers, and going for long runs, making love in the sand at dawn before anyone else had woken up.

"I love you," she whispered to Jake now, and part of her wished that everyone in the room would vanish except the two of them.

By the time dessert arrived, Celia was plastered.

"That was the most adorable toast I've ever heard," she said to Jake, louder than she needed to, her words slightly garbled. "Are you guys gonna get a dog? Oh, I'll be so jealous! I'd do anything to have a dog, but I live in a shoe box. Can I live in your attic and be the spinster aunt to your ten children, if I promise to take care of the dog?"

Sally felt slightly panicked, glancing over at Jake's relatives, but Jake just laughed. "Absolutely," he said, lifting his glass to toast Celia. "To spinster aunts!"

Celia clanked her glass hard against his, splashing red wine onto the tablecloth and down the front of her dress.

"Oopsie daisy," she said with a shrug. "Gonna dash to the ladies'! Be right back!"

They all watched her run off, silenced for a moment before the room once again filled with conversation. Everyone dug into the tiny chocolate éclairs and big bowls of sorbet. It was enough food for three times as many people, Sally thought happily. The dinner had been a success on the whole, although her wedding weekend was passing by far too fast.

Sally watched Anthony lean in toward April. She strained to hear their conversation.

"So you know Sal from college?" he asked.

"Yup," April said blandly.

He was a bit of a McSmarm, Sally knew, and of course April wasn't particularly interested in talking to him. But she didn't have to be rude. Unlike Celia, April was safe from his advances—men like that did not go for flat-chested white girls with dreadlocks and unshaved armpits.

"They're a great couple," he said, trying again.

"Mmm-hmm," April said, taking a bite of her sorbet and looking over her shoulder toward the steps, visibly willing Celia to return from the bathroom.

"My name's Anthony," he said. "Just in case you didn't catch it the first time."

"April," she said, her mouth full.

"Right. So what was your major at Smith?"

"Double major—government and SWAG," she said.

Sally sighed. *Oh brother, April.*

"What's SWAG?" he asked.

"The study of women and gender," she said, as if it should be obvious.

"Ahh, that's a specialty of mine as well," Anthony said, and then he winked.

Christ. She knew that April believed firmly that no man under sixty-five should ever wink, and that she had just decided without reservation that she hated him.

Just then, Celia returned, a wet spot running down her dress. "What are we talking about?" she said, leaning in.

Anthony looked relieved. "So, Celia, you work in publishing. Maybe you know my cousin. Her name's Andrea Panciacco. She's at Simon and Schuster."

Celia shrugged. "Nope, don't know her. I'm at Circus Books. But she probably knows this guy I used to work with. He went over to S and S last month."

Thus began several rounds of the *Maybe you know* game with Celia asking Anthony whether he knew her childhood friend who worked for Deutsche Bank in Boston, her high school boyfriend who graduated from Berkeley three years after he did, and her cousin who played in his soccer league (no, no, and no). Anthony, it turned out, had many former friends and acquaintances who worked in New York, though some of their last names escaped him: "You might know Liza something or other who's a producer for Chris Matthews or Keith Olbermann or one of those guys? She was in my Sunday school class as a kid."

Celia said she thought the name sounded familiar.

Finally, she and April switched seats. Sally was happy for that at least. She walked over to April's chair and squeezed her hand.

"Thank you for being here, sweetpea. It means the world to me," she said. "And thanks for not slugging Anthony over there."

"It was an effort," April said.

"I could tell," Sally said. "Believe me, I could tell."

She could be pissed at April, but what was the point? Sally wanted all the memories of her wedding to be special, joyous. Plus, she knew that April was out of her comfort zone here, just as she herself had been a year earlier, when she had flown to Chicago.

April had been begging her to come for months so they could have some time alone, just the two of them. They chose a week when Ronnie was supposed to be at a conference in Miami.

"Oh, drat, I was hoping to meet her," Sally had said over the phone, though in truth she hated the very idea of Ronnie— the danger she put April in, the way she demanded all of April's time, even forcing her to move in, the fact that she paid April next to nothing and never gave her any credit for her work. Sally couldn't imagine what she might say if they ever met.

But she wanted to see April's hometown. She pictured the two of them strolling along the water, taking one of those scenic bus tours, drinking frozen hot cocoa at Ethel's Chocolate Lounge. (She had found the place online, a little pink-and-purple oasis right in the middle of the city, with plush sofas and dim lighting and chocolate everything. Of course April had never heard of it, but she said she would go along.) Everyone always thought of April as this crazy counterculture hippie because that was what she projected to the world. But when Sally got her one-on-one, she was just April—sensitive and funny, smart and kind.

As soon as she saw April's face in the airport parking lot, Sally knew something was wrong.

"What is it?" she said.

"Ronnie's fucking livid," April said, breathless, not even giving her a hug. "The army is trying to block funding for our movie from going through, she canceled her trip, and she says we need to start working now, maybe get the ACLU involved, maybe bring a First Amendment suit if we have to."

There was a long pause before she said, "Sorry, Sal, I know this isn't what we had in mind for the weekend."

Sally could tell that April was under Ronnie's spell now, and there would be no snapping her out of it. "Don't worry," she said. "I can help you."

In the car, Sally looked down at her ring. Jake had proposed just one week earlier, and she was still in the habit of gazing at it for long stretches of time. She had told herself repeatedly on the plane not to be disappointed when April didn't notice it. Sally knew a ring just wasn't the sort of detail April would take in, let alone gush over. But for some reason, it still made her a little sad. They were best friends, but they were so very different in nearly every way, and the more time they spent out in the real world, the more apparent their differences became.

April and Ronnie's apartment reeked of cigarette smoke. The place was in a nice high-rise with a doorman at the front desk and a chandelier in the lobby. It was huge, with bright track lighting and wide windows. But as far as decorating went, they had only the necessities—a couch, a small dining table, a TV, and bookshelves sagging under the weight of bulky academic texts. There were no picture frames, no paintings or photographs, not even a carpet on the hardwood floor or lamps on the end tables. It looked exactly as Sally had expected.

She wished she could spend the weekend warming the place up, putting little accents here and there—some bright throw pillows on the sofa, maybe; a soft area rug, or perhaps a sisal; old Rosie the Riveter posters from the forties in worn gold frames. She was about to suggest this to April when Ronnie burst into the room, a cordless phone pressed to her cheek.

She had short, spiky hair, in such a deep shade of red that it looked almost purple. She wore faded jeans and a Smith sweatshirt with a patch on the sleeve, which Sally herself had sewed on.

"Isn't that yours?" she whispered to April.

April shrugged. "Our laundry gets mixed in all the time."

Sally grimaced. This wasn't normal, this relationship of theirs. She had tried many times to say so to April, but April never wanted to hear it.

"It's your own fucking department's report, Gerard," Ronnie yelled into the phone. "The Department of Defense openly admitted that one-third of female veterans had been raped during service, thirty-seven percent of them raped more than once, fourteen percent of them gang raped. Yet when a woman in your army brings charges, she only has a one-in-ten chance of getting justice. This is fucking *documented*, Gerard. I didn't pull these figures out of my ass. What, you think this doesn't qualify as post-traumatic stress? You're out of your fucking mind, Gerard, I swear."

She glanced in their direction, but she seemed not even to notice Sally. "April baby," she hissed. "Get me the DOD file from my bedside table. Now."

April ran down a corridor, and Sally stood there awkwardly, shuffling from one foot to the other. Farewell, Ethel's Chocolate Lounge.

They spent the next three days in the sort of frenzied state Sally imagined one might feel in an emergency room after a forty-car pileup. Ronnie talked on the phone constantly, and April pored over transcripts and videos of all her interviews.

Sally sat beside her on the couch and watched as these women—girls, really—explained in calm, measured tones what had happened to them in Iraq. One nineteen-year-old from a tiny town in Indiana had gone AWOL, refusing to join her company on their third deployment to Baghdad, because during her first two trips her direct supervisor had sexually assaulted her. It had started just one day after she saw a close friend killed in a car bombing. When she asked the sergeant where she should report for duty the following morning, he said, "Spread-eagle, tied up, in my bed." That night, he came to her while she lay sleeping and pulled her outside, ordering her to strip naked, then raping her in front of two of her fellow soldiers.

A mother told how her only daughter had committed suicide on her twenty-first birthday, shooting herself in the head after hearing that the army had dismissed gang-rape charges she had brought against five of her superiors, claiming that the bruises all over her body were not sufficient evidence for a court-martial. She had been given a rape kit in a military hospital the night of the attack, but hospital officials said it had been accidentally misplaced.

Sally cried as she watched this, texting Jake to tell him how upset she was.

Wow honey, he wrote back. *This sounds like the greatest vacation ever.*

Sally knew that anyone else would probably be annoyed with April, but she just wasn't. April had been there for her all through college, on those awful, lonely nights when she missed her mother and needed someone by her side.

Her friends from high school had been supportive the summer after her mother died, especially Monica Harris, her best friend since sixth grade. Monica would come by every day and stay on the phone with Sally for hours in the middle of the night. When she arrived at Smith, Sally assumed this would continue, but almost immediately Monica began to pull away from her—she was settling into college, too, after all. It was April who took her place, April who saved Sally from the humiliation of begging someone not to hang up, leaving her alone with her thoughts.

It often felt unbalanced because April never talked about pain in her life or asked for advice. Plus, Sally was in awe of

April, really, the fact that she could sit across from these people, recording their horrible stories without so much as tearing up. And the way she often convinced Sally that something that seemed ridiculous was in fact incredibly important. After all, it was April who had raised her consciousness about feminism (though April said that the term "consciousness raising" gave her the willies and made her think of a gaggle of 1970s housewives looking at their vaginas in hand mirrors before ripping into a cinnamon Danish).

She would have made an amazing journalist, Sally thought. If only stupid Ronnie hadn't gotten her hands on April first.

"How did you guys end up getting all these secret documents anyway?" Sally asked.

"Well, some of them aren't so secret, it's just that nobody's looking," April said, clearly not wanting to get into the details. She never wanted Sally to know about the more dangerous aspects of her work. But Sally pressed her now.

"And the others?"

"The others we sort of stole in a raid," April said with a big, proud smile.

Sally felt her stomach sink. "You raided a military office?"

"Yeah, it was awesome. Ronnie got caught, but I didn't," April said. Then, seeing the horror on Sally's face, she said, "Sal, don't worry about me. I'm fine, and Ronnie would never ask me to do anything seriously dangerous."

Sally knew this was a bold-faced lie. Ronnie reminded her a little of April's mother. She was old, yet not at all parental. She swore more than any person Sally had ever met (except, perhaps, April). She didn't make Sally feel safe and secure the way most adults did. Instead, she made her uneasy.

When the three of them sat down for dinner each night— always takeout from the Indian place across the street, or a Thai restaurant April loved—Ronnie downed glasses of wine like a marathoner chugging water after a long run. She talked only about the cause at hand, never once asking Sally where she lived or what she did for work, except on Sunday, the last night of Sally's trip. Sally was clearing the plates and had just picked up Ronnie's, when Ronnie grabbed her left hand, nearly sending the china sailing toward the floor.

"What is this?" Ronnie said, eyeing her engagement ring.

"I'm getting married!" Sally exclaimed. Even when talking to Ronnie, it was hard to hide how thrilled she felt. And at least someone had noticed her ring.

"Jesus," Ronnie said. "How old are you?"

"Twenty-four," Sally said.

"Oh, Christ, just what the world needs," Ronnie said to April.

April laughed, and Sally felt hurt by this, even as she told herself that April had no other option. Ronnie was her boss, after all.

Then, out of nowhere, Ronnie said, "One of every ten U.S. soldiers in Iraq is a woman, you know. There are one hundred sixty thousand of them over there."

Sally nodded, not sure how to respond. "Wow" was all she could muster.

She felt certain that something important was happening here, that April was doing exactly the sort of courageous work she had always dreamed of doing. But Sally was excited to fly home the following afternoon anyway, to see Jake and tell him everything that had gone on during this bizarre weekend.

On her last day in Chicago, April woke Sally early, before the sun had even come up. She had Sally's bag over her shoulder, and two travel mugs full of coffee in her hands.

"Come with me," she whispered. "Don't make a sound."

Sally followed April out of the apartment and into the elevator, before saying, "What's going on?"

"I'm stealing Ronnie's car for the morning and taking you on the tour of Chicago you deserve," April said. "I'm sorry it's so abbreviated."

Sally looked at her with a surprised smile. "Will Ronnie be pissed?" she asked.

"Probably, but she owes you this," April said.

"You're the best, lemon drop," Sally said. She felt relieved to see a bit of the old, independent pre-Ronnie April shining through.

In the car, they drank coffee and watched the sun rise and listened to a mix CD that April had made Sally for the plane. They drove past the Sears Tower and along the Magnificent Mile. They strolled down Clark Street, poking into little shops, and went to Wrigley Field so Sally could take a picture for Jake. Then April said, "Come on, we have brunch reservations."

Sally grinned. "Ethel's?" she said.

"Where else?" April said with a wink.

On the drive there, as Sally thought about strawberries dipped in chocolate fondue and how lucky she was to have such a weird and wonderful best friend and how much she wanted to kiss Jake, April said, "I know she's sort of bizarre and awkward, but isn't Ronnie fucking incredible?"

Sally was reminded of the tone women took when describing some terrible boyfriend to their friends. It was the sort of inflection she had once used when defending something embarrassing or conniving that Bill had done. Ronnie was April's equivalent of a bad boyfriend, and there was nothing Sally could say until April figured it out for herself. So she just smiled and looked out the window, pretending not to hear.

Later, when she told Celia this, Celia asked her if she thought April was in love with Ronnie, as Bree had long suspected.

"No," Sally told her. "Absolutely not. I think in some way she's like a mother to April."

"Not a very good one," Celia said.

"Yeah, but neither is her actual mother," Sally said.

She felt a little bit mean saying this, but it was the truth. Ronnie didn't really seem to care about April as anything other than an assistant, despite the weird intimacy of their life together. And April was willing to do anything to get Ronnie's approval.

"Their relationship is a little bit cultlike," Sally said.

"That's what I think, too," Celia said. "And I'm worried that no one's looking out for April."

Sally shot back quickly, "I am."

After they'd hung up, she wondered whether or not it was true. If April, willful and stubborn as she was, wanted to follow Ronnie down any and all of her dangerous paths, could anyone really stop her?

CELIA

Celia wasn't at all surprised that four years out of college, Sally still had her King House key on her key chain. They used it to sneak into the dining room for old time's sake after the rehearsal dinner. Lara, Jack and Jill, and the adults had gone to bed. Jake, his friends, and Sally's brother went to Packard's to play darts and drink beer.

Celia had suggested it as a joke: "Let's break into King House," she said, picturing them running up and down the hallways drunk, hugging first years in flannel pajamas and asking if they wanted to be snorkeled. (Snorkeling was a game that straight Quad girls used as a prelude to kissing. The person being snorkeled would lie flat on her back. The snorkeler would blow hard into her nose, so that a burst of air shot from the other girl's mouth.)

Sally jingled her keys. "Yes! We can sit at our old table and have some girl talk."

Celia had gotten to the point of drunkenness where she wasn't much interested in girl talk. She hadn't realized how hammered she was until she found herself in the Pizza Paradiso bathroom, mopping Chianti off her dress and singing "End of the Road" by Boyz II Men at the top of her lungs. Now, all she really wanted to do was go downtown and find some ridiculous townie to make out with, preferably on a pool table. But she reminded herself that this was Sally's weekend, and if she wanted girl talk in the King House dining hall, that's what she would get.

It was exam week. They could tell because the dining hall ladies had left out the usual enormous bowls of treats, each one inscribed with an FK for "Franklin King." There were M&M's in one bowl, packages of peanut-butter crackers in another, licorice whips, chocolate-covered pretzels, and a box of Munchkins from Dunkin' Donuts. It was as though the girls were bulking up for hibernation instead of studying for finals.

The dining room stood empty. It hadn't changed one bit since they had left, Celia thought. The gold chandeliers still sparkled, the long oak tables and chairs were the same ones they had carved their initials into the night before graduation, with Sally pointing out that this was rude and disrespectful, something that only twelve-year-old boys would do. (She added her carefully etched SPW all the same.)

The girls took their usual table in the corner, and Bree placed the box of doughnuts in the center.

"Looks like we got here just in time," she said, shoving one into her mouth and licking the cinnamon from her fingers. "The little piglets upstairs don't know there's a fresh batch of food here yet."

Like most things at Smith, the dining hall experience was extreme. Either you ate everything in sight, or you ate nothing. There were girls you did not want to sit with. They were called EDs, which was short for "eating disorders." EDs tended to compensate for not eating by talking excessively about food. They would go on all day about the pound cake on the dinner menu, and then take one tiny forkful before pronouncing it too rich. They'd stare at the contents of your plate, commenting that you must have a really fast metabolism if you took too much food, or warning you that you needed more sustenance if you didn't take enough.

Senior year someone puked in a second-floor shower stall every evening sometime between six and eight. No one ever heard her throw up, but there it would be, stuck to the tile in little globs, caked around the drain. Sally said she actually felt bad for whoever it was, because she must truly be a mess. Which, in turn, made everyone else think that Sally was probably doing the puking. After all, she had once admitted that she didn't always keep her food down, a very Sally way of saying that perhaps she was a touch bulimic.

The puker turned out to be an emaciated sophomore whom they called the Hare, because she kept a live rabbit in her closet and also had the worst Jennifer Aniston shag they'd ever seen.

"The way they used food as a substitute for sex here," Celia said now. "It was pretty amazing. No wonder I got so fat."

"You were never fat!" Sally protested, though they all knew Celia had gained a lot of weight during their years at Smith.

"Pleasingly plump, maybe," Bree said, and Celia burst out laughing.

It was something only your very best friend, or perhaps your mother, could get away with saying.

After college, Celia started doing Weight Watchers. She lost fourteen pounds in a month, but she dropped out because she could not stop laughing at the weekly meetings. She had sent the rest of them a long e-mail, detailing how she got scolded for bursting into giggles when the group leader—an Upper East Side woman in spandex—gave a lecture on emotional eating and warned them that the trick was to "Face your stuff, not stuff your face." After that, Celia just started counting calories on her own and avoided any carbs that did not come from beer.

"I don't know if I could have made it through exams without our nightly treat bowls," Bree said.

All four of them had graduated Phi Beta Kappa. There was a lot of pressure to succeed, to prepare yourself to *be* somebody down the line. In their graduating class there were four Fulbright scholars, three Saudi Arabian princesses, a girl who had written a bestselling book on overachieving females at the age of eighteen, and the heiress to the Mrs. Fields cookie fortune, who had already developed a business plan to triple the company's annual profits. There was a sense that if you were twenty-one and had yet to make a name for yourself, you had better get cracking. The feeling had only gotten stronger with each passing year since. Rhonda Lee, who had lived in their hall senior year, had already become a full professor at Harvard, for God's sake.

Celia had always dreamed of writing books. Ever since sixth grade she had fantasized about long days spent sitting in a country house somewhere, drinking tea and writing at the kitchen table, with a big furry dog at her feet. But how could she get there from here? How could you find the time and inspiration to sit down and write when you spent your days reading other people's crap, sending out rejection letter after rejection letter?

Whenever she set out to work on her novel, Celia found the task daunting. She wanted to write beautiful prose about characters steeped in tragedy, like the female authors she had always revered. She had already attempted a dozen plotlines, including a literary murder mystery set in Austin, a romantic tragedy about a woman who finds out her husband has a dark, criminal past, a historical novel about four mentally unstable sisters living in Victorian England, and so on. On occasion, she could get several pages out in one go and feel like she was flying afterward. But the next day, she would read over what she had written and see it for what it was: amateurish, ridiculous. She'd erase it all and start again from scratch. These days she was lucky if she was able to write the stupid "Class Notes" and get them into the *Quarterly* on time.

They all thought it was funny that Celia had ended up as secretary for the class of 2002. It was much more a Sally kind of thing, but in a brief burst of Smithie nostalgia, she had volunteered for the job right after graduation. It appealed to her love of snooping—she got to hear first what everyone in their class was up to. There had been six weddings so far, and already one divorce. It was some girl Celia had never heard of, and when she got the e-mail she wondered who on earth would feel the need to tell her entire college class that her young marriage had fallen apart after just ten months.

Celia always forwarded any juicy updates from their classmates to the other three, usually with some bitchy editorializing at the bottom. April said she was blown away by the achievements of their fellow alums. Bree confessed to Celia that she was secretly obsessed with finding out who had gotten married and had kids. Sally, in her sometimes morbid way, said she always skipped the class notes and flipped right to the obituaries at the back of the magazine.

Celia had started giggling at dinner, and now she could not stop. She reached into her oversize purse and pulled out the bottle of good champagne she had snagged from her boss's office after a Christmas party months earlier.

"To love!" Celia said, raising the bottle in the air. The rest of them raised imaginary glasses.

"To love!" Sally said, her face glowing. "And to you, my best friends. The first real loves of my life."

They passed the champagne around and competed to tell the best Smith stories—skinny-dipping in Paradise Pond under a full moon, attending the drag ball at the Davis Center in full tuxes and fake facial hair glued on by Bree, going to concerts at the Calvin Theatre, and filling the long walks home with songs and laughter.

By the time a couple of girls came down to forage for food a half hour later, they had finished off the champagne.

"Excuse me!" Celia called out to them, and Bree shushed her. "Hey, you, how old are you?"

The girls chuckled nervously. "Nineteen," one of them said.

"Jesus, you're infants!" Celia said.

"Don't mind her, she's shattered," Bree said.

The girls came closer and chatted with them for a while. One of them was a bio major, just like Sally had been; the other had something to do with women's studies, and April wrote down a list of books she should read on a dinner napkin. The girl looked like she might pass out when April told her that she worked for Ronnie Munro, and Celia had to stop herself from saying out loud that Ronnie was really a total asshole as a person, even if she had done good work for womankind.

Sally told them about her wedding the next day.

"It's so romantic to get married in the Quad!" one of the girls said, and Sally immediately invited her to the reception.

When the students had padded back upstairs, Celia reached into her bag again.

"I brought a little present for old time's sake."

It was a bottle of Bombay Sapphire gin, Sally's favorite drink back in college.

"Who are you, Mary Poppins?" April asked. "Do you have a lamp and a parakeet in that bag, too?"

Celia stuck out her tongue. "This will be your something blue, Sal," she joked.

Sally raised up her hand. "*No*, pumpkin," she said, laughing. "I'm too drunk already. I don't want to be a hungover bride!"

"Why not?" Celia said. "You're going to have three hungover bridesmaids."

"Good point," Sally said. She grabbed the bottle, unscrewed the cap, and took a long gulp.

"You guys, I know I'm young, but I love Jake so much. I just love the stuffing out of him," she said. "I cannot wait to be his wife."

April clapped her hands together, and Celia assumed she was trying to ignore the part about dying to be a wife. "Of all the tools I've seen come in and out of our lives, I'd have to say that you finally found yourself an amazing guy," April said.

"Remember the jerks I hooked up with in college?" Sally said. "The guy who liked to put staples in his arm when he got loaded? The kid who said he had a landscaping business, and then it turned out he went to Northampton High School and mowed lawns in the summer?"

They shrieked with laughter.

"Aren't you forgetting someone?" Bree asked.

"Who?" Sally said.

"Bill!" the other three said in unison, still laughing.

"I walked by his office this afternoon," Sally said, drawing out the words and pulling her feet up onto her chair.

"Why would you do that?" Bree said, sounding shocked, even though earlier she and Celia had made a bet about whether or not Sally would mention him. (Bree was the winner.)

Sally shrugged. "I've been thinking about him a lot. I've been having these ridiculous dreams about him, you know, sexual dreams. Part of me just wanted to see him again."

"For sex?" Celia said.

"Maybe," Sally said. "It wasn't really a conscious thing. Anyway, I didn't act on it. It's perfectly normal. Jill says before she married Jack she fantasized about all her exes."

"Now was that before or after they went up the hill to fetch a pail of water?" Celia said. She snorted with laughter, her head light and giddy.

"Are you having doubts about Jake?" April said.

"No!" Sally said. "Like I said, nothing happened."

They grew silent. Celia had been afraid April might say something like that, even though she had warned her not to.

Lately April had been obsessed with whether or not they should try to stop Sally from getting married, stating that she was too young and had no idea what she was getting herself into. It was absurd, Celia thought. Sally wasn't a child. Only in this little world were women in their midtwenties thought of as too young for marriage. All over the country, unmarried twenty-five-year-olds were considered old enough to be put out to pasture. Christ, by this age, her own mother had been married with a kid.

Celia picked up one of several pamphlets that had been left on the table, advertisements for upcoming campus events.

"Watch *Straight Eye for the Queer Girl* every Tuesday on Smith TV," she read aloud. "Oh, Lordy, how Smith is that?"

They all laughed, relaxing a bit.

Sally crawled into April's lap and wrapped her arms around her. "You've been awful quiet about yourself today, ladybug. What are you and crazy Ronnie up to these days?"

"We're about to start a new film. We're working with underage victims of sexual exploitation in Atlanta," April said.

Celia thought she sounded proud. She wished she could sound that way when she talked about her own job, but there wasn't a lot of pride to be taken in editing *How to Hang with a Hamptons Hunk: The Vacation-Crasher's Guide to Life.*

"You mean prostitutes?" Sally said.

April raised an eyebrow. "That's not the preferred word, but yes. We're making a documentary about the girls and their pimps. Do you know the average age of entrance into prostitution in this country is eleven years old? These fucking pimps recruit little girls in the streets, on the subway, at the mall. But also in places where you'd think kids are safe, like at school, or in shelters, or churches."

Sally shook her head. "Awful," she said.

"Right," April said. "So we're going to be following these girls, chronicling what they go through."

"Where will you stay?" Sally asked.

"Probably somewhere in the vicinity of where the girls live," April said. "Ronnie will figure out the details."

Celia wished they could be sober for this conversation. There were things she wanted to say; yet as soon as one of them landed in her head, she lost it again.

April went on. "Part of what we want to expose is how corrupt the cops are. Like half the time they arrest a girl, they tell her that she can go free if she'll give them a blow job."

"Half the time?" Bree asked skeptically.

"But why do you have to go to Atlanta?" Sally asked. "You don't even know anyone there. Isn't it just as bad in New York or Chicago?"

"Yeah, it's everywhere," April said. "Atlanta is one of the top places for it, because it's a hub for conventions and sports events, which, because men are pigs, means that the city has a very lucrative and *legal* adult entertainment industry: strip clubs, escort services, massage parlors, and all that shit. A lot of underage girls are kept hidden behind closed doors in these places. Or the pimps use Craigslist to sell them, because it's safer for them than putting the girls on the street."

Bree shifted in her seat. "I doubt it's all that bad," she said.

Celia gave her a little smile. She knew Bree felt strangely protective of the South, especially Georgia, as much as she herself sometimes made fun of it. It was almost like the unspoken rule that you can say whatever horrible things you want about your own family, but other people's families are totally off-limits.

"It's terrible, actually," April said. "The sexual exploitation of women and children is the third-largest moneymaker for organized crime in this country, after guns and drugs."

"You're never going to end prostitution," Bree said. "I mean, hello, the oldest profession in the world and all that."

April looked disgusted. "Jesus, Bree."

"What?" Bree said. "Show me one country in the world that doesn't have it."

"I can't, but that doesn't make it right," April said.

"Tell them about that article you sent me on the Swedish model," Sally said.

Swedish model? Celia pictured a tall blonde former sex worker who now did *Vogue* pictorials.

"In Sweden, they've created a really successful model where the behavior of the pimps and johns is criminalized, but the prostitutes are decriminalized—they see them as victims, which makes it much easier for women to go to the police and all that," April said.

"Well, isn't that a little sexist, provided the women are of age?" Bree said. "I mean, why should the government regulate what women do with their bodies? Isn't it just a slippery slope to abortion rights and everything else?"

The lawyer in Bree was getting fired up. Celia held her breath.

"Jesus fucking Christ, I can't talk about this anymore right now," April said. "Anyway, I am going to Atlanta, so that's that."

"It sounds dangerous," Bree said.

"I agree," Sally said. "What does your mother think?"

"She thinks it sounds great, really interesting," April said. "I'm doing it. We start next week."

"I think it's a terrible idea," Sally said.

"Why? It's not any more dangerous than anything else we've done," April said.

"Exactly," Sally said. "And after some of the shit Ronnie's made you do, you're lucky to be alive."

"Ronnie never *made* me do anything," April said.

"Honey, open your eyes," Sally said. "The woman is an extremist."

April sighed. "An extremist? She's not fucking Al Qaeda, okay?"

Celia could see the hurt on April's face, so in a lame attempt at smoothing things over, she said, "Well, I'm officially jealous. You have a job that actually makes a difference. Unlike me."

"Oh shut up," Bree said. "You have an awesome job, too. Stop freaking out just because you're not Danielle Steel yet. You'll get there."

"Thanks," Celia said. "I hate Danielle Steel, but I appreciate the sentiment."

"Maybe you should just quit your job and become a full-time writer," April said. "Life's short. You have to chase what matters most."

Bree rolled her eyes at this, but Celia smiled. This was the sort of thing that April was always saying, and it sounded lovely in theory. But April never seemed to think about paychecks or savings accounts or retirement funds. She lived her life as though each day might be her last, exactly the way people vowed to live in that brief moment after a near-death experience (right before promptly starting to act like they always had before).

"I don't know—I tell myself I don't write because I'm stifled at work, because I'm surrounded by all these loser wannabe writers and their bad self-help books all day," Celia said. "But maybe I'm just lazy. Losers or not, if I'm not going to write it now, then when will I ever do it?"

"Speaking of losers, Celia, I was watching you at dinner tonight with that awful Anthony," Sally said. "Sorry about him."

Celia swatted her away. "I'm fine," she said. "And he did give me a key to his room for later." She grinned to say that she was just kidding, but part of her was considering it.

"Don't you dare," Bree said.

"He was sort of cute," Celia said. "At least after several glasses of wine."

"You really have to watch yourself with the drinking, Cee," Sally said, in that preachy voice she sometimes got. "Jake and I worry about you!"

"I'm fine," Celia said.

"But really," Sally said. "Jake and I will be sitting at home some nights just watching TV or whatever, and I'll think to myself, Oh God, I hope Celia's not up to something she'll regret in the morning."

Celia felt stunned.

"Well, excuse me for not wanting to be an old married woman yet," she said. "Unlike some of us, I'm still young and I still like to go out and have a good time."

"So just because I'm getting married, I'm suddenly the girl who killed fun?" Sally said.

"Yeah basically," Celia said. She inhaled. "Look, maybe

there was a time when we were always together and it was okay for us to have an opinion on one another's every move, but that time has passed."

"I don't see why it has to be like that," Sally said. "I feel like all of you have just sort of pulled away from me ever since I met Jake. It's like you're punishing me for finally being happy in love because you're not."

Bree snorted. "Sal, that is the most self-satisfied thing you've ever said. We're busy. We have lives."

"Besides, Bree's in love," Celia said.

"I know that," Sally said with a sigh. "I just feel like—oh, never mind."

"No, what?" Bree challenged. "You've had no problem being honest so far."

"I just look at me and Jake. He makes me happy. He makes my life better, easier. Whereas, Lara, well, you know I love her, but . . ."

"Bullshit," Bree said. "You guys have never even liked Lara."

"Hey!" April said.

"I wasn't talking about you," Bree said.

April looked hurt.

Sally went on. "I like Lara just fine, tulip. What I don't like is watching one of my best friends ruin her relationship with her family and constantly feel miserable just to make a point."

"A point!" Bree sputtered. "What point is that?"

"That this Lara thing is for real," Sally said in a whisper.

Bree shook her head. "What makes you think you can say that to me? We keep our mouths shut about how totally fucked it is that you would go off looking for Bill. We never say a word about how you're marrying Jake just to make up for what your family doesn't give you."

"Looks like you just did," Sally said. "Besides, you think I couldn't feel that coming off of you since I met Jake? I saw that e-mail, you know. The one where you and April said that Jake's a moron because he hasn't read Proust. He is the love of my life. And if you'd ever bothered to get to know him, you'd already know that."

Celia saw April's mouth open, and she could feel the words coming in a sort of slow motion: "Sal, we know you love him, we're just worried he's not good enough for you."

Celia gasped.

"How dare you?" Sally said.

"What?" April looked truly befuddled. "You're allowed to tell me that my whole career is stupid, but I can't tell you what I honestly think about your boyfriend?"

"No," Sally said. "You can't do that, you idiot. And he's not my boyfriend. He's my husband."

She got up from her chair. "Thanks for making my wedding so special, guys," she said. "I can't tell you how long I've been wanting us all to be together again."

"Sal, don't go. We love you," Celia said.

She looked at the others for support, but she could see that wedding or not, they had no interest in making up.

They walked back to the hotel in silence.

They had had fights before, plenty of them. Theirs was not an easy friendship or a guiltless one. They had high expectations of one another and were sometimes disappointed. But in the past, they could never stay mad for long.

That night in the dining hall was different. Instead of one feeling hurt by another and venting to the remaining two, this time they had all been wounded.

Celia stayed up until morning, rolling over the things the others had said, as April snored away in the bed beside her.

She kept thinking about mothers—Sally's mother, dead and gone. Bree's mother, once a dear friend to her and now a virtual stranger. April's mother, that sad, selfish type, who defied what the rest of them knew. And Celia's own mother, whom she loved, worshipped, missed every day, even though they talked on the phone most mornings before work. She was so lucky, she thought, to have a mother in her life now, just as she always had. This separated her from the others. She remembered the night she told her mother she'd been raped. Celia was two years out of college then, and it was Thanksgiving. They were drinking gin and tonics in the kitchen after all the relatives had left, picking stuffing out of a bowl, and her mother was telling her about a teenager from the parish who had been attacked at gunpoint by two grown men in the high school parking lot late one night. She had done everything they said, but they slit her throat anyway, and now she was in critical condition at Mass General.

"They forced her to have sex," her mother said, with tears in her eyes. "Oh Celia, can you imagine? The poor girl was just a baby. All of us in the Legion of Mary have been praying for her every day, and we'll keep praying every day until she goes home."

Celia never thought that she would tell her parents what had happened to her at Dartmouth, but the visions came flying back at her then, just as they did when anyone mentioned rape, or sometimes when she tried to have sex—the blue condom, Rob Johann's dark skin against her pale arms, the heaviness of his body on hers.

She whispered, "I was raped. Back in college."

Her mother pulled Celia toward her and wrapped her arms around her.

"What happened?" she said.

Celia told her everything. Her mother held her close and listened without saying a word.

"Don't tell Daddy," Celia said when she was done. "I think it would kill him."

Soon after, her sister, Violet, swayed into the room, not yet twenty-one and drunk on Merlot. The conversation came to a halt, but later that night, Celia's mother crept into her bed and said, "What can I do, baby? What can I do?"

For so many reasons, none of the others could know their mothers as adults, with honesty. And so, Celia thought, they were searching, always, for something to take the place of that bond. At Smith, they had all tried to mother one another. But what had once seemed like genuine care and concern had now turned ugly—they could not stop judging, comparing.

Of course, this was true of all women, mothers and daughters, too. What daughter didn't hold her mother up as a measurement of all she hoped to be, or all she feared? What mother could look at her young daughter without a bit of longing for her own youth, her lost freedom?

Once, in the car with her mother when she was just nine or ten, Celia had asked, not unkindly, "Mom, when I grow up, will I have fat thighs like you?"

Her mother had a shocked look.

"Probably," she said at last.

They laughed looking back on it now, but Celia thought it was a telling moment: A kid who thinks her mother is just that—*hers*. A mother who is also a woman, an independent being, who doesn't want to be reminded by anyone, child or otherwise, of her tree-trunk thighs.

The world made women's private lives a public affair to people who knew them and even people who didn't. Back in New York, acquaintances would ask, "So, do you have a boyfriend?" On the rare occasion that the answer was yes, they would immediately demand to know: "When are you getting married?"

If it weren't for the feeling that everyone was watching, pitying, judging, would she even care that Sally was getting married while she herself was still single?

The next day, for Sally's sake, they posed for pictures, ate cake, danced in the rain, and gathered in the hotel lobby for a champagne toast and a storm of kisses before sending her off on her honeymoon. But they were smarting from the night before. Their good-byes were strained and, for the first time ever, not altogether unwelcome.

On the bus back to New York, Celia thought of how, during her junior year at Smith, she had taken a master class in fiction writing with the famed novelist Harold Lance. The whole thing was rather ridiculous. Lance's career had peaked in the sixties, and he made no secret of the fact that he was only teaching because he needed the money: His latest book had flopped, he said, and recently, after one too many scotches, he had left a cigarette burning in his family's farmhouse in Sturbridge, which had sent the two-hundred-year-old building toppling to the ground.

His presence was met with much fanfare anyway. Caterers set up trays of cookies and tea sandwiches at the blackboard. A reporter from *The Boston Globe* came to sit in. The college president even stopped by to tell the class how very honored they all should feel to be studying with a living legend.

Five years later, it was still the sort of ultra-Smith experience that Celia would mention when she wanted to impress a cute former English major over drinks.

"God, Harold Lance changed my life," he would inevitably say, and Celia would just smile, because she had never really liked his work—it was too masculine, too painstakingly *male*, the female characters merely victims or martyrs or whores.

There was, however, one vital thing Celia had learned from Harold Lance, something that helped her frame a story whenever she sat down to write: *Any good drama or tragedy is like a ball of yarn, made up of so many strands piled one upon another,* he had said. *You should be able to unwind the ball, to see every bit, right down to the start.*

Later, Celia would think back on Sally's wedding weekend as the start and wish it had all been different. If only they could have changed the beginning, she thought, maybe what happened next would never have come to pass.

PART TWO

Spring 2007 Class Notes

CLASS OF '02

Ladies, I hear wedding bells. Chapin House alum Robin Austin writes, "I am engaged to Chase Phillips III! We are trying to plan a winter wedding while also studying for the Bar Exam." . . . Noreen Jones gushes, "I'm in love! Mike and I are getting married in May—and we're also expecting our first daughter in June." A future Smithie in the making perhaps? . . . In non-wedding news, Nicole Johnson writes, "Monique Hilsen, Mary Gallagher, Caitlin Block-Rochelle and I all met up for an unforgettable long weekend in Paris! It was great to feel the Gillette House love again!" Oui oui. . . . Susanna Martinson is putting that doctorate in art history to good use as a professor of Japanese painting in Kyoto. . . . And my personal hero, April Adams, is working on her fourth documentary with famed artist (and Smith grad!) Ronnie Munro, due out in 2009. Fellow alums, you continue to impress and amaze me. Keep those updates coming!!!

> Your class secretary,
> Celia Donnelly
> (celiad@alumnae.smith.edu)

SALLY

Sally usually went for a run during her lunch break, but lately every time she broke a sweat she felt exhausted and her head ached. So instead she had taken to sitting at her desk with her boss's copy of *The Boston Globe* and reading it over salad and iced tea. The world was an absolute mess, and reading about it made her think of April, out there fighting for change, so genuinely concerned about making women's lives better—women most people didn't give a fig about, women April herself didn't even know. Sally regretted what she had said to April at the wedding, but every time she thought of calling her, she remembered what April had said about Jake and was once again filled with anger. She could not believe that in the year since her wedding, April still hadn't apologized, that she had never so much as called to see how the honeymoon went.

It was the Tuesday after Memorial Day, and Sally was worn

out from the weekend. They had spent it with Jake's family on the Cape, sailing and swimming and drinking sangria out on the porch. Each evening she had hoped that they might sneak off to her father's place in Chatham, which she knew would be empty, but Jake was caught up in watching golf on TV with his uncles, or listening to them tell their same old stories, which Sally had heard ten times over, and she imagined Jake had heard hundreds of times. It didn't seem to matter. He laughed like a madman all the same.

While Jake and his dad and uncles sat around, Rosemary and her sisters gossiped in the kitchen as they made a steady stream of food—onion dip, Swedish meatballs, bacon-wrapped scallops, boxed brownies, and ice cream. It shocked Sally how the women in Jake's family served the men. Jake's sister attended grad school out in Colorado, and Sally wondered if she would have joined in if she were around. She realized now that her own mother had been the same way, though Sally had hardly noticed it back then.

She couldn't win. If she went and sat on the couch with Jake, she would look like a moping princess to his mother. If she stayed in the kitchen and listened to one more story about the best lobster roll Jake's grandmother ever ate, she predicted she might go outside and drown herself in the Atlantic. Sally settled for volleying back and forth, shuttling the trays of hot food out to the guys, drinking too much wine, and lingering longer than she needed to in the TV room.

Sunday night she drank six glasses of Rosemary's home-made sangria. On the drive back home the next day, Jake had to pull over four times so she could vomit out the car window. She hadn't been feeling right for a while. At first, she thought she was just sick and exhausted because she had her period. But then days passed, without any change.

"Do you think you might be pregnant?" Jake said, sounding a little too hopeful at the prospect.

"No," Sally said. "I haven't skipped a single pill since my first year of college."

She didn't want him to know how terrified she felt. She thought of her mother, misdiagnosed by a doctor she trusted with her life. Bad headaches could mean anything—dehydration or impending blindness, stress or a brain tumor. Sally had gone to the doctor the previous week for blood work and gotten into a fight with Jake in the car afterward, when she asked him whether he thought she ought to call her father and tell him she was sick.

"You know, just in case the results are bad. Maybe I should prepare him," she said.

"I'm sure it's nothing," Jake said. "Don't worry. You're going to be fine."

"You're not a doctor, honey," she said.

"Well, I know you, and I know you're okay."

Sally sighed. In her own personal religion—a mix of Episcopalian and superstition—telling a sick person that she was just fine was akin to wishing death on her. Right when you decided not to worry, *right then,* was when everything would unravel. It was far more sensible not to taunt fate and to always always expect the worst.

The lab stood empty today; really, the entire Harvard campus was like a ghost town. Her boss had taken the whole week off, Jill had gone to Ogunquit with her sorority sisters, and the student interns had gone home for the summer.

This meant that Sally alone was there to do the day-to-day lab work: running western blots, making solutions for cell cultures, rinsing old glassware and ordering more. But it also meant she was free to read the paper with her feet up on the desk and *The Immaculate Collection* in the CD player. Sally opened the paper, scanning page one as she took a bite of her salad. She always wanted to skip right to the "Living/Arts" section, but forced herself to read the real stuff first. The front page was nothing but bad news: *Twelve GIs Killed by Roadside Bomb Outside Baghdad; As Deadly As Ever, Avian Flu Proves a Persistent Foe; Worn Crosswalks Lead to Deaths.*

She sighed. Jake always talked about the importance of keeping up on current events, but she had started to think that the whole endeavor was overrated. She was about to turn the page, when a small teaser at the bottom caught her eye: *Noted Smith College Professor Dies at 61.*

She flipped to the obituaries, curious. There, on the front page of the section, was a picture of Bill, looking handsome and young. She recognized it as the jacket photo from his first volume of poems.

William Lambert, age 61, gained national notoriety in the midseventies with his fine poetry collection, *Five Seasons.* Born in Newton, he graduated magna cum laude from Harvard University, earned his master's degree at Columbia, and published three books of poems before his thirtieth birthday. *The New York Times* called him "Inquisitive, inspired, and melancholy—the perfect blend for a young poet." In 1978, he married Janice DuPree (they divorced last year) and moved to Northampton, where he served as a visiting artist at Smith College for two years before joining the staff as a full professor. He never published again, but he was a beloved teacher and mentor. Mr. Lambert died from complications of pneumonia, according to his son, William Lambert Jr. He also leaves behind two other sons, Peter and Christopher.

Sally had to read it twice before she could be sure of what she had seen. Bill was dead. Her Bill. She reached for the phone to call Celia, pressing the receiver to her ear. There was no dial tone.

"Hello?" a man's voice said. "Hello?"

"Hello?" Sally said, confused. Ridiculously, she wondered if it might be Bill, calling to say that he wasn't really dead, that it was all part of some elaborate plan for them to be together again.

"Is this Sally Brown?" the man asked.

"Yes," she said. "Who is this?"

"This is Dr. Phillips from Beth Israel."

"Oh, Dr. Phillips, I'm so sorry. I've just gotten some bad news and the phone didn't even ring, and—"

He interrupted her, sounding rushed. "Sally, I'm going to need you to come into the office this afternoon," he said.

She felt a weight drop into her stomach. Suddenly everything came into focus. This was exactly how it had gone with her mother. First the doctor called instead of some receptionist, then he told her to come to the office to hear her results, then the death sentence—cancer.

Sally couldn't breathe. "Am I going to die?" she said quickly.

"Oh God no, Sally, but we have some test results here that I'd like to discuss with you," said Dr. Phillips, in a warm, soothing voice. He knew all about her mother, and he wanted to make this news as easy as possible for her, she thought.

She started to cry. Her whole body shook.

"Is it cancer?" she asked softly.

"No. Absolutely not. Sally, just come by. How's four o'clock? I'll have Bridget put you into the computer."

Four o'clock was three hours away.

"Please," she said. "I'll come in no matter what, but you have to tell me what's wrong."

Her crying turned into a steady sob.

He sighed.

"All right. I wouldn't normally do this," he said. "And I still want to see you at four. But you're perfectly healthy. Stop crying! Sally, you're not sick. You're about three months pregnant."

She felt like she had been shoved hard from behind. The thought had crossed her mind, of course, but she had ruled it out.

"I'm on the Pill," she said. "And I've gotten my period."

"It may have just been spotting," he said. "That's fairly common. As for the Pill, have you skipped any nights?"

"No," she said. "Absolutely not."

The doctor chuckled. "Well, I guess this little girl or guy just felt like being born."

Sally clenched her jaw. Now she wanted to shove him.

. . .

As soon as she saw Jake that night, she started to cry.

"Honey!" he said, laughing and wiping the tears from her cheeks. "Why are you crying? This is cause for celebration."

"I can't have a baby," she said. "I just graduated from college for God's sakes."

"Sal, you graduated five years ago," he said.

She calculated this in her head, alarmed as ever by how quickly time had passed.

"But still," she said. "This wasn't supposed to happen now. This wasn't the plan."

Jake pulled her toward him. "Screw the plan. This is going to be the greatest thing ever. You'll see."

"How are you so calm, baby?" she said, feeling slightly annoyed.

She had fallen in love with him partly because he always stayed composed and controlled while she was flipping out. But sometimes his calmness just made her feel crazier. When she had been with Bill, she had always been the sane one. Bill. Her heart felt like it dropped two feet. Bill was dead. She wanted to say something, but it didn't seem like the right time to tell Jake.

"How else am I going to be?" Jake said. "I know we weren't expecting this right this minute, but we'll figure it out. I was an accident, and look how much my mother loves me."

Sally sniffled, smiling in spite of herself. "You were not," she said.

"Sure was," he said. "Rosemary told me once when she was a little tipsy. One too many Nantucket Reds at brunch."

"What did she say?" Sally said.

"She said, 'Ellen was planned to the minute. Jakie was a pleasant surprise.' "

Sally couldn't help but laugh.

Jake leaned down, lifted up her shirt, and kissed her stomach. "If it's a girl, I think we should name her Eleanor after your mom," he said softly, and Sally began to cry again, but this time because she had married such a sweet, sweet man, and she felt more grateful for that than anything.

She was supposed to attend a NOW board meeting after dinner, but Sally decided she'd have to cancel. What was she going to tell those women? She had been saying for years that eventually she was going to go to med school. As time passed, it seemed less and less likely, and was less of what she wanted anyway. But the women at NOW always looked so pleased and proud when she said it. Most of them were about the age her mother would have been, and they had fought long and hard so that her generation could do whatever they wanted. What would they think about this? A bright twenty-six-year-old who just happened to be married was one thing, but pregnant? Suddenly it seemed like dozens of doors were slamming in her face, doors she hadn't even cared about until today. She would never be able to backpack across Europe, not that she really wanted to anyway. She would probably never become a doctor.

Later that night, she called Celia to tell her the news. She was the only one of the girls who had tried to make amends after Sally's wedding, sending a handwritten note of apology that Sally had saved in a box full of Smith keepsakes in the linen closet. As the phone rang, she put her hand over her belly and felt for a kick. She knew it was still way too early for that, but she wished she could see some sort of sign besides a pink line on a pee-soaked stick. (Between hanging up with the doctor and going to his office three hours later, she had done four home tests in the bathroom at work, all positive.)

"I have big news," she said when Celia answered. "Huge news, in fact."

"Huge like you got a new outfit on sale at Banana, or huge like your whole freaking world just got turned upside down?" Celia said.

"The latter," Sally said. "I'm pregnant."

There was a long pause before Celia spoke again, and Sally tried to picture the facial expression she was making. She imagined Celia standing in front of the mirror in her apartment, mouth open wide, in a sort of *oh shit* pantomime.

"Okay, Sal, don't take this the wrong way," Celia said. "But is this good news or bad news?"

Sally exhaled. "Oh thank you for saying that, sweetpea. I have absolutely no clue. Good news, I guess. Jake seems happy."

"What about you? Were you trying to get pregnant?" Celia asked.

"God no," Sally said. "We just got married a year ago! I'm only twenty-six! And I'm on the Pill. I don't know how the hell this could have happened."

"Well, what are you going to do?" Celia asked.

"What do you mean?" Sally said, and then realizing what Celia meant, she blurted out, "Oh God, I'm keeping it—I hadn't even thought."

"Sorry," Celia said. "I don't mean to be unsupportive. If

this is what you want, you've got an auntie here, ready and waiting. It's just that you sound scared."

"I'm terrified," Sally said.

Suddenly she remembered why the Smithies were her best friends. She knew that in the days to come, she would tell dozens of people that she was having a baby (Jesus Christ, a baby) and that every one of them would coo and ooh with delight, because she was married, and when married women got pregnant it was cause for cooing and oohing. But only the Smithies would have the guts to make sure she was really happy. The girls were the place she could go and always find herself.

Suddenly, Sally remembered. "Bill died," she said. "Oh my God, with all the craziness of this day, I almost forgot."

"What?!" Celia gasped. "Jesus, Sal, first you tell me you're pregnant and now this? Are you just conducting an experiment to see how quickly I can go into shock?"

Sally laughed. "It's true. What a day, huh?"

After they hung up, she closed the bedroom door and decided to call April. She tried twice, but April's cell phone went straight to voice mail. Sally didn't leave a message.

Since her wedding, she had wondered if she would ever speak to Bree or April again. That night in the King House dining hall had driven home the realization that perhaps they had all grown so far apart that their friendships no longer existed, simple as that. It felt strange, like leaving a lover whom you had shared everything with. It was an active falling away, not accidental or situational like the end of most friendships. Even if they saw each other on the street years later or caught one another's eye across the room at a party, they might just look away as if the moment had never passed.

But now Sally realized that she couldn't leave it like that, especially with April. She needed her friends too much to let them slip away. Sally knew they could mend things if they tried.

That night, she dreamed of April. In Sally's dream, the two of them coasted dangerously down a mountainside in Capri (she and Jake had been there once, and ever since she often dreamed of the island's gorgeous villas and lush lemon trees) in a tiny car, with no doors, and Sally told April that they had to jump out or they would crash. But April refused. She wanted to see the fish at the bottom of the ocean, and she said this car could take her there. Sally didn't want to leave her, but at the very last moment, she jumped. Then she watched the car, falling down down down through the air and into the sea. April waved from beneath the water, and beside her Bill floated along, waving also, looking young— dark haired and bearded just like in the picture that accompanied his obituary.

Sally called April before work the next day and then again on her lunch break. Both times she got a recording, and when she tried to leave a message, a mechanical voice told her that April's mailbox was full.

BREE

Lara had been wanting them to have dinner at her boss's house all summer, but Bree kept coming up with reasons why she couldn't make it. She knew they were hanging by a thread these days, and that an evening with Nora and Roseanna could lead to the kind of fight that might do them in completely. But in July there came a Sunday night when nothing else was going on—no soccer games or late meetings or season finales on TV. Bree had no choice but to go.

Nora ran an after-school program for low-income kids, where Lara was the program director. Her partner Roseanna had made tons of money in Silicon Valley in her twenties and gotten out just in time. She now stayed at home with their six-year-old son, Dylan, who was currently enrolled in a summer day camp for tap dancing.

They lived in a ridiculous house in the suburbs—seven bedrooms and four baths, with a flagstone patio and a swimming pool out back, lined with a huge fresco of a lounging naked woman. They hung the rainbow flag from a pole in the front yard and drove matching hers-and-hers Priuses.

It was July, and lilacs bloomed in the back garden. The smell reminded Bree of her mother.

Over dinner, when Lara asked Dylan what he wanted to be when he grew up, Dylan looked thoughtful. "A fireperson," he said. "Or an astronaut, or an aesthetician or a doctor."

Fireperson? Bree thought. *Aesthetician?* Jesus. When her little brothers were six they had wanted to be dinosaurs.

"Why not all four?" Lara asked.

"Nooo!" he said, dissolving into giggles.

"No? Why not?" Lara asked.

"When would I sleep?" Dylan slapped his palm against his forehead, making the rest of them laugh.

After coffee and dessert, they brought their glasses of wine into the playroom while Dylan prepared to put on a show for them. Bree glanced around at his toys—a Barbie Dream House and matching pink minivan, a kitchen set with a pretend dishwasher, and a dress-up corner.

"It's really important to us that he be exposed to gender-neutral toys," Roseanna said.

Nora patted her knee. "Someday his future wife will thank us for raising a man who washes the dishes and knows how to cook a soufflé—a plastic soufflé, at least."

"I think that's great," Lara said. "Don't you think so, B.?"

"Huh?" Bree was pretending to be intrigued by an Angelina Ballerina book, and just then Dylan saved her from having to answer by jumping out from behind the door in a spangled purple cape. "The show's starting!" he said. "Mama, present me to the audience!"

On the train back to San Francisco, Bree gazed out the window, thinking about the night they'd just spent. She suddenly sputtered with laughter.

Lara looked up from her book. "What's funny?" she asked, brushing a strand of hair out of Bree's face.

"I was just thinking about Nora and Roseanna. They're such über-Smithies and they didn't even go to Smith. San Francisco really is Northampton West, isn't it?"

"What do you mean?" Lara asked.

"I mean, could they *be* any more gay?" Bree shook her head, laughing. "Gender-neutral toys? They're like a parody of themselves. And that hideous fresco. And the rainbow flag!"

"We have a rainbow flag in our kitchen," Lara pointed out.

"I know, but that's totally different. Ours is a wall hanging that we've had since college. Theirs is roughly the size of the Goodyear blimp."

"What's wrong with gender-neutral toys?" Lara asked.

"Nothing! But that kid's toys weren't gender neutral—it was all girl stuff! I bet you if they had a daughter, they wouldn't let her play with Barbies in a million years, you know? But here's poor Dylan, and it seems like a swell idea to load him up with pink plastic. His future wife will thank them? There ain't gonna be a future wife if he stays on this track."

"I think he's a really bright kid," Lara said.

"So do I." Bree laughed. "It's just—"

"Are you trying to pick a fight?" Lara said.

"No!" Bree said. "God, I thought you'd think it was funny too."

Bree knew there was a time when Lara would have laughed along with her. They had often joked over the years that they both came from the sort of Southern homes where political correctness goes to die. But lately things had gotten tenser than ever. It had started with Sally's wedding more than a year earlier and grown worse with every passing month.

"You know, you're so critical of my boss, but I've never even met anyone from your office," Lara said after a long pause.

She said it as if she had just thought of it, when in fact this complaint recurred on a near-weekly basis.

"The people I work with aren't like that," Bree said for perhaps the six-hundredth time.

"What do you mean? You all go out drinking together every week."

"Yeah, but people don't bring their significant others along. It's more for stress relief than bonding. It's like parallel play for adults."

"Do they even have significant others?" Lara asked.

Bree's coworkers at the firm were mostly single guys in their twenties and thirties, something she knew irked Lara.

"The partners are all married. But otherwise, I don't really know," Bree said.

"You don't *know*? How is that possible? You've worked there for two years!"

Bree shrugged. "Because we just don't talk about our personal lives."

Lara bit her lower lip. "So you're saying it's normal that none of them knows about me," she said.

Bree instantly felt terrible. "Like I told you, sweetie, that kind of stuff hardly ever comes up."

"I feel like you don't want me to meet them," Lara said. After a long pause, she added, "When are we ever just going to have a normal relationship?"

"Never," Bree snapped.

They rode in silence the rest of the way home.

In truth, she didn't really want her coworkers to know about Lara. When they all went out for beers after work on Thursdays, Bree actually put on makeup and flirted with her office mate Chris and their boss, Peter. She enjoyed feeling the appreciation of men once in a while. One night after too many margaritas, Chris told her he thought he had fallen for her. They ended up kissing in his car, though she never told anyone, not even Celia, because telling someone would make it real.

Bree had no idea why she had done it, and the guilt weighed heavily on her. When things with Lara were at their worst, she often thought back to their easy, happy days at Smith. Why couldn't they get back there again?

Some parts of their world accepted them as a couple—Lara's family and most of their college friends and the girls from their soccer team and book club. And some people just didn't get it—Bree's family and Celia to some extent, and, Bree assumed, the guys from work. She saw no point in shoving the relationship in their faces. Lara was out and proud of it wherever she went. But for Bree, it never felt that simple. She was in a lesbian relationship, but she was not a lesbian. She loved Lara, but could she really live in a house with a rainbow flag out front and raise sons who slept in canopy beds and played with baby dolls?

She realized that Nora and Roseanna were extreme—most lesbians they knew were pretty normal parents. She knew Lara wasn't asking her for a naked lady fresco, just for her commitment. But the older Bree got, the more conservative she felt, the more she understood and valued the very heteronormative (as April would say) way in which her parents had raised her. She had gone off to Smith and become a lawyer and found this person she loved, and yet a huge part of her just wanted to be home at night, cooking dinner while her husband read the paper at the kitchen table and the little boys played Tonka trucks at his feet.

On the Saturday following their dinner with Nora and Roseanna, Bree and Lara woke up early to go for a run. The night before they had had sex for the first time in two weeks, and they'd gone for a long dinner at a little French place in their neighborhood, drinking wine and holding hands, laughing at old stories, and flirting with the pretty Parisian waitress. These bursts of happiness never seemed to last very long, but each time they both hoped that maybe some spell had been broken and they would just be happy now, like old times.

As they headed out the door, the phone rang.

"Let it ring," Bree said, but Lara answered it, and then, looking puzzled, handed the receiver to Bree.

"It's Tim," she said.

Bree's brother was about to start his senior year of college. He had never gotten up before ten on a Saturday in his life. Besides that, they rarely corresponded except through e-mails—he would send Bree some inappropriate joke or a link to a disgusting video of a guy having sex with a horse, and she would write back telling him that he was probably going to get her fired if he didn't quit it.

"Timmy?" she said into the phone. He was breathing hard.

"Mom's in the hospital," her brother said.

He told her that their mother had had a heart attack while tending to her garden in the front yard. A neighbor saw her lift an enormous clay pot of tulips, and then suddenly collapse.

"Is she going to be okay?" Bree asked.

"We don't know yet," Tim said, his voice wavering. "She'll have to have surgery in a few days, once she's stable. I think you should come home."

Bree thought of how young he was. She should be making calls like this, not him.

"Of course," she said. "Tell Daddy I'll catch the first plane I can get. And tell everyone I love them. And Timmy, I love you."

He sort of grunted at that, and Bree smiled for a moment, thinking of him, goofy and unsentimental as ever. It felt vaguely comforting for some reason.

When she hung up the phone, she turned to Lara.

"My mom had a heart attack," she said.

"Oh sweetie!" Lara said. "How is she?"

Bree shook her head. "Tim said they don't know yet. I've got to get there."

She ran into the bedroom, pulled out Lara's old soccer bag from under the bed, and began filling it with clothes. Lara followed close behind.

"I'll book a flight right now," she said, and she wrapped

her arms around Bree. "It's going to be okay," Lara whispered. "Honey, it's okay."

"A heart attack," Bree said. "My mother? This is the kind of thing that should be happening twenty years from now. She's still so young."

"It's awful," Lara said.

A while later, Lara kissed her, then left the room and went to the computer to buy tickets. Bree sat down on the bed and thought of her father. He had met her mother in grade school and never spent a day away from her since. He couldn't do anything without her—tie a tie, or write a letter, or make a sandwich, or talk to one of his children about something important.

"Do you think we can make it to the airport for the nine o' clock?" Lara called from the den.

"We have to," Bree said, and just then she was struck by an image of her mother waking up to see the two of them standing over her together. She might have another heart attack right then and there.

On holidays and other occasions, Bree took a stand. She knew she couldn't be with both Lara and her parents, so she chose Lara. But this was different. Her mother needed her, the version of her that the family loved. She pulled her long hair over her shoulder, and then went to Lara. She knew this wasn't going to go over well, but what choice did she have?

"Baby, I think I need to do this solo," she said.

"What do you mean?" Lara said.

"I think I should go home alone. You know how they feel about us, and—"

Lara looked stricken. "You shouldn't have to be alone right now," she said.

"I won't be, I'll have my family there," Bree said.

"What if I just come and stay in a hotel by myself?" Lara said. "That way we wouldn't be sleeping in sin under their roof or anything."

Sleeping in sin. She had meant it sarcastically, and Bree found this enraging given the circumstances.

"I'm sorry, but I'm going alone," Bree said before she turned back into their room and finished packing.

Lara went into the bathroom and slammed the door.

Bree knew this habit of hers rankled Lara more than any other—her ability to make a decision and announce that there would be no further discussion was, in Lara's opinion, "Cruel and selfish behavior, the type usually enacted by men with small penises."

At the airport, Bree watched families pass through security and thought of how she had become an outcast in her own family five years earlier. The separation had been heartbreaking, and yet it had never seemed quite real to Bree. Now she was going home for the first time since leaving for law school. She wished it could be for any other reason.

Bree bought an enormous Hershey bar in the duty-free shop and started eating it square by square. This made her think of the way Sally used to nibble cookies like a mouse and, in turn, of how Sally had lost her mother at such a young age. If her own mother died, Bree thought, she would never forgive herself for these years of virtual silence they had wasted. For a moment, she wished Sally were there with her. They hadn't spoken in a year. Bree had not heard from

April either, but she heard of them through Celia, ever the peacekeeper. Bree kept meaning to call Sally, but she wanted to do it when she had good news to share, when she knew she could prove Sally wrong about Lara. Sally was pregnant now, five months along. Another mother born, Bree thought. She was hurt that Sally hadn't called her, that she had had to hear the news from Celia.

Bree felt tears forming in her eyes. She hated crying in public. She dug her cell phone out of her purse and called Celia, who always said the right thing. True to form, she sounded soothing but not patronizing. She didn't tell Bree not to cry or worry. She offered to come down to Savannah right away.

"Thank you, but I'll be okay," Bree said.

"Are you guys going to stay at your parents' house?" Celia asked.

"It's just me," Bree said. "Lara didn't come."

"Why not?"

"She wanted to, but I said no," Bree said. "I just thought it would be best to avoid all that family drama."

Celia grew silent.

"You think that's fucked?" Bree said.

"It's a really tough situation, and you should do whatever you need, sweetie," Celia said.

"But am I being awful to Lara here?" Bree said. "Come on, brutal honesty, please."

Celia sighed. "Look, you're my best friend, you're my priority. I'm not really concerned about whether you're being awful to Lara. I'm just thinking that one of the only reasons to have a significant other in the first place is so you don't have to be alone at times like this. If you're shutting her out now, well, then, what's the point?"

Bree didn't know how to respond.

"Listen, my plane's boarding," she said at last. "I'll call you when I land."

She hung up the phone and knew right away who she needed to call. Despite how long it had been, she dialed the number and listened to six rings, then seven. Finally, the machine picked up.

"You've reached the Browns!" Sally's recorded voice sounded tinny, but so so happy. "Leave a message for Sally or Jake after the tone."

Bree hung up.

A moment later, her cell phone rang.

"Bree?!" Sally said. "I was bringing in the groceries. I just missed you! What's going on?"

"It's my mom," Bree said, starting to cry.

She told Sally about her mother, about Lara. She asked about Sally's pregnancy, and Sally surprised her by sounding utterly unsentimental about the whole thing—she said that every morning she woke up feeling like she had thrown back a bottle of cheap tequila the night before.

Twenty minutes later, before she hung up the phone, Bree whispered, "I'm sorry for what happened at the wedding. And I'm sorry for not calling sooner."

"Love means never having to say you're sorry," Sally said dramatically, and they both burst out laughing, because of all the stock phrases in history, this one was the most ridiculous.

"Seriously, though, I'm sorry, too," Sally said.

"Thanks for making me laugh," Bree said.

"Anytime," Sally said.

At twenty-four, Bree's brother Roger had their father's long, lean body and dark hair. When she walked into the terminal in Savannah, he hugged her tight. Her brothers had visited her in San Francisco a few times, and each time she saw Roger he looked more and more like a man.

Bree's parents had never been to her apartment. It had been nearly six months since she last saw them, at a big family reunion in Tennessee. "Neutral territory, so hopefully World War Three won't break out," she had said to Lara, hoping she wouldn't ask to come along. She didn't, and when Bree saw her family alone like that, she felt overjoyed. Her father had kissed her cheeks. Her mother had held her hand like they were schoolgirls. She realized then that they still loved her, as much as ever.

"Oh, it is so damn good to see you," Roger said. Then, looking past her, he asked, "Where's L-Dog?"

L-Dog, Bree thought. As if the two of them were old poker buddies or something.

"She's not coming," Bree said.

He nodded. "Probably for the best, huh?"

Roger offered to take her to the house first for some lunch, but Bree wanted to go straight to the hospital.

"How's Daddy?" she asked, once they were in the car.

Roger shrugged. "I think he's in shock. Poor Tim had to call the ambulance and me and you. Dad is just kind of out of it."

"She's so young," Bree said.

"Fifty-two," her brother said, and Bree wasn't sure whether he was agreeing with her or disagreeing.

"Had she been sick?" Bree asked. Tears filled her eyes. What kind of daughter didn't know the answer to that question?

"No," Roger said. "Me and Emily were over there for a barbecue just last night."

"Emily?" Bree said.

"This chick I've been seeing," Roger said.

"Your girlfriend?" she asked teasingly.

"She wishes," he said with a grin. "Mama talked about you last night. She told Emily that she still makes her potato salad without paprika because when you were little, you thought it looked like red ants and refused to eat it."

Bree laughed.

"Anyway, Emily doesn't know anything about anything, so she asked when you were coming home again. Said she'd like to meet you. And Mama said she hoped you'd be coming home soon because she only has one daughter, and two smelly sons just don't cut it."

"She did not say that," Bree said with a smile. It was exactly the kind of thing her mother would say.

"Sure did," Roger said. "We've all missed you, but Mama most of all."

"Well then why the hell doesn't she ever call me or come visit?" she said, surprised to hear the words come out of her own mouth.

"You gave them both such a shock, Bree. You rubbed this new lifestyle of yours in their faces."

"That's absurd," she said. She hated when people referred to an actual life as a "lifestyle."

"Sleeping with her in your room all those times in college?" he said. "Pretending like y'all were just friends. And you never come home anymore. I mean, I know you're busy, but even at Christmas?"

Bree's hands formed two fists. "I live with my girlfriend, and she's not welcome in my parents' house. If I call them, they say two words to me and then hang up. What am I supposed to do?"

"I know, I know," he said. "I just think that if things had been handled differently, well—what the hell. Anyway, you're here now."

They were silent for a while, and then he said, "You know, they're real proud of you. Dad's always telling people that you're a lawyer out in sunny California."

Bree scoffed. She thought of the weekend, two years back, when they had come out to Stanford to see her graduate. Lara was hopeful that maybe it would be a turning point, but Bree couldn't stop thinking about her Smith graduation, about telling her parents she loved a woman in the middle of the Quad, and how they had reacted.

At Stanford, they lived in a cramped studio apartment, far too small for all their stuff. On the day Bree's parents arrived, Lara wanted them to come see the place. She had spent all week cleaning, making coffee cake, and buying flowers. But when Bree's family stepped into the apartment, her parents' eyes were drawn straight to the bed, stacked on one side with law books, and with back issues of *Sports Illustrated* on the other.

"I bet you can guess which one of us sleeps on which side," Lara said with a smile.

Bree's mother turned bright red.

At dinner after the graduation ceremony, her father made a toast. Roger, drunk on the ten or so beers he'd had over the course of the day, decided he should make a toast, too. When he had finished, Bree saw Lara begin to rise from her chair, and cringed.

"I guess I should say a few words, too," she said.

Bree's father looked aghast. Her mother excused herself and stayed in the ladies' room for twenty minutes.

After they dropped the family at the airport the next morning, Lara smiled at Bree and said, "Well, that was a shit show."

Bree wanted to scream. She wanted to ask why Lara had felt the need to point out again and again that they were a couple. She was livid with her family, too. Her mother, with that ridiculous escape to the ladies' room, as if she were a character in a goddamn melodrama. Bree was caught in the middle, and being driven mad by both sides.

Roger dropped her in the hospital's massive circular driveway and went to park the car.

"She's in room 481," he said.

Bree walked inside, inhaling shallowly in an attempt to avoid the stale medicinal smell of the hospital. She suddenly felt panicked about seeing her parents after all this time. She asked a white-haired security guard where the elevators were, and he pointed to a spot directly ahead of her.

"Duh," she said. "I'm out of it, I'm sorry."

"You're fine, dear," he said. He smiled warmly, making her want to cry.

This man must see dozens of people every day who were going through the worst time of their lives. She imagined him heading home at night to some Mrs. Claus–type wife, unloading his stories on her while she made hot cocoa. Or perhaps he was a widower who took comfort in this place, where so many others were experiencing the same sort of grief he was.

She went to the elevator bank. A moment later, the elevator doors in front of her opened, and a family stepped off. Bree looked down to see a little girl in a pink tutu and a sparkly purple bathing suit, with a cast on her arm and a baby doll dangling from her free hand. She had bright red pigtails and freckles across her nose.

Bree gave her a wave, and the little girl waved back with the two fingers not covered by the cast.

"I broked my arm at Madison's pool party," she blurted out in an adorable nasal twang.

"Oh my goodness," Bree said, looking upward to smile at the parents.

"Bree?" the man's voice said. "Is that you?"

Doug Anderson was holding a redheaded infant against his chest, with a cloth diaper draped over his shoulder. The last time they had spoken, she was calling him from her first-year dorm room at Smith to end their engagement. He had begged her to reconsider, but she had already made up her mind. At April's suggestion, she had even sent his ring back to him in a Jiffy envelope earlier that day so she wouldn't chicken out.

He looked exactly the same. He wore a Shooter Jennings

concert T-shirt and ratty jeans. He kicked at the carpet with his toe, and Bree could swear the last ten years had never passed.

"Wow Doug," was all she could manage to say.

By his side stood a petite redhead in a white wrap dress who reminded Bree of Wilma Flintstone.

"This is my wife, Carolyn. Formerly Carolyn Dempsey. She finished a year behind us at the high school," Doug said.

"Right, of course." Bree smiled and stretched out her hand, though she had no memory of the woman. She was just grateful that he hadn't married the little tramp who broke up their relationship, even though that unknown girl had probably done her the biggest favor of her life. "I'm Bree," she said.

"Oh, I know who you are," Carolyn said sweetly, in a particular Southern tone that Bree hadn't heard in years. Her brothers called it a razor blade in a spoonful of honey.

"And these are our children, Rose and Oliver," Doug said.

Bree did the math. He really hadn't wasted any time. She had to hand it to Doug. He was the kind of guy who wanted to be married with lots of babies, and he had gotten the exact life he'd always intended to have. She could not believe that they were the same age. There were so many ways to be twenty-six years old.

"So Bree, do you live in the area?" Carolyn asked.

"No, I live out in San Francisco," she said. "With my girl-friend."

What the hell, she thought. Doug raised his eyebrows.

"What are you up to these days?" Doug asked.

"I'm working at a firm out there."

"As an attorney?" he asked.

Bree nodded.

"And Stanford? Did that ever happen?"

She nodded, blushing. It was a sensation particular to women, she thought, to feel like a braggart just by stating a fact about yourself.

"Good for you," Doug said with a kind smile.

Bree shrugged. "How about you? Looks like you've had your hands full."

"That's the truth," he said. "I'm working in my dad's office now, as a sort of paralegal. I basically drive him to his golf dates and keep the coffee flowing. I'm still planning to get that JD one of these days."

Bree thought he looked a little embarrassed for a second, but then his face lit up. "You know, someday when I have more than ten seconds at a stretch to think, when I'm not chasing this little pumpkin around."

He ruffled his daughter's hair tenderly, a gesture that made Bree wish for just a second that they could go back in time, to the summers they had spent lying in the sun-scorched grass in his backyard, talking about all the babies they'd have one day. If things had been different, she would be in Carolyn's place right now. She didn't want that sort of existence, but there was something so attractive about the security of feeling like you had stopped moving toward your life, and actually arrived.

"You're pretty," Rose said. "Do you want to sign my cast?"

Bree laughed. "I'd love to."

She pulled a pen from her purse and bent down to write her name. She had woken up this morning with the intention of taking a run with Lara, going to the farmer's market for fresh avocados, making some guacamole, and spending the rest of the day watching baseball on TV. Now here she stood, three thousand miles away from where she had started, giving her autograph to Doug Anderson's daughter. This was officially the strangest day of her life. She suddenly wished Lara were there to see it.

"So is everything okay?" Doug asked.

For a moment she thought he was asking whether she felt okay with running into him like this, but then she recalled where they were and why she had come in the first place.

"My mother had a heart attack," she said. "I'm just on my way up to see her now."

"Oh God, I'm so sorry," Doug said. "Is there anything I can do?"

His wife shot him a venomous look, which she immediately tried to cover with a toothy smile. "Yes, please let us know if we can help. Don't be shy now," she said.

"No, it's okay," Bree said. "But I'd better get up there."

"Right. Well, great to see you again," Doug said.

"You too," she said.

The elevator doors opened, and she stepped inside, waving good-bye to Doug and his family, willing the doors to close fast.

When the elevator stopped on the fourth floor, Bree could hear her brother Tim's voice immediately. She followed the sound to a dim room at the end of the hall, and there they all were—her brother and father looking weary, her mother in a hospital bed, hooked up to an IV and a heart monitor, with a tube in her nose.

"Bree!" she said softly. "Angel, you came!"

"Of course I came," Bree said. "How are you feeling?"

"I'm okay," her mother said meekly. "Thank you, Jesus, I'm okay."

"Praise the Lord!" said Tim in a mocking preacher's voice as Bree went to hug her father.

"Hush!" her mother said. "It's no time to go angering Him."

"So what are the doctors saying?" Bree asked.

"She has a little recovering to do, but she's going to be fine," her father said. "In a day or two, they'll do the surgery, and a few days after that we'll take her home."

"What's the surgery?" she said.

"Bypass," her mother said, holding her hand to her forehead. "Triple bypass, Bree, can you believe it? No more pecan pie for this family."

Roger came in, then, his keys jangling in his hand.

"All of you, get together," Bree's mother said. "Go on, I want to take a picture."

"Honey, there's no camera," Bree's father said gently.

"Oh I know," she said. "I meant a mental picture. I want to see my whole family together again."

Bree's father and brothers huddled in around her, scrunching together so that they were crushing her from either side, just like they used to when they were kids.

"Oww!" she said, laughing.

"Stop that now, boys," their mother said.

Later, her brothers and father went to the cafeteria to investigate a rumor about red velvet cake that they had heard from another patient on the hall. Bree stayed behind. Her mother, groggy from the morphine, started talking nonsense on and off. It felt a little bit frightening to see her this way, but Bree tried as hard as she could to act normal.

"This one really scared me," her mother said. "You just go ploop, and then all of a sudden wheee."

"Right," Bree said as if this were the most sensible statement in the world.

"It's been a hard day's night," her mother said.

"Sure has," Bree said, smiling because although she knew her mother was just spouting words, these ones were fairly apt.

"I should be sleeping like a log," her mother said with a sigh.

Her face turned sad for a moment. She said, "You know what? You should have fought us. Fought, fought 'til the death. Here's a secret: You would have won."

"What do you mean?" Bree asked, wanting to hear more, but her mother closed her eyes and fell asleep.

After everyone had gone to bed that night, Bree crept out onto the front porch to think. Her parents had seemed so happy to see her, and yet they hadn't even asked about Lara. It was their way, she thought, of telling her that she could have all this back again if only she would give Lara up. They were her family, and she loved them, but how could they ask her to make a choice like that?

It was a hot, sticky July night. Purple clouds of Spanish moss dripped from the trees and glistened in the moonlight. Savannah was her true home, and still the most beautiful place she had ever been. Bree tried to imagine walking hand in hand with Lara down Congress Street, pushing a double stroller in the sunshine. She shook her head. Impossible.

A pair of headlights shone in the distance, the first she had seen all night. It was only eleven o'clock, but this neighborhood went to sleep early. The car came closer, an old Volvo station wagon. When it reached her house, the driver pulled over and stepped out, closing the door gently. Bree squinted in the darkness to see if she could make him out as he walked toward her.

"Heya," Doug said. "Fancy meeting you here."

"Hi," she said, rising to hug him. "This is a surprise."

"Not a bad one, I hope," he said. "I was picking up diapers for the baby at the Rite Aid down the road, and I thought I'd drive by and see if y'all were home and needed anything."

"That's sweet of you, thanks," she said.

They sat down side by side on the porch steps. He asked after her mother, and Bree gave him the update. They talked about Doug's parents, and his brother who was in rehab for cocaine addiction, though most people outside the family thought he had gone to fantasy baseball camp. Then there was an uncomfortable moment in which neither of them knew what to say.

"Wow," she finally said with a laugh. "Look at you."

"Look at *you*," he said. "You're like a totally different person."

"How so?" she said, though of course she knew.

"Well let's see," he said with a grin. "When you left here nine years ago, you were a good Southern girl who wore her homecoming-queen crown around the house for fun. You were obsessed with makeup and magazines. Not to mention, you were engaged."

"To you, as I recall," she said.

Was she actually flirting with her high school boyfriend?

"That's right," he said. "You broke my heart, lady."

"I broke *your* heart?" she said, raising an eyebrow.

"Of course," he said. "I could tell as soon as you got to Smith that I'd lost you to that coven of gals you lived with. You still talk to them?"

She smiled. "Yes. They're my best friends."

"Anyway," he said. "Not that it matters to you one bit anymore, but I wanted to say that I'm sorry for what I did. Really sorry, Bree. I panicked and I felt like things with us weren't what I thought they'd be, and I just reached for something—"

"Uncomplicated," she said, thinking of that stupid kiss with Chris from the office.

"Right," he said.

She waved this away with her hand. "Really, truly, it's okay," she said. "We were just kids."

She found with surprise and relief that she meant it: She wasn't angry with him. All of that seemed like a million years ago now. It amazed her how you could long for a certain conversation, an apology, and then, by the time you got it, feel like you didn't need it anymore.

"Speaking of kids," she said, "I cannot believe you're a dad."

"Me neither," Doug said. "I know everyone says this, but in my case it's the truth—I have the awesomest kids ever."

"The *awesomest*?" Bree laughed.

"All right, Miss Smith Stanford. Whatever the word is. Kids are amazing. The first few months, they're just like these loaves of bread that shit. You're wondering what the hell you got yourself into. But then, they turn into people. It's the most incredible thing I've ever seen."

"Loaves of bread that shit," Bree repeated. "What a beautiful thought."

He gave her a playful shove. "Get outta here, you know what I mean."

"Honestly, I think you're remarkable," she said. "Lara and I wanted to get a puppy last year, but ultimately decided we weren't ready for the commitment."

"That your lady friend?" he asked.

Bree nodded. "Yeah. I'm surprised you haven't heard about it all over town."

"I may have heard a thing or two," he said. "There might have been some mention of how I turned you gay. I can't really remember."

She grimaced. "I'm sorry."

Doug winked. "Don't worry about it," he said.

"Well, don't you want to ask me about her?" she said.

Doug shook his head. "It sure was weird to hear you say it earlier, though. *My girlfriend.* Wow. I thought Carolyn's head might pop off. Anyway, back to the baby thing. I think we're just different sorts of people, me and you. You're a planner. Everything has to be perfectly aligned before you make a move, or you're afraid the whole damn world will come crashing down. For me, it's more like, 'We're having a baby. Now what?' "

Bree laughed. "I envy you that."

"Maybe it makes things easier," he said with a shrug. "Not so much analysis."

"I think you're right," she said. "Three-quarters of my adult life has been spent analyzing. It gets exhausting."

She wondered what might have happened if she had simply demanded that her parents try to adjust to her life. *You should have fought us,* her mother had said. What if she had insisted on bringing Lara home at the holidays, on making her a part of the family? Would it have worked? She should have let Lara come along this time. Maybe it wasn't too late. Maybe she could fly out tomorrow. Roger would pick her up at the airport, show her around town.

Even as she pictured it, Bree knew it wouldn't happen. She still didn't have the guts to take the risk.

"So is Carolyn a planner?" she asked.

"She's a cruise director without a boat," Doug said. "She keeps our house running like a military barracks. With love, of course." He smiled.

"Well, of course," Bree said. "Does she stay home with the kids?"

He nodded. "She's great at it."

"What did she want to be, you know, before she had them?" Bree asked.

Doug shrugged. "A mom?" he said.

He gazed out over the yard. "I drive by here sometimes when I get stressed. Not in a creepy way. I just like to remember how easy it was for us back in high school, how much fun we had. And I think about these big dreams we always talked about. You made them come true for yourself, Bree. I'm proud of you."

"No matter what you choose, you have to give something else up," she said. "You have a wife, kids, a house, a goddamn Volvo. I can't tell you how far I am from all of that."

"Speaking of my goddamn Volvo, I should get going," Doug said. "Carolyn might think I've joined a biker gang or something."

Bree laughed. "Before you go, can I ask you a question?" she said.

"Ask me anything," he said.

"Would you let your son play with Barbies?"

"Hell no," he said without even thinking. "Would you give your cat a big ol' bone to chew on?"

"That's what I thought," Bree said.

He kissed her on the cheek, and they said good-bye, and she thought of how she would probably never see him again, not unless they ran into each other somewhere in town.

After he drove off, Bree went to her childhood bedroom, still decorated with pink ballet slippers and rosy chiffon curtains. She crawled under her comforter and called Lara. The phone in their apartment rang four times, then five, and Bree wondered if maybe she had gone out with friends.

But then she heard Lara's voice at the end of the line.

"Hi, sweetie," she said.

"Hi," Lara said. "How's your mom doing?"

"She's stable, which is good."

"Oh, thank God. Give her my best. Or don't, if that's easier," Lara said. "I was really worried. I wish you had called me sooner." The edge in her voice surprised Bree.

"It's been mayhem here," Bree said. "Oh my God, guess who I ran into. Doug Anderson! I saw him at the hospital with his wife and kids, and then he stopped by tonight."

"He stopped by?" Lara asked. "Huh." She paused for a moment. "Do you want me to call work for you, or anything? Or I can still come out there if you want."

"No, no," Bree said. "You really don't have to. I don't want to trouble you, babe."

"Whatever," Lara said.

"Are you mad at me?" Bree asked, indignant. She knew things had been rough between them, and maybe she was largely to blame. But her mother had just had a heart attack, for God's sake. She didn't need this now.

"I just don't know what I mean to you," Lara said.

"What are you talking about?" Bree said.

"Ever since we left Smith, I've been waiting for you to come around and be open about us to the people in your life. I kept thinking that if I just stayed patient, you'd get comfortable eventually. But I know now that's never going to happen."

"That is so unfair," Bree said. "Why are you mentioning this now, of all times?"

She could hear Lara starting to cry. "I know it's a terrible time, with your mom being in the hospital. And I would give anything for it not to be this way. But I can't do this anymore."

"Baby!" Bree said. "You don't mean that."

"I do," Lara said. "This isn't getting better. I just feel like it's over. Really over, you know? Your mother has a heart attack and you don't want me to be with you? You don't even call me, but you have time to hang out with your former fiancé? That's not the kind of relationship I want."

Bree felt panicked. "Oh come on, my former fiancé? We were just kids. And it's not like we went out for burgers and beers! He just came by the house for a minute."

Lara was silent.

"After eight years, you're just going to call it quits like that?" Bree said. "And right when I need you most?"

"I love you," Lara said. "I think you're probably the love of my life. But let's face it. I'm not the love of yours."

She hung up. Bree tried to call her right back, but Lara just let the phone ring and ring. When she arrived home a week later, Lara had moved out.

CELIA

Celia was certain that Manhattan in summertime was the closest approximation to hell on earth. The air grew thick and heavy with heat, the streets reeked of garbage, air conditioners dripped their murky water onto her cheeks, and her hair became an untamable disaster.

It was July, the middle of her fifth New York summer. This one was particularly excruciating because Kayla, her office mate and friend of four years, had gotten engaged over Memorial Day weekend. Overnight, their discussion topics had gone from gossip and politics to centerpieces and flower girls and the virtues of the Kleinfeld bridal super-store over the snooty Vera Wang boutique on Madison Avenue.

Celia felt proud that the city hadn't changed her much. Her New York friends did things that she and the Smithies had never done, like snort cocaine, talk seriously about dieting, give the evil eye to people who brought children into restaurants, follow the lives of celebrities with genuine interest, and buy single items of clothing that cost more than a week's pay. She now added "get frenzied about weddings" to the list.

After a week of Kayla's wedding talk, Celia called Sally to thank her for not being a bridezilla.

"Oh *really*?" Sally said playfully. "I thought you all thought I was kind of a bridezilla."

"Well, we did," Celia said. "But that's because we hadn't seen the alternative yet."

One afternoon, Celia and Kayla ate lunch at the crowded sandwich place downstairs from their office. Behind the counter, fat men in white T-shirts made Philly cheese steaks and chicken parm subs, while sweat dripped down their doughy faces. Young guys in suits dabbed at their foreheads with cheap paper napkins, and women gave up the ghost and tied their hair back in high ponytails. Kayla didn't seem to notice a bit of it. Her face was radiant and dry; her blonde bob fell neatly against her shoulders, causing Celia to wonder whether engagement was so powerful that it even affected sweat glands.

"By the way," Kayla said. "I went to a Mets game with Marc and his boys from the firm last night. There was this one really cute guy. I was thinking maybe we could go on a double date sometime."

Celia shrugged, trying to banish the thought that no one had gone on a double date since 1953.

"Sure," she said. "Set it up."

"I know this probably sounds selfish, but I want you to have a great date for my wedding," Kayla said.

She was right, Celia thought. It sounded totally selfish, and stupid as well.

"And who knows," Kayla went on. "Maybe you and this guy will hit it off and end up married."

"I honestly don't know if I'll ever get married," Celia said, mostly as a means of changing the subject.

Kayla edited the memoirs of retired right-wing senators and pundits, but she was a die-hard liberal who had majored in political science at Williams and hoped to work on truly important books someday. Celia wanted to ask her what she thought of Nancy Pelosi's latest speech, one of her first since becoming Speaker of the House, but Kayla went on.

"Oh sweetie!" she said. "Of course you'll get married. Girls like us always get married. You'll find someone, I promise."

Celia took in a long, deep breath. "I don't mean that I won't find anyone," she said. "I mean, maybe I don't want to get married."

Kayla's eyes grew wide for a moment, and then she broke into a smile. "We all have those moments of doubt before we meet the right guy," she said. "You'll see."

Celia didn't say so, but she was thinking of how her mother's friends kept getting left by their husbands for much younger women.

"Are you ever afraid Daddy would do that?" Celia had once asked her mother.

"God no," her mother said. "Because he knows I'd shoot him."

Marriage wasn't security, as Celia had always thought. Nor

did it necessarily mean happiness. When her mother and aunts visited New York, they'd ooh and ahh over her studio apartment, and the envy in their eyes looked exactly the same as the way her single friends looked when they saw some girl with a giant engagement ring registering for china at Bloomingdale's.

She had met plenty of women in Manhattan who freely admitted that they were only working as a way to pass the time until they got married. It seemed like something from a bad black-and-white movie, something from a million years ago. And yet, there they'd be—at parties and friends' birthday dinners and in the bathroom line at bars. They were usually tiny and pretty, and almost all of them worked in marketing, so that Celia began to think "marketing" was actually just code for single and seriously looking.

"My job's just not the be-all end-all," they'd say. Or "There's not really anything I want to do as much as I want a family."

Celia remembered a phone conversation she had had with April a few months before Sally's wedding.

"These fucking women really piss me off," April said. "Because instead of being elated by the thought of making their own happiness and chasing some crazy dream, all they want to do is narrow their options and do something safe."

"I sort of feel the same way, but wasn't the women's movement about choice?" Celia said. "So shouldn't we respect their decision?"

"What decision? The decision to make no decision at all?" April seethed. "The decision to play out some bad nineteen-fifties fantasy?"

"Oh wow," Celia had said. "I'm gonna need you to recite the Hippocratic oath every day until Sal gets married, and apply it to your role in her wedding."

"How so?" April said.

"First do no harm."

As usual when it came to April, Celia saw her point but suspected that for most women it wasn't all that simple. She occasionally looked at expensive real estate online, fantasizing about writing novels in a Brooklyn brownstone or on a farm in the Catskills. She had known what she wanted to name her children (Ella, Max, Charlie) since she was eleven and had never once wavered in that decision. At Sally's urging, she opened a 401(k) as soon as she started her job, and she had checked its status every Monday morning for the past five years.

So many aspects of what she wanted out of real life were clear to her, but for some reason it was hard even to imagine having a husband. Celia had never managed to feel as comfortable around a man as she did around her friends, and this seemed a fundamental problem. If she was going to spend her life with someone, shouldn't he make her feel completely herself? Shouldn't she be able to bring him home to her crazy, boisterous family and expect him to love them as much as she did? Shouldn't she be able to share her love of Frank Sinatra and old movies, her extreme clumsiness, or her total aversion to museums, without worrying that he'd find her silly or strange or uncultured?

It wasn't their fault, but around men who interested her, she always turned into Celia Version 2.0—similar to the real thing, but not quite as sharp or fully formed. She lost her ability to make a joke or be sarcastic. She couldn't develop an argument the way she could with the girls, and she was positively undiscerning when it came to whom she found attractive or interesting. She knew that Smith was partly to blame for her troubles in this area. During her four years there it had been virtually impossible to meet a man, and when she did she was not looking for a soul mate or a debate partner—she already had that in her friends. Men were simply for decoration, dissection, and making out.

The mentality had stuck with her ever since. She had a theory that women's college grads were like people who had lived through the Depression—even though they now had plenty of food, they still hoarded every last scrap. When she met a guy, any guy, she was too willing to accept his flaws because who knew where her next meal was coming from? But it was one thing to date losers, and another thing entirely to marry one.

When her friends began to get engaged, instead of feeling jealous or antsy to do the same, Celia realized something: There was a very real possibility that no one was coming to save her. She would have to make her own plan. If she wanted to someday leave her job and write books, then she'd have to write books to do it, not wait around for some hedge fund guy to finance her fantasies. When she felt ready to have kids, she wanted to have them, regardless of whether or not she had found lasting love.

It was hard for girls like Kayla and Sally to understand this—Celia got the sense that they thought she was just putting on a brave face to mask her disappointment and fear of being alone. But what scared her far more than loneliness was the thought of waking up one day and realizing that she had attached herself to the wrong person, out of fear or pressure or God knows what. As a result, she had decided to view men as fun and nothing more, at least for now.

The night of her lunch with Kayla, Celia went out with friends and met a film producer named Daryl. He was thirty-two years old and a bit chubby, but not altogether unattractive. They were at a trendy bar on the Lower East Side, and he asked her if she wanted to take a walk. Hand in hand, they traversed the streets, and (only slightly drunk) she thought it was actually sort of romantic.

They stopped somewhere for a game of pool and shots— Jameson for him, and lemon drops for her. He knew a lot of people in publishing. He made her laugh with his pitch-perfect impressions of various writers and editors, and he had great taste in books. She took him home to Brooklyn, where they had brief but enjoyable sex on the sofa. He was gone before she woke up.

This was what a lot of New York men did. They fucked you and then left before breakfast, which was fine by Celia. She had emerged pretty much unscathed so far. There had been one terribly embarrassing case of chlamydia, which she prayed would stay away for good (while realizing that of all the things one could pray for, this would probably piss God off the most). And then there was the morning she woke up covered in her own blood, horrified for an instant before blurrily remembering what had happened—he was the singer in the band, they made out in a phone booth, she said he could come home with her, but then remembered that she had her period.

"It's cool," he said. "That's kind of my thing."

"He should have at least stayed to help you wash the sheets," Sally said the next day, when Celia told her the story. Celia could not think of anything more mortifying than washing her bloody sheets with last night's one-night stand.

After Daryl had gone, Celia took a long shower and then pulled her hair up into a wet ponytail. He was the fifteenth man she had slept with in her life, though she had stopped her official count at ten, and always reported her number as such when asked. Most of her friends' numbers topped out at seven. If she didn't meet the right guy soon, she was in very real danger of hitting twenty. At Smith, they never used words like "slut"—it still shocked Celia to hear people say it. But twenty sex partners. Wowsa. She knew for a fact that her mother had slept with only two men in her life: her father, and a college boyfriend who later became a priest.

Celia dressed, drank a cup of coffee standing up at the window, and then made her way to the subway. Her head throbbed. She could have done without the shots.

High Street station felt like a brick oven. She was already beginning to sweat through her linen top.

The A train came quickly, as it always did at rush hour. Celia stepped into the crowded car and sucked in the burst of air-conditioning. She closed her eyes as the train screeched to its next stop. Outwardly she was a very peaceful person. But the rage she felt daily on the New York City subway hinted at the possibility that the only difference between her and those raving-mad homeless people in the car was that she knew enough to keep quiet. All types of train behavior bugged her, and she liked to fling silent insults at passengers accordingly.

To the sleazoids who unabashedly stared at her breasts: *You're sweeping me off my feet here. Wanna get off the train and screw?*

To the Wall Street douche bags in pinstripes who sat down and then hid behind their copies of the *Financial Times,* so as not to see the standing pregnant women and old ladies with canes and young assistants teetering in stilettos: *Attention, passengers! Is every able-bodied man sitting comfortably? Well thank fuck for that.*

Today she had managed to get a seat on her own, leaving her relatively unannoyed. Celia watched a very Brooklyn mother (long straight hair with bits of gray mixed in, toned calves and arms, Birkenstocks) trying to negotiate with her two-year-old, coaxing him to sit down as he writhed about, nearly knocking out his teeth on the metal arm rail.

"How can I help you, Luca?" his mother kept saying in a loud, breathy voice.

How can I help you, as if she were his waitress at T.G.I. Friday's instead of his goddamn parent. This was one of a million reasons why Celia would never raise children in the city: parenthood as performance art. She wanted to reserve the right to tell little Luca to sit his butt down if he ever cared to see the Teletubbies again, without the fear that twenty-nine strangers might call Child Protective Services.

The train rolled past Thirty-fourth Street, where tourist families with fanny packs and matching smiles piled into the car. Their blond children held on to the poles, swaying this way and that, thrilled by every jolt and bump of the train. Celia thought for a moment of how strange it felt to simply live—to work, and go to the gym, and buy groceries, and wait for trains—in a place where so many people were visiting and in awe of their surroundings.

She got off at Forty-second Street, smiling at a pair of twins in a double stroller boarding the train with an older black woman, probably the nanny.

Most people who lived in New York hated Times Square, but she loved watching strangers discover the bright lights and larger-than-life everything. It gave her a little thrill to see them having the time of their lives while she was just trying to get to her desk before ten.

Celia made her way through the crowds on Eighth Avenue. Her heels were killing her. She wished she had thought to bring flip-flops.

She was twenty minutes late. Inside her building, the air-conditioning roared. She walked past the security desk, saying good morning to the guards, and then pressed the elevator button repeatedly.

The doors opened, and she rode up to the seventeenth floor, praying that her boss had remembered his nine o'clock eye doctor's appointment and was still reading the *National Review* in a waiting room somewhere uptown. (*Hail Mary, full of grace . . .*) He had warned her about being late too often, even though he himself regularly rolled in after lunch.

She poked her head into his office. The lights were still off. She breathed a sigh of relief, and went to her cubicle.

Kayla hadn't arrived yet. Her desk was covered in little swatches of lace—*Veil possibilities!*

Celia rolled her eyes at the sight of them.

Her phone was already ringing, and she picked it up in a rush.

"Celia Donnelly," she said.

At the other end of the line, Bree struggled to get words out.

Celia's stomach flipped. Bree's mother had died; she was sure of it.

"Honey," she said weakly. "What's wrong? Is it—"

"I called you twenty times last night," Bree snapped. "Why don't you ever pick up your goddamn cell phone?"

"I'm so sorry," Celia said. "My battery died."

In truth, she had seen Bree's calls come in and ignored them. She was out at a noisy bar and figured she could call back later. Now, thinking clearly, she realized how selfish that had been. But Bree had told her that her mother was fine. The surgery had gone well, and Bree was supposed to have flown home to California the night before.

"Is it your mom?" Celia whispered.

"No." Bree gulped. "Lara left me."

"What do you mean, she left you?"

"I mean she's gone. All her stuff is gone. She took the sheets off the bed and everything. Her toothbrush. All of it."

Bree had told Celia a few days earlier that they had been fighting and that Lara was ignoring her calls. Celia thought it was selfish of Lara considering the situation with Bree's mom, but she had never imagined this.

"Did she leave a note?" she asked.

"No," Bree said. "She left a check for this next month's rent and that's it."

"Jesus," Celia said. "Well, have you called any of her friends?"

"Her stupid schmuckie work friend Jasmine, who, by the way, is totally in love with her, told me she's safe and happy but just can't be near me right now. Can you imagine? My mother could have died and I'd have no way of telling her."

"Oh, baby," Celia said.

"I can't handle this," Bree said. "First my mother and now Lara. I called work this morning. I told them I'm taking three more weeks off."

"Can you do that?" Celia asked.

"No, but I've worked my ass off for that firm, and I deserve it. Plus, I told them it's for my mother. They think I'm still in Savannah."

"Isn't that bad luck?" Celia said. She would never dream of telling a lie that involved the health of a loved one. In her mind that was just asking for tragedy, begging for it, in fact.

"I love my mother, but right now I'm so mad at my parents I could scream," Bree said. "They're the reason I'm in this position in the first place."

"Well, what if someone from work sees you?" Celia asked.

"I'm not planning on staying around here," Bree said. "Would you mind if I came and stayed with you?"

"Of course not," Celia said.

She adored having her own space in her small two-room apartment in Brooklyn Heights. The thought of sharing it with almost anyone horrified her. But Bree was different. She could move right in with her insanely huge shoe collection, and Celia would be happy to have her, luggage and all.

"But you hate New York and it's two hundred degrees here right now," Celia said.

"Yeah, but I need to see you. Oh, Celia. Why the hell did I treat her so badly?"

Celia paused, unsure what to say. She had always thought

that if they ever broke up it would be because Bree had finally caved to her parents, or met some guy. She never pictured it this way, with Lara leaving Bree and breaking her heart.

"Just get here," Celia said. "We'll figure it all out."

Bree arrived the following afternoon.

They ate an early dinner at a tiny Italian place on Cranberry Street and drank a bottle of red wine. Afterward, they got into Celia's bed and talked.

"I know you're not her biggest fan, but I should call Sally," Celia said after a while. "I think this whole pregnancy thing has her really scared. I've been meaning to go visit her up in Boston, and she's called me a few times recently, but I haven't called back. Suddenly I'm having major Catholic guilt about screening phone calls."

"Didn't I tell you? We made up," Bree said.

The day they flew home from Sally's wedding, Celia called Bree and said, "Wow, that was kind of a disaster. Let's analyze it to death." They laughed. Celia said she felt terrible for adding that sour note to the occasion, and Bree said she hoped Sally choked on a piece of leftover wedding cake.

Celia had been overcome with guilt, and at her mother's suggestion, she had written long letters to Sally and to April, asking for forgiveness, saying that she loved them more than anything in the world. Bree had chastised her for making amends with April and Sally, but Celia knew that eventually they would all come back to one another in their own ways. And in the meantime, she got to hear each of them trash the others.

"Should I tell her you say hi?" Celia asked now.

"Of course," Bree said.

Celia smirked. "I knew you two would get back together eventually."

"She's a judgmental little weirdo sometimes, but she's my judgmental little weirdo," Bree said. "Sally was right about me and Lara, wasn't she?"

Celia started to respond, but stopped herself. It seemed too late to say that, more and more lately, she had been remembering how in love they were in college, and thinking that Lara was good for Bree, that she still loved her, and maybe Bree just needed to take that leap.

"She wasn't right about that, but I think we need to love her anyway," Celia said finally.

Sally picked up on the first ring.

"How are you feeling, babe?" Celia asked, without saying hello.

"Awful," Sally moaned. "I can't stop throwing up. Everything hurts. Even my gums and my eyes are sore. I had to stop wearing my contacts and put on my hideous glasses from college. I look like a fat Harry Potter. And I'm peeing like every five seconds."

"Is that normal?" Celia said.

"I guess so. The doctor says it's all just part of pregnancy," Sally said. "Have you heard from April recently? I've been calling her for weeks. She doesn't even know about the baby."

Celia thought about this. It had been months since they had spoken.

"I only talked to her once, in the spring sometime," Celia said. "It's weird. I get the impression that freaker Ronnie doesn't really let her talk on the phone."

They talked about Celia's job and dates and Sally's new kitchen furniture, and Celia thought of how vastly different their lives had become. Sally and Jake had built a goddamn deck the previous fall, while Celia pondered whether or not to waste money on a new dish rack after finding mold all over the bottom of her old one.

Finally, Celia said, "I have a mystery guest here who wants to say hi."

Bree took the phone from Celia. "Sal?" she said. "It's me."

That night, before they fell asleep, Celia whispered to Bree, "We need another reunion. Just the four of us."

Bree yawned. "I'm game," she said. "I guess we can't stay mad forever. We're Smithies, after all, and Smith is thicker than water."

Celia snorted. "That is so dorky," she said.

"I should e-mail April," Bree said. "I guess I could have been more supportive about that crazy project of hers."

Celia laughed. "That doesn't sound very supportive."

"Oh, you know what I mean," Bree said. "How is she anyway?"

"I honestly get nervous that she's going to crack," Celia said. "She's just around all this awful stuff all the time now. Pimps and prostitutes and God knows what. I really don't understand why she has to live among these people to make a film, you know?"

"I know," Bree said.

Changing the subject, Celia said, "Are you friends with

anyone in California who just wants to get married and then sort of drop out of life?"

"What do you mean?" Bree said. "Like move to a commune or something?"

Celia laughed. "Uhh, no. Like quit their jobs and just be married."

Bree paused for a moment, thinking this over. "I went to high school with tons of girls like that," she said. "But everyone I know in California is a lawyer or a lesbian. Neither one of those groups tends toward the stay-at-home-mom thing. I remember the night I first met you at Smith, and you told me what your mom does. You sounded so proud of her. I wanted my kids to talk about me like that someday."

A phone vibrated for a moment on the dresser, a text message coming in. Bree sprung up, probably because she expected it to be Lara.

She sounded crestfallen. "It was your phone," she said.

Bree handed it to Celia. The message was from Daryl, her vanishing hookup from two nights before. Celia had already forgotten about him, which of course was why he had gotten in touch. If she had spent forty-eight hours thinking of him, she never would have heard from him again. That was just how these things went.

She read it: *Sorry for running out. I had an early meeting. Thanks for the sleepover. I'd love to have dinner with you next weekend—slumber party optional.*

"Who's it from?" Bree said sleepily, crawling back under the covers.

"Just my sister," Celia said. "She got a new pair of shoes. Pretty gripping, huh?"

"Riveting," Bree said. "Thank you for taking me in, lover."

"Anytime."

After Celia lay down, Bree whispered, "Can you believe Sal's pregnant?"

"It's kind of crazy, right?" Celia said. "She's really freaking out. When I told my mother that the doctor told Sally she was three months along, my mom said a woman only finds out about her own pregnancy that late in the game if she's in major denial."

"I don't blame her," Bree said. "Hey, do you remember what April said to us at graduation, right after we went up to get our diplomas?"

Celia smiled into the darkness. "Of course. She leaned over and said, 'Congratulations. You can officially never get pregnant in college.'"

APRIL

The little house Ronnie rented for them was teeming with roaches the size of tea saucers. Ronnie called them water bugs, but April had seen enough roaches in her life to know what they looked like. Usually, bugs and mice didn't bother her. But Georgia roaches were bold. They perched on her coffee mug and didn't scamper away when she lifted it to her lips. They climbed right into the sheets, so that she might wake up to the sound and feeling of one of them inching across her leg—when she swatted at it, it just stayed put for a minute, taunting her, then flew up toward the ceiling.

April thought it strange that Bree had never mentioned such a thing when she talked about Savannah, since surely this would be enough to make her throw herself from a rooftop. But then again, she would wager that Bree had never seen this side of Georgia. April had decided there were two Georgias. The polite, peach-eating Georgia, and the bigoted, misogynistic, revolting Georgia. Their place was right smack in the middle of the latter.

Ronnie said it was crucial to the whole project that they live on English Avenue, in a neighborhood called the Bluff, where lots of the girls and their pimps lived. As white women, they already stood out, and they couldn't risk raising any more suspicion. Luckily, Ronnie's friend Alexa lived in the neighborhood and knew about their plan. She was a sometimes prostitute who had left her pimp but still worked the streets now and then. (April had no idea how these two women had met, but anyway.) Alexa introduced them to some people. Their story was that Ronnie had been in the life since she was twelve, and that April (her daughter) had followed in her footsteps. Since this was a fairly common tale, everyone seemed to believe them. They spent a year just trying to blend in—Ronnie made April cut off her dreads and grow her hair into a ridiculous bob that made her feel like a spy in a James Bond movie. She had to stop wearing the faded corduroys and slogan T-shirts that Ronnie called "your hipster uniform." Instead, April wore tight, low-cut shirts and dresses for the first time in her life, and tried not to think about how much she missed her familiar flannel. She hung out with the girls on the corner, knowing all the pimps by name but pretending that she chose to work alone. She even stood beside them on Metropolitan Parkway, driving off in cars with men Ronnie had hired so the girls would believe she was working. This was the sort of information that Ronnie had forbidden her from sharing with the Smithies, because she knew how much they would disapprove.

The neighborhood was dangerous, and Ronnie kept a handgun in her nightstand for protection. She told April that if any of the pimps ever tried to mess with her or break into the house, she should shoot without hesitation. April wondered silently how she might manage to get to Ronnie's room before the guy shot her first, but that was another story.

It was much harder living with Ronnie this way than April had imagined. In Chicago, their place was huge, and they stayed out of each other's way when they wanted to. But here, the quarters were much too close—they fought, bickered, got bored, and drank too much. Ronnie had grown more watchful than ever. She took April's cell phone away. She followed her around the house, and at times April could feel someone watching her as she moved along the sidewalk—when she turned around, Ronnie would be there, trailing her unapologetically.

Ronnie's doubts about April's loyalty had never been so intense. This annoyed April because here she was, willing to risk everything for a project that Ronnie had claimed they would have equal say in, a project that April herself believed in with all her heart, and yet Ronnie still acted as though she couldn't completely trust April.

April had told Ronnie time and again that she understood why she couldn't tell the girls. Besides, she hadn't even spoken to Sally or Bree in more than a year. In part, she knew, she was doing all of this to prove something to them—that her mission with Ronnie was crucial, a matter of life and death. When the time came, they would know what she had done and why.

Ronnie and April kept mostly to themselves, though

occasionally April would walk to the market at the end of the block and talk to the girls working the street—or the track, as they called it—out front. They stayed there almost all day and all night, vanishing only between 4:00 and 6:00 a.m. They dressed in short shorts and strappy tops and heels. Businessmen would pull up in cars without looking at all ashamed, and the girls would get in and go off to God knows where. Sometimes cabs full of tourists in town for a basketball game or a bachelor party would swing by—the girls told her how cabdrivers took kickbacks from pimps to bring guys over to this side of town.

The girls told April everything. They were dying to tell. And besides, they thought of her as one of them. An older one, of course, because these girls were mostly thirteen, fourteen, seventeen years old. They had all gotten here through roughly the same route. Poverty, bad family life, probably some sexual abuse, absent parents. Then suddenly, a knight in shining armor appeared—a nice guy with a car who would take them out to dinner, tell them he loved them, shower them with compliments, then ask for a tiny favor.

He needed some money, he'd say, and if she would sleep with his best friend, the friend would give them five thousand bucks. Just this once, the girl would think. We're in this together. He loves me. So she'd sleep with the friend, who of course didn't really have five thousand dollars. But the girl would think, How easy. When her man asked her to do it again, more often, and sometimes with strangers, even if it made her feel wrong, she'd say yes. When he told her to dance topless in a club, and take strange men into the back room and do whatever they said, she'd obey.

Then would come the admission: "Baby, I'm a pimp. But I do love you." Some of them didn't even know what the word "pimp" meant. He would explain and reveal that he had other girls. He might bring her to live with them and, as an initiation, invite ten friends over to gang rape her in a bedroom, then have the more senior girls beat the shit out of her. But it didn't really matter what he did. By now, she was complicit in all of it, a criminal whom no one wanted to help. And she loved him. That was the real kick in the ass about it, April thought. Once a woman fell in love, a man could set her on fire and she'd refuse to see the bad in him.

At night, April would lie in bed staring at the cracked ceiling, thinking about everything the girls on English Avenue had said. Their words haunted her. In the past, she and Ronnie had traveled for a week or a month at a time to gather research for a film. But this time, they were living in the midst of their subjects. April had come to know and care about the girls at the corner store—Linette and Rochelle, a pair of teenage sisters who had turned to the street when their single mother died. Angelika, a sweet, deep-voiced girl who looked about thirteen years old. Shaliqua, tough and foulmouthed. On the day April met her, a john had broken her jaw, but she reported for duty all the same, fearing even worse treatment from her pimp if she went to the hospital or the police.

For the first time, April understood Sally's version of feminism, and why she went to the domestic violence shelter week after week, helping new women each time but never even making a dent in the larger problem. Because when the individual women looked you in the face, you couldn't help but want to make them safe immediately.

When two sisters, just fifteen and seventeen, explained calmly that their mother died of a highly curable cancer because she had no health insurance, and then you had to watch those sisters get into cars with strange men day in and day out, you couldn't help but want to rip the whole ugly, unjust world apart and start over from scratch.

One afternoon, when it began to pour, April invited the girls inside for coffee. All but Angelika declined.

Angelika walked next to April, smiling, talking about her life as if it were a happy tale. She was seventeen, born and raised in Baltimore, sold to Redd, her pimp, by a strip club owner back home when she was just fourteen.

When Ronnie saw the two of them come through the front door, she took April aside and hissed, "Too close, April. Get rid of her."

April invited the girl over three or four times after that, always when Ronnie was away. The two of them would sit at the kitchen table, exchanging stories. Everything April said about her childhood was true, but she still felt guilty for lying to Angelika about who she was. Angelika told her she had been using crack, and sometimes heroin, since she was fourteen.

People tended to think that girls turned to prostitution to pay for drugs. They had that backward—most of the girls April met hadn't touched drugs before they entered the life. But now they needed them to numb the pain, to keep themselves together. Ronnie said that post-traumatic stress disorder was more common among prostitutes than among veterans returning from combat.

"Motherfucking Red Lobster," Ronnie screamed one night as they drank a bottle of cheap red wine.

Red Lobster was the restaurant of choice for the pimps when they were recruiting girls.

"That's all it fucking takes to turn a child into a sex slave," Ronnie said, banging her fist on the table. "One basket of popcorn shrimp and a motherfucking Diet Coke, and these girls think it's love. It's not their fault, of course. They're children from the ghetto, for fuck's sake. Most of them have never been into a restaurant with forks and knives and actual menus. They think Red Lobster is the motherfucking Ritz-Carlton. These are babies we're talking about."

Alexa told them a story about a pair of sisters—just nine and ten years old—who had been incarcerated in Atlanta earlier that year. Cops picked them up on the Parkway and threw them into a locked facility after they approached an unmarked police car in traffic and asked if the undercover officers inside wanted blow jobs. One afternoon a few months later, two cops transported the sisters to the court-house in the back of a squad car. The younger one wore stilettos and clutched a baby doll.

When the cops stopped at a red light, the girls started shrieking in the backseat.

"What is it? What do you girls want?" one of the officers said, kindly. She was a woman with kids of her own.

The girls pointed at a McDonald's outside the window.

"Happy Meals!" the nine-year-old exclaimed. "Please?"

Happy Meals. Men were out there, buying sex from kids who still got giddy over Happy Meals.

Sometimes she couldn't bear the weight of it. Late one night, April crept into Ronnie's room while she was sleeping and gently pulled open the drawer where she knew her phone was stored, right beside Ronnie's gun.

She longed to talk to Sally most of all, but when she remembered what Sally had said—that this whole mission was stupid—April knew she couldn't do it. Sal would just tell her to leave, to go home to Chicago and get a boring desk job with Amnesty International or some shit. So she went to the kitchen and called Celia instead.

"It's just too much," April said. "We don't matter in this world. Girls and women are constantly in danger and no one cares."

Celia agreed. "Like what happened to me at Dartmouth," she said.

She had not mentioned it since the night she first told them the story back in college. She went on, "I've wondered lots of times how that relates to the rest of it—strip clubs and pornos and prostitutes and all that. Men just come to believe that women are these objects, these disposable things."

"How does it affect you now?" April asked.

There were girls she had met on the Parkway who had been raped innumerable times. One of them was truly gorgeous, leggy and lean, but all her teeth were missing. She told April that some john had taken her to a hotel room one night. She didn't remember what had happened, but when she woke up, she had been badly beaten. He had knocked out her teeth. How could that girl ever look a man in the eye again, let alone learn to love one?

"For a couple of years after, the few times I had sex, I'd have really bad flashbacks," Celia said. "I'd remember that stupid blue condom, and I wouldn't be able to breathe. I hated sex. I hated penises, as weird as that sounds. Just the look of them. But I got through it. My mom helped me, surprisingly. I learned to separate so that now I don't think about my rape as sex. Rape isn't sex. It's something else."

"What would you do if you were ever in that position again?" April asked.

Celia responded without skipping a beat, as if she had thought of this before. "My one regret is that I didn't even try to get away at Dartmouth. Not that you always have a choice, but I did. If I could, I'd kill a man before I ever let myself be raped again."

Celia sighed, as if she were letting go of something. Then her tone brightened a bit. "Now, I genuinely love sex. I'm not always so wise about who I have it with, but that's another story. I know Bree and Sally think that after what happened to me at Dartmouth I should only sleep with my future husband or something, but I refuse. I don't want to be afraid of sex anymore."

That was the problem, April thought. For women, sex would always offer pleasure and peril in equal parts.

She often wondered what the hell was wrong with men. Sex could be fun, natural, good. Why did they have to corrupt it? Why did so many of them prefer to have sex with a victim or a child rather than a willing partner? For that matter, why was it better to have sex with a stranger than with your own wife?

Alexa, their one real friend in the Bluff, had once lived in New York, where she married a john. He offered to take her away from the life, and she said yes, after watching a fellow prostitute and friend get shot in the head by a customer she had turned away.

They moved into a house in Queens. They had a baby girl.

Alexa's husband beat her with an electrical cord and engraved his initials into her breasts with a carving knife. One day she returned from picking their daughter up at school to find him fucking another woman right in their living room. "What are you looking at, bitch?" he said to her while their child was watching and he was still inside some stranger.

That's when Alexa decided to move to Atlanta, where her sister lived. The court wouldn't give her custody of her little girl because she had a long criminal record for prostitution and drugs. For the same reason, she couldn't find a job. She went back to turning tricks, though she swore she'd never give a penny of her money to another man as long as she lived.

Ronnie had been married once, too, to a semi-famous movie actor (she wouldn't say who). He left her for someone else, "a teenager," Ronnie said. "I mean that literally. A literal fucking teenager. I think she was nineteen, but still."

So many of the men that Americans considered great had been philanderers. John F. Kennedy and Martin Luther King Jr. and Albert Einstein and Bill Clinton. And April's own father, though of course very few people thought of him as anything special. Any shrink would probably say that it all went back to him—this stranger she had glanced at only once in the line for a port-o-potty, a man who had never come looking for her or sent her a birthday card or paid a dollar in child support.

Sex and power just go together; that was the party line. As if what these men had done was simply a lark, a bit of fun. In truth, they had treated women like things, like trash, and yet this did nothing to color the world's opinion of their achievements. Even the pimps weren't in much danger of being punished for their crimes. Most of them, Alexa said, had turned to pimping because it carried nowhere near the threat of arrest or jail time that drug dealing did. You could sell crack on the street and go to jail for decades. Or you could sell a woman, and be back out by morning.

CELIA

After just one week in New York, six men had asked Bree out. She kept saying no, but they kept asking. Celia had forgotten that Bree had this hold over guys. The last time she had had to compete with Bree for men was first year of college—back then it was a given that no matter how many girls went out, every guy at the party would want Bree most of all. Celia had decided then that feeling jealous of Bree would be like feeling jealous of the Venus de Milo: You were never going to be that beautiful, so why bother getting upset about it? (Though when Bree met Lara sophomore year and stopped partying with guys altogether, Celia had felt somewhat relieved by the thought of finally being seen as herself, rather than the plain Jane standing beside the movie star.)

Bree always looked gorgeous, of course, but it was more

than just that. She exuded confidence and fun, even when she felt miserable and heartbroken.

They went out every night now, and every night new men pursued Bree. They didn't want to take her home or kiss her sloppily behind the fire door. They actually wanted to call her and ask her out on proper dates. Celia had never witnessed such a thing in a New York bar, and she found it highly annoying. But she tried to remind herself that Bree was her best friend, and that she was due for a little self-esteem boost after everything she had been through recently.

On Friday night, Celia returned home from work to find Bree in the bathroom, her makeup bag bursting. She was applying a hot pink lipstick that would have looked absurd on anyone else, but made her look like a Barbie doll.

"What's up?" Celia said, stepping into the cramped bathroom and perching on the edge of the tub.

"Remember that guy Adrian we met at the Ale House the other night?" Bree said.

"Yes." He looked like a Disney character—tall, broad, wavy dark hair, and a gorgeous smile. You half expected to see little cartoon birds floating around his shoulders. Celia had seen him out in her neighborhood dozens of times, and he had never approached her. But when Bree walked through the door of the bar, he was drawn to her like a dumb dog is drawn into traffic. Celia had the urge to scream *She's a lesbian!* and throw a beer right in his face.

"He's cute," Celia said now.

"Cute?" Bree said. "That boy could stop traffic in a gunnysack."

Celia raised an eyebrow.

"Okay, I stole that from a Dolly Parton song," Bree said. "But anyway, he asked me for my number while we talked, and I said I wasn't interested. But when I woke up this morning, I checked my work e-mail, and I saw that he had written me on the office account. He must have searched online to find my e-mail address. Cute, right?"

"Definitely cute," Celia said, trying to ignore her irritation. No man had ever searched for her. "So what did he say?"

"He asked me if I'd have dinner with him tonight," Bree said. "I e-mailed him back to see if he still wanted to meet, and he responded right away and said yes. He's picking me up at seven."

"He's picking you up?" Celia asked. It was another dating ritual that seemed impossible, prehistoric, in the city.

Bree nodded.

"Is it a date?" Celia asked.

"I guess so," Bree said. "It seems like a lot of trouble to go to if he just wants to be friends."

"Well, I know *he* wants it to be a date, but I'm asking if you want it to be one." Celia realized she was leaving out the most important question: *Are you a lesbian or what?*

Bree shrugged. "All I know is that the person I love decided to leave me without so much as a good-bye. If someone else wants to wine and dine me, who am I to stop him? It's just dinner; I'm not gonna marry the guy."

Celia smiled. *I'm not gonna marry the guy* was one of the lines most frequently uttered by single women who secretly wondered if they might be destined to marry the guy.

"Plus, you have your date with Barrel O'Daryl tonight, so if I don't go, I'll just be sitting home alone," Bree said.

"Please stop calling him that," Celia said. "I'm afraid I'll accidentally blurt out 'Barrel O'Daryl' over drinks."

"Or during sex," Bree said. "Oh Barrel O'Daryl! B.O.D.! Oh, take me now Barrel O'Daryl!"

Celia rolled her eyes. "I'm begging you to stop."

"Tell me about him," Bree said, dipping a gigantic blush brush into a huge vat of pink powder. "What does he do again?"

The rosy powder fell like fairy dust to the bathroom floor.

"He says he's a film producer, which probably means he shoots video footage of toy soldiers in his mom's basement in the Bronx," Celia said.

"Where did he go to school?" Bree asked.

"I don't know," Celia said. "Probably the University of Florida at Marzipan."

Bree snorted. "What the hell is that?"

"I just made it up. He seems like one of those guys who went to a college no one's ever heard of."

"Jeez, why are you so down on him already?" Bree said.

"I don't know, I guess I've learned not to get my hopes up," Celia said.

"Well, with an attitude like that, you're not going to get very far, missy," Bree said. Then she took her brush and swept it over Celia's nose for emphasis.

The next morning, Celia woke up to the sound of raindrops on the air conditioner. It was the first week of August, and even with the damn thing set to high, the apartment was sweltering. She slugged out of bed to find Bree sitting on the couch in her underwear, watching the *Today* show with a smear of white cream bleach over her lip.

Celia sat down beside her. "Morning, sexy."

"I have to get rid of my 'stache," Bree mumbled, trying not to move her lips too much.

"You're blonde, you don't have a 'stache," Celia said. "So? How was the big date?"

When she had returned from her own ill-fated date around midnight, Bree was still out.

Bree looked like she was about to speak. Instead, she raised a finger to let Celia know she would be right back, and then dashed into the bathroom. She returned a moment later with her face bleach-free.

"Coffee?" she asked. "I just made a pot."

Celia smiled. "Yes, please."

When Bree returned with the coffee, she was beaming.

"What's going on?" Celia said, reaching out to take one of the steaming mugs.

"Adrian is amazing," Bree said. "He's so funny and so sweet. He volunteers as a Big Brother, and he loves mountain biking and he does tons and tons of pro bono work at the firm. Oh! And his favorite movie is *Last Night*. Same as mine. And we both love sushi and Kurt Vonnegut and the Carpenters. What guy loves the Carpenters?"

Celia laughed, trying to disguise her creeping jealousy, and her thoughts about Bree and Lara, and her intense suspicion that Adrian would have said he loved Mussolini and Brussels sprouts if Bree liked them.

Bree sank into the couch and rested her feet on the coffee

table. "We talked all night. We sat on the promenade down by the water and watched the sun rise over the city. It was nice to just be romantic with someone again without all the baggage and the grief. You know? So. How was your date with B.O.D.?"

"B.O.D. is dead to me," Celia said.

"Uh-oh. How come?"

"Among other things, when the check arrived he said, and I quote, 'Celia, you're a word person. Do you know the derivation of the phrase 'going Dutch'?"

"He didn't."

"He did."

Bree whistled under her breath. "What a turd," she said.

"Do you think you'll see Adrian again while you're here?" Celia asked.

"He's taking me out tonight," Bree said. "I'm gonna take a look-see through your closet for something cute to wear, okay?"

A while later, Bree was trying on outfits in front of the bathroom mirror as Celia dozed on the couch. It was a lazy late morning, and outside the rain began to pour. Celia was half in a dream, and for some reason she kept hearing April's full name over and over: *April Adams, April Adams, April Adams.*

Suddenly, Bree was standing over her, shaking her awake.

"Oh my God, Celia. Look at this. Oh my God."

At first, Celia thought Bree was referring to her outfit—a long black halter over a pair of Seven jeans.

"That's a dress, not a top," Celia said, closing her eyes again.

"Cee, please wake up!" Bree said. She shook Celia hard, and as Celia came to she saw Bree running toward the television, turning the volume up. A picture of April filled the screen, with the word MISSING printed underneath. She was smiling wide and wearing her favorite red dress, the one that used to belong to her mother. Celia remembered the photograph instantly—she had taken it herself at Celebration of Sisterhood their senior year of college.

"The woman police are looking for is named April Adams," said a too-cheery news anchor with big blonde hair. "She was here in Atlanta to make a documentary about children in prostitution. She did not return home from an early evening walk last night, and no one has heard from her since. Police are worried that in a bizarre twist of fate, Ms. Adams herself may have been trafficked into this city's illegal sex trade."

Bree sat down beside Celia on the couch. They looked at each other for a moment, as if each of them thought this might be a dream.

"What the hell is going on?" Celia said. Her heart pounded.

A moment later, a black woman with short, cropped hair and crooked teeth appeared on the television. She seemed ageless in a way. She could have just as easily been forty or sixty-five. NEIGHBOR, it said at the bottom of the screen.

"Ms. Alexa Jones says she had become friendly with April Adams in the months that she lived here on English Avenue."

"April's a good, sweet girl," the woman said. To Celia, the idea that this woman even knew April, *her* April, was bizarre. "She's always down at the corner store talking to all the little girls. Last night, I seen April being pulled off by one of those young guys, a pimp. He just shoved her into his car and then drove away."

"Authorities are now looking for the man Ms. Jones saw, known to neighbors only by the name Redd," the news anchor said. "He may be driving a red Cadillac, and is thought to be just one of many pimps living in the area."

There were some stock photos of prostitutes walking in the city streets at night.

"Ms. Adams does not fit the typical profile of a sex trafficking victim," the anchor went on. "She is twenty-six years old, Caucasian, a graduate of Smith College in Massachusetts."

"I think I'm going to throw up," Celia said. "Is this really happening?"

Bree shook her head. "It must be a mistake. April would never let something like this happen to her."

"Maybe she didn't have a choice," Celia whispered.

"Well, where the hell was Ronnie?" Bree said.

Celia was silent. She thought of how many times Ronnie had left April to fend for herself.

"What do we do?" Celia asked. She was trying not to imagine the worst, but the worst kept coming into her head—April, dead at the hands of some horrible pimp, her body at the bottom of a murky pond or in a dumpster somewhere.

Bree looked composed. "We call the police."

After they had each been questioned by phone (When did they last see April? Hear from her? What was her state of mind? Did she fear anyone?), Bree, Celia, and Sally got on the phone with one another. The police officer they spoke to told Bree that they had conducted a massive search that morning, calling on dozens of local volunteers to comb the area for clues. There was nothing for the girls to do but wait.

Sally sounded hysterical. "I knew this was a terrible idea," she said, sobbing. "I told her not to do it. Oh God, you guys, I dreamed that April died."

"Sweetie, you've got to calm down," Celia said. "There's an explanation for all this, and we're going to figure it out. The police are doing everything they can."

"Are you home alone, Sal?" Bree asked.

"Yes," Sally said, choking on her tears. "Jake's away for a week for work. He just left an hour ago." Then, as if she thought they might question this, she added, "It's been on the calendar for months."

"Do you want to come out here for the weekend?" Celia asked. It was already four o'clock on Saturday, so there wasn't much weekend left.

"Yes," Sally said. She took a deep breath, but then started sobbing again. "Oh God, I don't think I can drive. And I don't want to be that crazy lady weeping on the Acela Express."

"Do you want us to come to you?" Celia asked, and Bree shot her a look of surprise.

"Could you?" Sally said.

"Fuck it, my boss is going to be on vacation all week," Celia said. "And Bree's here until next Sunday."

"And Jake's away!" Sally said.

"Yup. The three of us can be together for the week, maybe get down to Georgia if we have to and help search for her,"

Celia said. She thought of the dozens of news shows about missing girls she had watched over the years. Each time the search parties went out hopeful and came up with nothing at all or, worse, a body. "But I'm sure we won't get to that point," she said, trying to shake off the thought. "She'll be home soon."

Sally and Jake lived in a gorgeous old three-story Victorian that reminded Celia of her childhood dollhouse. It was the kind of home, Celia thought, that even her mother would look at with terrible envy. The outside was painted a pale yellow, and there was an actual swing on the front porch. Inside, the shiny hardwood floors were covered by thick Oriental rugs in shades of deep cranberry and inky blue. ("My mom's," Sally said proudly.) Their furniture was solid wood, with soft pillows thrown here and there, and long heavy curtains in every room.

"So I guess you guys skipped that whole Ikea phase of life, huh?" Celia said, as they drank lemonade in the kitchen late on Saturday night. The room was full of sleek, brand-new appliances—a stainless-steel fridge, marble countertops, the works.

Sally kept crying.

Celia wondered if Sally was more emotional because she knew what it was like to lose someone you loved, or because she and April had always been so close but had stubbornly ignored each other this past year. Or maybe her hormones were already going crazy from the pregnancy and the additional stress was just too much. (Even as she considered this, Celia thought of how April would have called it sexist.

"A woman can't express any emotions without being asked, 'Do you have your period?' " she always said when she had her period and felt enraged.)

Sally's house had five bedrooms, and she had turned down the beds in her two favorite guest rooms for Celia and Bree. But in the end, none of them could sleep that first night, and they huddled in Sally and Jake's bed and talked about April instead.

"I missed her so much all year, but I couldn't bring myself to make the first call," Sally said. "I kept thinking about what she said about Jake, and I just couldn't forgive her."

"I missed her, too," Bree said. "I always felt like she was one person who really stood behind my choices, no matter what. And I always thought we would make up eventually, put that stupid fight behind us."

"You will," Celia said. "As soon as they find her."

Later, they talked about Lara leaving Bree, and Bree (too tired for self-censorship, Celia thought) said, "I think she was the love of my life, and I just pushed her away." They talked about Sally's marriage, how it was exactly and not at all what she had expected. She admitted that Jake had wanted to cancel his business trip and stay home with her after they found out about April, but Sally had forced him to go. "Ever since I got pregnant, he treats me like I'm made of glass," she said. "If he said 'Everything will be okay, babe' one more time I might have exploded."

"He's just worried about you, sweetie," Bree said. "You have to let the people who love you take care of you."

"It's weird not having four of us in the bed," Sally said.

"I know," Bree said. "And even weirder that there *are* four of us." She pointed at Sally's round tummy.

They fell silent for a while before starting up the conversation again. Celia didn't tell the other two, but in her head she prayed to Saint Anthony, the patron saint of lost things, for April to call them now and just say the whole thing had been a big misunderstanding.

The phone didn't ring.

As soon as the sun came up, Bree called the Atlanta police department. She kept calling, at least once an hour. The detectives liked her familiar accent, so they didn't seem to mind, but each time they said the same thing: "Nothing new to report." Sally tried calling April's mother on her home phone, but it just rang and rang without ever going to a machine. A detective said she knew what had happened and was on her way to Atlanta. He would tell her they were looking for her when she arrived.

"Should we be coming, too? To help look?" Bree asked hopefully.

"No, ma'am. I already told you, there's no point in that," the detective said. "We've conducted a very thorough search already."

Everything definitive they heard, they got from the Georgia newspapers online or from Bree's parents, who read to them from *The Atlanta Journal-Constitution* over the phone. No one could find the pimp that Alexa Jones had mentioned the day before. His house had been raided, and cops had found cocaine and weed, as well as two eighteen-year-old girls beaten, bloodied, and tied to a radiator. This last fact scared them more than anything.

"Jesus, look what he's capable of," Celia whispered.

"Why wasn't this psychopath arrested sooner?" Bree said.

Sally was silent. At noon, she made grilled chicken sandwiches with pesto mayo and her mom's potato salad. None of them ate a bite.

It began to rain. The three of them huddled under a blanket on the couch, even though it was ninety degrees outside and not particularly cold in the house. If they had been here under any other circumstances, Celia thought, it would be a near-perfect way to spend the day. Instead, she felt nauseous and kept wishing that she might open her eyes and discover that the past two days had all been a dream.

Celia's parents stopped by that afternoon, and Celia felt a little guilty for not staying with them, since they only lived a few miles away. Violet had finished her senior year at UVM and stayed in Vermont with friends for the summer, and Celia knew they sometimes got lonely with no children left at home.

"We understand," her mother said. "You need to be with your friends now."

They had brought enough food for an army—a stuffed turkey, clam chowder, a Crock-Pot full of chili and corn bread, roast beef sandwiches, and a chocolate Entenmann's cake.

"In our family, when we're stressed out, we eat," Celia overheard her mother saying to Sally, as if it were an entirely novel concept.

The phone rang, and Sally hurried to answer it.

"Oh," she said. "Well, I don't think so, well—hold on please."

She laid the receiver on the counter and hissed at them, "Oh my God, it's someone from *Nancy Grace*. They want the three of us on the show tonight."

"No," Bree and Celia said simultaneously.

"I know, I know," Sally said. "But what do I tell *them*?" She pointed at the phone.

Celia's mother reached for it. "Hello," she said. "Listen, these girls are not going to talk to you at this time. They are going through something simply awful, and I know you'll understand when I now hang up on you. Good-bye."

The girls stood back, impressed. Celia felt proud. Sometimes she forgot what a hard-ass her mother could be; that in addition to hosting bake sales and teaching Sunday school and listening to her daughters' man problems, she was also vice president of the second-largest ad agency in Boston.

When Celia got home from work most nights, it was all she could do to flop onto the couch, switch on the television, and order sushi from the place downstairs, all the while feeling awash in Catholic guilt for not turning on the computer and writing something. How had her mother gone through all those long days at the office only to spend her nights cooking dinner and making school lunches and breaking up squabbles and correcting math homework?

She had once said that she believed the women's liberation movement of the sixties and seventies was actually a ploy by men to get women to do more.

"I make as much money as your father, and I still do about ninety percent of the housework," she said. "Which one of us has a higher quality of life because I work? I'll give you a clue: It's not me."

After a while, her parents started packing up to leave.

"You girls let me know if you need anything," her mother said to Sally and Bree as they said good-bye at the door.

Celia had the strongest urge to crawl into her raincoat and hide, like she had on the first day of kindergarten in 1986. Instead she just said, "Thanks, Mommy."

"My legion from church is going to pray for April every day, okay?" her mother said as Celia walked them out to their car.

Celia smiled. "Thank you."

Her mother took her hand and whispered, "Just so you know, miracles can happen."

Celia nodded, though she didn't believe it for a second.

"I feel weird leaving you," her mother said. "Are you girls going to be okay?"

"Of course," Celia said. "Sally's practically a grown up, after all."

"I can't believe she is going to have a baby," her mother said.

"Neither can I," Celia said.

"I already bought her four onesies and an adorable little tutu at the Treasure Chest in town." Her mother beamed.

"What if she has a boy?" asked Celia's father.

"Then I'll keep the tutu for my first granddaughter," she said.

"Or you could just put it on Molly," her father said. Molly was their springer spaniel.

"Will you guys come back tomorrow?" Celia said as they opened the car doors and slid inside.

"Absolutely," her mother said, "I have a nine o'clock conference call, and then I'm bringing you a pumpkin cheesecake."

. . .

Later that night, Ronnie Munro's face was all over the news channels on TV. After just one day, April's disappearance had made headlines.

In an interview on CNN, Ronnie spoke of the documentary they were making and actually cried each time they showed April's face. "If I had known what would become of her, I never would have brought April to this place. But here's what we have to remember—most girls out here aren't as lucky as April. They're teenagers, missing from home, but there's never been a single Amber Alert put out for them. They are sexual slaves in their own homeland, and we do nothing."

"Most girls aren't as *lucky*? I want to kill that woman with my bare hands," Sally said. "She's using April to sell her stupid movie and her stupid fucking cause."

Celia and Bree stared. It took a lot for Sally to use the F-word.

Ronnie continued on about child prostitutes. "You need look no further than Metropolitan Parkway or the Atlanta Hilton, or Craigslist on your home computer, to see the thousands of innocent children being forced into prostitution every day."

"Who fucking cares?" Sally snapped. "April's not a child prostitute!"

Bree patted her knee. "It's okay, sweetie. At least they're showing her picture and talking about her."

Sally changed the channel anyway.

"An anonymous donor has come forth offering one million dollars for the safe return of April Adams," said a news anchor with shellacked hair. "It is the largest sum of money ever put forth in a case like this one, just another way in which April Adams's story differs from that of most domestically trafficked women—the majority are young, poor, and African American, with few resources and little support."

And off he went, into yet another story about sex trafficking in America.

"A million dollars!" Celia said in amazement.

She looked over at Sally, who was busying herself with the leftover dinner plates, trying hard not to make eye contact. Celia often forgot that Sally had that kind of money. Despite the nice house and fancy furnishings, she never quite seemed like a millionaire.

"Sal?" Celia said.

Sally just shrugged. "I didn't know what else I could do."

"You're an amazing woman," Bree said.

Sally shook her head. "April's an amazing woman."

Then no one said anything for a long, long time.

BREE

Bree didn't go back to California at the end of their week at Sally's house. She couldn't face the empty apartment, the closet and dresser only half full, the bare kitchen cabinets gathering dust where Lara's copper pots and ceramic mixing bowls once sat. Instead she went home to Savannah, taking a full leave of absence from work and hardly even caring that they would probably fire her if and when she returned. She had called her parents from Sally's house and told them about the breakup and about April.

"Come home to us and we'll take care of you, baby," her mother had said. The offer was too good to refuse. Bree had talked to them more often than usual since her mother's heart attack. She realized of course that this had coincided with Lara's leaving, and so she couldn't be sure which event had led them back to her.

Adrian, the guy she had met in a bar in Celia's neighborhood in Brooklyn, a guy she hardly even knew, had called or e-mailed several times since April's disappearance. The excitement she had felt after their first date had faded quickly, and though Bree knew he meant well, she never answered his calls. They were only a painful reminder that Lara had not been in touch. She assumed that by now Lara must have heard about April. And yet there had been no calls, nothing. Wasn't Lara even thinking about her, or had she simply moved on to something or—this made Bree sick to imagine—*someone* else? Before she went to sleep at night, she called Lara's cell phone even though she knew what would happen. Each time, a recorded voice told her that the number had been changed.

Bree's father picked her up at the airport on Sunday evening. She made him switch the car radio to an AM news channel, and he looked at her sadly and said, "There's been no update. But listen, those guys in the Atlanta PD are some tough buzzards. They're gonna find your girl."

When they got home, her mother had set the table with her best china and heaping bowls of all Bree's favorites— mashed potatoes, biscuits, fried chicken, collard greens, creamed corn, and strawberry pie.

"No butter on the collards," her mother said. This was her version of a heart-healthy diet.

She hugged Bree close. "I'm only going to have a taste, don't worry. At a time like this, you deserve some comfort food," she said. Bree wasn't sure whether she was referring to April or Lara or both.

"Are the boys coming?" Bree asked, sitting down at the table and taking a warm biscuit from a bowl.

"Nope, it's just the three of us," her mother said.

Bree couldn't remember the last time the three of them had been alone together. Probably not since the summer she was nine, when she broke her leg and had to stay home while her brothers went to camp in the Berkshires.

She looked around the kitchen, at the familiar pale wooden cabinets and sky-blue walls, the wicker ceiling fan that hummed at night, and the faded yellow carpet. In this room, she had studied for countless spelling tests, baked a thousand coconut cakes with her mother, and hidden in the crawl space in the pantry where the dogs slept so she could talk to Doug Anderson on the cordless phone all night long. Here, it didn't really matter that she had graduated in the top 3 percent of her law school class or that she could afford an apartment with a guest room in the nicest part of San Francisco, or even that she had probably pissed away her entire career in the span of the last three weeks. Here she would always be adored for building a cardboard-box village for her She-Ra figurines and getting up early to fix her father cereal before work and forcing her brothers to let her paint their toenails. When she came back to her parents' home, she became a simpler, younger version of herself again in an instant.

In the years since graduation, Bree had forced herself to forget that this level of comfort existed, so that her family's absence wouldn't hurt so much. And now, just like that, she had them back. But her Lara was gone.

Over dinner, they talked about April and the investigation. Bree's dad knew a few of the cops in the Atlanta police department, guys who had transferred from Savannah years ago. He was pressing them for information, he said, but no one knew anything. The police questioned the pimp everyone suspected and then allowed him to go free—something Bree could not understand for a minute. Neighborhood girls interviewed on CNN said he walked the streets of the Bluff with his head held high now, the same as ever. The two teenagers police had found chained to a radiator in his home had refused to appear in front of a grand jury and said that they would deny all the accusations made against him. After five days, the police had nothing to hold him on, and so he was set free.

When talk of April got too hard, they discussed Bree's brothers—Roger and Emily were getting serious and had just gone to the beach house off the coast of Charleston for the weekend.

"They'll be home in the morning, and you'll finally get to meet our Emily," her mother said.

Our Emily. That made Bree want to cry. Why couldn't she ever have seen Lara that way?

Tim was living at the beach with friends for the summer, working as a pizza delivery boy, which scared Bree's mother because, as she said, "I followed him in the station wagon once, and he turned left on red three times! When I yelled at him about it later, he just said, 'What? You're not supposed to do that?' "

After dinner, Bree's father cut each of them a fat slice of strawberry pie. When he set her mother's piece down on the table in front of her, she turned her face toward him, her eyes brightened, and they kissed. It lasted just a second, but it reminded Bree of a photo from their wedding album—her mother's face tilted up adoringly toward her new husband, who was making a toast, raising a glass of champagne.

Bree felt her throat tighten. Her chest began to ache.

Could she tell them how much she missed Lara? Would they understand? She wished more than ever that the special person in her life were a man. Then her mother would soothe and coddle her to her heart's delight, her father would offer practical advice for winning her boyfriend back.

Bree's mother may have been wishing the same thing, because at that moment, she put down her fork and said, "Oh, guess who I ran into in the deli line at the Food Lion this morning. Betsy Anderson, Doug's mom."

Bree smiled. "Oh?"

"Yes, and she was just so precious, asking after all of us, but especially you. She said Doug was blown away when he saw you again. He said you looked more beautiful than ever."

Bree rolled her eyes, but her cheeks grew pink. Had he really said that to his mother, or was Bree's mother just meddling?

"He did not say that," she said at last.

"He did!" her mother said. "I think he's still sweet on you."

"Mom!" Bree laughed. "We talked for all of five minutes. He's married, for God's sake."

Her mother sighed. "His wife's a bit controlling from what I've heard. I wonder if he's happy with her."

"Dad!" Bree said. "Will you help me out here, please?"

Her father raised a hand. "Sweetie, when she gets like this, I find it best to just let her roll with the crazy."

Her mother went on, ignoring him. "Some marriages are meant to be, and some aren't. There's no shame in it. I knew I was going to marry your father in third grade. Everyone was picking on this nerdy kid with glasses—oh, what was his name?—anyway, your father got up from his chair, and I'll always remember this, he scooted right up next to what's his name and acted like they were the best of friends. You should have seen the grateful smile on what's his name's face. I'll never forget it, Bree. I leaned over to Patsy Foster, and—this is true, you can ask her yourself—I said to Patsy, I am going to marry Steven Miller."

"And you did," Bree said. She had heard the story a hundred times.

"And I did," her mother said proudly.

"Okay then, you've convinced me," Bree said. "I'm going to drive over to Doug's house right this instant and demand that he run away with me."

"Oh hush," her mother said, swatting at Bree with her napkin. "Honestly! As if I'd ever suggest such a thing."

Her father just shook his head and laughed.

He looked at Bree. "More pie?" he said. "Lord knows you deserve it."

The next morning, Bree woke early, planning to drive out to Atlanta to see April's mother, Lydia. Bree figured she could at least give her a hug and take her to lunch. She had never been alone with Lydia before. She hadn't ever come to Parents' Weekend, and they had met just once, at graduation. Sally warned her that Lydia was odd.

"Odd like April?" Bree had asked.

"Much odder," Sally said. "April's just a Dixie cup of crazy. Lydia's more like a twenty-gallon tank."

It had been over a week since April went missing. Bree knew from watching *48 Hours Mystery* that after a day the chances of finding a missing person alive almost disappeared. She tried hard to put thoughts like this one from her mind, but it was impossible to think of much else.

She was showered and dressed by seven and in the kitchen brewing coffee five minutes later. Her father had already gone to the office for the day, and her mother was out tending to the back garden, her favorite morning occupation. Bree sat at the table and listened to her mother singing through the screen door. It was a song by Patsy Cline, Bree thought, though she could not name it. The smell of coffee and something sweet in the oven filled her nostrils. She wished she could stay here, just like this, all morning long, then accompany her mother to the country club for lunch and spend the afternoon reading on the front porch. Instead, she would have to walk the street that April had last been seen on. She would have to look April's very strange mother in the eye and lie to her, saying that everything would be okay in the end.

Bree went to the cabinet under the old stone sink to get her mother's spare set of keys. They hung there, on the same red shoelace on the same little hook, right beside the rose-covered gardening gloves Bree had given her on Mother's Day in ninth grade. She was struck by the way nothing ever changed here. It was so unlike her own life and the lives of her friends, which seemed to change every day, every instant.

Outside, she heard her mother talking to someone, a man. Bree walked to the screen door, and there was her brother Roger, taking the hedge clippers from their mother's hands and snipping off a branch of something.

"Oh, thank you, darling, I could not cut those ones— they're so darn thick. Would you like to take some to Emily?

It may not look like much now, but if she cares for it, it'll be just gorgeous come next spring."

"No thanks, Mama," Roger said.

He looked up and noticed Bree inside the door. "Emily doesn't know it, but she's actually dating Mom," he said.

Bree laughed.

"I'm so sorry about April, Biscuit," Roger said, using his childhood nickname for her. Bree had always hated it, but now it was the most comforting sound she could imagine.

"There's nothing to be sorry about," she said. "April's tough as nails. We're going to find her."

Roger walked up the stairs and past her into the kitchen. He went to the fridge and started lining up items on the counter—a box of English muffins, a jar of honey mustard, a package of chicken breasts, half of last night's pie wrapped in tinfoil.

"What are you doing?" Bree said.

"Food shopping," he said.

"Mama!" she called outside. "Roger's taking all your food."

"So Mom said Doug Anderson paid you a visit last time you were here," Roger said teasingly.

"Not really," Bree said. "We sort of just bumped into each other."

"Bumped into each other on our front stoop as I heard it," he said. "Sounds like he *lurves* you."

"Shut up," she said. "I swear, Mom still thinks he's the One, even though he's married with two kids."

"Well, what do you think?" Roger said.

"I think she's nuts," Bree said. "But do you ever feel like Mama has this power over you? Like you just want to make her proud so badly that you'd do anything."

He raised an eyebrow. "I'm her oldest son, Biscuit. I don't have to work that hard. I know what you mean, though. I cried like a baby when I heard about the heart attack. I don't think I had cried for a decade before that. That's what Mama will do to you."

"You hadn't cried in a decade?" Bree said. This was one of those amazing things about men that made her thankful not to be one of them. Imagine not crying for ten years.

"It's like I almost want Doug to be the One, because I know how happy Mom would be if he was," Bree said.

"Sounds pretty romantic," he said.

She laughed, then said in a hush so her mother wouldn't hear, "It just makes me so sad to see how much they love Emily. Why couldn't they have ever loved Lara like that?"

"So you miss her," he said.

She told him the story of how Lara had left, how devastating it had felt to walk into their empty apartment.

"Why don't you call her?" he asked.

"I've tried. She changed her number. I don't even know where she is," Bree said. "Plus, sometimes it just gets so bad that you can't imagine how it could ever get good again, you know?"

Their mother came in then and removed the ridiculous floppy garden hat she had been wearing.

Bree gave her a hug. "I should hit the road," she said.

"Wear your seatbelt and pull over and take a nap if you get tired," her mother said.

"I'm just going to Atlanta." Bree laughed. "It's a three-and-a-half-hour drive. How tired can I get?"

"Drowsiness accounts for more accidents than you might think."

Bree rolled her eyes.

When she stepped outside, the heat hit her like a brick wall.

On the road to Atlanta, she ate the warm molasses cookies her mother had made for the ride. She listened to the radio and tried not to cry when one of April's favorite Bob Dylan songs came on, but she cried anyway.

She thought about Doug Anderson every time she saw a Volvo on the highway. He had been on her mind more lately than he had in the last nine years combined. Her mother seemed to think it wasn't too late for the two of them to just pick up where they'd left off in college, despite the fact that the man had a wife and children. For a little while now, Bree allowed herself to imagine it: At night, she'd burrow into him just like her mother burrowed into her dad, clad in a thin cotton nightgown, the color of a seashell. They'd wake up each morning to the sound of two kids pattering down the hall, and then they'd feel the weight of the kids' bodies on top of their own in bed. She thought about brushing that little cutie pie's long red hair and pinning it up with butterfly barrettes. (Of course, the hair would always be a reminder of the birth mother who had died in a tragic shark attack, but Bree would manage.) She envisioned flipping pancakes and singing songs in the car and having fights over vegetables and bedtimes. She pictured long, warm evenings on the porch alone with Doug, talking about their parents and their teenage years. Perhaps that sort of common ground was what real togetherness was made of. Not struggle and passion and difference, but just plain and simple, *My mama knows your mama, and I remem-*

ber what you looked like the summer you got braces and lost all your freckles.

Finally, there was a blast of a truck horn. Bree took it as a sign to stop thinking this way. She switched the radio to NPR and pretended to be riveted by a debate about ethanol. Of course, she had no one to pretend for but herself, but that seemed like more than enough.

When Bree pulled up to the dingy hotel, April's mother was standing out front in jeans and a long, flowing top, smoking a cigarette. Lydia looked like she had aged twenty years since Bree had last seen her. Her face was covered in deep wrinkles, her hair pulled back in a severe ponytail. Bree almost didn't recognize her.

She didn't smile as she climbed into the passenger seat. Bree wondered if Lydia knew how things had been between her and April this past year. Had April told her mother about their stupid fight at Sally's wedding, about the way their friendship had fallen apart?

She decided not to wonder.

"It's good to see you," Bree said.

"Jesus, could it be any damn hotter outside?" Lydia said. "I'm sweating in places I didn't even know I had."

She sounded drunk. It was only eleven o'clock in the morning.

"I'm starving," Lydia said. "That hotel food is just rotgut crap. There's a diner by the highway that's not too bad."

They drove to the diner in near silence and took a booth by the window. A fluorescent lightbulb over their heads flickered on and off every minute or so. The red plastic seat stuck to the back of Bree's bare legs.

After she'd ordered her coffee and taken a few sips, Lydia seemed to soften.

"It was good of you to come out here and keep me company for the day," she said. "I really don't even know what I'm doing in Atlanta. There's no real way to help. But what was I gonna do? Sit and chain-smoke in my apartment at home?"

Bree gave her a sad smile. Despite how odd she had always found Lydia, she pitied her now. Her only child was missing, and she was powerless to do anything about it.

"My mother says you're welcome to come stay with us in Savannah," Bree said.

Lydia waved her hand in the air, dismissing the invitation. "Believe me, that wouldn't be good for anyone."

They ordered pancakes and bacon from a bored-looking teenager in a pink uniform that was about three sizes too big.

Lydia pulled two tiny white bottles from her purse and shook out a few pills from each, downing the whole handful with one gulp from her water glass.

"That Ronnie Munro is a hot ticket," Lydia said. "She met me for coffee yesterday. I would have killed for a job like hers, to have turned out as a real, serious woman artist. Making a difference, you know?"

Bree nodded, although she thought it was an incredibly strange thing to say. If it weren't for Ronnie, April would probably be safe and sound in some Teach for America classroom full of disobedient little monsters right now.

"Wow, does she love April," Lydia said. "It made me

proud to hear Ronnie talk about what a fighter April is. My little girl." She gazed off into space for a moment, before looking Bree straight in the eye. "You know, that call I got from the police saying she was missing—that was the first I'd heard of April being in Atlanta. As far as I knew, she was still living with Ronnie in Chicago. I guess that shows you how close we've been in recent years."

Bree was stunned. Hadn't April said her mother thought the Atlanta project was a great idea? Was it really possible that she hadn't spoken to her mother in a year, either?

"Have you talked to the police yet today?" Bree said.

Lydia nodded sadly. "Nothing new. You heard they drained a few local ponds?"

Bree gasped. "No," she said, and with that thought, it finally hit her—April was dead.

"I did get an alarming call from April's father, or whatever you want to call him," Lydia said. "He asked how he could help. How do you like that? He wanted to hire special detectives and offer more money for information. I told him to go fuck himself."

Bree tried to disguise how shocked she felt. She wished Celia were there. She would know exactly what to say.

The waitress arrived with the pancakes and a sticky pitcher of syrup on a tray in one hand and the coffeepot in the other.

"Breakfast is served," she said as she slid the plates onto the tabletop.

After they left the diner, Bree drove Lydia around the city, helping her talk to the police and taking her to the grocery store to stock up. On the way home to Savannah, she wept, thinking about how unfair it all was—why had something like this happened to April, someone who always wanted only the best for the world?

Bree stayed in Georgia through the rest of August and all of September. Everyone at her office back in San Francisco knew what had happened, and for a time they were sympathetic. Bree's parents' house became her cocoon, and she spent her days helping her mother in the garden, reading thick novels, driving over to her father's office to drop off his lunch when he accidentally left it at home.

Sally kept saying this wasn't healthy, that Bree needed to get back into a routine. She knew Sal was right, but when her boss finally called and gave her the ultimatum she'd been expecting ever since she left—get back to work immediately, or they'd have to replace her—she told him she understood completely, and that she'd have one of the paralegals clean out her desk.

Bree did not think about how much it had taken to get the job, or about how the firm had been her first choice from the start. She did not think about the long hours she had spent with Lara, trying on suits for her interview, as Lara pored over Web sites to try to glean any information she could about the partners—eventually discovering that Peter Morris had an Amazon.com wish list that revealed his love of books about golf, dogs, and true crime; that Katherine White had run the Big Sur half marathon the previous fall and had once sued her landlord. She did not think about the days and nights she had spent busting her butt at that office, feeling her blood pumping as she ripped into a new case.

When she told her parents that she wasn't going back to work, her father gasped.

"Bree," he said. "Sweetheart, do you want to come work with me?"

She smiled, thinking this over, imagining what it would be like to settle back into Savannah for good, taking a little apartment downtown, walking to the office every day, arguing cases side by side with her father. Tim wanted to go on to law school after graduation, and she pictured him coming on board, too. What would they call themselves? Miller, Miller, and Miller? Miller & Sons?

But Bree had made her decision. "I think I'm going to go back to New York and visit Celia for a while," she said.

To her surprise, neither of them protested.

Instead, her mother said, "When my dear grandma died, I went and stayed with your aunt Kitty for two weeks straight, and she fed me a steady diet of whiskey and grilled cheese sandwiches until I stopped crying. Sometimes a girl just needs her best friend."

And so, Bree returned to New York. The autumn set in. Cool breezes came, and the leaves turned bright shades of orange and yellow, reminding her of the falls they had spent at Smith, having leaf fights in the Quad, greeting trick-or-treaters at the front door of King House with Milky Ways and lollipops.

For weeks, Bree and Celia cooked dinners together out of Celia's copy of *The Silver Spoon* cookbook and played Scrabble in bed. They tried to train Celia's new puppy, Lola, and they drank so many bottles of wine that Celia decided to make a giant kitchen bulletin board out of the corks. During the day, Bree picked up groceries, took the dog to the park, and cleaned the parts of Celia's apartment that Celia herself would have never even noticed were dirty. She scrubbed the windowsills and polished the oven dials and rinsed the toothbrush holder. Celia said she loved having Bree there, but Bree knew that any houseguest who stayed indefinitely could begin to grate on a girl. She hadn't really given Celia a choice—Celia was the person Bree needed to be with now, and so she made an effort to earn her keep.

On brisk afternoons, Bree wandered around Brooklyn alone, chatting with lonely old ladies in cafés, touching every glass bottle in an antique shop on Montague Street, trying to put the events of the summer from her mind. But when Celia came home from work, they'd curl up on the sofa and talk about April and Lara.

"Are you missing Lara?" Celia said one night as they sat there with a bowl of popcorn between them, and the puppy gnawed away at a pig's ear on the floor.

Bree shrugged. "Can you believe she still hasn't called me? I'm sure she's heard about April."

"I saw a girl who looked just like April in the street today," Celia said. "She had long red hair, and she was wearing a very April-looking corduroy jumper, and just sort of bopping along, the way April would. And even though I knew it wasn't her—I mean, April doesn't even have that red hair anymore—I *wanted* it to be her so badly."

"That's happened to me, too," Bree said. "I keep thinking I'm seeing her everywhere I go."

Celia started to respond, but Bree wasn't listening. She

was looking out through the window at the Watchtower, the world headquarters of the Jehovah's Witnesses, which had been erected so that they might be the first to see Christ coming at the Apocalypse.

There were dozens of them in the neighborhood, always walking around in their Sunday best—the men in pressed suits, the women wearing long flowing skirts and hats. Bree had asked Celia once why they were always so dressed up.

"When you think today might be the day you meet your Maker, you put in a little extra effort," Celia said with a grin.

Bree had laughed at this, but now she was thinking of how in some ways, the Jehovah's Witnesses had it right. You never really knew what God or life had in store, and when it hit you without warning, without any preparation on your part, perhaps it stung you all the more for that.

SALLY

Sally let the towel drop to the bathroom floor and looked at her body in the mirror. She screamed at the top of her lungs, like some teenager in a horror film who's just seen an ax murderer emerge from the basement.

"Babe?" Jake called up the stairs, sounding only mildly concerned.

"Sorry, I just saw myself naked again," she yelled.

"Okey-dokey," he said. She could hear him walking back to the TV room.

She was seven months pregnant. At five months, every part of her had suddenly exploded. She hadn't known many pregnant women up close and personal, and she had assumed that the only part of a woman that changed was her stomach. But now Sally's body—which she had always worked so hard to keep under control—had expanded in every direction. Her breasts grew heavy. Her face got full and fat, like those Smith College sophomores who gorged themselves on pudding and pot roast in the dining hall. Her thighs were covered in red stretch marks that wove this way and that like routes on a road map. Her fingers and feet had swollen up so that her wedding ring no longer fit, and she could only wear flip-flops, even to work (she had no earthly idea what she would do when the weather turned bitter cold in another month).

Her doctor said he'd never seen someone experience such an intensely physical pregnancy. When she got the slightest chill, her legs and feet turned blue and splotchy. ("It's normal!" Jake said sunnily. "It's from all the extra estrogen you're producing!") Her back hurt, she felt constipated all the time, she had insane mood swings that came over her with no warning, and she sometimes wanted to murder Jake in his sleep for getting her into this position in the first place.

Sally had never cared all that much about food, but throughout her pregnancy she felt ravenous. She craved blood oranges and rare steaks and cheeseburgers and Devil Dogs (had she ever even had a Devil Dog before?) and milk shakes and cinnamon buns, the kind they only sold at the mall. Jake kept feeding her, and telling her she looked beautiful, but she had gained forty-eight pounds since she got the news that she was having a baby, which she knew was insane.

As Rosemary had so gently put it, "Slow down! You may be eating for two, honey, but neither one is a sumo wrestler."

"Babies whose mothers gain under twenty pounds are more likely to be premature and suffer retardation in the uterus," Jake replied. "The sensible and safe pregnancy weight gain is between twenty-five and thirty-five pounds, but Sally's fine. Our doctor said so. She was so in shape to begin with. Although with a major weight gain like hers, a vaginal birth might become difficult or impossible, and—"

Sally interrupted him. "Honey, shut up please."

Rosemary looked shocked by this, but Sally would not have her vagina talked about in mixed company, just because she was pregnant.

"He keeps quoting from *What to Expect When You're Expecting*," she said. "And it's driving me nuts."

Rosemary furrowed her brow. "Oh, that is annoying. Jake, keep that stuff to yourself."

Jake looked sad. Sally didn't care. He was so pumped about being a dad that sometimes he made her feel like she didn't even exist.

He didn't want to have sex anymore, because he was afraid they'd hurt the baby, even though all the books said they wouldn't.

A week earlier, she had awakened to find him rolling up the rug in the upstairs hall.

"What are you doing?" she said.

"I'm putting skidproof mats down under all the carpets today," he said.

"Why?" she asked.

"Well, *What to Expect* says it's a good idea, you know, because the bigger you get, the more your center of gravity will shift, and the more likely you are to suffer a fall."

Sally inhaled deeply. Was this supposed to thrill her? she wondered. Were there women out there who longed for husbands to care this much?

Later that day, she opened a jar of olives over the kitchen

sink, and was about to eat one, when Jake said, "Did that pop?"

"What?" she said irritably.

"The jar, I didn't hear it pop. Those olives might be spoiled, Sal. I think you need to throw them out. The smallest amount of bacteria could be lethal to the baby."

Sally lifted the jar to her mouth and shook it hard, until her cheeks were full of olives and the salty juice leaked onto her chin and down the front of her neck. She chewed and chewed, and when she finally swallowed, she screamed, "I'm not your motherfucking baby vessel! I'm your wife!" and stormed out of the room.

She had read somewhere that women became mothers the moment they found out they were pregnant, while men didn't become fathers until they saw their babies for the first time. In her marriage, the reverse seemed to be true. Personally, she worried about this. But intellectually, she found it fascinating and wished she had April there to talk to about it—nature versus nurture and gender roles and all of that. When she tried to engage Jake in this conversation, he just said, "Oh, honey, you're going to be an amazing mom," which she knew wasn't true, and anyway, it was beside the point.

Jake talked to the baby, he sang to the baby, he read to the baby—*Family Circus* and *Peanuts, The Boston Globe* music reviews, and *Sports Illustrated,* cover to cover.

Sally didn't talk to the baby at all. She couldn't quite imagine this blob in her stomach as an actual person. Of course, as Jake pointed out, she had learned about April just two months after she found out she was pregnant. It was impossible to know how each of these things affected the other, or how she would feel about the baby if April were there. This had always been true for Sally—with happy change came surprising despair. What would it have felt like to graduate from high school or start college without having just lost her mother? What would her wedding have been like if she hadn't gotten into that stupid drunken fight with the girls the night before? Sally would never know.

She went into the bedroom and lay down naked, pulling a sheet up over herself so she didn't have to look at her revolting body. They were due at Jake's parents' house for dinner in an hour, and Sally wondered if she might be able to get out of it, just this once. It would be fabulous to have the house all to herself for the evening. She could watch a bad Lifetime movie and have a little bit of red wine. (Jake would flip, but she knew for a fact that pregnant women in Paris drank two glasses of Cabernet a day, and their babies turned out fine.) She could call Bree and Celia and talk for as long as she wanted, without Jake giving her that puppy-dog stare he always developed when she ignored him for too long.

Bree's and Celia's lives had changed more in these past two months than in all the years since they left Smith. She believed that April's disappearance had had a strange effect on them both, different than she would have imagined. Of course they were all sad and on edge, dreading the inevitable news each time the phone rang. But it was more than just that. It was as if Celia and Bree now saw the entire world through the prism of this single event—April had disappeared and everything else followed from that.

Bree had gone back to New York, a city she didn't even like, to live with Celia. She had told Sally in an e-mail about her horrible breakfast with April's mother. "I understand the importance of family now more than ever," she wrote. "And so for that reason, I actually feel blessed by things that have happened in my life that might otherwise make me upset." Did she mean her mother's heart attack? Or April? Or Lara? Sally suspected it was some combination of the three.

She was shocked that Bree had quit her job. As much as Bree seemed perfectly content to flush all her hard work down the toilet, Sally thought it was criminal and wondered if perhaps Bree was having a nervous breakdown. The Bree she had known back at school once wept when she got an A-minus on a final exam, claiming that it would derail her entire career.

Celia had changed, too, and Sally couldn't tell whether the change was for the better. Her reaction to April's disappearance was understandable. Realizing the randomness and brevity of life, Celia had decided to do away with everything that didn't make her happy and satisfied in the here and now. She said she was working harder on her novel than she ever had before. She had stopped dieting and gained ten pounds. She cooked roasted chicken stuffed with lemon and garlic, or beef stew, or spaghetti and meatballs. She bought a Maltese, an adorable little ball of white fluff that had already eaten four pairs of heels, a Marc Jacobs purse, and a fifty-dollar bill, as well as pissing all over her couch. She was taking a man hiatus for at least six months, and she refused to clean her bathroom, the chore she dreaded above all others (though Sally suspected Bree was probably doing it for her).

Some nights Sally got into bed beside Jake and wanted to be with her friends instead. All of their lives had changed so quickly in so many ways, and she couldn't help but feel a bit jealous that Bree and Celia had been able to form a little shell around themselves to brace them against whatever might come.

The only person who seemed not to have changed in the weeks since April's disappearance was Ronnie. She was still the same self-promoting conniver she always had been. She had taken her sex-trafficking show on the road—appearing on *Charlie Rose* and *Larry King* and *Fresh Air* with Terry Gross. She had a book coming out on the topic, too. And then there was the movie they had planned from the start.

Sally knew it was a good thing that child prostitution and sex trafficking were finally getting covered in the news— April would have been proud of that. But the way Ronnie used April's disappearance as her vehicle for getting the word out sickened Sally. Every story started in the same way: "April Adams wasn't your typical sex-trafficking victim. She was white, well educated, and yadda yadda yadda." It made Sally cringe, because in truth there was no proof that April had been kidnapped by a pimp, other than the testimony of some old woman. She could be anywhere, with anyone.

Thinking it over as she pulled the sheets up to her chin, Sally felt overcome with anger—at that fucking Ronnie for taking advantage of April's idealism and making April yet another casualty of her mission. At April herself for being so naïve (wasn't she lucky enough to have made it through all of Ronnie's other stupid projects?). Sally was irrationally enraged at her mother, too, for leaving her alone before she had time to ask any of the important questions. For the first few years after her death, Sally could always predict exactly what she might have said in response to any given problem. Now she really had no clue. Would she have been delighted to become a grandmother so soon, or disappointed in Sally for not following through on her dreams of med school? Would she know what to do about April? Would she understand how guilty Sally felt for letting a year pass between them without so much as a word?

Jake pouted a little, but ultimately he agreed to tell his mother that Sally felt too sick to go out. Ten minutes after she heard his car pull out of the driveway, she went down to the kitchen in her bathrobe to forage for food. She felt giddy, like the first time her parents left her home alone when she was eleven. She could do whatever she wanted! Which for the moment only entailed putting on a Faith Hill CD, making two peanut-butter-and-banana sandwiches, pouring a huge glass of chocolate milk, and eating standing up at the counter. But even so.

Faith's voice echoed through the wide rooms of the first floor. *I believe in Peter Pan and miracles, anything I can to get by.*

The house was too big for just the two of them. It was too big even for the two of them plus a baby, really. Neither of them had ever owned an apartment let alone an entire house before, and the constant upkeep amazed them. While a leaky faucet or a broken pipe had previously meant a call to the landlord, now it was a whole new level of work. They went to Home Depot at least once every weekend.

"How do you stand it?" Celia had asked her once on the phone, and Sally said, "I honestly don't know. Believe me, I never thought I'd be pregnant and shopping at Home Depot at the age of twenty-six." As soon as the words came out of her mouth, she felt like she had betrayed Jake—she actually enjoyed their Sunday drives to the garden department and the paint center. Afterward they always stopped at Brigham's for a hot-fudge sundae, and Jake got unduly excited about blasting an old Bruce Springsteen album and singing along.

Sally's father loved their house. She saw more of him these days, which wasn't particularly enjoyable. He never asked about the baby or April, just about their property tax or how much Jake had paid for his golf clubs. He had taken up with a new woman, Barbara, and Sally assumed she was the instigating force behind trying to make them closer. She could not bring herself to refer to Barbara as her father's girlfriend. She was fat—there was no nice word for it. She had gray stringy hair, and even on her best day she could not hold a candle to Sally's mother on her worst. She was forty-seven and worked in the accounting office of a suburban nursing home and seemed to have absolutely no redeeming qualities whatsoever. Sally had no idea what her father saw in Barbara. Maybe, like her mother had said once, men just could not be alone.

"Women leave their marriages when they can't take any more," she had told Sally. "Men leave when they find someone new."

Sally took a bite of her sandwich and washed it down with a big gulp of milk. As she swallowed, she felt it—the very first kick from inside. She let out a little squeal. Then, another kick.

"Oh my God," she said with a laugh.

It was the weirdest and greatest thing she had ever felt. Her child, alive inside her.

For two months, the doctor and nurses had been asking her if she had felt anything. She hated that she grew guilty each time she told them no, as if she was an inadequate mother even when it came to being kicked in the stomach. And now, this. She could not wait to tell them.

"Do you like bananas?" she asked, and she felt a surge of love and panic and safety all at once.

The phone rang, and Sally reached for the cordless, hoping it was Jake. Maybe she ought to drag her butt over to his mother's house after all, though she was glad to have had this moment just for herself.

"Hello?" she said.

At first, Sally could only make out a crackling sound at the other end of the line. Then she thought she could hear a whisper.

"Sal?" came the faint voice.

"April?" Sally said in disbelief.

The phone clicked off. Silence.

She needed to sit down. She went to the kitchen table. The phone sounded again, and she answered it on the first ring. Again, she heard the crackling noise. Tears formed at the edges of her eyes.

"April, can you hear me?" she shouted.

"Sweetie, no, it's Celia. I'm sorry. Did you think—oh, I'm sorry."

Sally's heart sank. "Oh," she said.

"I was just calling because Bree and I are in a bar in my neighborhood, and they're playing your song. That one by the Supremes."

" 'You Keep Me Hanging On,' " Sally said.

"*What?*" Celia said.

In the background, Sally could hear faint music, and women chattering and some sort of whirring noise, like a fan.

"Never mind," Sally said. "Hey Cee, guess what. The baby just kicked."

"What?" Celia said.

"The baby kicked!" Sally shouted, rolling her eyes.

"Oh my God," Celia said, then to someone else she said, "The baby kicked! Bree says 'Oh my God,' too."

Sally heard the sound of a toilet flushing.

"Are you calling me from the ladies' room?" she said.

"Oh. Yeah. Bree saw that guy Adrian at the bar. We're trying to get out of here without him seeing us, so we're hatching an escape plan in the bathroom. Hey, sweetie, my reception is kind of awful in here, can I call you later to—"

The line went dead.

Sally went back to her sandwiches on the counter and took another enormous bite. She laughed, picturing Celia and Bree hiding from some guy in the bathroom of a bar. She was glad to be done with that part of her life, at least.

She rubbed her belly and texted Jake on his cell phone: *Can you come home, honeybun?*

He wrote back right away. *Of course. Is everything okay?*

Yes, she wrote. *I just want to see you.*

Jake pulled up twenty minutes later, and she met him at the door with a mug of chocolate milk. "Thanks," he said with a surprised smile. She knew she had been rough on him lately.

"You seem better," he said.

"The baby kicked," she said.

His eyes brightened. "What? I can't believe I missed it."

"Well, maybe she will do it again if we wait long enough," Sally said, taking his hand and drawing him toward the couch.

"She?" Jake said. At Sally's urging they had decided not to find out the sex, but now she felt certain that the kicker in her belly was a tiny little girl.

They sat down on the couch.

"How was your mom's, love?" she asked.

"Fine. Same old, same old. Everyone was asking for you." Jake wrapped his arm around her. "What's been going on here?"

Sally smiled. "I found out the baby likes bananas," she said.

She nuzzled in toward him.

"You know," he said, "I don't think you're just my baby vessel."

"I know you don't," she said. "I think we're both just a little bit freaked out."

"Yeah," Jake said. "Can you believe people do this every day? They just keep having kids. I was stuck in traffic yesterday, and I thought to myself, Holy shit. For every person on the expressway right now, some poor innocent woman had to go through what Sal's going through."

Sally laughed. Sometimes she envied the girls their freedom, their bad dates and rented apartments and crazy nights out. Sometimes, but not tonight.

BREE

ree and Celia sat in a booth at the Old Town Bar in
Union Square, drinking beers and waiting for Ronnie.
She had e-mailed Celia a week before to say that she
was coming to town for a taping of the *Montel Williams Show*
and wanted to meet up with them to talk about April. At first,
Bree refused to go—she couldn't bear the sight of that
woman. But Celia said that maybe this would help. Yes, Ronnie was a self-serving bitch, but every time she got on TV,
they flashed April's picture. Bree knew that Celia imagined
April living somewhere out in Utah, brainwashed or drawn
into a cult. All they needed, in Celia's mind, was for some
unsuspecting person to see April on TV and then run into
her at the market, wearing a bonnet and buying farm-fresh
eggs.

It had been two months since April disappeared. Bree

had known for a long time that she was dead. She felt it in her gut. Of course, she wouldn't dream of saying so to anyone, but it was as true to her as her own name. She was just waiting for the body to surface.

Newspaper reporters and TV news shows called them every few days, but Bree's father had advised the girls not to speak to the press. The story kept getting covered; Ronnie made sure of that. And though eight long weeks had passed, they were all still in shock. When Bree tried to picture herself under bright lights, talking about April—*her* April—to the world, she knew that she would be unable to say a word, that she would simply moan and thrash about and then they'd probably have to cut to a commercial break so someone could drag her off to the loony bin.

It was a Tuesday night, and the long, gleaming oak bar was practically empty but for a few guys watching a football game on the TV in the corner. A dim green lamp hung in the air between them, casting an ethereal glow across Celia's face. She seemed more like her old college self lately, her face grown soft and full. She had quit wearing her tight black pencil skirts and heels and returned to a wardrobe of jeans and ballet flats. She wrote page upon page on her laptop at night while Bree flipped through magazines on the couch, and occasionally she read passages out loud. Bree was impressed, just as she had been back in college, at Celia's ability to stir up her emotions with written words. She believed in Celia as a writer, and not just because they were best friends.

"I had ninety pages of my novel done as of last night, and you know what I did with it this morning?" Celia said now.

"What?" Bree said.

"I erased it," Celia said. "I realized that the reason it sucked so much was because I was making it all up. So I've decided to try something new—a book about a crazy Irish Catholic family in Boston. Totally fictional, of course."

Bree smiled. "I love it," she said. "Ooh, can Gwyneth Paltrow play the main character's best friend in the movie version?"

"I'm sure that could be arranged," Celia said.

Bree knew that she would soon have to leave New York. The city was dirty and crowded, unfriendly and cold. It had nothing to offer her, other than Celia. And she worried that perhaps she was asking too much of her—Celia hardly spent time with her other friends these days, instead coming straight home to Bree as if they were the sort of codependent couple that neither of them could stand in real life. The leaves were off the trees now, and a freeze had set in. Bree's bank account balance was dwindling, her days blurred one into the next, and she realized it was time to do something new—conquer an unknown city, or move home to Savannah and start the life she had always intended to have. As it stood, her mother had already set up two dates for Bree for the next time she came home, with the sons of friends from her country club.

"I'm gonna miss you when I go," Bree said now.

"Who says you have to go?" Celia said.

She looked over Bree's shoulder toward the entrance to the bar. Her face turned serious.

"That's Ronnie," Celia hissed.

Bree turned around in her seat. Out of all of them, she

knew and cared the least about Ronnie Munro. Back in college, she knew that Ronnie was the sort of icon you loved if you were a militant, and loathed if you were just your average run-of-the-mill feminist. (Bree herself was neither.) She had seen the woman on television since April vanished, but she had never seen her in person. She avoided Ronnie on her trips to Atlanta, afraid of what she might say if they ever came face-to-face.

Ronnie looked much smaller than she had imagined— thin and almost frail, like a bird. Her hair was the color of an overripe eggplant. She wore jeans and Converse All Stars and a black T-shirt.

"Over here," Celia called out to her.

Ronnie walked toward them, and as she came closer Bree saw that her face was etched with deep lines.

"Give me a minute," Ronnie said.

She went to the bar and ordered a whole bottle of red wine for herself. She didn't ask them if they wanted anything, even though their glasses were empty. She drank almost a full glass of wine standing there, before coming over to the table.

"Now," she said, scooting in beside Bree. "We meet at last."

Ronnie made her uneasy. She didn't ask them a thing about themselves, just jumped right into her theories about April—perhaps she had gotten into a fight with one of the pimps and he'd kidnapped her to teach her a lesson. She certainly wouldn't have gone off with one of them voluntarily, or even at gunpoint.

"April's distrust of men started early, of course," Ronnie

said. "It wasn't just the father. Oh, I'm sure it started there, it always does. But I think that she learned what can be expected from men even more from Gabriel."

"Who's Gabriel?" Celia asked. Any stranger would think she was just curious, but Bree could tell she wanted to throttle this woman for holding on to information about April as if it belonged to her.

"This bastard friend of her mother's who molested her when she was a kid," Ronnie said casually. She took an enormous sip of wine. "He got her pregnant and ran off."

Bree was speechless. She could not have been more relieved to have Celia there. Celia, who never said the wrong thing at a moment like this.

"Did Lydia tell you that?" Celia said.

"No. Poor April told me. I did ask Lydia about it in Atlanta, though. She was very forthcoming."

"How so?" Celia asked.

"Well, she was just very honest. Said she fell head over heels for the prick herself. If I had a dollar for every time I've heard this story. She suspected, of course, like they always do, but she wanted to believe that the guy was a knight in shining armor, so—" She threw up her hands as if to say *That explains it.*

Celia cleared her throat. "So you're saying Lydia told you that she knew this guy molested her daughter but she didn't do anything?" Her voice was fiery, as if she thought the whole thing was just an ugly lie. Bree wasn't so sure.

Ronnie stared at Celia. "There's knowing and then there's knowing," she said. "This culture has created a myth that once a woman becomes a mother she loses her right to herself—she can't have sexual desires or passions or dreams anymore. And it's simply not true. Motherhood doesn't transform the soul. It doesn't move molecules."

Celia was saying something about how in theory she agreed with Ronnie, but that certainly we could expect mothers to protect their children at the very least. Bree couldn't focus. Her anger was a physical thing now, making her whole body tense up. What was all this? This goddamn conversation. It wasn't about April, she thought. It was about Ronnie, her theories, her stupid feminist bullshit. As far as Bree had ever seen, motherhood might as well move molecules for how it changed a woman. She thought of her own mother, at home in Savannah. She would do anything for her children, absolutely anything. To call Lydia a mother and have it mean the same thing seemed absurd.

Then Bree thought of Lara, and of her mother's face on the day she told her they were in love. It sent a shiver up her neck. A mother's approval could chart the course of a lifetime if you let it.

Finally, she interrupted the debate. "Why did you want to see us?" she asked.

Ronnie shrugged. "I know how important you all are to April," she said. "So I wondered if you knew anything that might help us find her."

Whom did she mean by *us*? It was as if April was Ronnie's, not theirs, to worry about.

"Don't you think if we knew anything we would have told the police right away?" Celia said.

"I don't know you people from Adam," Ronnie snapped. She took a deep breath. "I'm just trying to do everything I can for April, and since I was going to be in town anyway, I thought it would be best to see you and find out what you know, and just clear the air between us."

"Consider it clear," Celia said, in the curt voice she reserved for special occasions such as this.

"April joined me because she wanted to, you know," Ronnie said. "She wanted to make a real difference in the world. This didn't happen because of me. I didn't do this to her."

"You keep telling yourself that," Celia said abruptly. "Let's go, Bree."

Bree's heart fluttered as they got to their feet and made their way toward the door. She could never be that forceful, and furthermore, neither could Celia before coming to New York.

When they got out into the icy air, Celia let out a scream, her breath forming a white cotton-candy cloud in front of her face.

"I've never seen a guilty person try to explain her blame away so blatantly before, have you?" she said, as they made their way to the subway.

Bree shook her head, knowing that now was no time to argue with Celia. But secretly she wondered whether Ronnie had made a fair point—they'd all known that April was heading into dangerous territory, but she had done so anyway, against their advice. Had they been firm enough? Had they taken enough time to fight April, or had they just been distracted by their own silly drama?

Maybe April's death wasn't Ronnie's fault after all, but theirs.

.   .   .

The following weekend, Bree flew to San Francisco to empty out the old apartment. After two and a half months of living with her parents and then with Celia, she had continued to pay the rent. But now, finally, she had given her notice to Eddie, the landlord, and decided to take one final look.

She left at nine o'clock on a Saturday morning, with a return ticket for the red-eye back two days later. On the flight, Bree did everything she could to avoid thinking. It had been a tough summer, followed by an almost unbearable fall. She had decided that long stretches of time spent rolling it all over never did her any good. So she read the in-flight magazine and even bought her mother a ridiculous silk scarf from the shopping section. (Did people actually do this? she wondered. Shop while flying across the country at thirty-six thousand feet?) She watched two romantic comedies, both of which she'd seen with Celia on HBO the previous month. They had decided that these films were mediocre at best, and discussed at some length why it was so difficult for screenwriters to get it right. Why couldn't every romantic comedy be *When Harry Met Sally*? Was it really so hard? And wasn't that just like love itself, Celia had said philosophically after half a bottle of sauvignon blanc. It seemed like it should be effortless, a no-brainer, but it was all so much more complicated than that.

For the duration of the flight—six hours—Bree refused to let her thoughts take over. After the movies, she chatted with the elderly couple beside her. She read back issues of *Vogue*. She listened to Tom Petty on her iPod. She drank three sugary Cokes, calories be damned.

As soon as the plane landed in Oakland she started thinking about flights she and Lara had taken together into this airport, holding hands during takeoff and landing, but she warned herself to knock it off, or else. Even so, on the way to the old apartment, she remembered the time they had spent there together—painting the living room walls a pale blue, assembling the bookshelves and the coffee table.

Her parents were relieved that she was finally giving the place up.

"It's just an unnecessary drain on your finances, love," her mother said, though Bree suspected there was more to it than that. This was her last connection to Lara, the only physical proof of what they had shared.

When she told them that she was going back to collect her belongings, her father said he wanted her to call someone in San Francisco to keep her company, one of her old colleagues or a friend from the soccer team.

"I'm fine, Daddy," she had told him. "I'll have my cell phone."

"That cell phone won't be worth a plug nickel if you get mugged," he said. "I know you're an independent lady, but it's dangerous for a woman to be completely alone in a strange city."

Bree didn't think of San Francisco as strange. The steep inclines around Russian Hill, the Marina with its noisy tourists and snoozing sea lions, the tiny Mexican restaurants, and vendors selling Italian ices and fresh fried doughnuts were home to her in a way that no other place ever had been. The first home that she had chosen for herself. That she and Lara had chosen together. Bree didn't want company, for safety or any other reason. She wanted to walk through their old life like a ghost, without remembering that all of it—the apartment and the firm and, most of all, Lara—was still here, moving forward, without her.

Bree looked out the cab window at the familiar streets, streets she had walked with Lara so many times that it was a wonder their footprints weren't there in the cement.

The cab pulled onto Vallejo Street and right up in front of their old building. It was only one o'clock in the afternoon, and the sun shone brightly through the trees. Bree paid the driver and stepped out. Here it was, just like she had never left. She climbed the steps and inserted her key into the door. It gave its old familiar creak as she pushed it open.

She took the stairs to the second floor, and as she entered the apartment, she half expected Lara to be sitting at the kitchen table with a cup of coffee, listening to NPR and reading the paper. But the place was empty.

It looked exactly the same—their old furniture, Bree's cereal bowl and coffee cup in the dish drainer where she'd left them to dry back at the end of July, thinking she'd only be gone for the week to visit Celia. That was before April went missing. Before everything changed. The clock on the wall, left over from an old tenant, read 11:11 as it had ever since the battery died the same week they moved in. (Lara said it was good luck and they shouldn't touch it.)

Bree wandered from room to room, opening windows and letting the air in. The bed was still made, the sofa still covered in tissues from her crying fit upon returning from Savannah to find Lara gone. The water in the bathroom sink ran brown for a minute before turning clear, but otherwise it looked as if they had never left. Of course, Lara's things were missing. Her clothing from the closet and the mountain bike that was once wedged behind the couch. (Bree had always complained it was an eyesore.) All of it taken someplace new, wherever that was.

Lara had left their pictures fastened to the fridge with magnets, as if she didn't care to remember Bree at all. Black-and-white photo-booth shots taken at the Marina; Polaroids snapped on their holiday visits to Lara's family; old, curling color photos from their Smith days, both of them looking drunk and over the moon with happiness.

"How could you?" Bree said out loud, and then she laughed at herself for sounding like a bad TV movie. She could feel Celia's eyes roll from three thousand miles away.

Bree had to get out. She grabbed her keys and ran to the sidewalk, running, running, until she hit the end of the block. She walked quickly past the familiar row houses and neatly trimmed lawns. She walked past two-hundred-year-old oak trees and down the hill to the water, through neighborhoods she did not know, down streets full of children shouting on bicycles, where the smell of dinner cooking wafted out through open windows.

Darkness fell and the air grew heavy with moisture. Bree kept walking. Sally's wedding could have been a century ago for everything that had changed since. April was gone to them forever, though they now knew more about her than they ever had before. Sally would soon be a mother, responsible for a life besides her own. And Lara had vanished, like April, leaving no clue behind.

I have to let her go now, Bree thought.

Returning from her walk around nine o'clock that night, she passed the mailboxes by the old front gate, and then turned back. She had had the post office forward her mail to Celia's place in New York, but only her cell phone and electric bills and a subscription to *Runner's World* ever made it through.

Bree struggled to get the tiny door open. The box was stuffed full of flyers, for nail salons and the local sushi place and the gym down the block. She almost closed the door, but then she saw it—a small blue envelope, addressed to her, and in the upper-left corner, written so small that you could barely make it out, was the name Lara Matthews and a return address in Novato that seemed familiar, though Bree wasn't sure why.

She walked back to the apartment and poured herself a glass of water from the sink. She sat down at the kitchen table, and her hands shook as she ripped open the envelope. It had been postmarked the week April went missing.

It was a blue greeting card with a picture of Wonder Woman flying across the front. Inside, Lara had written:

I just heard about April, B. I am so sorry. But you are the strongest woman I know, and it will work out. I am here for you always if you want me. I love you, L.

Bree picked up the phone and called Celia.

"You'll never believe this," she said.

She read the card to Celia ten or twelve times, so they could parse it out, word by word. Lara had said she still loved her. She had said she would always be there. But if she really felt that way, why had she changed her phone number? Why hadn't she called?

"Maybe she needed to know that you'd come after her," Celia said.

"But what if I've waited too long now?" Bree said. "What if she's already engaged to some hot thing from her soccer team?"

"Umm, I'm gonna go ahead and doubt that she's engaged," Celia said. "Obviously, she was making a little gesture in the hopes that you would then make the grand gesture."

"Do you think I should make the grand gesture?" Bree asked.

"Well, what do you think?" Celia said.

"I don't know what I think," Bree said. "When I saw that card with her handwriting on it—I can't remember the last time I was so happy."

"That's gotta tell you something," Celia said.

"Yes, but it's not that simple."

"Sweetie, why do you think you even went out there, if not to get her back?" Celia asked.

"I came to clean out the apartment," Bree said. "You know that."

"Okay," Celia said.

"Okay, what?" Bree said. "Come on, Miss Psych 101, don't hold back your analysis now, when I need it most of all."

Celia laughed. "Do you have any liquor there? I think a shot of something might serve you well."

They talked for three hours, pausing only once so Celia could pee and take the dog outside for same.

Eventually, having reached no conclusion whatsoever, they said good night.

Bree couldn't sleep. She got out of bed and went to the kitchen, where she boiled water in the old teapot and pulled a bag of Earl Grey from the cupboard.

She took her tea and sat on the kitchen floor, looking up at the room. Had she ever seen it from this angle before?

Why now? Why the hell hadn't Lara just picked up the phone and called her? Why hadn't the card been forwarded to Celia's apartment with the rest of her mail? Had she gotten it sooner, would things be any different? Maybe she'd be living here now, in her same old life. Was it a blessing the way things had turned out? Or was the blessing the fact that she had found Lara's note and could still change her mind?

Bree looked over at the fridge, at one picture in particular: Lara laughing hysterically as she and a little boy named Devon Samuels from the after-school center crossed the finish line in a three-legged race.

Suddenly, Bree realized why she knew the return address on Lara's card—it was Nora and Roseanna's place out in the suburbs. She was surprised by how relieved she felt to know that Lara wasn't off with some hot single friend but instead in the home of her boss, her boss's wife, and their young son.

She drank down the rest of her tea and wished for morning to come quick.

Around 9:00 a.m. the next day, Bree showered and blew her hair dry in front of the bathroom mirror, where one Valentine's Day Lara had written her a dirty letter in red lipstick. She applied her makeup as carefully as she once had for her high school prom and spritzed her wrists with the Burberry perfume Lara liked, though she herself thought it was a bit too lemony. She hadn't brought anything terribly nice to wear, so she pulled an old sundress from college out of the closet, one of Lara's favorites.

Half an hour later, she was climbing into a taxi, her palms sweaty. The weather had changed, and now the sky was a pure blue, the unseasonable heat so strong that it made the sidewalk smell like a bread oven.

"Can you take me all the way out to Novato?" she asked the driver.

He eyed her in the rearview mirror. "For you, gorgeous, anything."

The row houses and sloping streets gave way to a highway lined with palm trees. Bree didn't know what she would say or even whether Lara was still staying there. No doubt, Nora and Roseanna saw her as the villain in all of this. She closed her eyes and took a series of long, deep breaths. She considered calling Celia, but decided against it: The decision needed to be all hers now.

Soon enough, they were surrounded by enormous homes, perched on the greenest lawns Bree had ever seen. And then Nora and Roseanna's place came into view, the rainbow flag billowing in the slight breeze.

"That's the one," she said, pointing.

She paid the driver, the price of the twenty-minute ride amounting to more than a quarter of what it had cost her to fly across the country. She knew she should have taken the train out, that perhaps it was a touch dramatic, but she did not want to wait any longer than she absolutely had to.

Bree walked slowly up the flagstone path. A few moments later, she stood at the front door and rang the bell. She smoothed her dress and counted to ten as she tried to keep from passing out or turning around and running down the driveway.

When the door opened, six-year-old Dylan stood on the other side in blue medical scrubs, a stethoscope hanging around his neck.

"Dylan!" Bree said happily.

He didn't seem to recognize her. "Dr. Dylan, yes," he said. "What seems to be the problem?"

"Who is it, sweetness?" Nora's voice came from close behind, and then she stood there in her red one-piece bathing suit, wiping her hands on a flowered dish towel.

She patted Dylan on the head. "Go out back and get Auntie Lara," she whispered.

"You mean Nurse Lara," he hissed.

"Yes, yes," she said. "Go."

Nora didn't invite Bree inside. Instead, she opened the screen door and stepped out onto the porch. She gave Bree an awkward hug.

"This is a surprise," she said. "How have you been?"

"I'm okay," Bree said. She looked inside the house. She could feel Lara's presence and wondered why Nora hadn't let her run straight to her side.

"I've been staying in New York with a friend," Bree said.

"Oh."

"I tried calling Lara so many times, but—" Bree trailed off. Why was she defending herself to this woman?

"It's really not my place, but I'll just say this," Nora started, glancing over her shoulder before she went on. "You have to be really certain, Bree. Don't do this to her if you're not sure."

Bree began to respond, but then the door opened, and Lara stood there. Lara! Tanned and toned, in an impossibly small navy-blue bikini, a beach towel wrapped around her waist. Bree stopped breathing for a moment as their eyes locked.

"I'll just give you two some space," Nora said. On her way back into the house, she touched Lara's arm. "There's coffee on the kitchen counter and fruit salad in the fridge if you want it."

"Thanks," Lara said.

And then it was just the two of them, at last.

"Hi," Bree said sheepishly.

A huge grin spread over Lara's face. "Hey there."

"You look amazing," Bree said. "You look more beautiful than ever."

Slowly, Lara wrapped her arms around Bree's back and buried her face in Bree's neck, her wet hair dripping onto both their shoulders.

"I missed you," Lara said.

"Me too," Bree said.

Across the street, a dad in khaki shorts and a T-shirt started up his lawn mower.

"How long have you been staying here?" Bree asked.

"Since I left," Lara said. "How's the old place?"

Bree shook her head. "I just saw it again for the first time yesterday," she said. "I'm giving it up, since neither of us has been living there."

"Where have you been?" Lara asked.

"With Celia."

"In New York?" Lara sounded surprised. "But you hate New York."

Bree laughed. "I know."

"I'm so sorry about April," Lara said. "I wanted to call you, but—"

"But what?" Bree asked.

"Oh, never mind."

"Okay, now you have to tell me."

"When this all started, way back when you were home with your mom, Nora and I had this long talk one night. She said she and Roseanna went through something really similar years ago. She said the best thing for both of us was for me to cut off all ties."

"Why would that be good for me?" Bree said. She had started to cry, realizing all at once how much she had missed this.

"Good for you because we both know how I feel, but you still needed to figure out your own feelings, without any help from me," Lara said.

Bree swallowed. Had she figured anything out? Was she wrong to have come?

Lara got dressed, and they took the train back into the city, holding hands and catching up the entire way, confessing to each other like little girls: Roseanna had set Lara up on a date with a woman who looked just like Bree, in the hopes of helping her move on, but Lara just wanted to cry each time she looked at her. Bree talked about how her mother had wanted her to get back together with her married high school boyfriend. Lara laughed, the entire ugly story underneath going unspoken, at least for now. They spent the day together curled up on the couch and went for a long dinner at a new Thai restaurant in the Trocadero.

It wasn't until late that night, when they were lying naked

in their old familiar bed, that Lara said, "What happens now?"

"I'm flying back to New York in the morning," Bree whispered.

"Do you have to?" Lara said. She sounded stricken, and Bree thought of Nora's words to her earlier that day: *Don't do this to her if you're not sure.*

"I want you to come home," Lara said. "I want us both to come home."

"I think I need some time to sort this out," Bree said finally. "Yesterday I didn't know if I would ever even see you again."

"Well, here I am," Lara said, not unkindly. "I'm here now, Bree."

SALLY

As usual, Sally was awakened by Jake singing in the shower. It was only the first week of November, but already he was singing Christmas carols with operatic gusto.

"We *wish* you a merry Christmas! We *wish* you a merry Christmas! We *wish* you a merry Christmas, and a happy New Year!"

His voice echoed through the master bath and into their bedroom, where Sally lay on her back in bed, with a pillow over her face.

"Honey!" she called, laughing. "I'm begging you to stop."

He went on, launching into the midpoint of "Jingle Bells": "Dashing through the snow, in a one horse open sleigh, o'er the fields we go, laughing all the way—ha! ha! ha!"

Sally groaned, but she couldn't help but smile. How on earth had she managed to attract a man who loved life and never seemed to worry? A man who started each day off with glee, as if he were a kindergartener on his way to the poster-paints table rather than a banker and a husband and a soon-to-be-father.

Early on in their dating life, when it had seemed like Jake might just be another one in a long line of men they talked about and nicknamed and then forgot, Celia had said he sounded like a golden retriever—always happy, friendly to everyone. Cee had meant it as a joke, but Sally thought it was actually a fairly apt description. She hoped she never forced that purity out of him.

Sally still had fifteen minutes left before her alarm went off, but she rolled out of bed and got to her feet—no small task, as her belly seemed roughly the size of a three-year-old child. She padded downstairs and started the coffee. Jake was drinking decaf with her in solidarity these days.

Sally opened the fridge and considered making him a big breakfast—eggs and bacon and toast and orange juice. But a second later, she felt exhausted from the mere thought of it, and unwrapped two of his Pop-Tarts instead.

When he came into the kitchen and saw what she'd done, Jake beamed. "You made me Pop-Tarts!" he said. "Thank you, baby."

This made Sally wish she had gone for the big breakfast. It was so easy to make Jake happy. Too easy. Sometimes she wanted to tell him that if he just complained a bit more, he could probably get a hell of a lot more out of this whole marriage situation.

Twenty minutes later he left the house, as usual kissing her first on her lips: "Good-bye, baby," he said. Then he kissed her belly: "And good-bye, baby," he said again.

"Have a good day at work, sweetpea," Sally said.

A month from now, she would be sending him off with an infant in her arms. She was only planning on taking a three-month maternity leave. Then she'd go right back to work. Jake's mother could not stop pointing out the obvious. "You don't need the money," she said again and again, as if Sally should quit her job and stay home sterilizing bottles and memorizing storybooks all day, just because she could afford to.

"You have a good day at work, too," Jake said now, and Sally held the door open for him with a smile.

Today would have been Bill's sixty-second birthday. Sally had been thinking about it, vaguely, for weeks. She wasn't going to work. She had asked her boss for the time off a full week earlier. She wanted to return—even just for a day—to the time when her love for him was the only thing she had to worry about, an exciting secret instead of a burden. In the weeks to come, everything would change. She would give birth, that petrifying, almost unbelievable prospect, the aftermath of which was even harder to picture. She had never missed her mother so much before. So perhaps that, too, was reason to have one more day alone, one more secret.

Sally remembered an afternoon, years ago; she must have been in middle school. Her mother and brother arrived in the station wagon to pick her up at a friend's house, and when Sally climbed into the backseat, her brother blurted out, "Guess what I just discovered?"

"What?" Sally pulled her heavy book bag in behind her and slammed the door.

"Mom has a dark secret," her brother said, dangling it, loving the power of knowing something that she did not.

"What?" Sally said. "What's he talking about?"

Her mother shrugged as she pulled the car out onto the street and past the rows of neat Colonials perched on sprawling green lawns.

"What *is* it?" Sally persisted. She was dying to know.

"What will you give me?" her brother said.

"How good is it?" Sally said.

"It's *good,*" her brother said. "I mean, really good."

Sally looked at her mother, who burst out laughing. "He's not lying," she said.

"Well, what do you want for it?" Sally asked her brother impatiently.

"You wash the dishes on my nights for a week," he said.

"Deal," Sally said, her heart speeding up.

"Mom drinks Dr Pepper," her brother said. "Like, a lot of it."

"*You* drink Dr Pepper?" Sally said with a gasp. It was as if she'd just learned that her mother was a heroin addict.

She had never let them have soda, not even their father was allowed it. When they protested in restaurants or at birthday parties, she would rattle off a long list of its dangers—everything from brown teeth to bone disease. The sugary substance had passed Sally's lips only three or four times in her life, and on each occasion she was struck with the sort of guilt that she imagined usually afflicted unfaithful husbands or first-time bank robbers.

"When I put my hockey stuff in the trunk after practice, I saw a whole garbage bag full of empty bottles," her brother said with glee. "She came clean pretty quick."

"I meant to take them to the recycling center today, but it

slipped my mind," her mother said. She shrugged again, as if they might just let the whole thing go.

"Mom!" Sally said. "I am shocked."

"Every woman needs secrets," her mother said with a smile then, her eyes meeting Sally's in the rearview mirror. "Remember that when you're old like me, pumpkin, because the world has a way of making a woman's life everyone else's business—you have to dig out a little place that's only yours."

Sally was proud of her mother for this one tiny secret, for being something other than exactly what they always expected her to be. She pictured her mother waiting for them in the wagon outside of school, sneaking sips from a red-and-white straw. She imagined her buying the week's groceries, her cart piled high with vegetables and chicken breasts and American cheese and apple juice and whole wheat bread. She would stop in the soda aisle, glance around to make sure no one was looking, and slip a six-pack under the rest of her purchases.

They fell silent as she slowed to let an elderly couple cross the street. The couple looked up and waved, and Sally's mother waved back, though Sally was certain she didn't know them. In that moment, a switch flipped inside of her, and the mother she knew returned.

"You both need to do your homework right away when we get home, because I have a meeting at the school tonight, and your father will be babysitting you, and I want everything to be settled," she said, almost absentmindedly. "Speaking of Daddy, let's not mention this little discovery of yours, okay?"

Sally had never forgotten her mother's words: *Every woman needs secrets,* she had said, though of course she meant something benign, like drinking soda, rather than sneaking off and lying to your husband about it when you were about to drop a baby at any moment.

Secrecy was the thing she most wanted to ask April about now. At Smith, Sally had believed that they shared everything. But April had never told her about being molested as a child—Sally had had to hear it from Bree, who heard it from Ronnie. Why had April kept this to herself? Sally wondered. And what more had she kept? She imagined a young, teenage April learning she was pregnant. Had she taken tests alone at home? Thrown up in gym class? Who besides awful Lydia did she share the news with? Sally imagined going back in time and putting her arms around April, scared and alone. The fact of being pregnant was almost too much to handle now, at the age of twenty-six. How had April made it through?

She spent the morning getting ready: applying a deep-conditioning treatment to her hair, reading *Vanity Fair* while she let it set in. She shaved her legs slowly, and rubbed cocoa butter into her skin, which she had read eliminated stretch marks. She put on makeup for the first time in weeks.

Sally left for Northampton that afternoon, with Bill's copy of the *Collected Poems of W. H. Auden* beside her on the passenger seat. There was a black-and-white photo of the poet on the book's cover. His face was lined with wrinkles; his eyes were small and sad. He had the look of a man who had seen much, felt much, said much. How different it was from

Bill's jacket photo—that handsome, vain smile, betraying nothing.

In the car, she sang along to the oldies station, belting out songs by the Beatles and Elton John. She thought of their Smith days, when a gentle knock on her dorm-room door might turn into Celia sliding across the floor in her under-wear, singing Cher into a hairbrush microphone and start-ing a ridiculous sing-along that would usually draw in a few other girls from the hall. Sally never sang like that anymore, unless she was alone. Why not? It wasn't that Jake would have discouraged such behavior but rather that she was unable to behave that way in front of him. Wives didn't do hairbrush serenades or jump up and down in bed in their underwear singing "If I Could Turn Back Time." Sally ran a palm over her belly and smiled. Mothers could be like that, though, she thought. Goofy and silly and bizarre, doing barnyard impressions and renditions of Broadway musi-cals, setting their children's heads tipping backward in delighted laughter. Whom had she ever laughed with the way she laughed with the Smithies? Her mother, and that was all.

Since feeling the baby's first kick, Sally had fallen in love. It seemed real; she was actually going to have a child. Her fears now centered on the agony of giving birth, and on who her child would be. There was something thrilling about the idea of a person made up of half of her stuff and half of Jake's. Sally hoped their baby would get the best of them both—Jake's sunny disposition and good sense and athletic ability. Her dark hair and cleanliness and that weird wild-card quality that made her who she was. But sometimes, especially when she was alone in the car like this, Sally imagined horrifying scenarios. What if their kid became a criminal, or a teen mother, or a Scientologist? What if she wanted to join the military?

Though Jake begged her not to, Sally had watched a rerun of Stone Phillips interviewing Jeffrey Dahmer's mother on TV a few nights earlier.

"What was he like as a boy?" Stone asked, in his concerned, rugged voice.

"Just like any other boy," she said. "I thought he was wonderful."

That was the problem, Sally told Jake. You would never know your own child was a cannibalistic serial killer until it was too late.

When she reached exit 18 and saw the familiar sign for Smith College, she rolled down her window. The mountain air was cool and sharp. She had come to think about Bill, and to remember April, not *one last time,* she decided, because *one last time* was bullshit. No one could ever say for sure whether they were doing something for the last time, unless they were dead. The day her mother died, they had stood in the hospital hall, by a too-familiar window that overlooked the Jamaicaway. Sally's brother was huddled up on the floor by the windowsill, his headphones blaring. Her father was talking to the doctor in hushed tones, signing papers on a clipboard. All of a sudden, a nurse with string-thin lips approached. Sally eyed her as she glanced from one of them to the next. When her eyes met Sally's, she smiled sadly and held out a plastic Baggie.

"Her effects," the nurse said in a thick Irish accent.

Sally gasped as she glanced down at her mother's engagement ring and watch, her house keys on that ugly Cape Cod
key chain, her red wallet still bulging with Stop & Shop
coupons. How many times had Sally looked at all this junk
without a second thought? And now it was all she had left of
her.

How could a person have and do all these stupid things—
clip coupons and double lock the front door—and then one
day just cease to exist? If April was dead, who would be the
one to get her belongings? What on earth would she even
have to show for her short, brave life?

When she got to the campus, Sally pulled the car to the
side of the road and got out, clutching Auden. She had read
that Bill was buried in the cemetery at the end of Main
Street, though the fact of it surprised her. She couldn't
remember if they had ever discussed it, but he did not seem
like the type to want to be buried. Sally wondered if maybe it
had been his children's idea. She remembered how unbearable it had been to think of her mother's familiar, warm
body burned up to ash. Though really, was it any better to
bury your parent in the ground, leaving him to decompose
like garbage, until he was nothing? She would never want to
see Bill like that, memorialized by a cold stone, a heap of
dirt, and some wilting flowers. Or worse, one of those stupid
miniature Christmas trees that people placed at gravesides
this time of year, as if the dead were twenty-somethings living in tiny studio apartments.

It was bitter cold. Sally tried to pull her woolen jacket over
her enormous stomach. Even though she was pregnant, she
was too vain to buy a maternity coat.

"I'll never wear it again!" she said to Jake when he told her she needed one on a recent trip to the mall for nursery furniture.

"What about when you're pregnant with our next kid?" he said.

"Oh, brother," she had snapped. "Can we get this one out into the light of day before we start talking about the next one, please?"

She pulled her mittens from her pockets now and began to walk the path through Center Campus toward the Quad.

"You okay?" she said to the baby. She hoped she wasn't slowly freezing her daughter to death. Once this kid came into the world, Sally knew, she would live in constant terror of somehow injuring or losing her. Having her tucked deep inside her belly was the safest she would ever feel about the child, and even that was scary.

Sally walked slowly. How many times had she taken this path with the girls, lazily gossiping on the way to class, or trudging arm in arm through the snow, or, on occasion, purposefully marching at a Take Back the Night rally or Celebration of Sisterhood, always with April leading the way. Smith had left its mark on her, so that the place would always feel like home, but she was a stranger here now. In each of her friends, her Smith College self would always live on. Maybe that was why they were all still so important to one another, even though so much had changed.

Two girls came toward her now, holding hands and whispering into each other's ears. They reminded her of Bree and Lara. Bree had called Sally a few days earlier to tell her how they had reunited in San Francisco. She said it felt magical, like one of the old movies Celia used to make them watch in college. But even so, Bree flew back to New York a day later, as planned.

When Sally asked what would happen next, Bree said, "I just don't know. Maybe I should move home and take that job my dad offered me. I could do worse, right? I had been dreaming of her for so long, Sal, but I need my family, too."

"Maybe you can have both," Sally had said gently.

"No," Bree said. "I really don't think so."

Sally paused in front of the library now, the site of her first conversation with Bill, the first place they ever made love. At her wedding, she had been afraid to go inside, because the passage of time had transformed him in her eyes. The thought of seeing him again, for what he really was, felt like too much. But now Bill was gone, and she could remember him just as he had been in those early days.

She walked inside and the familiar smell filled the air, a mix of leather and old paper and floor polish. She made her way toward Bill's office.

In the main room, Smithies sat alone at carrels, serious as monks, their faces down in their used copies of Thackeray and Joan Didion. Sally had a ridiculous urge to walk over to them, smooth their hair, and tell them to savor every minute of this. But none of the girls even looked up. Sally was twenty-six, which in college student years was borderline elderly. When you went to college in a town, you fancied it your own, but you never really knew the place in the way of the permanent residents—the cemeteries and the DMV, the public libraries and elementary schools. You just saw your campus as a world unto itself and thought of the townspeople as adorable extras. Did Harvard kids look at her that way now? Some old married pregnant lady, another nameless part of the safe backdrop that was Cambridge?

She took the stairs at the back of the room, her heart speeding up as she approached his office. She had imagined it many times these past few weeks—cardboard boxes overflowing with his books and papers, here and there a stray Post-it lying on the ground. But when she got there, she found the room completely bare but for his old steel desk and empty bookshelves. Everything familiar and personal—the wing chair, the lambskin rug—had been taken away. By whom? His children? His wife?

Sally stepped into the room and closed the door behind her. She sat on the floor and tried to find some trace of him, but even his smell had been erased. She opened up his old copy of Auden and read for nearly an hour—the epic poems, the love poems, the silly two-liners Auden had dashed off to other famous poets. Then she got to the one that reminded her most of Bill. It was one of the poems he had read to her over and over on those early nights in his office while they were cuddling on the rug, drinking wine from plastic cups meant to look like glass. Later, lying alone in her single bed, in a building full of girls lying alone in single beds, she would say the words out loud. She did this again now, reading it in a hushed voice to the empty room around her:

> Love like Matter is much
> odder than we thought.

> Love requires an Object,
> But this varies so much

Almost, I imagine,
Anything will do:
When I was a child, I
Loved a pumping-engine,
Thought it every bit as
Beautiful as you.

Bill had always said that every poem was different for every reader, because each person injected the poet's personal thoughts with his or her own, breathing new life into them. When Bill had read her that poem, she had imagined it to mean that he loved her in a way so pure and honest and absolute that it was as if he were a little boy again, running around in short-pants. The part she had ignored was the most important part: *Almost anything will do.*

She realized now, too late, that perhaps the poems he loved were his attempts at confessing. She lingered over this one, letting her finger trace each word slowly. When she finished, she laid the book on his desk and left the room, closing the door behind her.

Outside, it smelled like snow. As she walked toward the Quad and past the frozen pond, she imagined white flakes floating down, burying whatever remained of him.

By the time she reached King House, Sally was out of breath from walking, and she felt like her bladder was about to burst. She glanced around, but there were no students in sight, so she went right up to the back door of the house, prepared to use her old key to get inside and use the bathroom. When she saw the door, she jolted backward a bit—the keyhole had been covered over, and there was now a little cube of plastic in its place with a blinking red light, the sort of thing you would swipe a credit card through.

She thought of an old Joni Mitchell song that April used to play while they were studying. *Nothing lasts for long, nothing lasts for long.*

Sally rang the bell, but no one came, so she walked to the stone steps leading back down to the Quad and sat on the cold concrete. Where was April? she wondered for what felt like the millionth time. When would they ever know what really happened to her?

Sally felt the baby kick, and she let out a little laugh. "This is where I married your daddy," she said. Someday she would bring her little girl here. She thought of introducing her daughter to Celia and Bree, and to April, once she came back to them.

"Excuse me! Ma'am?" came a tinny voice from behind. Sally swiveled her head to see a young smiling girl with a backpack holding the door to the house open. She looked about eleven years old. "Did you want to come inside?" she asked, in a helpful, Girl Scout–like tone.

Sally thought about this for a moment. She imagined walking into King House, which was nothing without the girls by her side.

Finally, she shook her head. "No, thank you," she said. "I'm fine where I am."

CELIA

It was a brilliant, sunny Saturday in New York when they first heard the news. According to the television, the Atlanta police had been tipped off by an unidentified source that there were human remains—a woman's arm and calf—buried in the backyard of the pimp everyone thought had kidnapped April. The pimp himself had vanished. It would take a week or more to be certain it was her, but Celia had no doubt.

Celia and Bree sat side by side on the couch and cried all weekend.

Celia couldn't sleep, and on Monday she had to get Ambien from her doctor, a wiry guy who looked at her suspiciously, as if she had asked him for heroin. He eventually wrote the prescription (and gave her the number for a good shrink with an office right by her apartment) when she began to sob uncontrollably into his lab coat. Bree was leaving her soon, most likely returning home to Savannah to work in her father's firm, and the thought of being alone at night haunted Celia.

On Monday evening, their contact in the Atlanta police department called to say that the following afternoon they would conduct one final search.

"A search for what?" Celia asked.

"Whenever we come up with major evidence, such as remains, our search unit takes another look over the neighborhood where the evidence was found, and any outlying natural areas, just in case. We want to take every step we can to make sure this guy is put away, and sometimes that's as simple as finding a shell casing or a scrap of fabric."

The police were looking for civilian volunteers to help, so Celia and Bree bought two tickets for the first flight out in the morning. Celia's parents and sister planned to come down to Atlanta as well, and Bree's entire family did the same.

Celia kept thinking about the day just before Sally's wedding weekend, when April called to say that she had been beaten up, while Ronnie simply ran off.

She just needed to protect herself, April had said in Ronnie's defense.

What would have been different if Celia had said, *Oh yeah? Well, I just need to protect you and I demand that you quit.*

April probably would have laughed. But now, Celia would never know.

"What should we pack?" Bree asked. She was congested from crying, and her voice sounded foggy.

Celia knew what she was thinking, but could not bring

herself to say out loud: that they were, in fact, going to Georgia for April's funeral.

Sally's doctor had told her she absolutely could not fly this late in her pregnancy, but she was joining them in Atlanta anyway. Jake was panicked about this, but she hadn't given him any choice.

"He's freaking out because I've already fucking dropped," she said to Celia over the phone.

Now that she was pregnant, Sally swore as much as April ever had.

"What the hell does 'dropped' mean?" Celia asked.

"It just means the baby has descended down to my pelvis or something," Sally said. "Jake will tell you all about it when he sees you, I'm sure. But it could still be four weeks before I go into labor."

"Does it hurt when it drops?" Celia asked, cringing. When Sally talked about the specifics of her pregnancy, Celia always felt physically ill, which in turn made her feel like a bad female, but what could you do?

"Oh no," Sally said. "My stomach's just lower. Now I can breathe better, but I have to pee every ten minutes. Literally, Cee. Every ten freaking minutes."

"Eww," Celia said.

"Yeah, and that's not the half of it," Sally said. "I also have hemorrhoids. I'm twenty-six, and I have hemorrhoids. My gums are bleeding, my legs ache, my butt hurts. I am telling you right now, Celia. If you're smart, you'll just adopt."

It was pouring rain when they gathered outside the police station the next day. The search had been announced on television all across the country, and dozens of Smithies came to help, people Celia hadn't thought about in years and people she'd never even heard of, who had all been touched by April in some way or another. There was Jenna the Monster Truck, who had heralded them into Smith on their very first day. And Toby Jones, April's trans friend, who was now devastatingly handsome, good-looking enough to make Celia wonder whether any of the guys she had slept with in New York had once been a Lucy or a Tina.

Lara came, too. She and Bree had been talking by phone every night since Bree's return from California, and Celia wondered why they didn't just make it official already. Yes, there were complications. Of course. But she knew Bree well enough to know what would make her happy.

Outside the station, Lara stood by Bree's side, and the two of them held hands.

Celia looked over at Bree's parents, who were watching them.

"You're under surveillance," she said to Bree and Lara.

"I don't care," Bree said.

Lara's eyes grew wide.

"Well, maybe I care a little, but I'm trying not to," Bree said, and they laughed.

The search had also drawn locals and church and women's groups from all over the country, seventy people in all. April's mother was there, but there was no sign of Ronnie. The police captain brought them out to the parking lot and separated them into groups of ten.

"Thank you all for being here," he hollered into a sea of black umbrellas. "This kind of search needs to be exhaustive, and the police force just doesn't have the manpower to handle it alone. That's why we look to civilians like you to help us in times like this."

Volunteers handed out flyers printed with April's picture and a description of what she was wearing the last time she was seen. Celia stared down at the picture, wondering who had provided it—Ronnie?

The captain explained that they would be searching the neighborhood where April had lived and disappeared, as well as parks and fields and swamp areas. Each team would have a police officer to guide them.

"Many of you were here with us for our search on the morning of April's disappearance, but for those who weren't, here's the drill: Those of you in the less-developed areas should link arms and form a sort of human chain as you look at the ground and your surroundings," he said. "This way not a single inch will be missed."

The writer in Celia was amused by the vision of a human chain made of transgendered Smith grads and Catholic nuns and gray-haired second-wave feminists and Atlanta shopkeepers. She thought there was something in it that would please April, too, and for a moment, she smiled.

But then someone in the crowd called out, "What are we supposed to look for?"

The captain wiped a hand across his forehead, which was wet with rainwater despite his umbrella.

"Unfortunately, at this point, we aren't hoping to find April alive. We are searching for clues as to what happened to her," he said. "Anything that looks suspicious—clothing or a shoe or remains—should be reported immediately to your police liaison."

Celia willed herself not to look at April's mother.

He went on. "Those of you who will be searching the neighborhood, your job is to ask questions: Has anyone seen April? Has anyone heard anything we'd want to know?"

The idea of it scared Celia—what if she knocked on a door and then stood face-to-face with April's murderer? Would she know on some level that it was him? Would she scream or run or just burst into tears?

That's when the captain began to tell them where to go: Celia, Bree, Sally, and Jake were all part of the group assigned to search April's neighborhood, along with a police officer named Dan Daniels, who looked about her dad's age.

"Y'all were her closest friends," Officer Daniels said as they huddled together as a group. "We know you want to see justice happen here. I'm gonna tell you how to talk to these people in the neighborhood. They don't much love seeing cops on their block, so they're probably more likely to speak to you than to me."

They hardly said a word to one another as they knocked on doors along English Avenue and around the Bluff. In their collective imagination, Celia knew, they'd hoped to knock on some door and see April standing there with a cup of coffee in her hand. Or even just some sign of her: a pair of her corduroys slung over a banister, something.

But instead, when they got to the rows of tiny houses, only a few feet apart from one another, person after person said the same thing: They hadn't seen April, or even heard of her, and would Celia please kindly get off their stoop.

She had never felt so white in her entire life.

With each hour that passed, Celia grew at once more hopeless and more relieved.

She had been to countless wakes as a child, holding her father's hand as they gazed at the corpse of some old relative or another. The bodies never looked quite dead to Celia. If she stared at them long enough, she could swear they were taking shallow breaths. As a kid, she braced herself against the possibility that this was just like the really good haunted house they went to at Castle Island every Halloween, and that at any moment the person in the coffin would jump upright and scream, "Boo!"

But this wasn't some great-uncle she only saw at Christmas. This was April. Celia didn't want to see her body, or what remained of it. The thought alone was more than she could take.

Despite all their efforts, the volunteers and the police didn't turn up a thing that day. The rain had gotten heavier, and they were predicting thunderstorms for the following twenty-four hours. The police department decided to postpone the rest of the search and start it up again two days later.

That evening, all of them—Sally and Jake, Bree and Celia and their families—stood in front of the hotel, unsure of what to do next.

"We'd be happy to take everyone to dinner," Celia's father said. "If people are up for that."

But dinner never happened. Bree and Celia's families went off separately in search of something to eat; Bree said she was going to take a long walk alone; and Sally needed to lie down, so Celia and Jake accompanied her back to her room.

In the hotel room, Sally flopped onto the bed.

"Can you believe Ronnie didn't show up to help look for her?" she said. "That motherfucker. If I ever get my hands on her, Cee, I swear to God—"

"I'll get some ice," Jake said, grabbing the half-full bucket and hitting the hallway.

"Gotta love Jake," Celia said with a smile. "It's like the ninety-seventh time he's gotten ice since we've been here."

"I told him I was going to need a lot of alone time with you and Bree," Sally said. "I think he's a little bit afraid of me these days. I feel like I'm moving through quicksand, Celia. This all feels like a bad dream."

Celia nodded. "I know. I haven't slept much these past few days, have you?"

"Not really," Sally said softly. "I don't know if I can bring a child into such a terrible world."

Celia poked her belly. "I don't think you have much choice there," she said. "That child's coming into this world whether you like it or not."

"I know," Sally said. "I'm the fucking Goodyear blimp."

That night, Celia slept in bed with her sister and mother for the first time since she was in grade school.

Returning from Sally and Jake's room, she found her dad already asleep, snoring on a rollaway cot. Violet was sleeping, too, a copy of *Rolling Stone* magazine spread across her chest. Their mother was lying in bed beside her, with her eyes wide open. Celia nestled into her side, taking in the familiar scent of her nightgown, not wanting to ever have to go back to New York.

"What are you thinking about?" she asked.

"April's mom," her mother said. They had been on the same search team earlier that day, making their way through a huge park near April's old neighborhood. "It just ripped me up, watching her. I'm sure part of her wanted to find something of April's. And part of her didn't—part of her probably just pretends April lives in Tallahassee or something now, that she's out in an orange field, laughing at all of us for worrying."

Celia's oldest memory was of her mother baking circus cupcakes for her third birthday, each one topped with a tiny ballerina or a clown or a seal bouncing a red rubber ball on its nose. She was nine months pregnant with Violet, and her belly bumped against the kitchen counter as she mixed the hot pink icing. She seemed invincible, magical. Even now, if Celia called her complaining of a sore throat, her mother could tell if it was strep or just a virus merely from the sound of her voice. She always knew the answers to every little question—whether to tip the locksmith, what to give your boss for Christmas, how to handle a demanding agent or a creepy male superior at work, the length of time it took to make a perfect hard-boiled egg. As long as her mother was alive, Celia would feel protected, no matter how many miles stood between them. She thought now of how April had never known that sort of safety.

"Lydia's not really a mother like you are," Celia said. "She hadn't even spoken to April for over a year."

Her mother closed her eyes. "That might even make

things worse. When you have a daughter, this sort of thing is just your worst nightmare. It doesn't matter who you are. For the first time I can remember, I am actually angry at God. Why would He let something like this go on? I've never wanted you girls to walk through your lives thinking that bad things just happen for no reason, but—"

"Don't they?" Celia interrupted. "Isn't that the bitch of it?"

Her mother kissed her cheek. "Maybe. I don't know. Let's try to get some sleep."

A moment later, her voice tired and far away, she added, "And don't say 'bitch,' Cee Cee. That word is beneath you."

They were awakened by the sound of the phone ringing in the dark.

Violet jumped up first. "Wake-up call," she said. She picked up the phone and said, "Thank you," then hung up, and flopped back onto the bed.

It rang again.

"Jeez." Violet picked it up and said, "Yes?" After a moment, she let out a little scream and said, "Oh. Oh my God!"

Celia was still half in a dream, and her first thought was that maybe April wasn't really dead after all. Maybe the police were calling to say that the bones they had found were someone else's, that April was safe and warm in her bed.

But then Violet started shaking her. "Wake up!" she yelled. "Sally's having her baby!"

Celia opened her eyes and looked at the clock. It was four-fifteen in the morning.

Her mother sprang up and already had her shoes on

before Celia even put her feet on the floor. The hotel was huge. The two of them got to Sally's room five minutes later, panting from the run. When Celia knocked on the door, Jake answered it and gave them a pleading look, like he was being held hostage.

Behind him, Sally sat on the bed, calmly painting her toenails.

Celia's heart raced. "Umm, Sal, what are you doing?" she said.

"Getting ready," Sally said.

"But shouldn't you be on your way to the hospital?" Celia asked, looking at her mother for the answer.

"My contractions just started," Sally said. "We've got hours. Jake found an obstetrician in town who will take us. I just want to shave my legs and wash my hair and stuff. I don't even know this doctor, so I don't want to show up looking like a ragamuffin."

Celia's mouth formed a perfect O. So did Jake's.

Her mother went over and sat beside Sally on the bed. She gently ran her hand over Sally's hair. "You're right, sweetheart. You probably have time," she said. "But it's possible that you were already in labor in your sleep and didn't feel it, so you might be a lot more dilated than you think. That's what happened to me with Violet, and she was almost born in the back of a Cutlass Supreme."

"Oh God, really?" Sally said, suddenly sounding like herself.

Jake clapped his hands together. "Yes! That's exactly what I told her!"

"Baby, shut up," Sally snapped. She took a deep breath. "Sorry," she said. "Okay, let's go to the hospital."

They helped her to her feet.

Sally grabbed Celia's hand. "I want you and Bree in the room with us," she said. "Okay?"

Celia was stunned. "Yes!" she said with a laugh. "I'll go get Bree, and we'll meet you guys out front."

Before she left, Celia pulled Jake aside. "Are you okay?" she said. "Would you rather Bree and I didn't come?"

"This is Sally's show. I'm just along for the ride," he said. "Thanks for asking, though."

Celia squeezed his arm. "You're pretty great, you know. You're gonna be an amazing dad."

Jake smiled. "Thank you. Now go get Bree, before Sally stabs me to death with her nail file."

Bree's room was three flights above Sally's, and Celia took the stairs two at a time.

She knocked hard on the door.

"Bree!" she called. "Babe, come out here! Sally's about to pop."

When the door swung open a moment later, it was Lara who stood there, sleepy eyed and confused in her bra and boxers.

"Cee?" she said in a hoarse voice.

Celia just laughed. "I need Bree for a mission," she said.

Bree padded up behind Lara. "What kind of mission?" she said, squinting against the hallway light.

"Sally's going to have the baby, and she wants us in the room with her," Celia said.

"Oh my God," Bree said.

Celia cocked her head to the side. "You two look cozy," she said with a grin. "Have we made any decisions?"

Bree was pulling on jeans and a pair of flip-flops.

"Yeah yeah," she said, nonchalantly. "No time for that now."

But before they headed outside, she kissed Lara on the mouth and said, "I love you."

"She needs to stretch out in the backseat," Jake instructed as they got into the rental car. Celia sat in back, with Sally's head in her lap. Her water had broken sometime in the night, without even waking her up, and she was still leaking the sweet-smelling fluid now. Whoever drove this car next would be getting a lot more than they bargained for, Celia thought. She wished she could leave them a note: *Wear shoes in this vehicle at all times. Just trust me on this.*

They got lost trying to find the hospital. Bree called her father and woke him up for directions.

A few minutes later, they pulled up to a red light. Jake looked like he might start hyperventilating at any moment. "*Come on,* people! My wife is having a baby here!"

Bree turned around and smiled at Celia.

"Oh, Bree," Sally said. "Did you and Lara share a room last night?"

Bree laughed. "I'll tell you all the details later."

"No, tell us now," Sally said. "I need something to distract me from the fact that I'm about to push an eight-pound child out of a hole the size of a quarter."

Bree grinned. "Okay, then. So you know I went for a walk after the search. I was thinking about April and about how much of life is just out of our control. But this is something I can control. Lara is *here*. So I asked her to come to my room, and we talked for a long time. It was really nice."

"And then," Celia said.

Brec rolled her eyes. "And then we slept together."

Jake perked up at that. "Can I ask a question?" he asked sheepishly. "What exactly do you mean when you say you slept together? Like, did you—"

"Oh my God, shut up with that," Sally said.

Suddenly Jake pumped his fist in the air. "I am *the man!*" he shouted.

"Honey, you just found a hospital with directions from MapQuest," Sally said. "You didn't exactly discover the New World."

Jake laughed. "I sure am gonna miss all your pregnancy hormones," he said.

A nurse with spiky white hair took Sally into a private room to get her ready for the doctors. Celia, Bree, and Jake waited in the hall by the vending machines.

Celia still felt so young, like a kid. It seemed wrong somehow for the four of them to be here. She wished her mother had come along. She could only imagine how Sally felt. After all this, she would have a child, an actual person to take care of and raise.

After a while, an orderly approached them. "You can come in now," he said.

In the room, Sally was on her feet in her hospital gown, talking sharply to the white-haired nurse: "Listen, I want an enema," she said. "It's part of my birthing plan back home in Boston. Call my doctor there if you don't believe me."

The nurse smiled. "It's not that I don't believe you, dear," she said. "It's just not our policy to give enemas."

"Honey, why would you want an enema in the first place?"

Bree said, and Celia could not help but laugh—this was a word she had never expected to hear out of either of their mouths.

"So I don't take a big poop on the table while I'm giving birth!" Sally snapped.

Bree and Celia exchanged a look of horror. After this, Celia thought, it was quite possible that neither of them would ever be able to have a child.

The doctor said the baby's birth was still hours away. Sally had been right not to hurry. She could have stayed at the nice hotel in her fluffy white robe and painted a miniature replica of the Last Supper on each nail, and she still would have had time to spare. The four of them played cards and walked the halls and ate banana bread from the cafeteria. Sally panicked over not having her "birth bag," which was apparently a suitcase she had packed with her favorite nightgown, nice towels and lotion, a mix CD she and Jake had burned to listen to during the birth, a pink outfit from Rosemary to take the baby home in, and healthy snacks and water for Jake "so he doesn't pass out during delivery," Sally said.

They watched the rain fall and talked about April, and Sally said she hoped the baby came by Thursday morning, so that all of them could get back outside and search.

In the hours that followed, Celia got a real education, as her mother put it when Celia called her from the hospital lobby to give her an update at around 10:00 a.m.

When she got back upstairs, Bree was running toward her like a madwoman. "Her labor's over!" she said.

"Oh my God, she had the baby?" Celia said.

Bree laughed. "No, honey, she still has to deliver the baby. This is when the gore hits the fan. Didn't you ever take a health class in junior high?"

Celia shook her head. "Catholic school. They told us that babies were dropped into their cribs by teams of angels carrying fluffy pink or blue blankets."

When they reached Sally's room, the nurse was injecting the epidural into her spine. Celia had never seen such a huge needle in her life.

"Jesus, Mary, and Joseph," she said to Bree under her breath.

Sally was a trouper. She didn't scream as much as women in the movies usually did, because she said her doctor back home had told her it was a waste of energy and would make the birth longer than it needed to be. She squeezed Jake's hand with one of hers, and Celia's with the other.

"What was the first song on that mix CD you made?" Bree asked when Sally began to fade.

Between grunts, Sally said, "Supremes. 'Can't Hurry Love.' "

Celia, Bree, and Jake sang her the whole CD—"Don't Stop Believing" by Journey, "Manic Monday" by the Bangles—as the nurses looked on with a combination of annoyance and amusement.

There was more blood than Celia could have imagined. It was everywhere, and she was relieved that Sally didn't actually have to see it. She had always wondered why women gave birth lying down, with a sheet over their legs. This, evidently, was the reason.

After four hours of pushing, Sally was exhausted. She pushed and pushed until the blood vessels in her face popped, and she looked like she was bleeding from every pore. Celia and Bree were aghast; they couldn't help it. Here was their impeccable Sally—who never had a hair out of place, never so much as a wrinkle in her dress or a scuff on her shoe—looking like she'd just walked out of a boxing ring.

"What is it?" Sally said, squeezing hard, nearly crushing Celia's palm.

"Nothing," Celia said.

She turned to Jake. "Oh God, what happened? I look like shit, right?"

"You look beautiful. Honest," Jake said, and Celia almost burst into tears.

When the baby's head crowned, Sally screamed bloody murder.

Doctor's orders be damned, Celia thought. Had Sally's obstetrician back home, a man named Dr. Finkle, ever given birth? No. So what the hell did he know about screaming?

"Sally, we're having a little trouble getting the baby's shoulders out," the doctor said. "We're going to have to do a small episiotomy."

"How small?" she said.

"Small," the doctor said. "I promise. Seven stitches, max."

Stitches? Celia reminded herself to get on the waiting list for a couple of Romanian orphans as soon as she got home.

"No," Sally said, shaking her head. "I don't want it done."

Celia was about to speak up, about to say that these damn people needed to listen to Sally, and really, hadn't the poor girl been through enough without slicing her open?

"Babe," Jake said gently. "I know you didn't want one, but it will heal so much better than a jagged tear."

Bree's eyes nearly popped out of her head.

The doctor grinned. "I see Daddy here has been reading *What to Expect When You're Expecting.* He's right, I'm afraid."

"Oh okay," Sally said. "Just get this thing out of me." She put her head back, resigned.

The final pushes looked and sounded like agony, but moments later, there she was—Sally's daughter, April Eleanor Brown, with a shock of dark hair, just like her mother's. She was covered in goop, and Celia was surprised when the doctor laid her right on Sally's chest. Sally beamed, the most radiant smile Celia had ever seen, and that was really saying something when Sal's entire face was covered in bloody, red splotches.

Celia and Bree left Sally and Jake alone with the baby for a while and went to the cafeteria again to get some dinner.

Bree picked at her soggy Caesar salad. "So much has happened in the last two days that I feel like it's going to take a year to process all of it."

"Did Lara go back to San Francisco?" Celia asked.

"No, she's staying for the next round of searching," Bree said.

"And then what will you do?" Celia said.

"These past few weeks I've really believed that I'm going to end up back home in Savannah where I belong," Bree said. "But now—"

Celia grinned. "I think you're going to move back out to California," she said.

"Me too," Bree said. She whistled under her breath. "Oh man, this is gonna go over real big at my mom's house. Isn't it kind of funny that she'd prefer for me to break up Doug Anderson's marriage than for me to be a lesbian?"

They laughed.

"You never know, your parents might come around," Celia said. "Life is long."

It was a favorite phrase of her grandmother's, which she was only just beginning to understand.

They went to the gift shop for champagne and flowers and a dozen pink balloons. Celia knew that all of them felt strange celebrating, but she thought it was right that they should honor new life, now more than ever.

When they returned, each of them got to hold the baby. Celia felt like she might melt as she rocked the little thing in her arms.

"I'm your Auntie Celia," she whispered.

Jake opened the champagne, and they toasted. Sally had a few sips, but then handed the rest of her glass to Jake because she was breastfeeding. Celia thought that if she were in Sally's place, she'd ask to have the entire bottle fed into her IV. Or perhaps they should have started with the booze instead of ending with it.

"That was amazing to watch," Celia said of the birth, though she knew there were many other adjectives to describe it.

"And you two thought my wedding was painful," Sally said with a smile.

Bree laughed. "Oh my God, Sal. You're a mother."

"I'm a mother," Sally said. "I wish my mom was here to see this. And April, too."

Celia didn't know how to respond. If her mother were there, she'd say something like: *They are here, Sally; they're watching over you always.* But that felt about as unnatural to Celia as Sally saying the word "enema."

Finally, Bree said, "The baby has your mom's eyes."

"She does, doesn't she?" Sally said.

Celia gave Bree a smile. It was the perfect thing to say, she thought, though she had no idea whether or not it was true.

"So," Celia said, after their glasses had been emptied, the baby taken to the nursery to sleep. "Now what?"

"Now we all get a good night's rest so we can be bright and alert tomorrow, and find April," Sally said.

"Not you, though, right, honey?" Jake said nervously. "You're staying here, right?"

"We'll see how I feel," Sally said. "I'm not lugging around as much weight as I was yesterday. I should be much quicker on my feet by morning."

"Please tell me you're joking," Bree said.

"Or that it's the drugs talking," Celia said.

"Nope," Jake said. "That's just our Sally."

Celia and Bree exchanged a look.

"You're okay, Jake," Bree said. "You may even be the first male to earn the title of 'honorary Smithie.' "

"My husband, the Smithie." Sally beamed. A moment later, she closed her eyes and began to snore.

Jake ducked into the bathroom, and Bree turned to Celia.

"Is there any chance we might find her alive tomorrow?" she asked.

Celia shook her head sadly. "I think she's gone."

"So do I," Bree said. "And I hate that life just keeps going anyway."

APRIL

R onnie's plan was simple.

All over the country, little black girls left home each morning and never returned. They got killed by gang members or kidnapped by strangers and forced into prostitution. Yet no one ever issued an Amber Alert for them. The *Today* show never splashed their smiling photographs across America's TV screens. When an educated white girl went missing, the media couldn't get enough of the details.

Ronnie had a real gift for changing people's visions by using their own failings against them. She said she wanted to raise awareness about American child sex trafficking while also showing how little the country cares about anyone who's not privileged and white.

That was how April ended up telling her friends that they were making a documentary but leaving out the rest. And how she came to pack up her belongings and live with Ronnie in that shit hole on English Avenue.

After a year, just when April began to wonder whether they were doing the right thing, Ronnie announced that they were finally going to put the plan into action.

In the middle of the night one sticky Friday in August, April crept over to Alexa's house and silently crawled down a handmade rope ladder into a space under the parlor floorboards, about the size of the small walk-in closet she had at Smith. There was no light, the space smelled like mildew, and the floor was made of stone. Alexa had tried to make it nice. She filled it with pillows and a soft baby blanket. She told April not to worry—she had hidden girls there before, she said, when they were running from the police or their pimps. None of them had ever seen any roaches or mice, and Alexa said it was impossible to hear the girls from up above, even when one of them accidentally sneezed or coughed. Still, April had to press her palm hard against her mouth to keep from crying. She had never liked tight spaces, but she knew this was the only way.

The following morning, Ronnie told her that she had called April's mother and the Smith girls as planned to tell them what had happened. This way, Ronnie said, no one would be able to talk April out of the plan, but April would have her wish—those who loved her most would know she was safe.

Later that day, Ronnie reported April missing, and Alexa came forward to say that she had seen Redd shoving April into a car the night before. The last part was a flat-out lie like the rest of it, of course, but Ronnie and Alexa had decided that punishing Redd could be a special bonus of the project.

He was the worst of the worst in Atlanta, notorious in the neighborhood for beating his girls with a baseball bat, allowing them to be raped by dozens of men in a single night as part of a gang initiation, and once punishing a fifteen-year-old who refused to have sex with a drunk businessman by shoving a broken glass bottle into her vagina and biting a hole in her bottom lip. He was arrested on charges of aggravated assault and mayhem, but released on bail after just one month. No one seemed to know what had happened to the girl, but Alexa said Redd had been bragging to everyone that his friends finished her off.

The police saw these young girls as criminals, inhabiting the same vulgar world as their pimps, asking for what they got. What the cops and most people failed to recognize was that the pimps had made a choice, while the girls had been forced. Ronnie hoped the project would bring this to the attention of the general public. She referenced domestic violence, how forty years earlier no one talked about it—there was no movement, not even a name. But pioneering women had brought the issue to the forefront, and now they would do the same with sexual exploitation.

Sometimes April wondered if this project was Ronnie's final attempt at rehabilitating her reputation in the feminist community. Despite all the good she had done over the last three decades, she was usually thought of as a fringe figure, an outsider. Maybe she saw all this as her last best chance.

April was only supposed to be under Alexa's floor for a month. That was their agreement. In the beginning, Alexa would slip her a sandwich and a piece of fruit, or cookies and bottled water, during the day. If she had to pee, Alexa would bring a bedpan, though April tried with all her might not to put either of them in this position. She knew that Alexa believed in the cause as much as she and Ronnie did, and she knew that Ronnie was paying Alexa an ungodly amount to hide her, but even so.

After midnight, once everyone else in the house was behind closed doors, Alexa would let her out for a while, sneaking her up to her private quarters. There, April would shower and use the bathroom, stretch her legs, and eat a warm dinner at Alexa's little sewing table: fried chicken and red wine, spaghetti with garlic bread. It pained her to have to go back underground after an hour or so upstairs, but Alexa would always soothe her, saying, "Tomorrow night's gonna come so fast, you'll see."

Ronnie was insistent that even when it seemed like the pressure was off and no one was watching, April must never sleep upstairs. "Too risky," she insisted, and April thought this sounded accurate. Alexa gave her a bottle of prescription sleeping pills that some girl had left behind in the medicine cabinet, and April started taking one each night. They'd expired six months earlier, but they still worked just fine.

For the first four weeks, Ronnie brought an update every Monday night. At month's end, she said, they would tell everyone the truth—that April was alive and safe, that the whole thing was a work of art, a way of showing the world how ignorant people were about sexual exploitation and whom they chose to highlight in the press. Ronnie hoped some news outlets would report the disappearance. They never expected it would become such a major story.

When that first month came to an end, April sat across

from Ronnie in Alexa's bedroom, and Ronnie took her hand.

"Listen, kiddo," she said. "I know I said it would only be a month, but it's all going better than I ever could have hoped. I need you to do this just a little while longer."

As weeks passed, Ronnie's visits started to decrease. She was constantly off to New York or LA or Chicago to tape another TV segment on the dangers of domestic sex trafficking, and to promote a book she had now been commissioned to write on the topic. (She told April that once they came clean, they would write the book together and share the author credit.)

April tried to occupy her thoughts with other things—counting as high as she could, imagining what the girls were up to in their little corners of the world, translating English sentences into Spanish in an attempt to relearn the language she hadn't studied since senior year of high school.

The air down below the floor was stagnant and stale. April's legs ached from sitting still for so long, and her eyes stung from a lack of light. The waiting felt unbearable at times, and her mind wandered to all the farthest corners of loneliness—is this how housebound old ladies felt? she wondered. Or German shepherds who should be roaming the hills but instead were forced to stay gated up in the pantry all day while their stockbroker owners went to work? She decided that once she got out of there, she would get to know her elderly neighbors and that she'd never ever buy a dog, even if her (possible, as it was yet to be determined whether she wanted them) future children begged for one.

April could often hear muffled sounds from the room

above her, the TV and people talking. Sometimes, even after five, six, seven weeks, the television reports were about her disappearance—she heard police officers discussing the searches they were doing and residents expressing their concern for her. She felt guilty hearing this, and scared, too. She knew there would be legal repercussions when they finally told the truth about where she had been, perhaps even jail time. Ronnie said they would only get slapped with a huge fine, which she herself would pay. April wasn't so sure, but that hardly mattered anyway, if they could get their message out first. Her only solace was that the girls and her mother knew the truth.

Each time Ronnie came to visit, April would ask her whether she had heard from them.

"No," Ronnie said. "Not a thing."

April tried not to let Ronnie hear the disappointment in her voice. "I guess they want to help us by staying quiet," she said. "Or maybe they're all just still pissed off about that fight we had."

She thought about them often—Sally as a married woman, Bree and Lara perhaps planning a wedding of their own, and Celia, living her big brave scary lonely New York life. April regretted more than anything the way that she had left things with Sally. She wished she could go back to that last night in the King House dining hall and erase all of the stupid, petty words that had passed between them.

At the same time, she was sad and surprised that none of them had sent word through Ronnie. Maybe it was over, she thought. She remembered a time, all the way back in high school, when she had longed for friends like the King House girls. Now she knew the flip side of real friendship—that when it ended, it could sting you more than even the most bitter kind of loneliness.

One evening she heard a television ad overhead for a Halloween costume shop downtown, and when she checked with Alexa later that night she was shocked to find that it was early October. She had been down there for two months.

It was around this time that Ronnie began to get paranoid.

"I'm afraid the police might be on to us, and we are still generating so much interest," she said. "We can't stop now!"

She insisted that it would only be a little while longer, and she had one final request of April: "No more coming upstairs at night," she said. "You can use the bedpan and Alexa will bring you wet cloths to wash yourself, but you've gotta stay under the floorboards from here on out. It's just a few more days."

April could tell it wasn't up for debate. And since they had almost reached the end of this, why question Ronnie now?

Alexa's parlor was often full of girls who had run away from their pimps and now worked out of small bedrooms in her place for a fee. Sometimes when they chatted above her, April wanted to sit among them on the busted-up sofa, drinking sweet tea and gossiping about boys. (It always amazed her how some of the girls actually still dated and had normal crushes, even as a disgusting violent mockery of sex consumed their everyday lives. How could they look at men, any men, without contempt?)

April heard terrible things, too, things that she knew she would never be able to forget. The girls would meet their johns in the parlor, and then draw them upstairs.

"Hey, babycakes," April heard one of the johns say one night. His voice was booming and raspy. "I want you to wear this."

April couldn't make out the girl's response, but she could hear her tone—frightened, attempting to sound sweet and light. She wondered what the hell he wanted her to wear.

"Don't you like it?" he said. "It's my little girl's. I want to fuck you in this. I want you to call me Daddy, and I want you to be my little angel now, okay? You're gonna be my little girl, and Daddy's gonna be gentle with you."

Another night, right after Alexa brought dinner, a group of college boys in town for a football game came into the room. Their footsteps boomed through the floorboards so that April feared one of them might fall right through and be shocked to find her there, listening to them discuss a trip they'd taken to Mexico to watch a young girl have sex with a donkey onstage.

After that, April told Ronnie plainly that she could not fucking take this very much longer. It was one thing to be under the floorboards when she knew that she'd be able to come out once a day. But now it was increasingly making her feel sick and scared. "I'm starting to go nuts," she said. "You have to get me out of here."

"I will," Ronnie said, sounding almost annoyed, as if she herself had had to make the sacrifice. "Just be patient. April, we are doing so much good here, and it's all because of you."

One Thursday night, some of the girls from the corner store had gathered to watch music videos in the parlor. They were laughing, talking over one another, singing along with the TV. Just acting like normal teenagers for once. Among them, April could hear Angelika, one of Redd's girls, who had the low, seductive voice of an old jazz singer. She had been in the parlor a lot recently, and so April assumed she had left Redd for good.

After an hour or so, the girls quieted down. They made a comment here or there, laughing at a tampon commercial, moaning over Chris Brown, calling out to a friend in the kitchen to bring more tea and cigarettes. April felt relaxed for the first time in weeks.

A while later, someone new entered the room. April couldn't make out who she was from her voice, but she heard the girl say, "Turn on the news. They're reporting right outside on the street. They're looking for that missing white chick. You hear about how they found her bones a few days ago?"

Her body stiffened. She had seen Ronnie just yesterday, and Ronnie had made no mention of any of this. She strained to hear the television, willing the girls to shut up.

A smooth TV announcer's voice said, "After the grisly discovery of human remains believed to be those of April Adams, Atlanta police have called on volunteers from around the state and the country to help look for clues."

April thought of the girls, and then of her mother: Surely they had heard about this. How had they let it get so far? Or had Ronnie never told them about her in the first place? Were they each in their own little corners of the world right now, assuming her dead?

Before she could process any of it, there was the sound of

a slamming door overhead. The girls screamed. April heard them running out. Her heart sped up. Someone had a gun up there.

Then she heard his voice. "You fucking snitched," Redd said.

Angelika sounded panicked. "No, no, no, baby. It wasn't me."

"Bullshit! The cops say someone told them about that shit in my yard. I know it was you."

"I didn't tell them nothing, I swear," Angelika said, trying to sound soothing, though her voice shook.

"You lying to me now? They're gonna try to put me away for this shit. I never even touched that white bitch, but because you opened your big, fat fucking mouth—you are nothing," he screamed. "Remember that."

"I know, I know," Angelika said. "Please, you have to believe me."

"Fuck that," he said. "I saw you talking to her out on the track all the time, kissing her white ass. You even went over to her place. Now she's gone, and the fucking cops come after me."

Angelika sobbed. "They been asking me a lot of questions because some of the other girls told them I was her friend. But I swear, I didn't tell them nothing. Baby, I love you," she said.

"You get down on your fucking knees and you suck me off and maybe I'll forgive you," he said.

She was still crying. "Please put the gun down," she screamed.

"Do it!" Redd shouted, and she gave a little moan.

There was silence for a few moments. April shook. She

felt like she might vomit, imagining what was going on above. This was all happening because of her. If she climbed up through the floorboards and into the living room to help, he would probably shoot her. Through those silent moments, April willed the door to slam—either Redd would leave, or someone would come in to help Angelika. The other girls must have gone to call the police, after all. And Alexa had a handgun in the linen closet on the second floor.

Then she heard the shot.

Screams and weeping from elsewhere in the house started so quickly that it was as if they already knew what would happen. A few minutes later, she heard a lone siren, and then the paramedics in the living room. The screams did not die down.

Without seeing, April knew exactly what had passed. Redd had shot the girl dead and then walked out into the Atlanta evening, free as a bird. No one would ever tell the police what they had seen him do, for fear of being next. Hours later, she smelled the harsh, piercing scent of bleach and felt tiny acid drops of it leaking through the holes in the floor. Someone was weeping above her.

April could not sleep that night. She sat there, wide awake.

What a coward she had become. She had done nothing for Angelika. She had come here to help these girls, and now one of them was dead because of her. April cried silently into a pillow so no one would hear, remembering the sound of the gunshot, the moaning from inside the house.

How could anyone bear this? Men had all the power to make the world splendid but chose instead to ruin it, to shit on it, to turn women into their slaves and their punching bags. How could women like Sally marry men and merely hope that they wouldn't turn rotten someday—running away with their secretaries or, worse, seeking out some child on the city streets for sex they would not remember a week later, though the child would remember it for the rest of her life?

Men walked around like innocents, but most of them were destroyers of one sort or another. Waging wars or beating women or paying fifty dollars for a lap dance and a blow job after work before returning home to their wives to eat a chicken dinner and watch the evening news. April thought of her father, how he had never cared to see her face or hear her voice. How he had exchanged love and life and honor for sex. She thought of that asshole who had raped Celia in college, changing her forever, and then going forward with his life as if nothing had happened.

The activists were fighting—here in Atlanta and out in New York and LA and in Sweden and every place else, too. They were women, mostly. The few men involved were there because they had seen women they loved shattered by male violence. But what could these fighters really accomplish? They could pass laws and put up signs and send op-eds to *The New York Times* until they died. They no doubt *would* do all of these things. They would improve the world, even if just by inches. But as long as there were so-called upstanding men who believed it was okay to fuck little girls in exchange for cash, as long as there were men who were willing to sell those girls like they were nothing—what could any good person do?

And plenty of the good people were too caught up in being good anyway. So many of them huddled behind their awards and their TV appearances, feeling virtuous, accomplishing little. They got into squabbles about who would be president or treasurer, who would take notes, who would bring the lemon squares. Christ, even the feminists in their brownstone city apartments couldn't fight hard enough, because they were terrified of robbing anyone of her precious motherfucking *choices*, and who knew, maybe some women loved giving blow jobs to total strangers for ten dollars a pop. Meanwhile, miles away, little girls got shot in the head in the parlors of dingy brothels, and other little girls came along and cleaned their guts off the walls with a bottle of Clorox and a mop.

April knew she could leave anytime she wanted, just climb up the ladder and be done with all of this. She knew, too, that Ronnie would never forgive her, but who the fuck was Ronnie anyway? She was beginning to see that Ronnie had used her, ruined her. She closed her eyes against the darkness. It was simple: She couldn't do this anymore.

Hours later, when the house had long since fallen silent, April stole out. It was a struggle just to get up the rope ladder, and she realized with some alarm that her body had changed. The muscles around her upper arms and in her calves were gone. She now had the sagging skin of a much older woman, and her legs were dotted with sores from sitting still for so long. It took her several tries to push the loose floorboards up and climb out. She knew that she could not risk making a sound. She needed to talk to Ronnie before anyone else saw her.

Out of breath, she sat on the parlor floor for a moment, letting her eyes adjust to the light. The room, which she knew to be average size, looked simply enormous. The air was tinged with liquor and cigarette smoke, but it still smelled so fresh that April tried to suck it in by the barrelful.

She climbed to her feet; her legs wobbled at first, but after a few moments she got her balance. She crept down the hall. Behind one of the bedroom doors she could hear two voices arguing in hushed tones. Behind another, a young girl moaned, "Yes, yes, yes," in the most bored and sorrowful manner April had ever heard.

When she reached the front door, she held her breath as she pulled it toward her. A moment later, she was outside. The air smelled crisp. She noticed a tree's orange leaves in the streetlight and thought about the long walks she and Sally used to take around Paradise Pond in the fall.

There were a few pumpkins rotting out in the trash. Halloween must have passed now, she thought. It was November.

The street was empty, and all but silent. She knew that meant it was sometime after 4:00 a.m., because the girls were usually out until then. She wished she had thought to check the clock on Alexa's cable box.

When April reached the house, she went to the back door, hoping against hope that Ronnie had left it open, but it was locked.

April knocked gently at first, then harder. She thought she heard footsteps from inside, but a moment later all was still. She inhaled, trying to steady her mind. She didn't think she should risk going to the front door and ringing the bell.

Then the kitchen light switched on, the door opened, and there was Ronnie, standing before her in her old silk bathrobe, a gun in her hand.

"Jesus fucking Christ, April," she said. "What are you doing?"

Tears filled April's eyes. She was happy, relieved, to see Ronnie's face again, and this made her whole body ache. She hated to be that happy at the sight of someone who had wronged her, but then hadn't it been that way her whole life—her mother, her father, Gabriel. The only good people who had ever made her happy were Sally, Celia, and Bree.

"Get inside," Ronnie hissed. "Did anyone see you?"

April stepped into the familiar kitchen—the overhead fan rumbled in its flimsy setting, a half-empty bottle of wine and a few dried-up tomato slices sat on the table.

She began to sob, clutching Ronnie, burying her face in blue silk. Ronnie froze up as she did this, but April did not pull away.

"A girl got killed tonight because of me," April said. "Do you know what they're saying? They think they found my fucking body."

Ronnie didn't respond.

"What will happen now?" April said. "The police think Redd killed me. We're going to get in trouble. We might get killed. Why didn't you tell me any of this yesterday?"

Ronnie sighed, breaking apart from April and sitting down in a kitchen chair. She laid the gun on the table and traced the label on the bottle of wine with her fingers.

"I've been trying to decide what we should do next," Ronnie said. "I wanted to make a plan before I worried you."

April kept crying. "Ronnie, this isn't gonna be like the other times. We're in real trouble," she said. "We're going to have to turn ourselves in."

Ronnie shook her head. "I think we need to leave, and

start over. Pretend none of this ever happened. In a day or two, they'll know that body they found wasn't yours. After a few months, they'll give up the search altogether."

"And what will happen to me?" April said. "You expect me to just run off and start some new life without even telling my friends?"

"They're not your friends anymore anyway," Ronnie said sharply. "Or they won't be after this."

"You never told them, did you?" April said.

Ronnie was silent.

"Why?" April said. "Why the fuck did you do this to me?"

"I couldn't risk compromising all this," Ronnie said plainly.

"All this *what*?" April shouted. She looked down the hallway that led to the foyer and upstairs. Four suitcases were lined up at the bottom of the staircase.

"You were going to leave me here to deal by myself," April said.

"That's ridiculous," Ronnie said. "I'd never leave you."

April started moving down the hall and toward the front door.

Ronnie's chair screeched across the floor behind her. She got to her feet and pushed past April, shoving her into the wall as she got in front of the door.

"Where the fuck do you think you're going?" Ronnie said, spreading her arms out over the doorframe.

"I'm going to tell the police what happened," April said.

"Like hell you are," Ronnie said. "Look, you're not think-ing clearly. Let's just get a good night's sleep and we'll figure it all out in the morning." She cupped April's chin in the palm of her hand, holding on tight.

"Please," she said. "I'm begging you."

"It's fucking over," April said.

"You owe me this," Ronnie said.

April was filled with rage. "I owe you nothing," she said. "I believed in you, I thought that you cared about all of it. But you only ever cared about yourself. God, Ronnie, you used to stand for something so good, and now look at you."

Ronnie's gaze turned icy. She grabbed April by the arms.

"You're a child," Ronnie said. "Do what you want, but know this: If you go to the police, you'll spend your life in jail. And I will tell them that I had nothing to do with any of it, that you tricked me just like you tricked everyone else. You try to point them to one bit of evidence that I knew. You won't find it."

April shook out of her grip and ran up to Ronnie's bedroom, her legs burning beneath her. The room had been emptied of all Ronnie's belongings, but April pulled open the drawer in the nightstand, and there it was—her old cell phone. When she switched it on, the phone was almost out of power. She called Sally's home number, her whole body shaking.

A man answered on the second ring, sounding half asleep. In the background, April could hear the chirpy sounds of a sitcom on television, the soothing wave of a laugh track. Sally's house seemed to exist on a different planet from the one she was on here, and April longed to go there.

"Jake?" she said.

"No," the man said. "Who's this?"

"I'm a friend of Sally's," April said.

"Oh, this is her brother," he said. "They asked me to hang

at the house and do phone duty from here, in case anyone called about the baby."

"The baby," April said, her head swarming.

"Yes," he said. "She had her baby yesterday. Seven pounds, four ounces. A little girl."

"Oh my God," April said. "Is she in the hospital now? Can I call her there?"

"Umm, yeah," he said. "It's the Piedmont Hospital in Atlanta. Hold on, I can give you the number."

"She's at the Piedmont?" April said in disbelief.

"Yes," he said. "They were out there looking for a friend of hers when Sal went into labor."

April lost her signal then, the phone going dead.

Below her, she could hear Ronnie dragging her luggage onto the porch. She would be gone by dawn, and who knew where. April sat on the bed. She waited until she heard Ronnie's car pull out of the driveway and down the block before she left the house.

When April arrived at the hospital, the sun was rising over Atlanta, casting an orange glow across the lawn and over the heads of the orderlies smoking cigarettes by the entrance, making them look like angels in blue scrubs. It was the first sunrise she had seen in months. She wondered how long it would be before she saw another.

Her heart was thumping in her chest, and her hands shook as she made her way inside.

After so long underground, everything seemed brighter now, more crisp: the glossy magazines scattered around the hospital's main lounge, the giant silver doors of the elevator, gaping open so she could step inside. The maternity ward was on the fourth floor. April pressed the elevator button, and took a deep breath.

A man in a fancy suit got in on two and gave her a puzzled look, as though he knew her but couldn't say from where. She had gotten many of these looks this morning—from the bus driver who picked her up on the other side of town, from the woman out on the sidewalk selling carnations from a large plastic tub.

Soon it would all be over. She would go to the police and tell them everything and face whatever punishment might come. April had always thought that working with Ronnie was her ticket to the exact sort of life she had dreamed of in college. Now she saw, quite clearly, that she had given all of that away.

The scariest part was knowing that the girls might not forgive her; that perhaps she had gone too far this time and lost them for good. Sally had always said that it was the modern woman's joy and her burden to be given choices, endless choices. But she never said anything about what would happen if one of them made the wrong choice.

When the elevator opened on the fourth floor, April stepped out.

"Have a nice day," said the man in the suit.

"You too," she said.

The hallway smelled slightly sour. A baby cried somewhere in the distance. At a desk decorated with pink and blue teddy bears, a white-haired woman in scrubs sat alone playing poker online.

"Excuse me," April said. "I'm looking for Sally Werner's room. I'm sorry, Sally Brown."

The woman didn't look up from her computer screen.

"Seven B," she said.

April made her way past several open doors. She saw a young mother nursing an infant by the window in one room, a couple holding hands under a burst of blue balloons in another.

And then she heard them—Celia, Bree, and Sally, the sound of their laughter unmistakable, just as it had been from the hallway of the Autumn Inn when she arrived there for Sally's wedding. She stood just outside the door for a moment, taking in their conversation, remembering that first year when they lived in maids' quarters and the air was always alive with the noise of their chatter. She had never been so happy and so terrified at once.

A moment later, she stood in front of the open door and knocked on its frame.

The girls looked up. Sally's eyes grew so wide that April wished it were another time, another reality. She wished that she could make a joke.

"Is it you?" Sally said at last.

"It's me."

ACKNOWLEDGMENTS

Thank you to my wonderful friend and agent, Brettne Bloom, who encouraged me to write fiction and provided me with great insights (and many delicious home-cooked dinners) along the way; to my brilliant editor, Jenny Jackson, who cared about the characters as much as I did, and shared my vision for what this book should be. I am indebted to Jill Kneerim and Leslie Kaufmann at Kneerim & Williams, Jerry Bauer, Jenna Menard, Meghan Scott, and everyone at Knopf, especially Sarah Gelman, Andrea Robinson, Meghan Wilson, and Abby Weintraub.

Thank you to the generous friends who took the time to read this book before it was a book: Laura Smith, Aliya Pitts, Hilary Black, Laura Bonner, Noreen Kearney, Kate Sweeney, Becky Friedman, and most of all Lauren Semino, who was not only the first to read *Commencement,* but also the first to read every bad short story I wrote in high school, and beyond.

For those who have made my life infinitely richer through laughter, conversation, debate, understanding, encouragement, and advice, thanks to Karin Kringen, Caitlain McCarthy, Elizabeth Driscoll, Sara Stankiewicz, Cheryl Goss, Josh Friedman, Beth Mahon, Tim Melnyk, Erin Quinn, Olessa Pindak, Shilah Overmyer, Frances Lester, Theresa Gonzalez, Lucie Prinz, David Halpern, Amanda Millner-Fairbanks, Hilary Howard, Natasha Yefimov, Winter Miller, Liz Harris, Maureen Muenster, Ben Toff, Karen Oliver, Shelby Semino, Matt Semino, and while I'm at it, all the Seminos, and the Helds as well.

I will be forever grateful to my alma mater, Smith College, to the remarkable women I met in my time there, and to my inspiring teachers: among them, Maxine Rodburg, Michelle Chalfoun, Doug Bauer, Bill Oram, Michael Thurston, Craig Davis, and Michael Gorra.

For helping me understand the reality of sex trafficking in America, I owe thanks to Jane Manning, Rachel Lloyd, Melissa Farley, Stephanie Davis, the staff at Equality Now, and the writings of Catherine MacKinnon, Andrea Dworkin, Gloria Steinem, Robin Morgan, and so many others. For explaining and reexplaining all things medical, thank you to my friend and fellow Smith alum, Dr. Michelle Burke Noelck.

To Bob Herbert, who has taught me more about journalism, politics, decency, and the New York Jets than I ever could have hoped to learn; and to the staff of *The New York Times* editorial department, the kind of coworkers you actually miss come Sunday evening.

Thanks to the many members of my amazing extended family, storytellers all.

And a million thank-yous to Caroline Sullivan: a true artist, a quick wit, a warm heart, an incredible young woman. You are the best sister a girl could ask for, and then some.

Meet with Interesting People
Enjoy Stimulating Conversation
Discover Wonderful Books